Michael Strogoff;

Or, The Courier of the Czar

Jules Verne

Michael Strogoff; Or, The Courier of the Czar

The present edition is a reproduction of previous publication of this classic work. Minor typographical errors may have been corrected without note; however, for an authentic reading experience the spelling, punctuation, and capitalization have been retained from the original text.

ISBN: 978-1-63637-164-1

CONTENTS

BOOK I

BOOK II

CONTENTS

BOOK I

CHAPTER I
A FETE AT THE NEW PALACE

"SIRE, a fresh dispatch."

"Whence?"

"From Tomsk?"

"Is the wire cut beyond that city?"

"Yes, sire, since yesterday."

"Telegraph hourly to Tomsk, General, and keep me informed of all that occurs."

"Sire, it shall be done," answered General Kissoff.

These words were exchanged about two hours after midnight, at the moment when the fete given at the New Palace was at the height of its splendor.

During the whole evening the bands of the Preobra-jensky and Paulowsky regiments had played without cessation polkas, mazurkas, schottisches, and waltzes from among the choicest of their repertoires. Innumerable couples of dancers whirled through the magnificent saloons of the palace, which stood at a few paces only from the "old house of stones"—in former days the scene of so many terrible dramas, the echoes of whose walls were this night awakened by the gay strains of the musicians.

The grand-chamberlain of the court, was, besides, well seconded in his arduous and delicate duties. The grand-dukes and their aides-de-camp, the chamberlains-in-waiting and other officers of the palace, presided personally in the arrangement of the dances. The grand duchesses, covered with diamonds, the ladies-in-waiting in their most exquisite costumes, set the example to the wives of the military and civil dignitaries of the ancient "city of white stone." When, therefore, the signal for the "polonaise" resounded through the saloons, and the guests of all ranks took part in that measured promenade, which on occasions of this kind has all the importance of a national dance, the mingled costumes, the sweeping robes adorned with lace, and uniforms covered with orders, presented a scene of dazzling splendor, lighted by hundreds of lusters multiplied tenfold by the numerous mirrors adorning the walls.

The grand saloon, the finest of all those contained in the New Palace, formed to this procession of exalted personages and splendidly dressed women a frame worthy of the magnificence they displayed. The rich ceiling, with its gilding already softened by the touch of time, appeared

1

as if glittering with stars. The embroidered drapery of the curtains and doors, falling in gorgeous folds, assumed rich and varied hues, broken by the shadows of the heavy masses of damask.

Through the panes of the vast semicircular bay-windows the light, with which the saloons were filled, shone forth with the brilliancy of a conflagration, vividly illuminating the gloom in which for some hours the palace had been shrouded. The attention of those of the guests not taking part in the dancing was attracted by the contrast. Resting in the recesses of the windows, they could discern, standing out dimly in the darkness, the vague outlines of the countless towers, domes, and spires which adorn the ancient city. Below the sculptured balconies were visible numerous sentries, pacing silently up and down, their rifles carried horizontally on the shoulder, and the spikes of their helmets glittering like flames in the glare of light issuing from the palace. The steps also of the patrols could be heard beating time on the stones beneath with even more regularity than the feet of the dancers on the floor of the saloon. From time to time the watchword was repeated from post to post, and occasionally the notes of a trumpet, mingling with the strains of the orchestra, penetrated into their midst. Still farther down, in front of the facade, dark masses obscured the rays of light which proceeded from the windows of the New Palace. These were boats descending the course of a river, whose waters, faintly illumined by a few lamps, washed the lower portion of the terraces.

The principal personage who has been mentioned, the giver of the fete, and to whom General Kissoff had been speaking in that tone of respect with which sovereigns alone are usually addressed, wore the simple uniform of an officer of chasseurs of the guard. This was not affectation on his part, but the custom of a man who cared little for dress, his contrasting strongly with the gorgeous costumes amid which he moved, encircled by his escort of Georgians, Cossacks, and Circassians—a brilliant band, splendidly clad in the glittering uniforms of the Caucasus.

This personage, of lofty stature, affable demeanor, and physiognomy calm, though bearing traces of anxiety, moved from group to group, seldom speaking, and appearing to pay but little attention either to the merriment of the younger guests or the graver remarks of the exalted dignitaries or members of the diplomatic corps who represented at the Russian court the principal governments of Europe. Two or three of these astute politicians—physiognomists by virtue of their profession—failed not to detect on the countenance of their host symptoms of disquietude, the source of which eluded their penetration; but none ventured to interrogate him on the subject.

It was evidently the intention of the officer of chasseurs that his own anxieties should in no way cast a shade over the festivities; and, as he was a personage whom almost the population of a world in itself was wont to obey, the gayety of the ball was not for a moment checked.

Nevertheless, General Kissoff waited until the officer to whom he had just communicated the dispatch forwarded from Tomsk should give him permission to withdraw; but the latter still remained silent. He had taken the telegram, he had read it carefully, and his visage became even more clouded than before. Involuntarily he sought the hilt of his sword, and then passed his hand for an instant before his eyes, as though, dazzled by the brilliancy of the light, he wished to shade them, the better to see into the recesses of his own mind.

"We are, then," he continued, after having drawn General Kissoff aside towards a window, "since yesterday without intelligence from the Grand Duke?"

"Without any, sire; and it is to be feared that in a short time dispatches will no longer cross the Siberian frontier."

"But have not the troops of the provinces of Amoor and Irkutsk, as those also of the Trans-Balkan territory, received orders to march immediately upon Irkutsk?"

"The orders were transmitted by the last telegram we were able to send beyond Lake Baikal."

"And the governments of Yeniseisk, Omsk, Semipolatinsk, and Tobolsk—are we still in direct communication with them as before the insurrection?"

"Yes, sire; our dispatches have reached them, and we are assured at the present moment that the Tartars have not advanced beyond the Irtish and the Obi."

"And the traitor Ivan Ogareff, are there no tidings of him?"

"None," replied General Kissoff. "The head of the police cannot state whether or not he has crossed the frontier."

"Let a description of him be immediately dispatched to Nijni-Novgorod, Perm, Ekaterenburg, Kasirnov, Tioumen, Ishim, Omsk, Tomsk, and to all the telegraphic stations with which communication is yet open."

"Your majesty's orders shall be instantly carried out."

"You will observe the strictest silence as to this."

The General, having made a sign of respectful assent, bowing low, mingled with the crowd, and finally left the apartments without his departure being remarked.

The officer remained absorbed in thought for a few moments, when, recovering himself, he went among the various groups in the saloon, his countenance reassuming that calm aspect which had for an instant been disturbed.

Nevertheless, the important occurrence which had occasioned these rapidly exchanged words was not so unknown as the officer of the chasseurs of the guard and General Kissoff had possibly supposed. It was not spoken of officially, it is true, nor even officiously, since tongues were not free; but a few exalted personages had been informed, more or less exactly, of the events which had taken place beyond the frontier. At any rate, that which was only slightly known, that which was not matter of conversation even between members of the corps diplomatique, two guests, distinguished by no uniform, no decoration, at this reception in the New Palace, discussed in a low voice, and with apparently very correct information.

3

By what means, by the exercise of what acuteness had these two ordinary mortals ascertained that which so many persons of the highest rank and importance scarcely even suspected? It is impossible to say. Had they the gifts of foreknowledge and foresight? Did they possess a supplementary sense, which enabled them to see beyond that limited horizon which bounds all human gaze? Had they obtained a peculiar power of divining the most secret events? Was it owing to the habit, now become a second nature, of living on information, that their mental constitution had thus become really transformed? It was difficult to escape from this conclusion.

Of these two men, the one was English, the other French; both were tall and thin, but the latter was sallow as are the southern Provencals, while the former was ruddy like a Lancashire gentleman. The Anglo-Norman, formal, cold, grave, parsimonious of gestures and words, appeared only to speak or gesticulate under the influence of a spring operating at regular intervals. The Gaul, on the contrary, lively and petulant, expressed himself with lips, eyes, hands, all at once, having twenty different ways of explaining his thoughts, whereas his interlocutor seemed to have only one, immutably stereotyped on his brain.

The strong contrast they presented would at once have struck the most superficial observer; but a physiognomist, regarding them closely, would have defined their particular characteristics by saying, that if the Frenchman was "all eyes," the Englishman was "all ears."

In fact, the visual apparatus of the one had been singularly perfected by practice. The sensibility of its retina must have been as instantaneous as that of those conjurors who recognize a card merely by a rapid movement in cutting the pack or by the arrangement only of marks invisible to others. The Frenchman indeed possessed in the highest degree what may be called "the memory of the eye."

The Englishman, on the contrary, appeared especially organized to listen and to hear. When his aural apparatus had been once struck by the sound of a voice he could not forget it, and after ten or even twenty years he would have recognized it among a thousand. His ears, to be sure, had not the power of moving as freely as those of animals who are provided with large auditory flaps; but, since scientific men know that human ears possess, in fact, a very limited power of movement, we should not be far wrong in affirming that those of the said Englishman became erect, and turned in all directions while endeavoring to gather in the sounds, in a manner apparent only to the naturalist. It must be observed that this perfection of sight and hearing was of wonderful assistance to these two men in their vocation, for the Englishman acted as correspondent of the Daily Telegraph, and the Frenchman, as correspondent of what newspaper, or of what newspapers, he did not say; and when asked, he replied in a jocular manner that he corresponded with "his cousin Madeleine." This Frenchman, however, neath his careless surface, was wonderfully shrewd and sagacious. Even while speaking at random, perhaps the better to hide his desire to learn, he never forgot himself. His loquacity even helped him

4

to conceal his thoughts, and he was perhaps even more discreet than his confrere of the Daily Telegraph. Both were present at this fete given at the New Palace on the night of the 15th of July in their character of reporters.

It is needless to say that these two men were devoted to their mission in the world—that they delighted to throw themselves in the track of the most unexpected intelligence—that nothing terrified or discouraged them from succeeding—that they possessed the imperturbable sang froid and the genuine intrepidity of men of their calling. Enthusiastic jockeys in this steeplechase, this hunt after information, they leaped hedges, crossed rivers, sprang over fences, with the ardor of pure-blooded racers, who will run "a good first" or die!

Their journals did not restrict them with regard to money—the surest, the most rapid, the most perfect element of information known to this day. It must also be added, to their honor, that neither the one nor the other ever looked over or listened at the walls of private life, and that they only exercised their vocation when political or social interests were at stake. In a word, they made what has been for some years called "the great political and military reports."

It will be seen, in following them, that they had generally an independent mode of viewing events, and, above all, their consequences, each having his own way of observing and appreciating.

The French correspondent was named Alcide Jolivet. Harry Blount was the name of the Englishman. They had just met for the first time at this fete in the New Palace, of which they had been ordered to give an account in their papers. The dissimilarity of their characters, added to a certain amount of jealousy, which generally exists between rivals in the same calling, might have rendered them but little sympathetic. However, they did not avoid each other, but endeavored rather to exchange with each other the chat of the day. They were sportsmen, after all, hunting on the same ground. That which one missed might be advantageously secured by the other, and it was to their interest to meet and converse.

This evening they were both on the look out; they felt, in fact, that there was something in the air.

"Even should it be only a wildgoose chase," said Alcide Jolivet to himself, "it may be worth powder and shot."

The two correspondents therefore began by cautiously sounding each other.

"Really, my dear sir, this little fete is charming!" said Alcide Jolivet pleasantly, thinking himself obliged to begin the conversation with this eminently French phrase.

"I have telegraphed already, 'splendid!'" replied Harry Blount calmly, employing the word specially devoted to expressing admiration by all subjects of the United Kingdom.

"Nevertheless," added Alcide Jolivet, "I felt compelled to remark to my cousin—"

"Your cousin?" repeated Harry Blount in a tone of surprise, interrupting his brother of the pen.

5

"Yes," returned Alcide Jolivet, "my cousin Madeleine. It is with her that I correspond, and she likes to be quickly and well informed, does my cousin. I therefore remarked to her that, during this fete, a sort of cloud had appeared to overshadow the sovereign's brow."

"To me, it seemed radiant," replied Harry Blount, who perhaps, wished to conceal his real opinion on this topic.

"And, naturally, you made it 'radiant,' in the columns of the Daily Telegraph."

"Exactly."

"Do you remember, Mr. Blount, what occurred at Zakret in 1812?"

"I remember it as well as if I had been there, sir," replied the English correspondent.

"Then," continued Alcide Jolivet, "you know that, in the middle of a fete given in his honor, it was announced to the Emperor Alexander that Napoleon had just crossed the Niemen with the vanguard of the French army. Nevertheless the Emperor did not leave the fete, and notwithstanding the extreme gravity of intelligence which might cost him his empire, he did not allow himself to show more uneasiness."

"Than our host exhibited when General Kissoff informed him that the telegraphic wires had just been cut between the frontier and the government of Irkutsk."

"Ah! you are aware of that?"

"I am!"

"As regards myself, it would be difficult to avoid knowing it, since my last telegram reached Udinsk," observed Alcide Jolivet, with some satisfaction.

"And mine only as far as Krasnoiarsk," answered Harry Blount, in a no less satisfied tone.

"Then you know also that orders have been sent to the troops of Nikolaevsk?"

"I do, sir; and at the same time a telegram was sent to the Cossacks of the government of Tobolsk to concentrate their forces."

"Nothing can be more true, Mr. Blount; I was equally well acquainted with these measures, and you may be sure that my dear cousin shall know of them to-morrow."

"Exactly as the readers of the Daily Telegraph shall know it also, M. Jolivet."

"Well, when one sees all that is going on...."

"And when one hears all that is said...."

"An interesting campaign to follow, Mr. Blount."

"I shall follow it, M. Jolivet!"

"Then it is possible that we shall find ourselves on ground less safe, perhaps, than the floor of this ball-room."

"Less safe, certainly, but—"

"But much less slippery," added Alcide Jolivet, holding up his companion, just as the latter, drawing back, was about to lose his equilibrium.

Thereupon the two correspondents separated, pleased that the one had not stolen a march on the other.

At that moment the doors of the rooms adjoining the great reception saloon were thrown open, disclosing to view several immense tables beautifully laid out, and groaning under a profusion of valuable china and gold plate. On the central table, reserved for the princes, princesses, and members of the corps diplomatique, glittered an epergne of inestimable price, brought from London, and around this chef-d'oeuvre of chased gold reflected under the light of the lusters a thousand pieces of most beautiful service from the manufactories of Sevres.

The guests of the New Palace immediately began to stream towards the supper-rooms.

At that moment. General Kissoff, who had just re-entered, quickly approached the officer of chasseurs.

"Well?" asked the latter abruptly, as he had done the former time.

"Telegrams pass Tomsk no longer, sire."

"A courier this moment!"

The officer left the hall and entered a large antechamber adjoining. It was a cabinet with plain oak furniture, situated in an angle of the New Palace. Several pictures, amongst others some by Horace Vernet, hung on the wall.

The officer hastily opened a window, as if he felt the want of air, and stepped out on a balcony to breathe the pure atmosphere of a lovely July night. Beneath his eyes, bathed in moonlight, lay a fortified inclosure, from which rose two cathedrals, three palaces, and an arsenal. Around this inclosure could be seen three distinct towns: Kitai-Gorod, Beloi-Gorod, Zemlianai-Gorod—European, Tartar, and Chinese quarters of great extent, commanded by towers, belfries, minarets, and the cupolas of three hundred churches, with green domes, surmounted by the silver cross. A little winding river, here and there reflected the rays of the moon.

This river was the Moskowa; the town Moscow; the fortified inclosure the Kremlin; and the officer of chasseurs of the guard, who, with folded arms and thoughtful brow, was listening dreamily to the sounds floating from the New Palace over the old Muscovite city, was the Czar.

CHAPTER II
RUSSIANS AND TARTARS

THE Czar had not so suddenly left the ball-room of the New Palace, when the fete he was giving to the civil and military authorities and principal people of Moscow was at the height of its brilliancy, without ample cause; for he had just received information that serious events were taking place beyond the frontiers of the Ural. It had become evident that a formidable rebellion threatened to wrest the Siberian provinces from the Russian crown.

Asiatic Russia, or Siberia, covers a superficial area of 1,790,208 square miles, and contains nearly two millions of inhabitants. Extending from the Ural Mountains, which separate it from Russia in Europe, to the shores of the Pacific Ocean, it is bounded on the south by Turkestan and the Chinese Empire; on the north by the Arctic Ocean, from the Sea of Kara to Behring's Straits. It is divided into several governments or provinces, those of Tobolsk, Yeniseisk, Irkutsk, Omsk, and Yakutsk; contains two districts, Okhotsk and Kamtschatka; and possesses two countries, now under the Muscovite dominion—that of the Kirghiz and that of the Tshouktshes. This immense extent of steppes, which includes more than one hundred and ten degrees from west to east, is a land to which criminals and political offenders are banished.

Two governor-generals represent the supreme authority of the Czar over this vast country. The higher one resides at Irkutsk, the far capital of Eastern Siberia. The River Tchouna separates the two Siberias.

No rail yet furrows these wide plains, some of which are in reality extremely fertile. No iron ways lead from those precious mines which make the Siberian soil far richer below than above its surface. The traveler journeys in summer in a kibick or telga; in winter, in a sledge.

An electric telegraph, with a single wire more than eight thousand versts in length, alone affords communication between the western and eastern frontiers of Siberia. On issuing from the Ural, it passes through Ekaterenburg, Kasirnov, Tioumen, Ishim, Omsk, Elamsk, Kolyvan, Tomsk, Krasnoiarsk, Nijni-Udinsk, Irkutsk, Verkne-Nertschink, Strelink, Albazine, Blagowstenks, Radde, Orlomskaya, Alexandrowskoe, and Nikolaevsk; and six roubles and nineteen copecks are paid for every word sent from one end to the other. From Irkutsk there is a branch to Kiatka, on the Mongolian frontier; and from thence, for thirty copecks a word, the post conveys the dispatches to Pekin in a fortnight.

It was this wire, extending from Ekaterenburg to Nikolaevsk, which had been cut, first beyond Tomsk, and then between Tomsk and Kolyvan.

This was why the Czar, to the communication made to him for the second time by General Kissoff, had answered by the words, "A courier this moment!"

The Czar remained motionless at the window for a few moments, when the door was again opened. The chief of police appeared on the threshold.

"Enter, General," said the Czar briefly, "and tell me all you know of Ivan Ogareff."

"He is an extremely dangerous man, sire," replied the chief of police.

"He ranked as colonel, did he not?"

"Yes, sire."

"Was he an intelligent officer?"

"Very intelligent, but a man whose spirit it was impossible to subdue; and possessing an ambition which stopped at nothing, he became involved in secret intrigues, and was degraded from his rank by his Highness the Grand Duke, and exiled to Siberia."

"How long ago was that?"

"Two years since. Pardoned after six months of exile by your majesty's favor, he returned to Russia."

"And since that time, has he not revisited Siberia?"

"Yes, sire; but he voluntarily returned there," replied the chief of police, adding, and slightly lowering his voice, "there was a time, sire, when NONE returned from Siberia."

"Well, whilst I live, Siberia is and shall be a country whence men CAN return."

The Czar had the right to utter these words with some pride, for often, by his clemency, he had shown that Russian justice knew how to pardon.

The head of the police did not reply to this observation, but it was evident that he did not approve of such half-measures. According to his idea, a man who had once passed the Ural Mountains in charge of policemen, ought never again to cross them. Now, it was not thus under the new reign, and the chief of police sincerely deplored it. What! no banishment for life for other crimes than those against social order! What! political exiles returning from Tobolsk, from Yakutsk, from Irkutsk! In truth, the chief of police, accustomed to the despotic sentences of the ukase which formerly never pardoned, could not understand this mode of governing. But he was silent, waiting until the Czar should interrogate him further. The questions were not long in coming.

"Did not Ivan Ogareff," asked the Czar, "return to Russia a second time, after that journey through the Siberian provinces, the object of which remains unknown?"

"He did."

"And have the police lost trace of him since?"

"No, sire; for an offender only becomes really dangerous from the day he has received his pardon."

The Czar frowned. Perhaps the chief of police feared that he had gone rather too far, though the stubbornness of his ideas was at least equal to the boundless devotion he felt for his master. But the Czar, disdaining to reply to these indirect reproaches cast on his policy, continued his questions. "Where was Ogareff last heard of?"

"In the province of Perm."

"In what town?"

"At Perm itself."

"What was he doing?"

"He appeared unoccupied, and there was nothing suspicious in his conduct."

"Then he was not under the surveillance of the secret police?"

"No, sire."

"When did he leave Perm?"

"About the month of March?"

9

"To go...?"

"Where, is unknown."

"And it is not known what has become of him?"

"No, sire; it is not known."

"Well, then, I myself know," answered the Czar. "I have received anonymous communications which did not pass through the police department; and, in the face of events now taking place beyond the frontier, I have every reason to believe that they are correct."

"Do you mean, sire," cried the chief of police, "that Ivan Ogareff has a hand in this Tartar rebellion?"

"Indeed I do; and I will now tell you something which you are ignorant of. After leaving Perm, Ivan Ogareff crossed the Ural mountains, entered Siberia, and penetrated the Kirghiz steppes, and there endeavored, not without success, to foment rebellion amongst their nomadic population. He then went so far south as free Turkestan; there, in the provinces of Bokhara, Khokhand, and Koondooz, he found chiefs willing to pour their Tartar hordes into Siberia, and excite a general rising in Asiatic Russia. The storm has been silently gathering, but it has at last burst like a thunderclap, and now all means of communication between Eastern and Western Siberia have been stopped. Moreover, Ivan Ogareff, thirsting for vengeance, aims at the life of my brother!"

The Czar had become excited whilst speaking, and now paced up and down with hurried steps. The chief of police said nothing, but he thought to himself that, during the time when the emperors of Russia never pardoned an exile, schemes such as those of Ivan Ogareff could never have been realized. Approaching the Czar, who had thrown himself into an armchair, he asked, "Your majesty has of course given orders so that this rebellion may be suppressed as soon as possible?"

"Yes," answered the Czar. "The last telegram which reached Nijni-Udinsk would set in motion the troops in the governments of Yenisei, Irkutsk, Yakutsk, as well as those in the provinces of the Amoor and Lake Baikal. At the same time, the regiments from Perm and Nijni-Novgorod, and the Cossacks from the frontier, are advancing by forced marches towards the Ural Mountains; but some weeks must pass before they can attack the Tartars."

"And your majesty's brother, his Highness the Grand Duke, is now isolated in the government of Irkutsk, and is no longer in direct communication with Moscow?"

"That is so."

"But by the last dispatches, he must know what measures have been taken by your majesty, and what help he may expect from the governments nearest Irkutsk?"

"He knows that," answered the Czar; "but what he does not know is, that Ivan Ogareff, as well as being a rebel, is also playing the part of a traitor, and that in him he has a personal and bitter enemy. It is to the Grand Duke that Ogareff owes his first disgrace; and what is more serious is, that this man is not known to him. Ogareff's plan, therefore, is to go to

Irkutsk, and, under an assumed name, offer his services to the Grand Duke. Then, after gaining his confidence, when the Tartars have invested Irkutsk, he will betray the town, and with it my brother, whose life he seeks. This is what I have learned from my secret intelligence; this is what the Grand Duke does not know; and this is what he must know!"

"Well, sire, an intelligent, courageous courier..."

"I momentarily expect one."

"And it is to be hoped he will be expeditious," added the chief of police; "for, allow me to add, sire, that Siberia is a favorable land for rebellions."

"Do you mean to say. General, that the exiles would make common cause with the rebels?" exclaimed the Czar.

"Excuse me, your majesty," stammered the chief of police, for that was really the idea suggested to him by his uneasy and suspicious mind.

"I believe in their patriotism," returned the Czar.

"There are other offenders besides political exiles in Siberia," said the chief of police.

"The criminals? Oh, General, I give those up to you! They are the vilest, I grant, of the human race. They belong to no country. But the insurrection, or rather, the rebellion, is not to oppose the emperor; it is raised against Russia, against the country which the exiles have not lost all hope of again seeing—and which they will see again. No, a Russian would never unite with a Tartar, to weaken, were it only for an hour, the Muscovite power!"

The Czar was right in trusting to the patriotism of those whom his policy kept, for a time, at a distance. Clemency, which was the foundation of his justice, when he could himself direct its effects, the modifications he had adopted with regard to applications for the formerly terrible ukases, warranted the belief that he was not mistaken. But even without this powerful element of success in regard to the Tartar rebellion, circumstances were not the less very serious; for it was to be feared that a large part of the Kirghiz population would join the rebels.

The Kirghiz are divided into three hordes, the greater, the lesser, and the middle, and number nearly four hundred thousand "tents," or two million souls. Of the different tribes some are independent and others recognize either the sovereignty of Russia or that of the Khans of Khiva, Khokhand, and Bokhara, the most formidable chiefs of Turkestan. The middle horde, the richest, is also the largest, and its encampments occupy all the space between the rivers Sara Sou, Irtish, and the Upper Ishim, Lake Saisang and Lake Aksakal. The greater horde, occupying the countries situated to the east of the middle one, extends as far as the governments of Omsk and Tobolsk. Therefore, if the Kirghiz population should rise, it would be the rebellion of Asiatic Russia, and the first thing would be the separation of Siberia, to the east of the Yenisei.

It is true that these Kirghiz, mere novices in the art of war, are rather nocturnal thieves and plunderers of caravans than regular soldiers. As M. Levchine says, "a firm front or a square of good infantry could repel ten times the number of Kirghiz; and a single cannon might destroy a frightful number."

That may be; but to do this it is necessary for the square of good infantry to reach the rebellious country, and the cannon to leave the arsenals of the Russian provinces, perhaps two or three thousand versts distant. Now, except by the direct route from Ekaterenburg to Irkutsk, the often marshy steppes are not easily practicable, and some weeks must certainly pass before the Russian troops could reach the Tartar hordes.

Omsk is the center of that military organization of Western Siberia which is intended to overawe the Kirghiz population. Here are the bounds, more than once infringed by the half-subdued nomads, and there was every reason to believe that Omsk was already in danger. The line of military stations, that is to say, those Cossack posts which are ranged in echelon from Omsk to Semipolatinsk, must have been broken in several places. Now, it was to be feared that the "Grand Sultans," who govern the Kirghiz districts would either voluntarily accept, or involuntarily submit to, the dominion of Tartars, Mussulmen like themselves, and that to the hate caused by slavery was not united the hate due to the antagonism of the Greek and Mussulman religions. For some time, indeed, the Tartars of Turkestan had endeavored, both by force and persuasion, to subdue the Kirghiz hordes.

A few words only with respect to these Tartars. The Tartars belong more especially to two distinct races, the Caucasian and the Mongolian. The Caucasian race, which, as Abel de Remusat says, "is regarded in Europe as the type of beauty in our species, because all the nations in this part of the world have sprung from it," includes also the Turks and the Persians. The purely Mongolian race comprises the Mongols, Manchoux, and Thibetans.

The Tartars who now threatened the Russian Empire, belonged to the Caucasian race, and occupied Turkestan. This immense country is divided into different states, governed by Khans, and hence termed Khanats. The principal khanats are those of Bokhara, Khokhand, Koondooz, etc. At this period, the most important and the most formidable khanat was that of Bokhara. Russia had already been several times at war with its chiefs, who, for their own interests, had supported the independence of the Kirghiz against the Muscovite dominion. The present chief, Feofar-Khan, followed in the steps of his predecessors.

The khanat of Bokhara has a population of two million five hundred thousand inhabitants, an army of sixty thousand men, trebled in time of war, and thirty thousand horsemen. It is a rich country, with varied animal, vegetable, and mineral products, and has been increased by the accession of the territories of Balkh, Aukoi, and Meimaneh. It possesses nineteen large towns. Bokhara, surrounded by a wall measuring more than eight English miles, and flanked with towers, a glorious city, made illustrious by Avicenna and other learned men of the tenth century, is regarded as the center of Mussulman science, and ranks among the most celebrated cities of Central Asia. Samarcand, which contains the tomb of

Tamerlane and the famous palace where the blue stone is kept on which each new khan must seat himself on his accession, is defended by a very strong citadel. Karschi, with its triple cordon, situated in an oasis, surrounded by a marsh peopled with tortoises and lizards, is almost impregnable, Is-chardjoui is defended by a population of twenty thousand souls. Protected by its mountains, and isolated by its steppes, the khanat of Bokhara is a most formidable state; and Russia would need a large force to subdue it.

The fierce and ambitious Feofar now governed this corner of Tartary. Relying on the other khans—principally those of Khokhand and Koondooz, cruel and rapacious warriors, all ready to join an enterprise so dear to Tartar instincts—aided by the chiefs who ruled all the hordes of Central Asia, he had placed himself at the head of the rebellion of which Ivan Ogareff was the instigator. This traitor, impelled by insane ambition as much as by hate, had ordered the movement so as to attack Siberia. Mad indeed he was, if he hoped to rupture the Muscovite Empire. Acting under his suggestion, the Emir—which is the title taken by the khans of Bokhara—had poured his hordes over the Russian frontier. He invaded the government of Semipolatinsk, and the Cossacks, who were only in small force there, had been obliged to retire before him. He had advanced farther than Lake Balkhash, gaining over the Kirghiz population on his way. Pillaging, ravaging, enrolling those who submitted, taking prisoners those who resisted, he marched from one town to another, followed by those impedimenta of Oriental sovereignty which may be called his household, his wives and his slaves—all with the cool audacity of a modern Ghengis-Khan. It was impossible to ascertain where he now was; how far his soldiers had marched before the news of the rebellion reached Moscow; or to what part of Siberia the Russian troops had been forced to retire. All communication was interrupted. Had the wire between Kolyvan and Tomsk been cut by Tartar scouts, or had the Emir himself arrived at the Yeniseisk provinces? Was all the lower part of Western Siberia in a ferment? Had the rebellion already spread to the eastern regions? No one could say. The only agent which fears neither cold nor heat, which can neither be stopped by the rigors of winter nor the heat of summer, and which flies with the rapidity of lightning—the electric current—was prevented from traversing the steppes, and it was no longer possible to warn the Grand Duke, shut up in Irkutsk, of the danger threatening him from the treason of Ivan Ogareff.

A courier only could supply the place of the interrupted current. It would take this man some time to traverse the five thousand two hundred versts between Moscow and Irkutsk. To pass the ranks of the rebels and invaders he must display almost superhuman courage and intelligence. But with a clear head and a firm heart much can be done.

"Shall I be able to find this head and heart?" thought the Czar.

13

CHAPTER III
MICHAEL STROGOFF MEETS THE CZAR

THE door of the imperial cabinet was again opened and General Kissoff was announced.

"The courier?" inquired the Czar eagerly.

"He is here, sire," replied General Kissoff.

"Have you found a fitting man?"

"I will answer for him to your majesty."

"Has he been in the service of the Palace?"

"Yes, sire."

"You know him?"

"Personally, and at various times he has fulfilled difficult missions with success."

"Abroad?"

"In Siberia itself."

"Where does he come from?"

"From Omsk. He is a Siberian."

"Has he coolness, intelligence, courage?"

"Yes, sire; he has all the qualities necessary to succeed, even where others might possibly fail."

"What is his age?"

"Thirty."

"Is he strong and vigorous?"

"Sire, he can bear cold, hunger, thirst, fatigue, to the very last extremities."

"He must have a frame of iron."

"Sire, he has."

"And a heart?"

"A heart of gold."

"His name?"

"Michael Strogoff."

"Is he ready to set out?"

"He awaits your majesty's orders in the guard-room."

"Let him come in," said the Czar.

In a few moments Michael Strogoff, the courier, entered the imperial library. He was a tall, vigorous, broad-shouldered, deep-chested man. His powerful head possessed the fine features of the Caucasian race. His well-knit frame seemed built for the performance of feats of strength. It would have been a difficult task to move such a man against his will, for when his feet were once planted on the ground, it was as if they had taken root. As he doffed his Muscovite cap, locks of thick curly hair fell over his broad, massive forehead. When his ordinarily pale face became at all flushed, it arose solely from a more rapid action of the heart. His eyes, of a deep blue, looked with clear, frank, firm gaze. The slightly-contracted eyebrows indicated lofty heroism—"the hero's cool courage," according to the definition of the physiologist. He possessed a fine nose, with large nostrils; and a well-shaped mouth, with the slightly-projecting lips which denote a generous and noble heart.

Michael Strogoff had the temperament of the man of action, who does not bite his nails or scratch his head in doubt and indecision. Sparing of gestures as of words, he always stood motionless like a soldier before his superior; but when he moved, his step showed a firmness, a freedom of movement, which proved the confidence and vivacity of his mind.

Michael Strogoff wore a handsome military uniform something resembling that of a light-cavalry officer in the field—boots, spurs, half tightly-fitting trousers, brown pelisse, trimmed with fur and ornamented with yellow braid. On his breast glittered a cross and several medals.

Michael Strogoff belonged to the special corps of the Czar's couriers, ranking as an officer among those picked men. His most discernible characteristic—particularly in his walk, his face, in the whole man, and which the Czar perceived at a glance—was, that he was "a fulfiller of orders." He therefore possessed one of the most serviceable qualities in Russia—one which, as the celebrated novelist Tourgueneff says, "will lead to the highest positions in the Muscovite empire."

In short, if anyone could accomplish this journey from Moscow to Irkutsk, across a rebellious country, surmount obstacles, and brave perils of all sorts, Michael Strogoff was the man.

A circumstance especially favorable to the success of his plan was, that he was thoroughly acquainted with the country which he was about to traverse, and understood its different dialects—not only from having traveled there before, but because he was of Siberian origin.

His father—old Peter Strogoff, dead ten years since—inhabited the town of Omsk, situated in the government of the same name; and his mother, Marfa Strogoff, lived there still. There, amid the wild steppes of the provinces of Omsk and Tobolsk, had the famous huntsman brought up his son Michael to endure hardship. Peter Strogoff was a huntsman by profession. Summer and winter—in the burning heat, as well as when the cold was sometimes fifty degrees below zero—he scoured the frozen plains, the thickets of birch and larch, the pine forests; setting traps; watching for small game with his gun, and for large game with the spear or knife. The large game was nothing less than the Siberian bear, a formidable and ferocious animal, in size equaling its fellow of the frozen seas. Peter Strogoff had killed more than thirty-nine bears—that is to say, the fortieth had fallen under his blows; and, according to Russian legends, most huntsmen who have been lucky enough up to the thirty-ninth bear, have succumbed to the fortieth.

Peter Strogoff had, however, passed the fatal number without even a scratch. From that time, his son Michael, aged eleven years, never failed to accompany him to the hunt, carrying the ragatina or spear to aid his father, who was armed only with the knife. When he was fourteen, Michael Strogoff had killed his first bear, quite alone—that was nothing; but after stripping it he dragged the gigantic animal's skin to his father's

15

house, many versts distant, exhibiting remarkable strength in a boy so young.

This style of life was of great benefit to him, and when he arrived at manhood he could bear any amount of cold, heat, hunger, thirst, or fatigue. Like the Yakout of the northern countries, he was made of iron. He could go four-and-twenty hours without eating, ten nights without sleeping, and could make himself a shelter in the open steppe where others would have been frozen to death. Gifted with marvelous acuteness, guided by the instinct of the Delaware of North America, over the white plain, when every object is hidden in mist, or even in higher latitudes, where the polar night is prolonged for many days, he could find his way when others would have had no idea whither to turn. All his father's secrets were known to him. He had learnt to read almost imperceptible signs—the forms of icicles, the appearance of the small branches of trees, mists rising far away in the horizon, vague sounds in the air, distant reports, the flight of birds through the foggy atmosphere, a thousand circumstances which are so many words to those who can decipher them. Moreover, tempered by snow like a Damascus blade in the waters of Syria, he had a frame of iron, as General Kissoff had said, and, what was no less true, a heart of gold.

The only sentiment of love felt by Michael Strogoff was that which he entertained for his mother, the aged Marfa, who could never be induced to leave the house of the Strogoffs, at Omsk, on the banks of the Irtish, where the old huntsman and she had lived so long together. When her son left her, he went away with a full heart, but promising to come and see her whenever he could possibly do so; and this promise he had always religiously kept.

When Michael was twenty, it was decided that he should enter the personal service of the Emperor of Russia, in the corps of the couriers of the Czar. The hardy, intelligent, zealous, well-conducted young Siberian first distinguished himself especially, in a journey to the Caucasus, through the midst of a difficult country, ravaged by some restless successors of Schamyl; then later, in an important mission to Petropolowski, in Kamtschatka, the extreme limit of Asiatic Russia. During these long journeys he displayed such marvelous coolness, prudence, and courage, as to gain him the approbation and protection of his chiefs, who rapidly advanced him in his profession.

The furloughs which were his due after these distant missions, he never failed to devote to his old mother. Having been much employed in the south of the empire, he had not seen old Marfa for three years—three ages!—the first time in his life he had been so long absent from her. Now, however, in a few days he would obtain his furlough, and he had accordingly already made preparations for departure for Omsk, when the events which have been related occurred. Michael Strogoff was therefore introduced into the Czar's presence in complete ignorance of what the emperor expected from him.

The Czar fixed a penetrating look upon him without uttering a word, whilst Michael stood perfectly motionless.

The Czar, apparently satisfied with his scrutiny, motioned to the chief of police to seat himself, and dictated in a low voice a letter of not more than a few lines.

The letter penned, the Czar re-read it attentively, then signed it, preceding his name with the words "Byt po semou," which, signifying "So be it," constitutes the decisive formula of the Russian emperors.

The letter was then placed in an envelope, which was sealed with the imperial arms.

The Czar, rising, told Michael Strogoff to draw near.

Michael advanced a few steps, and then stood motionless, ready to answer.

The Czar again looked him full in the face and their eyes met. Then in an abrupt tone, "Thy name?" he asked.

"Michael Strogoff, sire."

"Thy rank?"

"Captain in the corps of couriers of the Czar."

"Thou dost know Siberia?"

"I am a Siberian."

"A native of?"

"Omsk, sire."

"Hast thou relations there?"

"Yes sire."

"What relations?"

"My old mother."

The Czar suspended his questions for a moment. Then, pointing to the letter which he held in his hand, "Here is a letter which I charge thee, Michael Strogoff, to deliver into the hands of the Grand Duke, and to no other but him."

"I will deliver it, sire."

"The Grand Duke is at Irkutsk."

"I will go to Irkutsk."

"Thou wilt have to traverse a rebellious country, invaded by Tartars, whose interest it will be to intercept this letter."

"I will traverse it."

"Above all, beware of the traitor, Ivan Ogareff, who will perhaps meet thee on the way."

"I will beware of him."

"Wilt thou pass through Omsk?"

"Sire, that is my route."

"If thou dost see thy mother, there will be the risk of being recognized. Thou must not see her!"

Michael Strogoff hesitated a moment.

"I will not see her," said he.

"Swear to me that nothing will make thee acknowledge who thou art, nor whither thou art going."

"I swear it."

"Michael Strogoff," continued the Czar, giving the letter to the young

17

courier, "take this letter; on it depends the safety of all Siberia, and perhaps the life of my brother the Grand Duke."

"This letter shall be delivered to his Highness the Grand Duke."

"Then thou wilt pass whatever happens?"

"I shall pass, or they shall kill me."

"I want thee to live."

"I shall live, and I shall pass," answered Michael Strogoff.

The Czar appeared satisfied with Strogoff's calm and simple answer.

"Go then, Michael Strogoff," said he, "go for God, for Russia, for my brother, and for myself!"

The courier, having saluted his sovereign, immediately left the imperial cabinet, and, in a few minutes, the New Palace.

"You made a good choice there, General," said the Czar.

"I think so, sire," replied General Kissoff; "and your majesty may be sure that Michael Strogoff will do all that a man can do."

"He is indeed a man," said the Czar.

CHAPTER IV
FROM MOSCOW TO NIJNI-NOVGOROD

THE distance between Moscow and Irkutsk, about to be traversed by Michael Strogoff, was three thousand four hundred miles. Before the telegraph wire extended from the Ural Mountains to the eastern frontier of Siberia, the dispatch service was performed by couriers, those who traveled the most rapidly taking eighteen days to get from Moscow to Irkutsk. But this was the exception, and the journey through Asiatic Russia usually occupied from four to five weeks, even though every available means of transport was placed at the disposal of the Czar's messengers.

Michael Strogoff was a man who feared neither frost nor snow. He would have preferred traveling during the severe winter season, in order that he might perform the whole distance by sleighs. At that period of the year the difficulties which all other means of locomotion present are greatly diminished, the wide steppes being leveled by snow, while there are no rivers to cross, but simply sheets of glass, over which the sleigh glides rapidly and easily.

Perhaps certain natural phenomena are most to be feared at that time, such as long-continuing and dense fogs, excessive cold, fearfully heavy snow-storms, which sometimes envelop whole caravans and cause their destruction. Hungry wolves also roam over the plain in thousands. But it would have been better for Michael Strogoff to face these risks; for during the winter the Tartar invaders would have been stationed in the towns, any movement of their troops would have been impracticable, and he could consequently have more easily performed his journey. But it was not in his power to choose either weather or time. Whatever the circumstances, he must accept them and set out.

Such were the difficulties which Michael Strogoff boldly confronted and prepared to encounter.

In the first place, he must not travel as a courier of the Czar usually would. No one must even suspect what he really was. Spies swarm in a rebellious country; let him be recognized, and his mission would be in danger. Also, while supplying him with a large sum of money, which was sufficient for his journey, and would facilitate it in some measure, General Kissoff had not given him any document notifying that he was on the Emperor's service, which is the Sesame par excellence. He contented himself with furnishing him with a "podorojna."

This podorojna was made out in the name of Nicholas Korpanoff, merchant, living at Irkutsk. It authorized Nicholas Korpanoff to be accompanied by one or more persons, and, moreover, it was, by special notification, made available in the event of the Muscovite government forbidding natives of any other countries to leave Russia.

The podorojna is simply a permission to take post-horses; but Michael Strogoff was not to use it unless he was sure that by so doing he would not excite suspicion as to his mission, that is to say, whilst he was on European territory. The consequence was that in Siberia, whilst traversing the insurgent provinces, he would have no power over the relays, either in the choice of horses in preference to others, or in demanding conveyances for his personal use; neither was Michael Strogoff to forget that he was no longer a courier, but a plain merchant, Nicholas Korpanoff, traveling from Moscow to Irkutsk, and, as such exposed to all the impediments of an ordinary journey.

To pass unknown, more or less rapidly, but to pass somehow, such were the directions he had received.

Thirty years previously, the escort of a traveler of rank consisted of not less than two hundred mounted Cossacks, two hundred foot-soldiers, twenty-five Baskir horsemen, three hundred camels, four hundred horses, twenty-five wagons, two portable boats, and two pieces of cannon. All this was requisite for a journey in Siberia.

Michael Strogoff, however, had neither cannon, nor horsemen, nor foot-soldiers, nor beasts of burden. He would travel in a carriage or on horseback, when he could; on foot, when he could not.

There would be no difficulty in getting over the first thousand miles, the distance between Moscow and the Russian frontier. Railroads, post-carriages, steamboats, relays of horses, were at everyone's disposal, and consequently at the disposal of the courier of the Czar.

Accordingly, on the morning of the 16th of July, having doffed his uniform, with a knapsack on his back, dressed in the simple Russian costume—tightly-fitting tunic, the traditional belt of the Moujik, wide trousers, gartered at the knees, and high boots—Michael Strogoff arrived at the station in time for the first train. He carried no arms, openly at least, but under his belt was hidden a revolver and in his pocket, one of those large knives, resembling both a cutlass and a yataghan, with which a Siberian hunter can so neatly disembowel a bear, without injuring its precious fur.

A crowd of travelers had collected at the Moscow station. The stations on the Russian railroads are much used as places for meeting, not only by those who are about to proceed by the train, but by friends who come to see them off. The station resembles, from the variety of characters assembled, a small news exchange.

The train in which Michael took his place was to set him down at Nijni-Novgorod. There terminated at that time, the iron road which, uniting Moscow and St. Petersburg, has since been continued to the Russian frontier. It was a journey of under three hundred miles, and the train would accomplish it in ten hours. Once arrived at Nijni-Novgorod, Strogoff would either take the land route or the steamer on the Volga, so as to reach the Ural Mountains as soon as possible.

Michael Strogoff ensconced himself in his corner, like a worthy citizen whose affairs go well with him, and who endeavors to kill time by sleep. Nevertheless, as he was not alone in his compartment, he slept with one eye open, and listened with both his ears.

In fact, rumor of the rising of the Kirghiz hordes, and of the Tartar invasion had transpired in some degree. The occupants of the carriage, whom chance had made his traveling companions, discussed the subject, though with that caution which has become habitual among Russians, who know that spies are ever on the watch for any treasonable expressions which may be uttered.

These travelers, as well as the large number of persons in the train, were merchants on their way to the celebrated fair of Nijni-Novgorod;—a very mixed assembly, composed of Jews, Turks, Cossacks, Russians, Georgians, Kalmucks, and others, but nearly all speaking the national tongue.

They discussed the pros and cons of the serious events which were taking place beyond the Ural, and those merchants seemed to fear lest the government should be led to take certain restrictive measures, especially in the provinces bordering on the frontier—measures from which trade would certainly suffer. They apparently thought only of the struggle from the single point of view of their threatened interests. The presence of a private soldier, clad in his uniform—and the importance of a uniform in Russia is great—would have certainly been enough to restrain the merchants' tongues. But in the compartment occupied by Michael Strogoff, there was no one who seemed a military man, and the Czar's courier was not the person to betray himself. He listened, then.

"They say that caravan teas are up," remarked a Persian, known by his cap of Astrakhan fur, and his ample brown robe, worn threadbare by use.

"Oh, there's no fear of teas falling," answered an old Jew of sullen aspect. "Those in the market at Nijni-Novgorod will be easily cleared off by the West; but, unfortunately, it won't be the same with Bokhara carpets."

"What! are you expecting goods from Bokhara?" asked the Persian.

"No, but from Samarcand, and that is even more exposed. The idea of reckoning on the exports of a country in which the khans are in a state of revolt from Khiva to the Chinese frontier!"

"Well," replied the Persian, "if the carpets do not arrive, the drafts will not arrive either, I suppose."

"And the profits, Father Abraham!" exclaimed the little Jew, "do you reckon them as nothing?"

"You are right," said another; "goods from Central Asia run a great risk in the market, and it will be the same with the tallow and shawls from the East."

"Why, look out, little father," said a Russian traveler, in a bantering tone; "you'll grease your shawls terribly if you mix them up with your tallow."

"That amuses you," sharply answered the merchant, who had little relish for that sort of joke.

"Well, if you tear your hair, or if you throw ashes on your head," replied the traveler, "will that change the course of events? No; no more than the course of the Exchange."

"One can easily see that you are not a merchant," observed the little Jew.

"Faith, no, worthy son of Abraham! I sell neither hops, nor eider-down, nor honey, nor wax, nor hemp-seed, nor salt meat, nor caviare, nor wood, nor wool, nor ribbons, nor, hemp, nor flax, nor morocco, nor furs."

"But do you buy them?" asked the Persian, interrupting the traveler's list.

"As little as I can, and only for my own private use," answered the other, with a wink.

"He's a wag," said the Jew to the Persian.

"Or a spy," replied the other, lowering his voice. "We had better take care, and not speak more than necessary. The police are not over-particular in these times, and you never can know with whom you are traveling."

In another corner of the compartment they were speaking less of mercantile affairs, and more of the Tartar invasion and its annoying consequences.

"All the horses in Siberia will be requisitioned," said a traveler, "and communication between the different provinces of Central Asia will become very difficult."

"Is it true," asked his neighbor, "that the Kirghiz of the middle horde have joined the Tartars?"

"So it is said," answered the traveler, lowering his voice; "but who can flatter themselves that they know anything really of what is going on in this country?"

"I have heard speak of a concentration of troops on the frontier. The Don Cossacks have already gathered along the course of the Volga, and they are to be opposed to the rebel Kirghiz."

"If the Kirghiz descend the Irtish, the route to Irkutsk will not be safe," observed his neighbor. "Besides, yesterday I wanted to send a telegram to Krasnoiarsk, and it could not be forwarded. It's to be feared that before long the Tartar columns will have isolated Eastern Siberia."

"In short, little father," continued the first speaker, "these merchants have good reason for being uneasy about their trade and transactions. After requisitioning the horses, they will take the boats, carriages, every means of transport, until presently no one will be allowed to take even one step in all the empire."

"I'm much afraid that the Nijni-Novgorod fair won't end as brilliantly as it has begun," responded the other, shaking his head. "But the safety and integrity of the Russian territory before everything. Business is business."

If in this compartment the subject of conversation varied but little— nor did it, indeed, in the other carriages of the train—in all it might have been observed that the talkers used much circumspection. When they did happen to venture out of the region of facts, they never went so far as to attempt to divine the intentions of the Muscovite government, or even to criticize them.

This was especially remarked by a traveler in a carriage at the front part of the train. This person—evidently a stranger—made good use of his eyes, and asked numberless questions, to which he received only evasive answers. Every minute leaning out of the window, which he would keep down, to the great disgust of his fellow-travelers, he lost nothing of the views to the right. He inquired the names of the most insignificant places, their position, what were their commerce, their manufactures, the number of their inhabitants, the average mortality, etc., and all this he wrote down in a note-book, already full.

This was the correspondent Alcide Jolivet, and the reason of his putting so many insignificant questions was, that amongst the many answers he received, he hoped to find some interesting fact "for his cousin." But, naturally enough, he was taken for a spy, and not a word treating of the events of the day was uttered in his hearing.

Finding, therefore, that he could learn nothing of the Tartar invasion, he wrote in his book, "Travelers of great discretion. Very close as to political matters."

Whilst Alcide Jolivet noted down his impressions thus minutely, his confrere, in the same train, traveling for the same object, was devoting himself to the same work of observation in another compartment. Neither of them had seen each other that day at the Moscow station, and they were each ignorant that the other had set out to visit the scene of the war. Harry Blount, speaking little, but listening much, had not inspired his companions with the suspicions which Alcide Jolivet had aroused. He was not taken for a spy, and therefore his neighbors, without constraint, gossiped in his presence, allowing themselves even to go farther than their natural caution would in most cases have allowed them. The correspondent of the Daily Telegraph had thus an opportunity of observing

22

how much recent events preoccupied the merchants of Nijni-Novgorod, and to what a degree the commerce with Central Asia was threatened in its transit.

He therefore noted in his book this perfectly correct observation, "My fellow-travelers extremely anxious. Nothing is talked of but war, and they speak of it, with a freedom which is astonishing, as having broken out between the Volga and the Vistula."

The readers of the Daily Telegraph would not fail to be as well informed as Alcide Jolivet's "cousin." But as Harry Blount, seated at the left of the train, only saw one part of the country, which was hilly, without giving himself the trouble of looking at the right side, which was composed of wide plains, he added, with British assurance, "Country mountainous between Moscow and Wladimir."

It was evident that the Russian government purposed taking severe measures to guard against any serious eventualities even in the interior of the empire. The rebel lion had not crossed the Siberian frontier, but evil influences might be feared in the Volga provinces, so near to the country of the Kirghiz.

The police had as yet found no traces of Ivan Ogareff. It was not known whether the traitor, calling in the foreigner to avenge his personal rancor, had rejoined Feofar-Khan, or whether he was endeavoring to foment a revolt in the government of Nijni-Novgorod, which at this time of year contained a population of such diverse elements. Perhaps among the Persians, Armenians, or Kalmucks, who flocked to the great market, he had agents, instructed to provoke a rising in the interior. All this was possible, especially in such a country as Russia. In fact, this vast empire, 4,000,000 square miles in extent, does not possess the homogeneousness of the states of Western Europe. The Russian territory in Europe and Asia contains more than seventy millions of inhabitants. In it thirty different languages are spoken. The Sclavonian race predominates, no doubt, but there are besides Russians, Poles, Lithuanians, Courlanders. Add to these, Finns, Laplanders, Esthonians, several other northern tribes with unpronounceable names, the Permiaks, the Germans, the Greeks, the Tartars, the Caucasian tribes, the Mongol, Kalmuck, Samoid, Kamtschatkan, and Aleutian hordes, and one may understand that the unity of so vast a state must be difficult to maintain, and that it could only be the work of time, aided by the wisdom of many successive rulers.

Be that as it may, Ivan Ogareff had hitherto managed to escape all search, and very probably he might have rejoined the Tartar army. But at every station where the train stopped, inspectors came forward who scrutinized the travelers and subjected them all to a minute examination, as by order of the superintendent of police, these officials were seeking Ivan Ogareff. The government, in fact, believed it to be certain that the traitor had not yet been able to quit European Russia. If there appeared cause to suspect any traveler, he was carried off to explain himself at the police station, and in the meantime the train went on its way, no person troubling himself about the unfortunate one left behind.

With the Russian police, which is very arbitrary, it is absolutely useless to argue. Military rank is conferred on its employees, and they act in military fashion. How can anyone, moreover, help obeying, unhesitatingly, orders which emanate from a monarch who has the right to employ this formula at the head of his ukase: "We, by the grace of God, Emperor and Autocrat of all the Russias of Moscow, Kiev, Wladimir, and Novgorod, Czar of Kasan and Astrakhan, Czar of Poland, Czar of Siberia, Czar of the Tauric Chersonese, Seignior of Pskov, Prince of Smolensk, Lithuania, Volkynia, Podolia, and Finland, Prince of Esthonia, Livonia, Courland, and of Semigallia, of Bialystok, Karelia, Sougria, Perm, Viatka, Bulgaria, and many other countries; Lord and Sovereign Prince of the territory of Nijni-Novgorod, Tchemigoff, Riazan, Polotsk, Rostov, Jaroslavl, Bielozersk, Oudoria, Obdoria, Kondinia, Vitepsk, and of Mstislaf, Governor of the Hyperborean Regions, Lord of the countries of Iveria, Kartalinia, Grou-zinia, Kabardinia, and Armenia, Hereditary Lord and Suzerain of the Scherkess princes, of those of the mountains, and of others; heir of Norway, Duke of Schleswig-Holstein, Stormarn, Dittmarsen, and Oldenburg." A powerful lord, in truth, is he whose arms are an eagle with two heads, holding a scepter and a globe, surrounded by the escutcheons of Novgorod, Wladimir, Kiev, Kasan, Astrakhan, and of Siberia, and environed by the collar of the order of St. Andrew, surmounted by a royal crown!

As to Michael Strogoff, his papers were in order, and he was, consequently, free from all police supervision.

At the station of Wladimir the train stopped for several minutes, which appeared sufficient to enable the correspondent of the Daily Telegraph to take a twofold view, physical and moral, and to form a complete estimate of this ancient capital of Russia.

At the Wladimir station fresh travelers joined the train. Among others, a young girl entered the compartment occupied by Michael Strogoff. A vacant place was found opposite the courier. The young girl took it, after placing by her side a modest traveling-bag of red leather, which seemed to constitute all her luggage. Then seating herself with downcast eyes, not even glancing at the fellow-travelers whom chance had given her, she prepared for a journey which was still to last several hours.

Michael Strogoff could not help looking attentively at his newly-arrived fellow-traveler. As she was so placed as to travel with her back to the engine, he even offered her his seat, which he might prefer to her own, but she thanked him with a slight bend of her graceful neck.

The young girl appeared to be about sixteen or seventeen years of age. Her head, truly charming, was of the purest Sclavonic type—slightly severe, and likely in a few summers to unfold into beauty rather than mere prettiness. From beneath a sort of kerchief which she wore on her head escaped in profusion light golden hair. Her eyes were brown, soft, and expressive of much sweetness of temper. The nose was straight, and attached to her pale and somewhat thin cheeks by delicately mobile nostrils. The lips were finely cut, but it seemed as if they had long since forgotten how to smile.

The young traveler was tall and upright, as far as could be judged of her figure from the very simple and ample pelisse that covered her. Although she was still a very young girl in the literal sense of the term, the development of her high forehead and clearly-cut features gave the idea that she was the possessor of great moral energy—a point which did not escape Michael Strogoff. Evidently this young girl had already suffered in the past, and the future doubtless did not present itself to her in glowing colors; but she had surely known how to struggle still with the trials of life. Her energy was evidently both prompt and persistent, and her calmness unalterable, even under circumstances in which a man would be likely to give way or lose his self-command.

Such was the impression which she produced at first sight. Michael Strogoff, being himself of an energetic temperament, was naturally struck by the character of her physiognomy, and, while taking care not to cause her annoyance by a too persistent gaze, he observed his neighbor with no small interest. The costume of the young traveler was both extremely simple and appropriate. She was not rich—that could be easily seen; but not the slightest mark of negligence was to be discerned in her dress. All her luggage was contained in the leather bag which, for want of room, she held on her lap.

She wore a long, dark pelisse, gracefully adjusted at the neck by a blue tie. Under this pelisse, a short skirt, also dark, fell over a robe which reached the ankles. Half-boots of leather, thickly soled, as if chosen in anticipation of a long journey, covered her small feet.

Michael Strogoff fancied that he recognized, by certain details, the fashion of the costume of Livonia, and thought his neighbor a native of the Baltic provinces.

But whither was this young girl going, alone, at an age when the fostering care of a father, or the protection of a brother, is considered a matter of necessity? Had she now come, after an already long journey, from the provinces of Western Russia? Was she merely going to Nijni-Novgorod, or was the end of her travels beyond the eastern frontiers of the empire? Would some relation, some friend, await her arrival by the train? Or was it not more probable, on the contrary, that she would find herself as much isolated in the town as she was in this compartment? It was probable.

In fact, the effect of habits contracted in solitude was clearly manifested in the bearing of the young girl. The manner in which she entered the carriage and prepared herself for the journey, the slight disturbance she caused among those around her, the care she took not to incommode or give trouble to anyone, all showed that she was accustomed to be alone, and to depend on herself only.

Michael Strogoff observed her with interest, but, himself reserved, he sought no opportunity of accosting her. Once only, when her neighbor— the merchant who had jumbled together so imprudently in his remarks

25

tallow and shawls—being asleep, and threatening her with his great head, which was swaying from one shoulder to the other, Michael Strogoff awoke him somewhat roughly, and made him understand that he must hold himself upright.

The merchant, rude enough by nature, grumbled some words against "people who interfere with what does not concern them," but Michael Strogoff cast on him a glance so stern that the sleeper leant on the opposite side, and relieved the young traveler from his unpleasant vicinity.

The latter looked at the young man for an instant, and mute and modest thanks were in that look.

But a circumstance occurred which gave Strogoff a just idea of the character of the maiden. Twelve versts before arriving at Nijni-Novgorod, at a sharp curve of the iron way, the train experienced a very violent shock. Then, for a minute, it ran onto the slope of an embankment.

Travelers more or less shaken about, cries, confusion, general disorder in the carriages—such was the effect at first produced. It was to be feared that some serious accident had happened. Consequently, even before the train had stopped, the doors were opened, and the panic-stricken passengers thought only of getting out of the carriages.

Michael Strogoff thought instantly of the young girl; but, while the passengers in her compartment were precipitating themselves outside, screaming and struggling, she had remained quietly in her place, her face scarcely changed by a slight pallor.

She waited—Michael Strogoff waited also.

Both remained quiet.

"A determined nature!" thought Michael Strogoff.

However, all danger had quickly disappeared. A breakage of the coupling of the luggage-van had first caused the shock to, and then the stoppage of, the train, which in another instant would have been thrown from the top of the embankment into a bog. There was an hour's delay. At last, the road being cleared, the train proceeded, and at half-past eight in the evening arrived at the station of Nijni-Novgorod.

Before anyone could get out of the carriages, the inspectors of police presented themselves at the doors and examined the passengers.

Michael Strogoff showed his podorojna, made out in the name of Nicholas Korpanoff. He had consequently no difficulty. As to the other travelers in the compartment, all bound for Nijni-Novgorod, their appearance, happily for them, was in nowise suspicious.

The young girl in her turn, exhibited, not a passport, since passports are no longer required in Russia, but a permit indorsed with a private seal, and which seemed to be of a special character. The inspector read the permit with attention. Then, having attentively examined the person whose description it contained:

"You are from Riga?" he said.

"Yes," replied the young girl.

"You are going to Irkutsk?"

"Yes."

"By what route?"

"By Perm."

"Good!" replied the inspector. "Take care to have your permit vised, at the police station of Nijni-Novgorod."

The young girl bent her head in token of assent.

Hearing these questions and replies, Michael Strogoff experienced a mingled sentiment both of surprise and pity. What! this young girl, alone, journeying to that far-off Siberia, and at a time when, to its ordinary dangers, were added all the perils of an invaded country and one in a state of insurrection! How would she reach it? What would become of her?

The inspection ended, the doors of the carriages were then opened, but, before Michael Strogoff could move towards her, the young Livonian, who had been the first to descend, had disappeared in the crowd which thronged the platforms of the railway station.

CHAPTER V
THE TWO ANNOUNCEMENTS

NIJNI-NOVGOROD, Lower Novgorod, situate at the junction of the Volga and the Oka, is the chief town in the district of the same name. It was here that Michael Strogoff was obliged to leave the railway, which at the time did not go beyond that town. Thus, as he advanced, his traveling would become first less speedy and then less safe.

Nijni-Novgorod, the fixed population of which is only from thirty to thirty-five thousand inhabitants, contained at that time more than three hundred thousand; that is to say, the population was increased tenfold. This addition was in consequence of the celebrated fair, which was held within the walls for three weeks. Formerly Makariew had the benefit of this concourse of traders, but since 1817 the fair had been removed to Nijni-Novgorod.

Even at the late hour at which Michael Strogoff left the platform, there was still a large number of people in the two towns, separated by the stream of the Volga, which compose Nijni-Novgorod. The highest of these is built on a steep rock, and defended by a fort called in Russia "kreml."

Michael Strogoff expected some trouble in finding a hotel, or even an inn, to suit him. As he had not to start immediately, for he was going to take a steamer, he was compelled to look out for some lodging; but, before doing so, he wished to know exactly the hour at which the steamboat would start. He went to the office of the company whose boats plied between Nijni-Novgorod and Perm. There, to his great annoyance, he found that no boat started for Perm till the following day at twelve o'clock. Seventeen hours to wait! It was very vexatious to a man so pressed for time. However, he never senselessly murmured. Besides, the fact was that no other conveyance could take him so quickly either to Perm or Kasan. It would be better, then, to wait for the steamer, which would enable him to regain lost time.

Here, then, was Michael Strogoff, strolling through the town and quietly looking out for some inn in which to pass the night. However, he troubled himself little on this score, and, but that hunger pressed him, he would probably have wandered on till morning in the streets of Nijni-Novgorod. He was looking for supper rather than a bed. But he found both at the sign of the City of Constantinople. There, the landlord offered him a fairly comfortable room, with little furniture, it is true, but not without an image of the Virgin, and a few saints framed in yellow gauze.

A goose filled with sour stuffing swimming in thick cream, barley bread, some curds, powdered sugar mixed with cinnamon, and a jug of kwass, the ordinary Russian beer, were placed before him, and sufficed to satisfy his hunger. He did justice to the meal, which was more than could be said of his neighbor at table, who, having, in his character of "old believer" of the sect of Raskalniks, made the vow of abstinence, rejected the potatoes in front of him, and carefully refrained from putting sugar in his tea.

His supper finished, Michael Strogoff, instead of going up to his bedroom, again strolled out into the town. But, although the long twilight yet lingered, the crowd was already dispersing, the streets were gradually becoming empty, and at length everyone retired to his dwelling.

Why did not Michael Strogoff go quietly to bed, as would have seemed more reasonable after a long railway journey? Was he thinking of the young Livonian girl who had been his traveling companion? Having nothing better to do, he WAS thinking of her. Did he fear that, lost in this busy city, she might be exposed to insult? He feared so, and with good reason. Did he hope to meet her, and, if need were, to afford her protection? No. To meet would be difficult. As to protection—what right had he—

"Alone," he said to himself, "alone, in the midst of these wandering tribes! And yet the present dangers are nothing compared to those she must undergo. Siberia! Irkutsk! I am about to dare all risks for Russia, for the Czar, while she is about to do so—For whom? For what? She is authorized to cross the frontier! The country beyond is in revolt! The steppes are full of Tartar bands!"

Michael Strogoff stopped for an instant, and reflected.

"Without doubt," thought he, "she must have determined on undertaking her journey before the invasion. Perhaps she is even now ignorant of what is happening. But no, that cannot be; the merchants discussed before her the disturbances in Siberia—and she did not seem surprised. She did not even ask an explanation. She must have known it then, and knowing it, is still resolute. Poor girl! Her motive for the journey must be urgent indeed! But though she may be brave—and she certainly is so—her strength must fail her, and, to say nothing of dangers and obstacles, she will be unable to endure the fatigue of such a journey. Never can she reach Irkutsk!"

Indulging in such reflections, Michael Strogoff wandered on as chance led him; being well acquainted with the town, he knew that he could easily retrace his steps.

Having strolled on for about an hour, he seated himself on a bench against the wall of a large wooden cottage, which stood, with many others, on a vast open space. He had scarcely been there five minutes when a hand was laid heavily on his shoulder.

"What are you doing here?" roughly demanded a tall and powerful man, who had approached unperceived.

"I am resting," replied Michael Strogoff.

"Do you mean to stay all night on the bench?"

"Yes, if I feel inclined to do so," answered Michael Strogoff, in a tone somewhat too sharp for the simple merchant he wished to personate.

"Come forward, then, so I can see you," said the man.

Michael Strogoff, remembering that, above all, prudence was requisite, instinctively drew back. "It is not necessary," he replied, and calmly stepped back ten paces.

The man seemed, as Michael observed him well, to have the look of a Bohemian, such as are met at fairs, and with whom contact, either physical or moral, is unpleasant. Then, as he looked more attentively through the dusk, he perceived, near the cottage, a large caravan, the usual traveling dwelling of the Zingaris or gypsies, who swarm in Russia wherever a few copecks can be obtained.

As the gypsy took two or three steps forward, and was about to interrogate Michael Strogoff more closely, the door of the cottage opened. He could just see a woman, who spoke quickly in a language which Michael Strogoff knew to be a mixture of Mongol and Siberian.

"Another spy! Let him alone, and come to supper. The papluka is waiting for you."

Michael Strogoff could not help smiling at the epithet bestowed on him, dreading spies as he did above all else.

In the same dialect, although his accent was very different, the Bohemian replied in words which signify, "You are right, Sangarre! Besides, we start to-morrow."

"To-morrow?" repeated the woman in surprise.

"Yes, Sangarre," replied the Bohemian; "to-morrow, and the Father himself sends us—where we are going!"

Thereupon the man and woman entered the cottage, and carefully closed the door.

"Good!" said Michael Strogoff, to himself; "if these gipsies do not wish to be understood when they speak before me, they had better use some other language."

From his Siberian origin, and because he had passed his childhood in the Steppes, Michael Strogoff, it has been said, understood almost all the languages in usage from Tartary to the Sea of Ice. As to the exact signification of the words he had heard, he did not trouble his head. For why should it interest him?

29

It was already late when he thought of returning to his inn to take some repose. He followed, as he did so, the course of the Volga, whose waters were almost hidden under the countless number of boats floating on its bosom.

An hour after, Michael Strogoff was sleeping soundly on one of those Russian beds which always seem so hard to strangers, and on the morrow, the 17th of July, he awoke at break of day.

He had still five hours to pass in Nijni-Novgorod; it seemed to him an age. How was he to spend the morning unless in wandering, as he had done the evening before, through the streets? By the time he had finished his breakfast, strapped up his bag, had his podorojna inspected at the police office, he would have nothing to do but start. But he was not a man to lie in bed after the sun had risen; so he rose, dressed himself, placed the letter with the imperial arms on it carefully at the bottom of its usual pocket within the lining of his coat, over which he fastened his belt; he then closed his bag and threw it over his shoulder. This done, he had no wish to return to the City of Constantinople, and intending to breakfast on the bank of the Volga near the wharf, he settled his bill and left the inn. By way of precaution, Michael Strogoff went first to the office of the steam-packet company, and there made sure that the Caucasus would start at the appointed hour. As he did so, the thought for the first time struck him that, since the young Livonian girl was going to Perm, it was very possible that her intention was also to embark in the Caucasus, in which case he should accompany her.

The town above with its kremlin, whose circumference measures two versts, and which resembles that of Moscow, was altogether abandoned. Even the governor did not reside there. But if the town above was like a city of the dead, the town below, at all events, was alive.

Michael Strogoff, having crossed the Volga on a bridge of boats, guarded by mounted Cossacks, reached the square where the evening before he had fallen in with the gipsy camp. This was somewhat outside the town, where the fair of Nijni-Novgorod was held. In a vast plain rose the temporary palace of the governor-general, where by imperial orders that great functionary resided during the whole of the fair, which, thanks to the people who composed it, required an ever-watchful surveillance.

This plain was now covered with booths symmetrically arranged in such a manner as to leave avenues broad enough to allow the crowd to pass without a crush.

Each group of these booths, of all sizes and shapes, formed a separate quarter particularly dedicated to some special branch of commerce. There was the iron quarter, the furriers' quarter, the woolen quarter, the quarter of the wood merchants, the weavers' quarter, the dried fish quarter, etc. Some booths were even built of fancy materials, some of bricks of tea, others of masses of salt meat—that is to say, of samples of the goods which the owners thus announced were there to the purchasers—a singular, and somewhat American, mode of advertisement.

In the avenues and long alleys there was already a large assemblage of people—the sun, which had risen at four o'clock, being well above the horizon—an extraordinary mixture of Europeans and Asiatics, talking, wrangling, haranguing, and bargaining. Everything which can be bought or sold seemed to be heaped up in this square. Furs, precious stones, silks, Cashmere shawls, Turkey carpets, weapons from the Caucasus, gauzes from Smyrna and Ispahan. Tiflis armor, caravan teas. European bronzes, Swiss clocks, velvets and silks from Lyons, English cottons, harness, fruits, vegetables, minerals from the Ural, malachite, lapis-lazuli, spices, perfumes, medicinal herbs, wood, tar, rope, horn, pumpkins, watermelons, etc—all the products of India, China, Persia, from the shores of the Caspian and the Black Sea, from America and Europe, were united at this corner of the globe.

It is scarcely possible truly to portray the moving mass of human beings surging here and there, the excitement, the confusion, the hubbub; demonstrative as were the natives and the inferior classes, they were completely outdone by their visitors. There were merchants from Central Asia, who had occupied a year in escorting their merchandise across its vast plains, and who would not again see their shops and counting-houses for another year to come. In short, of such importance is this fair of Nijni-Novgorod, that the sum total of its transactions amounts yearly to nearly a hundred million dollars.

On one of the open spaces between the quarters of this temporary city were numbers of mountebanks of every description; gypsies from the mountains, telling fortunes to the credulous fools who are ever to be found in such assemblies; Zingaris or Tsiganes—a name which the Russians give to the gypsies who are the descendants of the ancient Copts—singing their wildest melodies and dancing their most original dances; comedians of foreign theaters, acting Shakespeare, adapted to the taste of spectators who crowded to witness them. In the long avenues the bear showmen accompanied their four-footed dancers, menageries resounded with the hoarse cries of animals under the influence of the stinging whip or red-hot irons of the tamer; and, besides all these numberless performers, in the middle of the central square, surrounded by a circle four deep of enthusiastic amateurs, was a band of "mariners of the Volga," sitting on the ground, as on the deck of their vessel, imitating the action of rowing, guided by the stick of the master of the orchestra, the veritable helmsman of this imaginary vessel! A whimsical and pleasing custom!

Suddenly, according to a time-honored observance in the fair of Nijni-Novgorod, above the heads of the vast concourse a flock of birds was allowed to escape from the cages in which they had been brought to the spot. In return for a few copecks charitably offered by some good people, the bird-fanciers opened the prison doors of their captives, who flew out in hundreds, uttering their joyous notes.

It should be mentioned that England and France, at all events, were this year represented at the great fair of Nijni-Novgorod by two of the most distinguished products of modern civilization, Messrs. Harry Blount and Alcide Jolivet. Jolivet, an optimist by nature, found everything agreeable, and as by chance both lodging and food were to his taste, he jotted down in his book some memoranda particularly favorable to the town of Nijni-Novgorod. Blount, on the contrary, having in vain hunted for a supper, had been obliged to find a resting-place in the open air. He therefore looked at it all from another point of view, and was preparing an article of the most withering character against a town in which the landlords of the inns refused to receive travelers who only begged leave to be flayed, "morally and physically."

Michael Strogoff, one hand in his pocket, the other holding his cherry-stemmed pipe, appeared the most indifferent and least impatient of men; yet, from a certain contraction of his eyebrows every now and then, a careful observer would have seen that he was burning to be off.

For two hours he kept walking about the streets, only to find himself invariably at the fair again. As he passed among the groups of buyers and sellers he discovered that those who came from countries on the confines of Asia manifested great uneasiness. Their trade was visibly suffering. Another symptom also was marked. In Russia military uniforms appear on every occasion. Soldiers are wont to mix freely with the crowd, the police agents being almost invariably aided by a number of Cossacks, who, lance on shoulder, keep order in the crowd of three hundred thousand strangers. But on this occasion the soldiers, Cossacks and the rest, did not put in an appearance at the great market. Doubtless, a sudden order to move having been foreseen, they were restricted to their barracks.

Moreover, while no soldiers were to be seen, it was not so with their officers. Since the evening before, aides-decamp, leaving the governor's palace, galloped in every direction. An unusual movement was going forward which a serious state of affairs could alone account for. There were innumerable couriers on the roads both to Wladimir and to the Ural Mountains. The exchange of telegraphic dispatches with Moscow was incessant.

Michael Strogoff found himself in the central square when the report spread that the head of police had been summoned by a courier to the palace of the governor-general. An important dispatch from Moscow, it was said, was the cause of it.

"The fair is to be closed," said one.

"The regiment of Nijni-Novgorod has received the route," declared another.

"They say that the Tartars menace Tomsk!"

"Here is the head of police!" was shouted on every side. A loud clapping of hands was suddenly raised, which subsided by degrees, and finally was succeeded by absolute silence. The head of police arrived in the middle of the central square, and it was seen by all that he held in his hand a dispatch.

Then, in a loud voice, he read the following announcements: "By order of the Governor of Nijni-Novgorod.

"1st. All Russian subjects are forbidden to quit the province upon any pretext whatsoever.

32

"2nd. All strangers of Asiatic origin are commanded to leave the province within twenty-four hours."

CHAPTER VI
BROTHER AND SISTER

HOWEVER disastrous these measures might be to private interests, they were, under the circumstances, perfectly justifiable.

"All Russian subjects are forbidden to leave the province;" if Ivan Ogareff was still in the province, this would at any rate prevent him, unless with the greatest difficulty, from rejoining Feofar-Khan, and becoming a very formidable lieutenant to the Tartar chief.

"All foreigners of Asiatic origin are ordered to leave the province in four-and-twenty hours;" this would send off in a body all the traders from Central Asia, as well as the bands of Bohemians, gipsies, etc., having more or less sympathy with the Tartars. So many heads, so many spies—undoubtedly affairs required their expulsion.

It is easy to understand the effect produced by these two thunder-claps bursting over a town like Nijni-Novgorod, so densely crowded with visitors, and with a commerce so greatly surpassing that of all other places in Russia. The natives whom business called beyond the Siberian frontier could not leave the province for a time at least. The tenor of the first article of the order was express; it admitted of no exception. All private interests must yield to the public weal. As to the second article of the proclamation, the order of expulsion which it contained admitted of no evasion either. It only concerned foreigners of Asiatic origin, but these could do nothing but pack up their merchandise and go back the way they came. As to the mountebanks, of which there were a considerable number, they had nearly a thousand versts to go before they could reach the nearest frontier. For them it was simply misery.

At first there rose against this unusual measure a murmur of protestation, a cry of despair, but this was quickly suppressed by the presence of the Cossacks and agents of police. Immediately, what might be called the exodus from the immense plain began. The awnings in front of the stalls were folded up; the theaters were taken to pieces; the fires were put out; the acrobats' ropes were lowered; the old broken-winded horses of the traveling vans came back from their sheds. Agents and soldiers with whip or stick stimulated the tardy ones, and made nothing of pulling down the tents even before the poor Bohemians had left them.

Under these energetic measures the square of Nijni-Novgorod would, it was evident, be entirely evacuated before the evening, and to the tumult of the great fair would succeed the silence of the desert.

It must again be repeated—for it was a necessary aggravation of these severe measures—that to all those nomads chiefly concerned in the order of expulsion even the steppes of Siberia were forbidden, and they would be obliged to hasten to the south of the Caspian Sea, either to Persia, Turkey, or the plains of Turkestan. The post of the Ural, and the mountains which form, as it were, a prolongation of the river along the Russian frontier, they were not allowed to pass. They were therefore under the necessity of traveling six hundred miles before they could tread a free soil.

Just as the reading of the proclamation by the head of the police came to an end, an idea darted instinctively into the mind of Michael Strogoff. "What a singular coincidence," thought he, "between this proclamation expelling all foreigners of Asiatic origin, and the words exchanged last evening between those two gipsies of the Zingari race. 'The Father himself sends us where we wish to go,' that old man said. But 'the Father' is the emperor! He is never called anything else among the people. How could those gipsies have foreseen the measure taken against them? how could they have known it beforehand, and where do they wish to go? Those are suspicious people, and it seems to me that to them the government proclamation must be more useful than injurious."

But these reflections were completely dispelled by another which drove every other thought out of Michael's mind. He forgot the Zingaris, their suspicious words, the strange coincidence which resulted from the proclamation. The remembrance of the young Livonian girl suddenly rushed into his mind. "Poor child!" he thought to himself. "She cannot now cross the frontier."

In truth the young girl was from Riga; she was Livonian, consequently Russian, and now could not leave Russian territory! The permit which had been given her before the new measures had been promulgated was no longer available. All the routes to Siberia had just been pitilessly closed to her, and, whatever the motive taking her to Irkutsk, she was now forbidden to go there.

This thought greatly occupied Michael Strogoff. He said to himself, vaguely at first, that, without neglecting anything of what was due to his important mission, it would perhaps be possible for him to be of some use to this brave girl; and this idea pleased him. Knowing how serious were the dangers which he, an energetic and vigorous man, would have personally to encounter, he could not conceal from himself how infinitely greater they would prove to a young unprotected girl. As she was going to Irkutsk, she would be obliged to follow the same road as himself, she would have to pass through the bands of invaders, as he was about to attempt doing himself. If, moreover, she had at her disposal only the money necessary for a journey taken under ordinary circumstances, how could she manage to accomplish it under conditions which made it not only perilous but expensive?

"Well," said he, "if she takes the route to Perm, it is nearly impossible but that I shall fall in with her. Then, I will watch over her without her suspecting it; and as she appears to me as anxious as myself to reach Irkutsk, she will cause me no delay."

But one thought leads to another. Michael Strogoff had till now thought only of doing a kind action; but now another idea flashed into his brain; the question presented itself under quite a new aspect.

"The fact is," said he to himself, "that I have much more need of her than she can have of me. Her presence will be useful in drawing off suspicion from me. A man traveling alone across the steppe, may be easily guessed to be a courier of the Czar. If, on the contrary, this young girl accompanies me, I shall appear, in the eyes of all, the Nicholas Korpanoff of my podorojna. Therefore, she must accompany me. Therefore, I must find her again at any cost. It is not probable that since yesterday evening she has been able to get a carriage and leave Nijni-Novgorod. I must look for her. And may God guide me!"

Michael left the great square of Nijni-Novgorod, where the tumult produced by the carrying out of the prescribed measures had now reached its height. Recriminations from the banished strangers, shouts from the agents and Cossacks who were using them so brutally, together made an indescribable uproar. The girl for whom he searched could not be there. It was now nine o'clock in the morning. The steamboat did not start till twelve. Michael Strogoff had therefore nearly two hours to employ in searching for her whom he wished to make his traveling companion.

He crossed the Volga again and hunted through the quarters on the other side, where the crowd was much less considerable. He entered the churches, the natural refuge for all who weep, for all who suffer. Nowhere did he meet with the young Livonian.

"And yet," he repeated, "she could not have left Nijni-Novgorod yet. We'll have another look." He wandered about thus for two hours. He went on without stopping, feeling no fatigue, obeying a potent instinct which allowed no room for thought. All was in vain.

It then occurred to him that perhaps the girl had not heard of the order—though this was improbable enough, for such a thunder-clap could not have burst without being heard by all. Evidently interested in knowing the smallest news from Siberia, how could she be ignorant of the measures taken by the governor, measures which concerned her so directly?

But, if she was ignorant of it, she would come in an hour to the quay, and there some merciless agent would refuse her a passage! At any cost, he must see her beforehand, and enable her to avoid such a repulse.

But all his endeavors were in vain, and he at length almost despaired of finding her again. It was eleven o'clock, and Michael thought of presenting his podorojna at the office of the head of police. The proclamation evidently did not concern him, since the emergency had been foreseen for him, but he wished to make sure that nothing would hinder his departure from the town.

Michael then returned to the other side of the Volga, to the quarter in which was the office of the head of police. An immense crowd was collected there; for though all foreigners were ordered to quit the province, they had notwithstanding to go through certain forms before they could depart.

Without this precaution, some Russian more or less implicated in the Tartar movement would have been able, in a disguise, to pass the frontier—just those whom the order wished to prevent going. The strangers were sent away, but still had to gain permission to go.

Mountebanks, gypsies, Tsiganes, Zingaris, mingled with merchants from Persia, Turkey, India, Turkestan, China, filled the court and offices of the police station.

Everyone was in a hurry, for the means of transport would be much sought after among this crowd of banished people, and those who did not set about it soon ran a great risk of not being able to leave the town in the prescribed time, which would expose them to some brutal treatment from the governor's agents.

Owing to the strength of his elbows Michael was able to cross the court. But to get into the office and up to the clerk's little window was a much more difficult business. However, a word into an inspector's ear and a few judiciously given roubles were powerful enough to gain him a passage. The man, after taking him into the waiting-room, went to call an upper clerk. Michael Strogoff would not be long in making everything right with the police and being free in his movements.

Whilst waiting, he looked about him, and what did he see? There, fallen, rather than seated, on a bench, was a girl, prey to a silent despair, although her face could scarcely be seen, the profile alone being visible against the wall. Michael Strogoff could not be mistaken. He instantly recognized the young Livonian.

Not knowing the governor's orders, she had come to the police office to get her pass signed. They had refused to sign it. No doubt she was authorized to go to Irkutsk, but the order was peremptory—it annulled all previous au-thorizations, and the routes to Siberia were closed to her. Michael, delighted at having found her again, approached the girl.

She looked up for a moment and her face brightened on recognizing her traveling companion. She instinctively rose and, like a drowning man who clutches at a spar, she was about to ask his help.

At that moment the agent touched Michael on the shoulder, "The head of police will see you," he said.

"Good," returned Michael. And without saying a word to her for whom he had been searching all day, without reassuring her by even a gesture, which might compromise either her or himself, he followed the man.

The young Livonian, seeing the only being to whom she could look for help disappear, fell back again on her bench.

Three minutes had not passed before Michael Strogoff reappeared, accompanied by the agent. In his hand he held his podorojna, which threw open the roads to Siberia for him. He again approached the young Livonian, and holding out his hand: "Sister," said he.

She understood. She rose as if some sudden inspiration prevented her from hesitating a moment.

"Sister," repeated Michael Strogoff, "we are authorized to continue our journey to Irkutsk. Will you come with me?"

"I will follow you, brother," replied the girl, putting her hand into that of Michael Strogoff. And together they left the police station.

CHAPTER VII
GOING DOWN THE VOLGA

A LITTLE before midday, the steamboat's bell drew to the wharf on the Volga an unusually large concourse of people, for not only were those about to embark who had intended to go, but the many who were compelled to go contrary to their wishes. The boilers of the Caucasus were under full pressure; a slight smoke issued from its funnel, whilst the end of the escape-pipe and the lids of the valves were crowned with white vapor. It is needless to say that the police kept a close watch over the departure of the Caucasus, and showed themselves pitiless to those travelers who did not satisfactorily answer their questions.

Numerous Cossacks came and went on the quay, ready to assist the agents, but they had not to interfere, as no one ventured to offer the slightest resistance to their orders. Exactly at the hour the last clang of the bell sounded, the powerful wheels of the steamboat began to beat the water, and the Caucasus passed rapidly between the two towns of which Nijni-Novgorod is composed.

Michael Strogoff and the young Livonian had taken a passage on board the Caucasus. Their embarkation was made without any difficulty. As is known, the podorojna, drawn up in the name of Nicholas Korpanoff, authorized this merchant to be accompanied on his journey to Siberia. They appeared, therefore, to be a brother and sister traveling under the protection of the imperial police. Both, seated together at the stern, gazed at the receding town, so disturbed by the governor's order. Michael had as yet said nothing to the girl, he had not even questioned her. He waited until she should speak to him, when that was necessary. She had been anxious to leave that town, in which, but for the providential intervention of this unexpected protector, she would have remained imprisoned. She said nothing, but her looks spoke her thanks.

The Volga, the Rha of the ancients, the largest river in all Europe, is almost three thousand miles in length. Its waters, rather unwholesome in its upper part, are improved at Nijni-Novgorod by those of the Oka, a rapid affluent, issuing from the central provinces of Russia. The system of Russian canals and rivers has been justly compared to a gigantic tree whose branches spread over every part of the empire. The Volga forms the trunk of this tree, and it has for roots seventy mouths opening into the Caspian Sea. It is navigable as far as Rjef, a town in the government of Tver, that is, along the greater part of its course.

The steamboats plying between Perm and Nijni-Novgorod rapidly perform the two hundred and fifty miles which separate this town from the town of Kasan. It is true that these boats have only to descend the Volga, which adds nearly two miles of current per hour to their own speed; but on arriving at the confluence of the Kama, a little below Kasan, they are obliged to quit the Volga for the smaller river, up which they ascend to Perm. Powerful as were her machines, the Caucasus could not thus, after entering the Kama, make against the current more than ten miles an hour. Including an hour's stoppage at Kasan, the voyage from Nijni-Novgorod to Perm would take from between sixty to sixty-two hours.

The steamer was very well arranged, and the passengers, according to their condition or resources, occupied three distinct classes on board. Michael Strogoff had taken care to engage two first-class cabins, so that his young companion might retire into hers whenever she liked.

The Caucasus was loaded with passengers of every description. A number of Asiatic traders had thought it best to leave Nijni-Novgorod immediately. In that part of the steamer reserved for the first-class might be seen Armenians in long robes and a sort of miter on their heads; Jews, known by their conical caps; rich Chinese in their traditional costume, a very wide blue, violet, or black robe; Turks, wearing the national turban; Hindoos, with square caps, and a simple string for a girdle, some of whom, hold in their hands all the traffic of Central Asia; and, lastly, Tartars, wearing boots, ornamented with many-colored braid, and the breast a mass of embroidery. All these merchants had been obliged to pile up their numerous bales and chests in the hold and on the deck; and the transport of their baggage would cost them dear, for, according to the regulations, each person had only a right to twenty pounds' weight.

In the bows of the Caucasus were more numerous groups of passengers, not only foreigners, but also Russians, who were not forbidden by the order to go back to their towns in the province. There were mujiks with caps on their heads, and wearing checked shirts under their wide pelisses; peasants of the Volga, with blue trousers stuffed into their boots, rose-colored cotton shirts, drawn in by a cord, felt caps; a few women, habited in flowery-patterned cotton dresses, gay-colored aprons, and bright handkerchiefs on their heads. These were principally third-class passengers, who were, happily, not troubled by the prospect of a long return voyage. The Caucasus passed numerous boats being towed up the stream, carrying all sorts of merchandise to Nijni-Novgorod. Then passed rafts of wood interminably long, and barges loaded to the gunwale, and nearly sinking under water. A bootless voyage they were making, since the fair had been abruptly broken up at its outset.

The waves caused by the steamer splashed on the banks, covered with flocks of wild duck, who flew away uttering deafening cries. A little farther, on the dry fields, bordered with willows, and aspens, were scattered a few cows, sheep, and herds of pigs. Fields, sown with thin buckwheat and rye, stretched away to a background of half-cultivated hills, offering no remarkable prospect. The pencil of an artist in quest of the picturesque would have found nothing to reproduce in this monotonous landscape.

The Caucasus had been steaming on for almost two hours, when the young Livonian, addressing herself to Michael, said, "Are you going to Irkutsk, brother?"

"Yes, sister," answered the young man. "We are going the same way. Consequently, where I go, you shall go."

"To-morrow, brother, you shall know why I left the shores of the Baltic to go beyond the Ural Mountains."

"I ask you nothing, sister."

"You shall know all," replied the girl, with a faint smile. "A sister should hide nothing from her brother. But I cannot to-day. Fatigue and sorrow have broken me."

"Will you go and rest in your cabin?" asked Michael Strogoff.

"Yes—yes; and to-morrow—"

"Come then—"

He hesitated to finish his sentence, as if he had wished to end it by the name of his companion, of which he was still ignorant.

"Nadia," said she, holding out her hand.

"Come, Nadia," answered Michael, "and make what use you like of your brother Nicholas Korpanoff." And he led the girl to the cabin engaged for her off the saloon.

Michael Strogoff returned on deck, and eager for any news which might bear on his journey, he mingled in the groups of passengers, though without taking any part in the conversation. Should he by any chance be questioned, and obliged to reply, he would announce himself as the merchant Nicholas Korpanoff, going back to the frontier, for he did not wish it to be suspected that a special permission authorized him to travel to Siberia.

The foreigners in the steamer could evidently speak of nothing but the occurrences of the day, of the order and its consequences. These poor people, scarcely recovered from the fatigue of a journey across Central Asia, found themselves obliged to return, and if they did not give loud vent to their anger and despair, it was because they dared not. Fear, mingled with respect, restrained them. It was possible that inspectors of police, charged with watching the passengers, had secretly embarked on board the Caucasus, and it was just as well to keep silence; expulsion, after all, was a good deal preferable to imprisonment in a fortress. Therefore the men were either silent, or spoke with so much caution that it was scarcely possible to get any useful information.

Michael Strogoff thus could learn nothing here; but if mouths were often shut at his approach—for they did not know him—his ears were soon struck by the sound of one voice, which cared little whether it was heard or not.

The man with the hearty voice spoke Russian, but with a French accent; and another speaker answered him more reservedly. "What," said the first, "are you on board this boat, too, my dear fellow; you whom I met at the imperial fete in Moscow, and just caught a glimpse of at Nijni-Novgorod?"

39

"Yes, it's I," answered the second drily.

"Really, I didn't expect to be so closely followed."

"I am not following you sir; I am preceding you."

"Precede! precede! Let us march abreast, keeping step, like two soldiers on parade, and for the time, at least, let us agree, if you will, that one shall not pass the other."

"On the contrary, I shall pass you."

"We shall see that, when we are at the seat of war; but till then, why, let us be traveling companions. Later, we shall have both time and occasion to be rivals."

"Enemies."

"Enemies, if you like. There is a precision in your words, my dear fellow, particularly agreeable to me. One may always know what one has to look for, with you."

"What is the harm?"

"No harm at all. So, in my turn, I will ask your permission to state our respective situations."

"State away."

"You are going to Perm—like me?"

"Like you."

"And probably you will go from Perm to Ekaterenburg, since that is the best and safest route by which to cross the Ural Mountains?"

"Probably."

"Once past the frontier, we shall be in Siberia, that is to say in the midst of the invasion."

"We shall be there."

"Well! then, and only then, will be the time to say, Each for himself, and God for—"

"For me."

"For you, all by yourself! Very well! But since we have a week of neutral days before us, and since it is very certain that news will not shower down upon us on the way, let us be friends until we become rivals again."

"Enemies."

"Yes; that's right, enemies. But till then, let us act together, and not try and ruin each other. All the same, I promise you to keep to myself all that I can see—"

"And I, all that I can hear."

"Is that agreed?"

"It is agreed."

"Your hand?"

"Here it is." And the hand of the first speaker, that is to say, five wide-open fingers, vigorously shook the two fingers coolly extended by the other.

"By the bye," said the first, "I was able this morning to telegraph the very words of the order to my cousin at seventeen minutes past ten."

"And I sent it to the Daily Telegraph at thirteen minutes past ten."

"Bravo, Mr. Blount!"

"Very good, M. Jolivet."

"I will try and match that!"

"It will be difficult."

"I can try, however."

So saying, the French correspondent familiarly saluted the Englishman, who bowed stiffly. The governor's proclamation did not concern these two news-hunters, as they were neither Russians nor foreigners of Asiatic origin. However, being urged by the same instinct, they had left Nijni-Novgorod together. It was natural that they should take the same means of transport, and that they should follow the same route to the Siberian steppes. Traveling companions, whether enemies or friends, they had a week to pass together before "the hunt would be open." And then success to the most expert! Alcide Jolivet had made the first advances, and Harry Blount had accepted them though he had done so coldly.

That very day at dinner the Frenchman open as ever and even too loquacious, the Englishman still silent and grave, were seen hobnobbing at the same table, drinking genuine Cliquot, at six roubles the bottle, made from the fresh sap of the birch-trees of the country. On hearing them chatting away together, Michael Strogoff said to himself: "Those are inquisitive and indiscreet fellows whom I shall probably meet again on the way. It will be prudent for me to keep them at a distance."

The young Livonian did not come to dinner. She was asleep in her cabin, and Michael did not like to awaken her. It was evening before she reappeared on the deck of the Caucasus. The long twilight imparted a coolness to the atmosphere eagerly enjoyed by the passengers after the stifling heat of the day. As the evening advanced, the greater number never even thought of going into the saloon. Stretched on the benches, they inhaled with delight the slight breeze caused by the speed of the steamer. At this time of year, and under this latitude, the sky scarcely darkened between sunset and dawn, and left the steersman light enough to guide his steamer among the numerous vessels going up or down the Volga.

Between eleven and two, however, the moon being new, it was almost dark. Nearly all the passengers were then asleep on the deck, and the silence was disturbed only by the noise of the paddles striking the water at regular intervals. Anxiety kept Michael Strogoff awake. He walked up and down, but always in the stern of the steamer. Once, however, he happened to pass the engine-room. He then found himself in the part reserved for second and third-class passengers.

There, everyone was lying asleep, not only on the benches, but also on the bales, packages, and even the deck itself. Some care was necessary not to tread on the sleepers, who were lying about everywhere. They were chiefly mujiks, accustomed to hard couches, and quite satisfied with the planks of the deck. But no doubt they would, all the same, have soundly abused the clumsy fellow who roused them with an accidental kick.

Michael Strogoff took care, therefore, not to disturb anyone. By going thus to the end of the boat, he had no other idea but that of striving against sleep by a rather longer walk. He reached the forward deck, and was already climbing the forecastle ladder, when he heard someone speaking near him. He stopped. The voices appeared to come from a group of passengers enveloped in cloaks and wraps. It was impossible to recognize them in the dark, though it sometimes happened that, when the steamer's chimney sent forth a plume of ruddy flames, the sparks seemed to fall amongst the group as though thousands of spangles had been suddenly illuminated.

Michael was about to step up the ladder, when a few words reached his ear, uttered in that strange tongue which he had heard during the night at the fair. Instinctively he stopped to listen. Protected by the shadow of the forecastle, he could not be perceived himself. As to seeing the passengers who were talking, that was impossible. He must confine himself to listening.

The first words exchanged were of no importance—to him at least— but they allowed him to recognize the voices of the man and woman whom he had heard at Nijni-Novgorod. This, of course, made him redouble his attention. It was, indeed, not at all impossible that these same Tsiganes, now banished, should be on board the Caucasus.

And it was well for him that he listened, for he distinctly heard this question and answer made in the Tartar idiom: "It is said that a courier has set out from Moscow for Irkutsk."

"It is so said, Sangarre; but either this courier will arrive too late, or he will not arrive at all."

Michael Strogoff started involuntarily at this reply, which concerned him so directly. He tried to see if the man and woman who had just spoken were really those whom he suspected, but he could not succeed.

In a few moments Michael Strogoff had regained the stern of the vessel without having been perceived, and, taking a seat by himself, he buried his face in his hands. It might have been supposed that he was asleep.

He was not asleep, however, and did not even think of sleeping. He was reflecting, not without a lively apprehension: "Who is it knows of my departure, and who can have any interest in knowing it?"

CHAPTER VIII
GOING UP THE KAMA

THE next day, the 18th of July, at twenty minutes to seven in the morning, the Caucasus reached the Kasan quay, seven versts from the town.

Kasan is situated at the confluence of the Volga and Kasanka. It is an important chief town of the government, and a Greek archbishopric, as well as the seat of a university. The varied population preserves an Asiatic character. Although the town was so far from the landing-place, a large crowd was collected on the quay. They had come for news. The governor of the province had published an order identical with that of Nijni-Novgorod. Police officers and a few Cossacks kept order among the crowd, and cleared the way both for the passengers who were disembarking and also for those who were embarking on board the Caucasus, minutely examining both classes of travelers. The one were the Asiatics who were being expelled; the other, mujiks stopping at Kasan.

Michael Strogoff unconcernedly watched the bustle which occurs at all quays on the arrival of a steam vessel. The Caucasus would stay for an hour to renew her fuel. Michael did not even think of landing. He was unwilling to leave the young Livonian girl alone on board, as she had not yet reappeared on deck.

The two journalists had risen at dawn, as all good huntsmen should do. They went on shore and mingled with the crowd, each keeping to his own peculiar mode of proceeding; Harry Blount, sketching different types, or noting some observation; Alcide Jolivet contenting himself with asking questions, confiding in his memory, which never failed him.

There was a report along all the frontier that the insurrection and invasion had reached considerable proportions. Communication between Siberia and the empire was already extremely difficult. All this Michael Strogoff heard from the new arrivals. This information could not but cause him great uneasiness, and increase his wish of being beyond the Ural Mountains, so as to judge for himself of the truth of these rumors, and enable him to guard against any possible contingency. He was thinking of seeking more direct intelligence from some native of Kasan, when his attention was suddenly diverted.

Among the passengers who were leaving the Caucasus, Michael recognized the troop of Tsiganes who, the day before, had appeared in the Nijni-Novgorod fair. There, on the deck of the steamboat were the old Bohemian and the woman. With them, and no doubt under their direction, landed about twenty dancers and singers, from fifteen to twenty years of age, wrapped in old cloaks, which covered their spangled dresses. These dresses, just then glancing in the first rays of the sun, reminded Michael of the curious appearance which he had observed during the night. It must have been the glitter of those spangles in the bright flames issuing from the steamboat's funnel which had attracted his attention.

"Evidently," said Michael to himself, "this troop of Tsiganes, after remaining below all day, crouched under the forecastle during the night. Were these gipsies trying to show themselves as little as possible? Such is not according to the usual custom of their race."

Michael Strogoff no longer doubted that the expressions he had heard, had proceeded from this tawny group, and had been exchanged between the old gypsy and the woman to whom he gave the Mongolian name of Sangarre. Michael involuntarily moved towards the gangway, as the Bohemian troop was leaving the steamboat.

The old Bohemian was there, in a humble attitude, little conformable with the effrontery natural to his race. One would have said that he was endeavoring rather to avoid attention than to attract it. His battered hat, browned by the suns of every clime, was pulled forward over his wrinkled face. His arched back was bent under an old cloak, wrapped closely round him, notwithstanding the heat. It would have been difficult, in this miserable dress, to judge of either his size or face. Near him was the Tsigane, Sangarre, a woman about thirty years old. She was tall and well made, with olive complexion, magnificent eyes, and golden hair.

Many of the young dancers were remarkably pretty, all possessing the clear-cut features of their race. These Tsiganes are generally very attractive, and more than one of the great Russian nobles, who try to vie with the English in eccentricity, has not hesitated to choose his wife from among these gypsy girls. One of them was humming a song of strange rhythm, which might be thus rendered:

> *"Glitters brightly the gold*
> *In my raven locks streaming*
> *Rich coral around*
> *My graceful neck gleaming;*
> *Like a bird of the air,*
> *Through the wide world I roam."*

The laughing girl continued her song, but Michael Strogoff ceased to listen. It struck him just then that the Tsigane, Sangarre, was regarding him with a peculiar gaze, as if to fix his features indelibly in her memory.

It was but for a few moments, when Sangarre herself followed the old man and his troop, who had already left the vessel. "That's a bold gypsy," said Michael to himself. "Could she have recognized me as the man whom she saw at Nijni-Novgorod? These confounded Tsiganes have the eyes of a cat! They can see in the dark; and that woman there might well know—"

Michael Strogoff was on the point of following Sangarre and the gypsy band, but he stopped. "No," thought he, "no unguarded proceedings. If I were to stop that old fortune teller and his companions my incognito would run a risk of being discovered. Besides, now they have landed, before they can pass the frontier I shall be far beyond it. They may take the route from Kasan to Ishim, but that affords no resources to travelers. Besides a tarantass, drawn by good Siberian horses, will always go faster than a gypsy cart! Come, friend Korpanoff, be easy."

By this time the man and Sangarre had disappeared.

Kasan is justly called the "Gate of Asia" and considered as the center of Siberian and Bokharian commerce; for two roads begin here and lead across the Ural Mountains. Michael Strogoff had very judiciously chosen the one by Perm and Ekaterenburg. It is the great stage road, well supplied with relays kept at the expense of the government, and is prolonged from Ishim to Irkutsk.

It is true that a second route—the one of which Michael had just spoken—avoiding the slight detour by Perm, also connects Kasan with Ishim. It is perhaps shorter than the other, but this advantage is much diminished by the absence of post-houses, the bad roads, and lack of villages. Michael Strogoff was right in the choice he had made, and if, as appeared probable, the gipsies should follow the second route from Kasan to Ishim, he had every chance of arriving before them.

An hour afterwards the bell rang on board the Caucasus, calling the new passengers, and recalling the former ones. It was now seven o'clock in the morning. The requisite fuel had been received on board. The whole vessel began to vibrate from the effects of the steam. She was ready to start. Passengers going from Kasan to Perm were crowding on the deck.

Michael noticed that of the two reporters Blount alone had rejoined the steamer. Was Alcide Jolivet about to miss his passage?

But just as the ropes were being cast off, Jolivet appeared, tearing along. The steamer was already sheering off, the gangway had been drawn onto the quay, but Alcide Jolivet would not stick at such a little thing as that, so, with a bound like a harlequin, he alighted on the deck of the Caucasus almost in his rival's arms.

"I thought the Caucasus was going without you," said the latter.

"Bah!" answered Jolivet, "I should soon have caught you up again, by chartering a boat at my cousin's expense, or by traveling post at twenty copecks a verst, and on horseback. What could I do? It was so long a way from the quay to the telegraph office."

"Have you been to the telegraph office?" asked Harry Blount, biting his lips.

"That's exactly where I have been!" answered Jolivet, with his most amiable smile.

"And is it still working to Kolyvan?"

"That I don't know, but I can assure you, for instance, that it is working from Kasan to Paris."

"You sent a dispatch to your cousin?"

"With enthusiasm."

"You had learnt then—?"

"Look here, little father, as the Russians say," replied Alcide Jolivet, "I'm a good fellow, and I don't wish to keep anything from you. The Tartars, and Feofar-Khan at their head, have passed Semipolatinsk, and are descending the Irtish. Do what you like with that!"

What! such important news, and Harry Blount had not known it; and his rival, who had probably learned it from some inhabitant of Kasan, had already transmitted it to Paris. The English paper was distanced! Harry Blount, crossing his hands behind him, walked off and seated himself in the stern without uttering a word.

About ten o'clock in the morning, the young Livonian, leaving her cabin, appeared on deck. Michael Strogoff went forward and took her hand. "Look, sister!" said he, leading her to the bows of the Caucasus.

The view was indeed well worth seeing. The Caucasus had reached the confluence of the Volga and the Kama. There she would leave the former river, after having descended it for nearly three hundred miles, to ascend the latter for a full three hundred.

The Kama was here very wide, and its wooded banks lovely. A few white sails enlivened the sparkling water. The horizon was closed by a line of hills covered with aspens, alders, and sometimes large oaks.

But these beauties of nature could not distract the thoughts of the young Livonian even for an instant. She had left her hand in that of her companion, and turning to him, "At what distance are we from Moscow?" she asked.

"Nine hundred versts," answered Michael.

"Nine hundred, out of seven thousand!" murmured the girl.

The bell now announced the breakfast hour. Nadia followed Michael Strogoff to the restaurant. She ate little, and as a poor girl whose means are small would do. Michael thought it best to content himself with the fare which satisfied his companion; and in less than twenty minutes he and Nadia returned on deck. There they seated themselves in the stern, and without preamble, Nadia, lowering her voice to be heard by him alone, began:

"Brother, I am the daughter of an exile. My name is Nadia Fedor. My mother died at Riga scarcely a month ago, and I am going to Irkutsk to rejoin my father and share his exile."

"I, too, am going to Irkutsk," answered Michael, "and I shall thank Heaven if it enables me to give Nadia Fedor safe and sound into her father's hands."

"Thank you, brother," replied Nadia.

Michael Strogoff then added that he had obtained a special podorojna for Siberia, and that the Russian authorities could in no way hinder his progress.

Nadia asked nothing more. She saw in this fortunate meeting with Michael a means only of accelerating her journey to her father.

"I had," said she, "a permit which authorized me to go to Irkutsk, but the new order annulled that; and but for you, brother, I should have been unable to leave the town, in which, without doubt, I should have perished."

"And dared you, alone, Nadia," said Michael, "attempt to cross the steppes of Siberia?"

"The Tartar invasion was not known when I left Riga. It was only at Moscow that I learnt the news."

"And despite it, you continued your journey?"

"It was my duty."

The words showed the character of the brave girl.

She then spoke of her father, Wassili Fedor. He was a much-esteemed physician at Riga. But his connection with some secret society having been asserted, he received orders to start for Irkutsk. The police who brought the order conducted him without delay beyond the frontier.

Wassili Fedor had but time to embrace his sick wife and his

46

daughter, so soon to be left alone, when, shedding bitter tears, he was led away. A year and a half after her husband's departure, Madame Fedor died in the arms of her daughter, who was thus left alone and almost penniless. Nadia Fedor then asked, and easily obtained from the Russian government, an authorization to join her father at Irkutsk. She wrote and told him she was starting. She had barely enough money for this long journey, and yet she did not hesitate to undertake it. She would do what she could. God would do the rest.

CHAPTER IX
DAY AND NIGHT IN A TARANTASS

THE next day, the 19th of July, the Caucasus reached Perm, the last place at which she touched on the Kama.

The government of which Perm is the capital is one of the largest in the Russian Empire, and, extending over the Ural Mountains, encroaches on Siberian territory. Marble quarries, mines of salt, platina, gold, and coal are worked here on a large scale. Although Perm, by its situation, has become an important town, it is by no means attractive, being extremely dirty, and without resources. This want of comfort is of no consequence to those going to Siberia, for they come from the more civilized districts, and are supplied with all necessaries.

At Perm travelers from Siberia resell their vehicles, more or less damaged by the long journey across the plains. There, too, those passing from Europe to Asia purchase carriages, or sleighs in the winter season.

Michael Strogoff had already sketched out his programme. A vehicle carrying the mail usually runs across the Ural Mountains, but this, of course, was discontinued. Even if it had not been so, he would not have taken it, as he wished to travel as fast as possible, without depending on anyone. He wisely preferred to buy a carriage, and journey by stages, stimulating the zeal of the postillions by well-applied "na vodkou," or tips.

Unfortunately, in consequence of the measures taken against foreigners of Asiatic origin, a large number of travelers had already left Perm, and therefore conveyances were extremely rare. Michael was obliged to content himself with what had been rejected by others. As to horses, as long as the Czar's courier was not in Siberia, he could exhibit his podorojna, and the postmasters would give him the preference. But, once out of Europe, he had to depend alone on the power of his roubles.

But to what sort of a vehicle should he harness his horses? To a telga or to a tarantass? The telga is nothing but an open four-wheeled cart, made entirely of wood, the pieces fastened together by means of strong rope. Nothing could be more primitive, nothing could be less comfortable; but, on the other hand, should any accident happen on the way, nothing could be more easily repaired. There is no want of firs on the Russian frontier, and axle-trees grow naturally in forests. The post extraordinary, known by the name of "perck-ladnoi," is carried by the telga, as any road is good enough for it. It must be confessed that sometimes the ropes which fasten the concern together break, and whilst the hinder part remains stuck in some bog, the fore-part arrives at the post-house on two wheels; but this result is considered quite satisfactory.

Michael Strogoff would have been obliged to employ a telga, if he had not been lucky enough to discover a tarantass. It is to be hoped that the invention of Russian coach-builders will devise some improvement in this last-named vehicle. Springs are wanting in it as well as in the telga; in the absence of iron, wood is not spared; but its four wheels, with eight or nine feet between them, assure a certain equilibrium over the jolting rough roads. A splash-board protects the travelers from the mud, and a strong leathern hood, which may be pulled quite over the occupiers, shelters them from the great heat and violent storms of the summer. The tarantass is as solid and as easy to repair as the telga, and is, moreover, less addicted to leaving its hinder part in the middle of the road.

It was not without careful search that Michael managed to discover this tarantass, and there was probably not a second to be found in all Perm. He haggled long about the price, for form's sake, to act up to his part as Nicholas Korpanoff, a plain merchant of Irkutsk.

Nadia had followed her companion in his search after a suitable vehicle. Although the object of each was different, both were equally anxious to arrive at their goal. One would have said the same will animated them both.

"Sister," said Michael, "I wish I could have found a more comfortable conveyance for you."

"Do you say that to me, brother, when I would have gone on foot, if need were, to rejoin my father?"

"I do not doubt your courage, Nadia, but there are physical fatigues a woman may be unable to endure."

"I shall endure them, whatever they be," replied the girl. "If you ever hear a complaint from me you may leave me in the road, and continue your journey alone."

Half an hour later, the podorojna being presented by Michael, three post-horses were harnessed to the tarantass. These animals, covered with long hair, were very like long-legged bears. They were small but spirited, being of Siberian breed. The way in which the iemschik harnessed them was thus: one, the largest, was secured between two long shafts, on whose farther end was a hoop carrying tassels and bells; the two others were simply fastened by ropes to the steps of the tarantass. This was the complete harness, with mere strings for reins.

Neither Michael Strogoff nor the young Livonian girl had any baggage. The rapidity with which one wished to make the journey, and the more than modest resources of the other, prevented them from embarrassing themselves with packages. It was a fortunate thing, under the circumstances, for the tarantass could not have carried both baggage

48

and travelers. It was only made for two persons, without counting the iemschik, who kept his equilibrium on his narrow seat in a marvelous manner.

The iemschik is changed at every relay. The man who drove the tarantass during the first stage was, like his horses, a Siberian, and no less shaggy than they; long hair, cut square on the forehead, hat with a turned-up brim, red belt, coat with crossed facings and buttons stamped with the imperial cipher. The iemschik, on coming up with his team, threw an inquisitive glance at the passengers of the tarantass. No luggage!—and had there been, where in the world could he have stowed it? Rather shabby in appearance too. He looked contemptuous.

"Crows," said he, without caring whether he was overheard or not; "crows, at six copecks a verst!"

"No, eagles!" said Michael, who understood the iemschik's slang perfectly; "eagles, do you hear, at nine copecks a verst, and a tip besides."

He was answered by a merry crack of the whip.

In the language of the Russian postillions the "crow" is the stingy or poor traveler, who at the post-houses only pays two or three copecks a verst for the horses. The "eagle" is the traveler who does not mind expense, to say nothing of liberal tips. Therefore the crow could not claim to fly as rapidly as the imperial bird.

Nadia and Michael immediately took their places in the tarantass. A small store of provisions was put in the box, in case at any time they were delayed in reaching the post-houses, which are very comfortably provided under direction of the State. The hood was pulled up, as it was insupportably hot, and at twelve o'clock the tarantass left Perm in a cloud of dust.

The way in which the iemschik kept up the pace of his team would have certainly astonished travelers who, being neither Russians nor Siberians, were not accustomed to this sort of thing. The leader, rather larger than the others, kept to a steady long trot, perfectly regular, whether up or down hill. The two other horses seemed to know no other pace than the gallop, though they performed many an eccentric curvette as they went along. The iemschik, however, never touched them, only urging them on by startling cracks of his whip. But what epithets he lavished on them, including the names of all the saints in the calendar, when they behaved like docile and conscientious animals! The string which served as reins would have had no influence on the spirited beasts, but the words "na pravo," to the right, "na levo," to the left, pronounced in a guttural tone, were more effectual than either bridle or snaffle.

And what amiable expressions! "Go on, my doves!" the iemschik would say. "Go on, pretty swallows! Fly, my little pigeons! Hold up, my cousin on the left! Gee up, my little father on the right!"

But when the pace slackened, what insulting expressions, instantly understood by the sensitive animals! "Go on, you wretched snail! Confound you, you slug! I'll roast you alive, you tortoise, you!"

Whether or not it was from this way of driving, which requires the iemschiks to possess strong throats more than muscular arms, the tarantass flew along at a rate of from twelve to fourteen miles an hour. Michael Strogoff was accustomed both to the sort of vehicle and the mode of traveling. Neither jerks nor jolts incommoded him. He knew that a Russian driver never even tries to avoid either stones, ruts, bogs, fallen trees, or trenches, which may happen to be in the road. He was used to all that. His companion ran a risk of being hurt by the violent jolts of the tarantass, but she would not complain.

For a little while Nadia did not speak. Then possessed with the one thought, that of reaching her journey's end, "I have calculated that there are three hundred versts between Perm and Ekaterenburg, brother," said she. "Am I right?"

"You are quite right, Nadia," answered Michael; "and when we have reached Ekaterenburg, we shall be at the foot of the Ural Mountains on the opposite side."

"How long will it take to get across the mountains?"

"Forty-eight hours, for we shall travel day and night. I say day and night, Nadia," added he, "for I cannot stop even for a moment; I go on without rest to Irkutsk."

"I shall not delay you, brother; no, not even for an hour, and we will travel day and night."

"Well then, Nadia, if the Tartar invasion has only left the road open, we shall arrive in twenty days."

"You have made this journey before?" asked Nadia.

"Many times."

"During winter we should have gone more rapidly and surely, should we not?"

"Yes, especially with more rapidity, but you would have suffered much from the frost and snow."

"What matter! Winter is the friend of Russia."

"Yes, Nadia, but what a constitution anyone must have to endure such friendship! I have often seen the temperature in the Siberian steppes fall to more than forty degrees below freezing point! I have felt, notwithstanding my reindeer coat, my heart growing chill, my limbs stiffening, my feet freezing in triple woolen socks; I have seen my sleigh horses covered with a coating of ice, their breath congealed at their nostrils. I have seen the brandy in my flask change into hard stone, on which not even my knife could make an impression. But my sleigh flew like the wind. Not an obstacle on the plain, white and level farther than the eye could reach! No rivers to stop one! Hard ice everywhere, the route open, the road sure! But at the price of what suffering, Nadia, those alone could say, who have never returned, but whose bodies have been covered up by the snow storm."

"However, you have returned, brother," said Nadia.

"Yes, but I am a Siberian, and, when quite a child, I used to follow my father to the chase, and so became inured to these hardships. But when you said to me, Nadia, that winter would not have stopped you, that you would have gone alone, ready to struggle against the frightful Siberian

50

climate, I seemed to see you lost in the snow and falling, never to rise again."

"How many times have you crossed the steppe in winter?" asked the young Livonian.

"Three times, Nadia, when I was going to Omsk."

"And what were you going to do at Omsk?"

"See my mother, who was expecting me."

"And I am going to Irkutsk, where my father expects me. I am taking him my mother's last words. That is as much as to tell you, brother, that nothing would have prevented me from setting out."

"You are a brave girl, Nadia," replied Michael. "God Himself would have led you."

All day the tarantass was driven rapidly by the iemschiks, who succeeded each other at every stage. The eagles of the mountain would not have found their name dishonored by these "eagles" of the highway. The high price paid for each horse, and the tips dealt out so freely, recommended the travelers in a special way. Perhaps the postmasters thought it singular that, after the publication of the order, a young man and his sister, evidently both Russians, could travel freely across Siberia, which was closed to everyone else, but their papers were all en regle and they had the right to pass.

However, Michael Strogoff and Nadia were not the only travelers on their way from Perm to Ekaterenburg. At the first stages, the courier of the Czar had learnt that a carriage preceded them, but, as there was no want of horses, he did not trouble himself about that.

During the day, halts were made for food alone. At the post-houses could be found lodging and provision. Besides, if there was not an inn, the house of the Russian peasant would have been no less hospitable. In the villages, which are almost all alike, with their white-walled, green-roofed chapels, the traveler might knock at any door, and it would be opened to him. The moujik would come out, smiling and extending his hand to his guest. He would offer him bread and salt, the burning charcoal would be put into the "samovar," and he would be made quite at home. The family would turn out themselves rather than that he should not have room. The stranger is the relation of all. He is "one sent by God."

On arriving that evening Michael instinctively asked the postmaster how many hours ago the carriage which preceded them had passed that stage.

"Two hours ago, little father," replied the postmaster.

"Is it a berlin?"

"No, a telga."

"How many travelers?"

"Two."

"And they are going fast?"

"Eagles!"

"Let them put the horses to as soon as possible."

Michael and Nadia, resolved not to stop even for an hour, traveled all night. The weather continued fine, though the atmosphere was heavy and becoming charged with electricity. It was to be hoped that a storm would not burst whilst they were among the mountains, for there it would be terrible. Being accustomed to read atmospheric signs, Michael Strogoff knew that a struggle of the elements was approaching.

The night passed without incident. Notwithstanding the jolting of the tarantass, Nadia was able to sleep for some hours. The hood was partly raised so as to give as much air as there was in the stifling atmosphere.

Michael kept awake all night, mistrusting the iemschiks, who are apt to sleep at their posts. Not an hour was lost at the relays, not an hour on the road.

The next day, the 20th of July, at about eight o'clock in the morning, they caught the first glimpse of the Ural Mountains in the east. This important chain which separates Russia from Siberia was still at a great distance, and they could not hope to reach it until the end of the day. The passage of the mountains must necessarily be performed during the next night. The sky was cloudy all day, and the temperature was therefore more bearable, but the weather was very threatening.

It would perhaps have been more prudent not to have ascended the mountains during the night, and Michael would not have done so, had he been permitted to wait; but when, at the last stage, the iemschik drew his attention to a peal of thunder reverberating among the rocks, he merely said:

"Is a telga still before us?"

"Yes."

"How long is it in advance?"

"Nearly an hour."

"Forward, and a triple tip if we are at Ekaterenburg to-morrow morning."

CHAPTER X
A STORM IN THE URAL MOUNTAINS

THE Ural Mountains extend in a length of over two thousand miles between Europe and Asia. Whether they are called the Urals, which is the Tartar, or the Poyas, which is the Russian name, they are correctly so termed; for these names signify "belt" in both languages. Rising on the shores of the Arctic Sea, they reach the borders of the Caspian. This was the barrier to be crossed by Michael Strogoff before he could enter Siberian Russia. The mountains could be crossed in one night, if no accident happened. Unfortunately, thunder muttering in the distance announced that a storm was at hand. The electric tension was such that it could not be dispersed without a tremendous explosion, which in the peculiar state of the atmosphere would be very terrible.

Michael took care that his young companion should be as well protected as possible. The hood, which might have been easily blown away, was fastened more securely with ropes, crossed above and at the back. The traces were doubled, and, as an additional precaution, the nave-boxes were stuffed with straw, as much to increase the strength of the wheels as to lessen the jolting, unavoidable on a dark night. Lastly, the fore and hinder parts, connected simply by the axles to the body of the tarantass, were joined one to the other by a crossbar, fixed by means of pins and screws.

Nadia resumed her place in the cart, and Michael took his seat beside her. Before the lowered hood hung two leathern curtains, which would in some degree protect the travelers against the wind and rain. Two great lanterns, suspended from the iemschik's seat, threw a pale glimmer scarcely sufficient to light the way, but serving as warning lights to prevent any other carriage from running into them.

It was well that all these precautions were taken, in expectation of a rough night. The road led them up towards dense masses of clouds, and should the clouds not soon resolve into rain, the fog would be such that the tarantass would be unable to advance without danger of falling over some precipice.

The Ural chain does not attain any very great height, the highest summit not being more than five thousand feet. Eternal snow is there unknown, and what is piled up by the Siberian winter is soon melted by the summer sun. Shrubs and trees grow to a considerable height. The iron and copper mines, as well as those of precious stones, draw a considerable number of workmen to that region. Also, those villages termed "gavody" are there met with pretty frequently, and the road through the great passes is easily practicable for post-carriages.

But what is easy enough in fine weather and broad daylight, offers difficulties and perils when the elements are engaged in fierce warfare, and the traveler is in the midst of it. Michael Strogoff knew from former experience what a storm in the mountains was, and perhaps this would be as terrible as the snowstorms which burst forth with such vehemence in the winter.

Rain was not yet falling, so Michael raised the leathern curtains which protected the interior of the tarantass and looked out, watching the sides of the road, peopled with fantastic shadows, caused by the wavering light of the lanterns. Nadia, motionless, her arms folded, gazed forth also, though without leaning forward, whilst her companion, his body half out of the carriage, examined both sky and earth.

The calmness of the atmosphere was very threatening, the air being perfectly still. It was just as if Nature were half stifled, and could no longer breathe; her lungs, that is to say those gloomy, dense clouds, not being able to perform their functions. The silence would have been complete but for the grindings of the wheels of the tarantass over the road, the creaking of the axles, the snorting of the horses, and the clattering of their iron hoofs among the pebbles, sparks flying out on every side.

The road was perfectly deserted. The tarantass encountered neither pedestrians nor horsemen, nor a vehicle of any description, in the narrow defiles of the Ural, on this threatening night. Not even the fire of a charcoal-burner was visible in the woods, not an encampment of miners near the mines, not a hut among the brushwood.

Under these peculiar circumstances it might have been allowable to postpone the journey till the morning. Michael Strogoff, however, had not hesitated, he had no right to stop, but then—and it began to cause him some anxiety—what possible reason could those travelers in the telga ahead have for being so imprudent?

Michael remained thus on the look-out for some time. About eleven o'clock lightning began to blaze continuously in the sky. The shadows of huge pines appeared and disappeared in the rapid light. Sometimes when the tarantass neared the side of the road, deep gulfs, lit up by the flashes, could be seen yawning beneath them. From time to time, on their vehicle giving a worse lurch than usual, they knew that they were crossing a bridge of roughly-hewn planks thrown over some chasm, thunder appearing actually to be rumbling below them. Besides this, a booming sound filled the air, which increased as they mounted higher. With these different noises rose the shouts of the iemschik, sometimes scolding, sometimes coaxing his poor beasts, who were suffering more from the oppression of the air than the roughness of the roads. Even the bells on the shafts could no longer rouse them, and they stumbled every instant.

"At what time shall we reach the top of the ridge?" asked Michael of the iemschik.

"At one o'clock in the morning if we ever get there at all," replied he, with a shake of his head.

"Why, my friend, this will not be your first storm in the mountains, will it?"

"No, and pray God it may not be my last!"

"Are you afraid?"

"No, I'm not afraid, but I repeat that I think you were wrong in starting."

"I should have been still more wrong had I stayed."

"Hold up, my pigeons!" cried the iemschik; it was his business to obey, not to question.

Just then a distant noise was heard, shrill whistling through the atmosphere, so calm a minute before. By the light of a dazzling flash, almost immediately followed by a tremendous clap of thunder, Michael could see huge pines on a high peak, bending before the blast. The wind was unchained, but as yet it was the upper air alone which was disturbed. Successive crashes showed that many of the trees had been unable to resist the burst of the hurricane. An avalanche of shattered trunks swept across the road and dashed over the precipice on the left, two hundred feet in front of the tarantass.

The horses stopped short.

"Get up, my pretty doves!" cried the iemschik, adding the cracking of his whip to the rumbling of the thunder.

Michael took Nadia's hand. "Are you asleep, sister?"

"No, brother."

"Be ready for anything; here comes the storm!"

"I am ready."

Michael Strogoff had only just time to draw the leathern curtains, when the storm was upon them.

The iemschik leapt from his seat and seized the horses' heads, for terrible danger threatened the whole party.

The tarantass was at a standstill at a turning of the road, down which swept the hurricane; it was absolutely necessary to hold the animals' heads to the wind, for if the carriage was taken broadside it must infallibly capsize and be dashed over the precipice. The frightened horses reared, and their driver could not manage to quiet them. His friendly expressions had been succeeded by the most insulting epithets. Nothing was of any use. The unfortunate animals, blinded by the lightning, terrified by the incessant peals of thunder, threatened every instant to break their traces and flee. The iemschik had no longer any control over his team.

At that moment Michael Strogoff threw himself from the tarantass and rushed to his assistance. Endowed with more than common strength, he managed, though not without difficulty, to master the horses.

The storm now raged with redoubled fury. A perfect avalanche of stones and trunks of trees began to roll down the slope above them.

"We cannot stop here," said Michael.

"We cannot stop anywhere," returned the iemschik, all his energies apparently overcome by terror. "The storm will soon send us to the bottom of the mountain, and that by the shortest way."

"Take you that horse, coward," returned Michael, "I'll look after this one."

A fresh burst of the storm interrupted him. The driver and he were obliged to crouch upon the ground to avoid being blown down. The carriage, notwithstanding their efforts and those of the horses, was gradually blown back, and had it not been stopped by the trunk of a tree, it would have gone over the edge of the precipice.

"Do not be afraid, Nadia!" cried Michael Strogoff.

"I'm not afraid," replied the young Livonian, her voice not betraying the slightest emotion.

The rumbling of the thunder ceased for an instant, the terrible blast had swept past into the gorge below.

"Will you go back?" said the iemschik.

"No, we must go on! Once past this turning, we shall have the shelter of the slope."

"But the horses won't move!"

"Do as I do, and drag them on."

"The storm will come back!"

"Do you mean to obey?"

"Do you order it?"

"The Father orders it!" answered Michael, for the first time invoking the all-powerful name of the Emperor.

"Forward, my swallows!" cried the iemschik, seizing one horse, while Michael did the same to the other.

Thus urged, the horses began to struggle onward. They could no longer rear, and the middle horse not being hampered by the others, could keep in the center of the road. It was with the greatest difficulty that either man or beasts could stand against the wind, and for every three steps they took in advance, they lost one, and even two, by being forced backwards. They slipped, they fell, they got up again. The vehicle ran a great risk of being smashed. If the hood had not been securely fastened, it would have been blown away long before. Michael Strogoff and the iemschik took more than two hours in getting up this bit of road, only half a verst in length, so directly exposed was it to the lashing of the storm. The danger was not only from the wind which battered against the travelers, but from the avalanche of stones and broken trunks which were hurtling through the air.

Suddenly, during a flash of lightning, one of these masses was seen crashing and rolling down the mountain towards the tarantass. The iemschik uttered a cry.

Michael Strogoff in vain brought his whip down on the team, they refused to move.

A few feet farther on, and the mass would pass behind them! Michael saw the tarantass struck, his companion crushed; he saw there was no time to drag her from the vehicle.

Then, possessed in this hour of peril with superhuman strength, he threw himself behind it, and planting his feet on the ground, by main force placed it out of danger.

The enormous mass as it passed grazed his chest, taking away his breath as though it had been a cannon-ball, then crushing to powder the flints on the road, it bounded into the abyss below.

"Oh, brother!" cried Nadia, who had seen it all by the light of the flashes.

"Nadia!" replied Michael, "fear nothing!"

"It is not on my own account that I fear!"

"God is with us, sister!"

"With me truly, brother, since He has sent thee in my way!" murmured the young girl.

The impetus the tarantass had received was not to be lost, and the tired horses once more moved forward. Dragged, so to speak, by Michael and the iemschik, they toiled on towards a narrow pass, lying north and south, where they would be protected from the direct sweep of the tempest. At one end a huge rock jutted out, round the summit of which whirled an eddy. Behind the shelter of the rock there was a comparative calm; yet once within the circumference of the cyclone, neither man nor beast could resist its power.

Indeed, some firs which towered above this protection were in a trice shorn of their tops, as though a gigantic scythe had swept across them. The storm was now at its height. The lightning filled the defile, and the thunderclaps had become one continued peal. The ground, struck by the concussion, trembled as though the whole Ural chain was shaken to its foundations.

Happily, the tarantass could be so placed that the storm might strike it obliquely. But the counter-currents, directed towards it by the slope, could not be so well avoided, and so violent were they that every instant it seemed as though it would be dashed to pieces.

Nadia was obliged to leave her seat, and Michael, by the light of one of the lanterns, discovered an excavation bearing the marks of a miner's pick, where the young girl could rest in safety until they could once more start.

Just then—it was one o'clock in the morning—the rain began to fall in torrents, and this in addition to the wind and lightning, made the storm truly frightful. To continue the journey at present was utterly impossible. Besides, having reached this pass, they had only to descend the slopes of the Ural Mountains, and to descend now, with the road torn up by a thousand mountain torrents, in these eddies of wind and rain, was utter madness.

"To wait is indeed serious," said Michael, "but it must certainly be done, to avoid still longer detentions. The very violence of the storm makes me hope that it will not last long. About three o'clock the day will begin to break, and the descent, which we cannot risk in the dark, we shall be able, if not with ease, at least without such danger, to attempt after sunrise."

"Let us wait, brother," replied Nadia; "but if you delay, let it not be to spare me fatigue or danger."

"Nadia, I know that you are ready to brave everything, but, in exposing both of us, I risk more than my life, more than yours, I am not fulfilling my task, that duty which before everything else I must accomplish."

"A duty!" murmured Nadia.

Just then a bright flash lit up the sky; a loud clap followed. The air was filled with sulphurous suffocating vapor, and a clump of huge pines, struck by the electric fluid, scarcely twenty feet from the tarantass, flared up like a gigantic torch.

The iemschik was struck to the ground by a counter-shock, but, regaining his feet, found himself happily unhurt.

Just as the last growlings of the thunder were lost in the recesses of the mountain, Michael felt Nadia's hand pressing his, and he heard her whisper these words in his ear: "Cries, brother! Listen!"

CHAPTER XI
TRAVELERS IN DISTRESS

DURING the momentary lull which followed, shouts could be distinctly heard from farther on, at no great distance from the tarantass. It was an earnest appeal, evidently from some traveler in distress.

Michael listened attentively. The iemschik also listened, but shook his head, as though it was impossible to help.

"They are travelers calling for aid," cried Nadia.

"They can expect nothing," replied the iemschik.

"Why not?" cried Michael. "Ought not we do for them what they would for us under similar circumstances?"

"Surely you will not risk the carriage and horses!"

"I will go on foot," replied Michael, interrupting the iemschik.

"I will go, too, brother," said the young girl.

"No, remain here, Nadia. The iemschik will stay with you. I do not wish to leave him alone."

"I will stay," replied Nadia.

"Whatever happens, do not leave this spot."

"You will find me where I now am."

Michael pressed her hand, and, turning the corner of the slope, disappeared in the darkness.

"Your brother is wrong," said the iemschik.

"He is right," replied Nadia simply.

Meanwhile Strogoff strode rapidly on. If he was in a great hurry to aid the travelers, he was also very anxious to know who it was that had not been hindered from starting by the storm; for he had no doubt that the cries came from the telga, which had so long preceded him.

The rain had stopped, but the storm was raging with redoubled fury. The shouts, borne on the air, became more distinct. Nothing was to be seen of the pass in which Nadia remained. The road wound along, and the squalls, checked by the corners, formed eddies highly dangerous, to pass which, without being taken off his legs, Michael had to use his utmost strength.

He soon perceived that the travelers whose shouts he had heard were at no great distance. Even then, on account of the darkness, Michael could not see them, yet he heard distinctly their words.

This is what he heard, and what caused him some surprise: "Are you coming back, blockhead?"

"You shall have a taste of the knout at the next stage."

"Do you hear, you devil's postillion! Hullo! Below!"

"This is how a carriage takes you in this country!"

"Yes, this is what you call a telga!"

"Oh, that abominable driver! He goes on and does not appear to have discovered that he has left us behind!"

"To deceive me, too! Me, an honorable Englishman! I will make a complaint at the chancellor's office and have the fellow hanged."

This was said in a very angry tone, but was suddenly interrupted by a burst of laughter from his companion, who exclaimed, "Well! this is a good joke, I must say."

"You venture to laugh!" said the Briton angrily.

"Certainly, my dear confrere, and that most heartily. 'Pon my word I never saw anything to come up to it."

Just then a crashing clap of thunder re-echoed through the defile, and then died away among the distant peaks. When the sound of the last growl had ceased, the merry voice went on: "Yes, it undoubtedly is a good joke. This machine certainly never came from France."

"Nor from England," replied the other.

On the road, by the light of the flashes, Michael saw, twenty yards from him, two travelers, seated side by side in a most peculiar vehicle, the wheels of which were deeply imbedded in the ruts formed in the road.

He approached them, the one grinning from ear to ear, and the other gloomily contemplating his situation, and recognized them as the two reporters who had been his companions on board the Caucasus.

"Good-morning to you, sir," cried the Frenchman. "Delighted to see you here. Let me introduce you to my intimate enemy, Mr. Blount."

The English reporter bowed, and was about to introduce in his turn his companion, Alcide Jolivet, in accordance with the rules of society, when Michael interrupted him.

"Perfectly unnecessary, sir; we already know each other, for we traveled together on the Volga."

"Ah, yes! exactly so! Mr.—"

"Nicholas Korpanoff, merchant, of Irkutsk. But may I know what has happened which, though a misfortune to your companion, amuses you so much?"

"Certainly, Mr. Korpanoff," replied Alcide. "Fancy! our driver has gone off with the front part of this confounded carriage, and left us quietly seated in the back part! So here we are in the worse half of a telga; no driver, no horses. Is it not a joke?"

"No joke at all," said the Englishman.

"Indeed it is, my dear fellow. You do not know how to look at the bright side of things."

"How, pray, are we to go on?" asked Blount.

"That is the easiest thing in the world," replied Alcide. "Go and harness yourself to what remains of our cart; I will take the reins, and call you my little pigeon, like a true iemschik, and you will trot off like a real post-horse."

"Mr. Jolivet," replied the Englishman, "this joking is going too far, it passes all limits and—"

"Now do be quiet, my dear sir. When you are done up, I will take your place; and call me a broken-winded snail and faint-hearted tortoise if I don't take you over the ground at a rattling pace."

Alcide said all this with such perfect good-humor that Michael could not help smiling. "Gentlemen," said he, "here is a better plan. We have now reached the highest ridge of the Ural chain, and thus have merely to descend the slopes of the mountain. My carriage is close by, only two hundred yards behind. I will lend you one of my horses, harness it to the remains of the telga, and to-mor-how, if no accident befalls us, we will arrive together at Ekaterenburg."

"That, Mr. Korpanoff," said Alcide, "is indeed a generous proposal."

"Indeed, sir," replied Michael, "I would willingly offer you places in my tarantass, but it will only hold two, and my sister and I already fill it."

"Really, sir," answered Alcide, "with your horse and our demi-telga we will go to the world's end."

"Sir," said Harry Blount, "we most willingly accept your kind offer. And, as to that iemschik—"

"Oh! I assure you that you are not the first travelers who have met with a similar misfortune," replied Michael.

"But why should not our driver come back? He knows perfectly well that he has left us behind, wretch that he is!"

"He! He never suspected such a thing."

"What! the fellow not know that he was leaving the better half of his telga behind?"

"Not a bit, and in all good faith is driving the fore part into Ekaterenburg."

"Did I not tell you that it was a good joke, confrere?" cried Alcide.

"Then, gentlemen, if you will follow me," said Michael, "we will return to my carriage, and—"

"But the telga," observed the Englishman.

"There is not the slightest fear that it will fly away, my dear Blount!" exclaimed Alcide; "it has taken such good root in the ground, that if it were left here until next spring it would begin to bud."

"Come then, gentlemen," said Michael Strogoff, "and we will bring up the tarantass."

The Frenchman and the Englishman, descending from their seats, no longer the hinder one, since the front had taken its departure, followed Michael.

Walking along, Alcide Jolivet chattered away as usual, with his invariable good-humor. "Faith, Mr. Korpanoff," said he, "you have indeed got us out of a bad scrape."

"I have only done, sir," replied Michael, "what anyone would have done in my place."

"Well, sir, you have done us a good turn, and if you are going farther we may possibly meet again, and—"

Alcide Jolivet did not put any direct question to Michael as to where he was going, but the latter, not wishing it to be suspected that he had anything to conceal, at once replied, "I am bound for Omsk, gentlemen."

"Mr. Blount and I," replied Alcide, "go where danger is certainly to be found, and without doubt news also."

"To the invaded provinces?" asked Michael with some earnestness.

"Exactly so, Mr. Korpanoff; and we may possibly meet there."

"Indeed, sir," replied Michael, "I have little love for cannon-balls or lance points, and am by nature too great a lover of peace to venture where fighting is going on."

"I am sorry, sir, extremely sorry; we must only regret that we shall separate so soon! But on leaving Ekaterenburg it may be our fortunate fate to travel together, if only for a few days?"

"Do you go on to Omsk?" asked Michael, after a moment's reflection.

"We know nothing as yet," replied Alcide; "but we shall certainly go as far as Ishim, and once there, our movements must depend on circumstances."

"Well then, gentlemen," said Michael, "we will be fellow-travelers as far as Ishim."

Michael would certainly have preferred to travel alone, but he could not, without appearing at least singular, seek to separate himself from the two reporters, who were taking the same road that he was. Besides, since Alcide and his companion intended to make some stay at Ishim, he thought it rather convenient than otherwise to make that part of the journey in their company.

Then in an indifferent tone he asked, "Do you know, with any certainty, where this Tartar invasion is?"

"Indeed, sir," replied Alcide, "we only know what they said at Perm. Feofar-Khan's Tartars have invaded the whole province of Semipolatinsk, and for some days, by forced marches, have been descending the Irtish. You must hurry if you wish to get to Omsk before them."

"Indeed I must," replied Michael.

"It is reported also that Colonel Ogareff has succeeded in passing the frontier in disguise, and that he will not be slow in joining the Tartar chief in the revolted country."

"But how do they know it?" asked Michael, whom this news, more or less true, so directly concerned.

"Oh! as these things are always known," replied Alcide; "it is in the air."

"Then have you really reason to think that Colonel Ogareff is in Siberia?"

"I myself have heard it said that he was to take the road from Kasan to Ekaterenburg."

"Ah! you know that, Mr. Jolivet?" said Harry Blount, roused from his silence.

"I knew it," replied Alcide.

"And do you know that he went disguised as a gypsy!" asked Blount.

"As a gypsy!" exclaimed Michael, almost involuntarily, and he suddenly remembered the look of the old Bohemian at Nijni-Novgorod, his voyage on board the Caucasus, and his disembarking at Kasan.

"Just well enough to make a few remarks on the subject in a letter to my cousin," replied Alcide, smiling.

"You lost no time at Kasan," dryly observed the Englishman.

"No, my dear fellow! and while the Caucasus was laying in her supply of fuel, I was employed in obtaining a store of information."

Michael no longer listened to the repartee which Harry Blount and Alcide exchanged. He was thinking of the gypsy troupe, of the old Tsigane, whose face he had not been able to see, and of the strange woman who accompanied him, and then of the peculiar glance which she had cast at him. Suddenly, close by he heard a pistol-shot.

"Ah! forward, sirs!" cried he.

"Hullo!" said Alcide to himself, "this quiet merchant who always avoids bullets is in a great hurry to go where they are flying about just now!"

Quickly followed by Harry Blount, who was not a man to be behind in danger, he dashed after Michael. In another instant the three were opposite the projecting rock which protected the tarantass at the turning of the road.

The clump of pines struck by the lightning was still burning. There was no one to be seen. However, Michael was not mistaken. Suddenly a dreadful growling was heard, and then another report.

"A bear;" cried Michael, who could not mistake the growling. "Nadia; Nadia!" And drawing his cutlass from his belt, Michael bounded round the buttress behind which the young girl had promised to wait.

The pines, completely enveloped in flames, threw a wild glare on the scene. As Michael reached the tarantass, a huge animal retreated towards him.

It was a monstrous bear. The tempest had driven it from the woods, and it had come to seek refuge in this cave, doubtless its habitual retreat, which Nadia then occupied.

Two of the horses, terrified at the presence of the enormous creature, breaking their traces, had escaped, and the iemschik, thinking only of his beasts, leaving Nadia face to face with the bear, had gone in pursuit of them.

But the brave girl had not lost her presence of mind. The animal, which had not at first seen her, was attacking the remaining horse. Nadia, leaving the shelter in which she had been crouching, had run to the carriage, taken one of Michael's revolvers, and, advancing resolutely towards the bear, had fired close to it.

The animal, slightly wounded in the shoulder, turned on the girl, who rushed for protection behind the tarantass, but then, seeing that the horse was attempting to break its traces, and knowing that if it did so, and the others were not recovered, their journey could not be continued, with the most perfect coolness she again approached the bear, and, as it raised its paws to strike her down, gave it the contents of the second barrel.

This was the report which Michael had just heard. In an instant he was on the spot. Another bound and he was between the bear and the girl. His arm made one movement upwards, and the enormous beast, ripped up by that terrible knife, fell to the ground a lifeless mass. He had executed in splendid style the famous blow of the Siberian hunters, who endeavor not to damage the precious fur of the bear, which fetches a high price.

"You are not wounded, sister?" said Michael, springing to the side of the young girl.

"No, brother," replied Nadia.

At that moment the two journalists came up. Alcide seized the horse's head, and, in an instant, his strong wrist mastered it. His companion and he had seen Michael's rapid stroke. "Bravo!" cried Alcide; "for a simple merchant, Mr. Korpanoff, you handle the hunter's knife in a most masterly fashion."

"Most masterly, indeed," added Blount.

"In Siberia," replied Michael, "we are obliged to do a little of everything."

Alcide regarded him attentively. Seen in the bright glare, his knife dripping with blood, his tall figure, his foot firm on the huge carcass, he was indeed worth looking at.

"A formidable fellow," said Alcide to himself. Then advancing respectfully, he saluted the young girl.

Nadia bowed slightly.

Alcide turned towards his companion. "The sister worthy of the brother!" said he. "Now, were I a bear, I should not meddle with two so brave and so charming."

Harry Blount, perfectly upright, stood, hat in hand, at some distance. His companion's easy manners only increased his usual stiffness.

At that moment the iemschik, who had succeeded in recapturing his two horses, reappeared. He cast a regretful glance at the magnificent animal lying on the ground, loth to leave it to the birds of prey, and then proceeded once more to harness his team.

Michael acquainted him with the travelers' situation, and his intention of loaning one of the horses.

"As you please," replied the iemschik. "Only, you know, two carriages instead of one."

"All right, my friend," said Alcide, who understood the insinuation, "we will pay double."

"Then gee up, my turtle-doves!" cried the iemschik.

Nadia again took her place in the tarantass. Michael and his companions followed on foot. It was three o'clock. The storm still swept with terrific violence across the defile. When the first streaks of daybreak appeared the tarantass had reached the telga, which was still conscientiously imbedded as far as the center of the wheel. Such being the case, it can be easily understood how a sudden jerk would separate the front from the hinder part. One of the horses was now harnessed by means of cords to the remains of the telga, the reporters took their place on the singular equipage, and the two carriages started off. They had now only to descend the Ural slopes, in doing which there was not the slightest difficulty.

Six hours afterwards the two vehicles, the tarantass preceding the telga, arrived at Ekaterenburg, nothing worthy of note having happened in the descent.

The first person the reporters perceived at the door of the post-house was their iemschik, who appeared to be waiting for them. This worthy Russian had a fine open countenance, and he smilingly approached the travelers, and, holding out his hand, in a quiet tone he demanded the usual "pour-boire."

This very cool request roused Blount's ire to its highest pitch, and had not the iemschik prudently retreated, a straight-out blow of the fist, in true British boxing style, would have paid his claim of "na vodkou."

Alcide Jolivet, at this burst of anger, laughed as he had never laughed before.

"But the poor devil is quite right!" he cried. "He is perfectly right, my dear fellow. It is not his fault if we did not know how to follow him!"

Then drawing several copecks from his pocket, "Here my friend," said he, handing them to the iemschik; "take them. If you have not earned them, that is not your fault."

This redoubled Mr. Blount's irritation. He even began to speak of a lawsuit against the owner of the telga.

"A lawsuit in Russia, my dear fellow!" cried Alcide. "Things must indeed change should it ever be brought to a conclusion! Did you never hear the story of the wet-nurse who claimed payment of twelve months' nursing of some poor little infant?"

"I never heard it," replied Harry Blount.

"Then you do not know what that suckling had become by the time judgment was given in favor of the nurse?"

"What was he, pray?"

"Colonel of the Imperial Guard!"

At this reply all burst into a laugh.

Alcide, enchanted with his own joke, drew out his notebook, and in it wrote the following memorandum, destined to figure in a forthcoming French and Russian dictionary: "Telga, a Russian carriage with four wheels, that is when it starts; with two wheels, when it arrives at its destination."

CHAPTER XII

PROVOCATION

EKATERENBURG, geographically, is an Asiatic city; for it is situated beyond the Ural Mountains, on the farthest eastern slopes of the chain. Nevertheless, it belongs to the government of Perm; and, consequently, is included in one of the great divisions of European Russia. It is as though a morsel of Siberia lay in Russian jaws.

Neither Michael nor his companions were likely to experience the slightest difficulty in obtaining means of continuing their journey in so large a town as Ekaterenburg. It was founded in 1723, and has since become a place of considerable size, for in it is the chief mint of the empire. There also are the headquarters of the officials employed in the management of the mines. Thus the town is the center of an important district, abounding in manufactories principally for the working and refining of gold and platina.

Just now the population of Ekaterenburg had greatly increased; many Russians and Siberians, menaced by the Tartar invasion, having collected there. Thus, though it had been so troublesome a matter to find horses and vehicles when going to Ekaterenburg, there was no difficulty in leaving it; for under present circumstances few travelers cared to venture on the Siberian roads.

So it happened that Blount and Alcide had not the slightest trouble in replacing, by a sound telga, the famous demi-carriage which had managed to take them to Ekaterenburg. As to Michael, he retained his tarantass, which was not much the worse for its journey across the Urals; and he had only to harness three good horses to it to take him swiftly over the road to Irkutsk.

As far as Tioumen, and even up to Novo-Zaimskoe, this road has slight inclines, which gentle undulations are the first signs of the slopes of the Ural Mountains. But after Novo-Zaimskoe begins the immense steppe.

At Ichim, as we have said, the reporters intended to stop, that is at about four hundred and twenty miles from Ekaterenburg. There they intended to be guided by circumstances as to their route across the invaded country, either together or separately, according as their news-hunting instinct set them on one track or another.

This road from Ekaterenburg to Ichim—which passes through Irkutsk—was the only one which Michael could take. But, as he did not run after news, and wished, on the contrary, to avoid the country devastated by the invaders, he determined to stop nowhere.

"I am very happy to make part of my journey in your company," said he to his new companions, "but I must tell you that I am most anxious to reach Omsk; for my sister and I are going to rejoin our mother. Who can say whether we shall arrive before the Tartars reach the town! I must therefore stop at the post-houses only long enough to change horses, and must travel day and night."

"That is exactly what we intend doing," replied Blount.

"Good," replied Michael; "but do not lose an instant. Buy or hire a carriage whose—"

"Whose hind wheels," added Alcide, "are warranted to arrive at the same time as its front wheels."

Half an hour afterwards the energetic Frenchman had found a tarantass in which he and his companion at once seated themselves.

Michael and Nadia once more entered their own carriage, and at twelve o'clock the two vehicles left the town of Ekaterenburg together.

Nadia was at last in Siberia, on that long road which led to Irkutsk. What must then have been the thoughts of the young girl? Three strong swift horses were taking her across that land of exile where her parent was condemned to live, for how long she knew not, and so far from his native land. But she scarcely noticed those long steppes over which the tarantass was rolling, and which at one time she had despaired of ever seeing, for her eyes were gazing at the horizon, beyond which she knew her banished father was. She saw nothing of the country across which she was traveling at the rate of fifteen versts an hour; nothing of these regions of Western Siberia, so different from those of the east. Here, indeed, were few cultivated fields; the soil was poor, at least at the surface, but in its bowels lay hid quantities of iron, copper, platina, and gold. How can hands be found to cultivate the land, when it pays better to burrow beneath the earth? The pickaxe is everywhere at work; the spade nowhere.

However, Nadia's thoughts sometimes left the provinces of Lake Baikal, and returned to her present situation. Her father's image faded away, and was replaced by that of her generous companion as he first appeared on the Vladimir railroad. She recalled his attentions during that journey, his arrival at the police-station, the hearty simplicity with which he had called her sister, his kindness to her in the descent of the Volga, and then all that he did for her on that terrible night of the storm in the Urals, when he saved her life at the peril of his own.

Thus Nadia thought of Michael. She thanked God for having given her such a gallant protector, a friend so generous and wise. She knew that she was safe with him, under his protection. No brother could have done more than he. All obstacles seemed cleared away; the performance of her journey was but a matter of time.

Michael remained buried in thought. He also thanked God for having brought about this meeting with Nadia, which at the same time enabled him to do a good action, and afforded him additional means for concealing his true character. He delighted in the young girl's calm intrepidity. Was she not indeed his sister? His feeling towards his beautiful and brave companion was rather respect than affection. He felt that hers was one of those pure and rare hearts which are held by all in high esteem.

However, Michael's dangers were now beginning, since he had reached Siberian ground. If the reporters were not mistaken, if Ivan Ogareff had really passed the frontier, all his actions must be made with extreme caution. Things were now altered; Tartar spies swarmed in the Siberian provinces. His incognito once discovered, his character as courier of the Czar known, there was an end of his journey, and probably of his life. Michael felt now more than ever the weight of his responsibility.

While such were the thoughts of those occupying the first carriage, what was happening in the second? Nothing out of the way. Alcide spoke in sentences; Blount replied by monosyllables. Each looked at everything in his own light, and made notes of such incidents as occurred on the journey—few and but slightly varied—while they crossed the provinces of Western Siberia.

At each relay the reporters descended from their carriage and found themselves with Michael. Except when meals were to be taken at the post-houses, Nadia did not leave the tarantass. When obliged to breakfast or dine, she sat at table, but was always very reserved, and seldom joined in conversation.

Alcide, without going beyond the limits of strict propriety, showed that he was greatly struck by the young girl. He admired the silent energy which she showed in bearing all the fatigues of so difficult a journey.

The forced stoppages were anything but agreeable to Michael; so he hastened the departure at each relay, roused the innkeepers, urged on the iemschiks, and expedited the harnessing of the tarantass. Then the hurried meal over—always much too hurried to agree with Blount, who was a methodical eater—they started, and were driven as eagles, for they paid like princes.

It need scarcely be said that Blount did not trouble himself about the girl at table. That gentleman was not in the habit of doing two things at once. She was also one of the few subjects of conversation which he did not care to discuss with his companion.

Alcide having asked him, on one occasion, how old he thought the girl, "What girl?" he replied, quite seriously.

"Why, Nicholas Korpanoff's sister."

"Is she his sister?"

"No; his grandmother!" replied Alcide, angry at his indifference. "What age should you consider her?"

"Had I been present at her birth I might have known."

Very few of the Siberian peasants were to be seen in the fields. These peasants are remarkable for their pale, grave faces, which a celebrated traveler has compared to those of the Castilians, without the haughtiness of the latter. Here and there some villages already deserted indicated the approach of the Tartar hordes. The inhabitants, having driven off their flocks of sheep, their camels, and their horses, were taking refuge in the plains of the north. Some tribes of the wandering Kirghiz, who remained faithful, had transported their tents beyond the Irtych, to escape the depredations of the invaders.

Happily, post traveling was as yet uninterrupted; and telegraphic communication could still be effected between places connected with the wire. At each relay horses were to be had on the usual conditions. At each telegraphic station the clerks transmitted messages delivered to them, delaying for State dispatches alone.

Thus far, then, Michael's journey had been accomplished satisfactorily. The courier of the Czar had in no way been impeded; and, if he could only get on to Krasnoiarsk, which seemed the farthest point attained by Feofar-Khan's Tartars, he knew that he could arrive at Irkutsk, before them. The day after the two carriages had left Ekaterenburg they reached the small town of Toulouguisk at seven o'clock in the morning, having covered two hundred and twenty versts, no event worthy of mention having occurred. The same evening, the 22d of July, they arrived at Tioumen.

Tioumen, whose population is usually ten thousand inhabitants, then contained double that number. This, the first industrial town established by the Russians in Siberia, in which may be seen a fine metal-refining factory and a bell foundry, had never before presented such an animated appearance. The correspondents immediately went off after news. That brought by Siberian fugitives from the seat of war was far from reassuring. They said, amongst other things, that Feofar-Khan's army was rapidly approaching the valley of the Ichim, and they confirmed the report that the Tartar chief was soon to be joined by Colonel Ogareff, if he had not been so already. Hence the conclusion was that operations would be pushed in Eastern Siberia with the greatest activity. However, the loyal Cossacks of the government of Tobolsk were advancing by forced marches towards Tomsk, in the hope of cutting off the Tartar columns.

At midnight the town of Novo-Saimsk was reached; and the travelers now left behind them the country broken by tree-covered hills, the last remains of the Urals.

Here began the regular Siberian steppe which extends to the neighborhood of Krasnoiarsk. It is a boundless plain, a vast grassy desert; earth and sky here form a circle as distinct as that traced by a sweep of the compasses. The steppe presents nothing to attract notice but the long line of the telegraph posts, their wires vibrating in the breeze like the strings of a harp. The road could be distinguished from the rest of the plain only by the clouds of fine dust which rose under the wheels of the tarantass. Had it not been for this white riband, which stretched away as far as the eye could reach, the travelers might have thought themselves in a desert.

Michael and his companions again pressed rapidly forward. The horses, urged on by the iemschik, seemed to fly over the ground, for there was not the slightest obstacle to impede them. The tarantass was going straight for Ichim, where the two correspondents intended to stop, if nothing happened to make them alter their plans.

A hundred and twenty miles separated Novo-Saimsk from the town of Ichim, and before eight o'clock the next evening the distance could and should be accomplished if no time was lost. In the opinion of the iemschiks, should the travelers not be great lords or high functionaries, they were worthy of being so, if it was only for their generosity in the matter of "na vodkou."

On the afternoon of the next day, the 23rd of July, the two carriages were not more than thirty versts from Ichim. Suddenly Michael caught sight of a carriage—scarcely visible among the clouds of dust—preceding them along the road. As his horses were evidently less fatigued than those of the other traveler, he would not be long in overtaking it. This was neither a tarantass nor a telga, but a post-berlin, which looked as if it had made a long journey. The postillion was thrashing his horses with all his might, and only kept them at a gallop by dint of abuse and blows. The berlin had certainly not passed through Novo-Saimsk, and could only have struck the Irkutsk road by some less frequented route across the steppe.

Our travelers' first thought, on seeing this berlin, was to get in front of it, and arrive first at the relay, so as to make sure of fresh horses. They said a word to their iemschiks, who soon brought them up with the berlin.

Michael Strogoff came up first. As he passed, a head was thrust out of the window of the berlin.

He had not time to see what it was like, but as he dashed by he distinctly heard this word, uttered in an imperious tone: "Stop!"

But they did not stop; on the contrary, the berlin was soon distanced by the two tarantasses.

It now became a regular race; for the horses of the berlin—no doubt excited by the sight and pace of the others—recovered their strength and kept up for some minutes. The three carriages were hidden in a cloud of dust. From this cloud issued the cracking of whips mingled with excited shouts and exclamations of anger.

Nevertheless, the advantage remained with Michael and his companions, which might be very important to them if the relay was poorly provided with horses. Two carriages were perhaps more than the postmaster could provide for, at least in a short space of time.

Half an hour after the berlin was left far behind, looking only a speck on the horizon of the steppe.

It was eight o'clock in the evening when the two carriages reached Ichim. The news was worse and worse with regard to the invasion. The town itself was menaced by the Tartar vanguard; and two days before the authorities had been obliged to retreat to Tobolsk. There was not an officer nor a soldier left in Ichim.

On arriving at the relay, Michael Strogoff immediately asked for horses. He had been fortunate in distancing the berlin. Only three horses were fit to be harnessed. The others had just come in worn out from a long stage.

As the two correspondents intended to stop at Ichim, they had not to trouble themselves to find transport, and had their carriage put away. In ten minutes Michael was told that his tarantass was ready to start.

"Good," said he.

Then turning to the two reporters: "Well, gentlemen, the time is come for us to separate."

"What, Mr. Korpanoff," said Alcide Jolivet, "shall you not stop even for an hour at Ichim?"

"No, sir; and I also wish to leave the post-house before the arrival of the berlin which we distanced."

"Are you afraid that the traveler will dispute the horses with you?"

"I particularly wish to avoid any difficulty."

"Then, Mr. Korpanoff," said Jolivet, "it only remains for us to thank you once more for the service you rendered us, and the pleasure we have had in traveling with you."

"It is possible that we shall meet you again in a few days at Omsk," added Blount.

"It is possible," answered Michael, "since I am going straight there."

"Well, I wish you a safe journey, Mr. Korpanoff," said Alcide, "and Heaven preserve you from telgas."

The two reporters held out their hands to Michael with the intention of cordially shaking his, when the sound of a carriage was heard outside. Almost immediately the door was flung open and a man appeared.

It was the traveler of the berlin, a military-looking man, apparently about forty years of age, tall, robust in figure, broad-shouldered, with a strongly-set head, and thick mus-taches meeting red whiskers. He wore a plain uniform. A cavalry saber hung at his side, and in his hand he held a short-handled whip.

"Horses," he demanded, with the air of a man accustomed to command.

"I have no more disposable horses," answered the postmaster, bowing.

"I must have some this moment."

"It is impossible."

"What are those horses which have just been harnessed to the tarantass I saw at the door?"

"They belong to this traveler," answered the postmaster, pointing to Michael Strogoff.

"Take them out!" said the traveler in a tone which admitted of no reply.

Michael then advanced.

"These horses are engaged by me," he said.

"What does that matter? I must have them. Come, be quick; I have no time to lose."

"I have no time to lose either," replied Michael, restraining himself with difficulty.

Nadia was near him, calm also, but secretly uneasy at a scene which it would have been better to avoid.

"Enough!" said the traveler. Then, going up to the postmaster, "Let the horses be put into my berlin," he exclaimed with a threatening gesture.

The postmaster, much embarrassed, did not know whom to obey, and looked at Michael, who evidently had the right to resist the unjust demands of the traveler.

Michael hesitated an instant. He did not wish to make use of his podorojna, which would have drawn attention to him, and he was most unwilling also, by giving up his horses, to delay his journey, and yet he must not engage in a struggle which might compromise his mission.

The two reporters looked at him ready to support him should he appeal to them.

"My horses will remain in my carriage," said Michael, but without raising his tone more than would be suitable for a plain Irkutsk merchant.

The traveler advanced towards Michael and laid his hand heavily on his shoulder. "Is it so?" he said roughly. "You will not give up your horses to me?"

"No," answered Michael.

"Very well, they shall belong to whichever of us is able to start. Defend yourself; I shall not spare you!"

So saying, the traveler drew his saber from its sheath, and Nadia threw herself before Michael.

Blount and Alcide Jolivet advanced towards him.

"I shall not fight," said Michael quietly, folding his arms across his chest.

"You will not fight?"

"No."

"Not even after this?" exclaimed the traveler. And before anyone could prevent him, he struck Michael's shoulder with the handle of the whip. At this insult Michael turned deadly pale. His hands moved convulsively as if he would have knocked the brute down. But by a tremendous effort he mastered himself. A duel! it was more than a delay; it was perhaps the failure of his mission. It would be better to lose some hours. Yes; but to swallow this affront!

"Will you fight now, coward?" repeated the traveler, adding coarseness to brutality.

"No," answered Michael, without moving, but looking the other straight in the face.

"The horses this moment," said the man, and left the room.

The postmaster followed him, after shrugging his shoulders and bestowing on Michael a glance of anything but approbation.

The effect produced on the reporters by this incident was not to Michael's advantage. Their discomfiture was visible. How could this strong young man allow himself to be struck like that and not demand satisfaction for such an insult? They contented themselves with bowing to him and retired, Jolivet remarking to Harry Blount

"I could not have believed that of a man who is so skillful in finishing up Ural Mountain bears. Is it the case that a man can be courageous at one time and a coward at another? It is quite incomprehensible."

A moment afterwards the noise of wheels and whip showed that the berlin, drawn by the tarantass' horses, was driving rapidly away from the post-house.

Nadia, unmoved, and Michael, still quivering, remained alone in the room. The courier of the Czar, his arms crossed over his chest was seated motionless as a statue. A color, which could not have been the blush of shame, had replaced the paleness on his countenance.

Nadia did not doubt that powerful reasons alone could have allowed him to suffer so great a humiliation from such a man. Going up to him as he had come to her in the police-station at Nijni-Novgorod:

"Your hand, brother," said she.

And at the same time her hand, with an almost maternal gesture, wiped away a tear which sprang to her companion's eye.

71

CHAPTER XIII
DUTY BEFORE EVERYTHING

NADIA, with the clear perception of a right-minded woman, guessed that some secret motive directed all Michael Strogoff's actions; that he, for a reason unknown to her, did not belong to himself; and that in this instance especially he had heroically sacrificed to duty even his resentment at the gross injury he had received.

Nadia, therefore, asked no explanation from Michael. Had not the hand which she had extended to him already replied to all that he might have been able to tell her?

Michael remained silent all the evening. The postmaster not being able to supply them with fresh horses until the next morning, a whole night must be passed at the house. Nadia could profit by it to take some rest, and a room was therefore prepared for her.

The young girl would no doubt have preferred not to leave her companion, but she felt that he would rather be alone, and she made ready to go to her room.

Just as she was about to retire she could not refrain from going up to Michael to say good-night.

"Brother," she whispered. But he checked her with a gesture. The girl sighed and left the room.

Michael Strogoff did not lie down. He could not have slept even for an hour. The place on which he had been struck by the brutal traveler felt like a burn.

"For my country and the Father," he muttered as he ended his evening prayer.

He especially felt a great wish to know who was the man who had struck him, whence he came, and where he was going. As to his face, the features of it were so deeply engraven on his memory that he had no fear of ever forgetting them.

Michael Strogoff at last asked for the postmaster. The latter, a Siberian of the old type, came directly, and looking rather contemptuously at the young man, waited to be questioned.

"You belong to the country?" asked Michael.

"Yes."

"Do you know that man who took my horses?"

"No."

"Had you never seen him before?"

"Never."

"Who do you think he was?"

"A man who knows how to make himself obeyed."

Michael fixed his piercing gaze upon the Siberian, but the other did not quail before it.

"Do you dare to judge me?" exclaimed Michael.

"Yes," answered the Siberian, "there are some things even a plain merchant cannot receive without returning."

"Blows?"

"Blows, young man. I am of an age and strength to tell you so."

Michael went up to the postmaster and laid his two powerful hands on his shoulders.

Then in a peculiarly calm tone, "Be off, my friend," said he: "be off! I could kill you."

The postmaster understood. "I like him better for that," he muttered and retired without another word.

At eight o'clock the next morning, the 24th of July, three strong horses were harnessed to the tarantass. Michael Strogoff and Nadia took their places, and Ichim, with its disagreeable remembrances, was soon left far behind.

At the different relays at which they stopped during the day Strogoff ascertained that the berlin still preceded them on the road to Irkutsk, and that the traveler, as hurried as they were, never lost a minute in pursuing his way across the steppe.

At four o'clock in the evening they reached Abatskaia, fifty miles farther on, where the Ichim, one of the principal affluents of the Irtych, had to be crossed. This passage was rather more difficult than that of the Tobol. Indeed the current of the Ichim was very rapid just at that place. During the Siberian winter, the rivers being all frozen to a thickness of several feet, they are easily practicable, and the traveler even crosses them without being aware of the fact, for their beds have disappeared under the snowy sheet spread uniformly over the steppe; but in summer the difficulties of crossing are sometimes great.

In fact, two hours were taken up in making the passage of the Ichim, which much exasperated Michael, especially as the boatmen gave them alarming news of the Tartar invasion. Some of Feofar-Khan's scouts had already appeared on both banks of the lower Ichim, in the southern parts of the government of Tobolsk. Omsk was threatened. They spoke of an engagement which had taken place between the Siberian and Tartar troops on the frontier of the great Kirghese horde—an engagement not to the advantage of the Russians, who were weak in numbers. The troops had retreated thence, and in consequence there had been a general emigration of all the peasants of the province. The boatmen spoke of horrible atrocities committed by the invaders—pillage, theft, incendiarism, murder. Such was the system of Tartar warfare.

The people all fled before Feofar-Khan. Michael Strogoff's great fear was lest, in the depopulation of the towns, he should be unable to obtain the means of transport. He was therefore extremely anxious to reach Omsk. Perhaps there they would get the start of the Tartar scouts, who were coming down the valley of the Irtych, and would find the road open to Irkutsk.

Just at the place where the tarantass crossed the river ended what is called, in military language, the "Ichim chain"—a chain of towers, or little

73

wooden forts, extending from the southern frontier of Siberia for a distance of nearly four hundred versts. Formerly these forts were occupied by detachments of Cossacks, and they protected the country against the Kirghese, as well as against the Tartars. But since the Muscovite Government had believed these hordes reduced to absolute submission, they had been abandoned, and now could not be used; just at the time when they were needed. Many of these forts had been reduced to ashes; and the boatmen even pointed out the smoke to Michael, rising in the southern horizon, and showing the approach of the Tartar advance-guard.

As soon as the ferryboat landed the tarantass on the right bank of the Ichim, the journey across the steppe was resumed with all speed. Michael Strogoff remained very silent. He was, however, always attentive to Nadia, helping her to bear the fatigue of this long journey without break or rest; but the girl never complained. She longed to give wings to the horses. Something told her that her companion was even more anxious than herself to reach Irkutsk; and how many versts were still between!

It also occurred to her that if Omsk was entered by the Tartars, Michael's mother, who lived there, would be in danger, and that this was sufficient to explain her son's impatience to get to her.

Nadia at last spoke to him of old Marfa, and of how unprotected she would be in the midst of all these events.

"Have you received any news of your mother since the beginning of the invasion?" she asked.

"None, Nadia. The last letter my mother wrote to me contained good news. Marfa is a brave and energetic Siberian woman. Notwithstanding her age, she has preserved all her moral strength. She knows how to suffer."

"I shall see her, brother," said Nadia quickly. "Since you give me the name of sister, I am Marfa's daughter."

And as Michael did not answer she added:

"Perhaps your mother has been able to leave Omsk?"

"It is possible, Nadia," replied Michael; "and I hope she may have reached Tobolsk. Marfa hates the Tartars. She knows the steppe, and would have no fear in just taking her staff and going down the banks of the Irtych. There is not a spot in all the province unknown to her. Many times has she traveled all over the country with my father; and many times I myself, when a mere child, have accompanied them across the Siberian desert. Yes, Nadia, I trust that my mother has left Omsk."

"And when shall you see her?"

"I shall see her—on my return."

"If, however, your mother is still at Omsk, you will be able to spare an hour to go to her?"

"I shall not go and see her."

"You will not see her?"

"No, Nadia," said Michael, his chest heaving as he felt he could not go on replying to the girl's questions.

"You say no! Why, brother, if your mother is still at Omsk, for what reason could you refuse to see her?"

"For what reason, Nadia? You ask me for what reason," exclaimed Michael, in so changed a voice that the young girl started. "For the same reason as that which made me patient even to cowardice with the villain who—" He could not finish his sentence.

"Calm yourself, brother," said Nadia in a gentle voice. "I only know one thing, or rather I do not know it, I feel it. It is that all your conduct is now directed by the sentiment of a duty more sacred—if there can be one—than that which unites the son to the mother."

Nadia was silent, and from that moment avoided every subject which in any way touched on Michael's peculiar situation. He had a secret motive which she must respect. She respected it.

The next day, July 25th, at three o'clock in the morning, the tarantass arrived at Tioukalmsk, having accomplished a distance of eighty miles since it had crossed the Ichim. They rapidly changed horses. Here, however, for the first time, the iemschik made difficulties about starting, declaring that detachments of Tartars were roving across the steppe, and that travelers, horses, and carriages would be a fine prize for them.

Only by dint of a large bribe could Michael get over the unwillingness of the iemschik, for in this instance, as in many others, he did not wish to show his podorojna. The last ukase, having been transmitted by telegraph, was known in the Siberian provinces; and a Russian specially exempted from obeying these words would certainly have drawn public attention to himself—a thing above all to be avoided by the Czar's courier. As to the iemschik's hesitation, either the rascal traded on the traveler's impatience or he really had good reason to fear.

However, at last the tarantass started, and made such good way that by three in the afternoon it had reached Koulatsinskoe, fifty miles farther on. An hour after this it was on the banks of the Irtych. Omsk was now only fourteen miles distant.

The Irtych is a large river, and one of the principal of those which flow towards the north of Asia. Rising in the Altai Mountains, it flows from the southeast to the northwest and empties itself into the Obi, after a course of four thousand miles.

At this time of year, when all the rivers of the Siberian basin are much swollen, the waters of the Irtych were very high. In consequence the current was changed to a regular torrent, rendering the passage difficult enough. A swimmer could not have crossed, however powerful; and even in a ferryboat there would be some danger.

But Michael and Nadia, determined to brave all perils whatever they might be, did not dream of shrinking from this one. Michael proposed to his young companion that he should cross first, embarking in the ferryboat with the tarantass and horses, as he feared that the weight of this load would render it less safe. After landing the carriage he would return and fetch Nadia.

The girl refused. It would be the delay of an hour, and she would not, for her safety alone, be the cause of it.

The embarkation was made not without difficulty, for the banks were partly flooded and the boat could not get in near enough. However, after half an hour's exertion, the boatmen got the tarantass and the three horses on board. The passengers embarked also, and they shoved off.

For a few minutes all went well. A little way up the river the current was broken by a long point projecting from the bank, and forming an eddy easily crossed by the boat. The two boatmen propelled their barge with long poles, which they handled cleverly; but as they gained the middle of the stream it grew deeper and deeper, until at last they could only just reach the bottom. The ends of the poles were only a foot above the water, which rendered their use difficult. Michael and Nadia, seated in the stern of the boat, and always in dread of a delay, watched the boatmen with some uneasiness.

"Look out!" cried one of them to his comrade.

The shout was occasioned by the new direction the boat was rapidly taking. It had got into the direct current and was being swept down the river. By diligent use of the poles, putting the ends in a series of notches cut below the gunwale, the boatmen managed to keep the craft against the stream, and slowly urged it in a slanting direction towards the right bank.

They calculated on reaching it some five or six versts below the landing place; but, after all, that would not matter so long as men and beasts could disembark without accident. The two stout boatmen, stimulated moreover by the promise of double fare, did not doubt of succeeding in this difficult passage of the Irtych.

But they reckoned without an accident which they were powerless to prevent, and neither their zeal nor their skill-fulness could, under the circumstances, have done more.

The boat was in the middle of the current, at nearly equal distances from either shore, and being carried down at the rate of two versts an hour, when Michael, springing to his feet, bent his gaze up the river.

Several boats, aided by oars as well as by the current, were coming swiftly down upon them.

Michael's brow contracted, and a cry escaped him.

"What is the matter?" asked the girl.

But before Michael had time to reply one of the boatmen exclaimed in an accent of terror:

"The Tartars! the Tartars!"

There were indeed boats full of soldiers, and in a few minutes they must reach the ferryboat, it being too heavily laden to escape from them.

The terrified boatmen uttered exclamations of despair and dropped their poles.

"Courage, my friends!" cried Michael; "courage! Fifty roubles for you if we reach the right bank before the boats overtake us."

Incited by these words, the boatmen again worked manfully but it soon become evident that they could not escape the Tartars.

It was scarcely probable that they would pass without attacking them. On the contrary, there was everything to be feared from robbers such as these.

"Do not be afraid, Nadia," said Michael; "but be ready for anything."

"I am ready," replied Nadia.

"Even to leap into the water when I tell you?"

"Whenever you tell me."

"Have confidence in me, Nadia."

"I have, indeed!"

The Tartar boats were now only a hundred feet distant. They carried a detachment of Bokharian soldiers, on their way to reconnoiter around Omsk.

The ferryboat was still two lengths from the shore. The boatmen redoubled their efforts. Michael himself seized a pole and wielded it with superhuman strength. If he could land the tarantass and horses, and dash off with them, there was some chance of escaping the Tartars, who were not mounted.

But all their efforts were in vain. "Saryn na kitchou!" shouted the soldiers from the first boat.

Michael recognized the Tartar war-cry, which is usually answered by lying flat on the ground. As neither he nor the boatmen obeyed a volley was let fly, and two of the horses were mortally wounded.

At the next moment a violent blow was felt. The boats had run into the ferryboat.

"Come, Nadia!" cried Michael, ready to jump overboard.

The girl was about to follow him, when a blow from a lance struck him, and he was thrown into the water. The current swept him away, his hand raised for an instant above the waves, and then he disappeared.

Nadia uttered a cry, but before she had time to throw herself after him she was seized and dragged into one of the boats. The boatmen were killed, the ferryboat left to drift away, and the Tartars continued to descend the Irtych.

CHAPTER XIV
MOTHER AND SON

OMSK is the official capital of Western Siberia. It is not the most important city of the government of that name, for Tomsk has more inhabitants and is larger. But it is at Omsk that the Governor-General of this the first half of Asiatic Russia resides. Omsk, properly so called, is composed of two distinct towns: one which is exclusively inhabited by the authorities and officials; the other more especially devoted to the Siberian merchants, although, indeed, the trade of the town is of small importance.

77

This city has about 12,000 to 13,000 inhabitants. It is defended by walls, but these are merely of earth, and could afford only insufficient protection. The Tartars, who were well aware of this fact, consequently tried at this period to carry it by main force, and in this they succeeded, after an investment of a few days.

The garrison of Omsk, reduced to two thousand men, resisted valiantly. But driven back, little by little, from the mercantile portion of the place, they were compelled to take refuge in the upper town.

It was there that the Governor-General, his officers, and soldiers had entrenched themselves. They had made the upper quarter of Omsk a kind of citadel, and hitherto they held out well in this species of improvised "kreml," but without much hope of the promised succor. The Tartar troops, who were descending the Irtych, received every day fresh reinforcements, and, what was more serious, they were led by an officer, a traitor to his country, but a man of much note, and of an audacity equal to any emergency. This man was Colonel Ivan Ogareff.

Ivan Ogareff, terrible as any of the most savage Tartar chieftains, was an educated soldier. Possessing on his mother's side some Mongolian blood, he delighted in deceptive strategy and ambuscades, stopping short of nothing when he desired to fathom some secret or to set some trap. Deceitful by nature, he willingly had recourse to the vilest trickery; lying when occasion demanded, excelling in the adoption of all disguises and in every species of deception. Further, he was cruel, and had even acted as an executioner. Feofar-Khan possessed in him a lieutenant well capable of seconding his designs in this savage war.

When Michael Strogoff arrived on the banks of the Irtych, Ivan Ogareff was already master of Omsk, and was pressing the siege of the upper quarter of the town all the more eagerly because he must hasten to Tomsk, where the main body of the Tartar army was concentrated.

Tomsk, in fact, had been taken by Feofar-Khan some days previously, and it was thence that the invaders, masters of Central Siberia, were to march upon Irkutsk.

Irkutsk was the real object of Ivan Ogareff. The plan of the traitor was to reach the Grand Duke under a false name, to gain his confidence, and to deliver into Tartar hands the town and the Grand Duke himself. With such a town, and such a hostage, all Asiatic Siberia must necessarily fall into the hands of the invaders. Now it was known that the Czar was acquainted with this conspiracy, and that it was for the purpose of baffling it that a courier had been intrusted with the important warning. Hence, therefore, the very stringent instructions which had been given to the young courier to pass incognito through the invaded district.

This mission he had so far faithfully performed, but now could he carry it to a successful completion?

The blow which had struck Michael Strogoff was not mortal. By swimming in a manner by which he had effectually concealed himself, he had reached the right bank, where he fell exhausted among the bushes.

When he recovered his senses, he found himself in the cabin of a mujik, who had picked him up and cared for him. For how long a time had he been the guest of this brave Siberian? He could not guess. But when he opened his eyes he saw the handsome bearded face bending over him, and regarding him with pitying eyes. "Do not speak, little father," said the mujik, "Do not speak! Thou art still too weak. I will tell thee where thou art and everything that has passed."

And the mujik related to Michael Strogoff the different incidents of the struggle which he had witnessed—the attack upon the ferry by the Tartar boats, the pillage of the tarantass, and the massacre of the boatmen.

But Michael Strogoff listened no longer, and slipping his hand under his garment he felt the imperial letter still secured in his breast. He breathed a sigh of relief.

But that was not all. "A young girl accompanied me," said he.

"They have not killed her," replied the mujik, anticipating the anxiety which he read in the eyes of his guest. "They have carried her off in their boat, and have continued the descent of Irtych. It is only one prisoner more to join the many they are taking to Tomsk!"

Michael Strogoff was unable to reply. He pressed his hand upon his heart to restrain its beating. But, notwithstanding these many trials, the sentiment of duty mastered his whole soul. "Where am I?" asked he.

"Upon the right bank of the Irtych, only five versts from Omsk," replied the mujik.

"What wound can I have received which could have thus prostrated me? It was not a gunshot wound?"

"No; a lance-thrust in the head, now healing," replied the mujik. "After a few days' rest, little father, thou wilt be able to proceed. Thou didst fall into the river; but the Tartars neither touched nor searched thee; and thy purse is still in thy pocket."

Michael Strogoff gripped the mujik's hand. Then, recovering himself with a sudden effort, "Friend," said he, "how long have I been in thy hut?"

"Three days."

"Three days lost!"

"Three days hast thou lain unconscious."

"Hast thou a horse to sell me?"

"Thou wishest to go?"

"At once."

"I have neither horse nor carriage, little father. Where the Tartar has passed there remains nothing!"

"Well, I will go on foot to Omsk to find a horse."

"A few more hours of rest, and thou wilt be in a better condition to pursue thy journey."

"Not an hour!"

"Come now," replied the mujik, recognizing the fact that it was useless to struggle against the will of his guest, "I will guide thee myself. Besides," he added, "the Russians are still in great force at Omsk, and thou couldst, perhaps, pass unperceived."

"Friend," replied Michael Strogoff, "Heaven reward thee for all thou hast done for me!"

"Only fools expect reward on earth," replied the mujik.

Michael Strogoff went out of the hut. When he tried to walk he was seized with such faintness that, without the assistance of the mujik, he would have fallen; but the fresh air quickly revived him. He then felt the wound in his head, the violence of which his fur cap had lessened. With the energy which he possessed, he was not a man to succumb under such a trifle. Before his eyes lay a single goal—far-distant Irkutsk. He must reach it! But he must pass through Omsk without stopping there.

"God protect my mother and Nadia!" he murmured. "I have no longer the right to think of them!"

Michael Strogoff and the mujik soon arrived in the mercantile quarter of the lower town. The surrounding earthwork had been destroyed in many places, and there were the breaches through which the marauders who followed the armies of Feofar-Khan had penetrated. Within Omsk, in its streets and squares, the Tartar soldiers swarmed like ants; but it was easy to see that a hand of iron imposed upon them a discipline to which they were little accustomed. They walked nowhere alone, but in armed groups, to defend themselves against surprise.

In the chief square, transformed into a camp, guarded by many sentries, 2,000 Tartars bivouacked. The horses, picketed but still saddled, were ready to start at the first order. Omsk could only be a temporary halting-place for this Tartar cavalry, which preferred the rich plains of Eastern Siberia, where the towns were more wealthy, and, consequently, pillage more profitable.

Above the mercantile town rose the upper quarter, which Ivan Ogareff, notwithstanding several assaults vigorously made but bravely repelled, had not yet been able to reduce. Upon its embattled walls floated the national colors of Russia.

It was not without a legitimate pride that Michael Strogoff and his guide, vowing fidelity, saluted them.

Michael Strogoff was perfectly acquainted with the town of Omsk, and he took care to avoid those streets which were much frequented. This was not from any fear of being recognized. In the town his old mother only could have called him by name, but he had sworn not to see her, and he did not. Besides—and he wished it with his whole heart—she might have fled into some quiet portion of the steppe.

The mujik very fortunately knew a postmaster who, if well paid, would not refuse at his request either to let or to sell a carriage or horses. There remained the difficulty of leaving the town, but the breaches in the fortifications would, of course, facilitate his departure.

The mujik was accordingly conducting his guest straight to the posting-house, when, in a narrow street, Michael Strogoff, coming to a sudden stop sprang behind a jutting wall.

"What is the matter?" asked the astonished mujik.

"Silence!" replied Michael, with his finger on his lips. At this moment a detachment debouched from the principal square into the street which Michael Strogoff and his companion had just been following.

At the head of the detachment, composed of twenty horsemen, was an officer dressed in a very simple uniform. Although he glanced rapidly from one side to the other he could not have seen Michael Strogoff, owing to his precipitous retreat.

The detachment went at full trot into the narrow street. Neither the officer nor his escort concerned themselves about the inhabitants. Several unlucky ones had scarcely time to make way for their passage. There were a few half-stifled cries, to which thrusts of the lance gave an instant reply, and the street was immediately cleared.

When the escort had disappeared, "Who is that officer?" asked Michael Strogoff. And while putting the question his face was pale as that of a corpse.

"It is Ivan Ogareff," replied the Siberian, in a deep voice which breathed hatred.

"He!" cried Michael Strogoff, from whom the word escaped with a fury he could not conquer. He had just recognized in this officer the traveler who had struck him at the posting-house of Ichim. And, although he had only caught a glimpse of him, it burst upon his mind, at the same time, that this traveler was the old Zingari whose words he had overheard in the market place of Nijni-Novgorod.

Michael Strogoff was not mistaken. The two men were one and the same. It was under the garb of a Zingari, mingling with the band of Sangarre, that Ivan Ogareff had been able to leave the town of Nijni-Novgorod, where he had gone to seek his confidants. Sangarre and her Zingari, well paid spies, were absolutely devoted to him. It was he who, during the night, on the fair-ground had uttered that singular sentence, which Michael Strogoff could not understand; it was he who was voyaging on board the Caucasus, with the whole of the Bohemian band; it was he who, by this other route, from Kasan to Ichim, across the Urals, had reached Omsk, where now he held supreme authority.

Ivan Ogareff had been barely three days at Omsk, and had it not been for their fatal meeting at Ichim, and for the event which had detained him three days on the banks of the Irtych, Michael Strogoff would have evidently beaten him on the way to Irkutsk.

And who knows how many misfortunes would have been avoided in the future! In any case—and now more than ever—Michael Strogoff must avoid Ivan Ogareff, and contrive not to be seen. When the moment of encountering him face to face should arrive, he knew how to meet it, even should the traitor be master of the whole of Siberia.

The mujik and Michael resumed their way and arrived at the posting-house. To leave Omsk by one of the breaches would not be difficult after nightfall. As for purchasing a carriage to replace the tarantass, that was impossible. There were none to be let or sold. But what want had Michael Strogoff now for a carriage? Was he not alone, alas? A horse would suffice him; and, very fortunately, a horse could be had. It was an animal of strength and mettle, and Michael Strogoff, accomplished horseman as he was, could make good use of it.

It was four o'clock in the afternoon. Michael Strogoff, compelled to wait till nightfall, in order to pass the fortifications, but not desiring to show himself, remained in the posting-house, and there partook of food.

There was a great crowd in the public room. They were talking of the expected arrival of a corps of Muscovite troops, not at Omsk, but at Tomsk—a corps intended to recapture that town from the Tartars of Feofar-Khan.

Michael Strogoff lent an attentive ear, but took no part in the conversation. Suddenly a cry made him tremble, a cry which penetrated to the depths of his soul, and these two words rushed into his ear: "My son!"

His mother, the old woman Marfa, was before him! Trembling, she smiled upon him. She stretched forth her arms to him. Michael Strogoff arose. He was about to throw himself—

The thought of duty, the serious danger for his mother and himself in this unfortunate meeting, suddenly stopped him, and such was his command over himself that not a muscle of his face moved. There were twenty people in the public room. Among them were, perhaps, spies, and was it not known in the town that the son of Marfa Strogoff belonged to the corps of the couriers of the Czar?

Michael Strogoff did not move.

"Michael!" cried his mother.

"Who are you, my good lady?" Michael Strogoff stammered, unable to speak in his usual firm tone.

"Who am I, thou askest! Dost thou no longer know thy mother?"

"You are mistaken," coldly replied Michael Strogoff. "A resemblance deceives you."

The old Marfa went up to him, and, looking straight into his eyes, said, "Thou art not the son of Peter and Marfa Strogoff?"

Michael Strogoff would have given his life to have locked his mother in his arms; but if he yielded it was all over with him, with her, with his mission, with his oath! Completely master of himself, he closed his eyes, in order not to see the inexpressible anguish which agitated the revered countenance of his mother. He drew back his hands, in order not to touch those trembling hands which sought him. "I do not know in truth what it is you say, my good woman," he replied, stepping back.

"Michael!" again cried his aged mother.

"My name is not Michael. I never was your son! I am Nicholas Korpanoff, a merchant at Irkutsk."

And suddenly he left the public room, whilst for the last time the words re-echoed, "My son! my son!"

Michael Strogoff, by a desperate effort, had gone. He did not see his old mother, who had fallen back almost inanimate upon a bench. But when the postmaster hastened to assist her, the aged woman raised herself. Suddenly a thought occurred to her. She denied by her son! It was not possible. As for being herself deceived, and taking another for him, equally

82

impossible. It was certainly her son whom she had just seen; and if he had not recognized her it was because he would not, it was because he ought not, it was because he had some cogent reasons for acting thus! And then, her mother's feelings arising within her, she had only one thought—"Can I, unwittingly, have ruined him?"

"I am mad," she said to her interrogators. "My eyes have deceived me! This young man is not my child. He had not his voice. Let us think no more of it; if we do I shall end by finding him everywhere."

Less than ten minutes afterwards a Tartar officer appeared in the posting-house. "Marfa Strogoff?" he asked.

"It is I," replied the old woman, in a tone so calm, and with a face so tranquil, that those who had witnessed the meeting with her son would not have known her.

"Come," said the officer.

Marfa Strogoff, with firm step, followed the Tartar. Some moments afterwards she found herself in the chief square in the presence of Ivan Ogareff, to whom all the details of this scene had been immediately reported.

Ogareff, suspecting the truth, interrogated the old Siberian woman. "Thy name?" he asked in a rough voice.

"Marfa Strogoff."

"Thou hast a son?"

"Yes."

"He is a courier of the Czar?"

"Yes."

"Where is he?"

"At Moscow."

"Thou hast no news of him?"

"No news."

"Since how long?"

"Since two months."

"Who, then, was that young man whom thou didst call thy son a few moments ago at the posting-house?"

"A young Siberian whom I took for him," replied Marfa Strogoff. "This is the tenth man in whom I have thought I recognized my son since the town has been so full of strangers. I think I see him everywhere."

"So this young man was not Michael Strogoff?"

"It was not Michael Strogoff."

"Dost thou know, old woman, that I can torture thee until thou avowest the truth?"

"I have spoken the truth, and torture will not cause me to alter my words in any way."

"This Siberian was not Michael Strogoff?" asked a second time Ivan Ogareff.

"No, it was not he," replied a second time Marfa Strogoff. "Do you think that for anything in the world I would deny a son whom God has given me?"

Ivan Ogareff regarded with an evil eye the old woman who braved him to the face. He did not doubt but that she had recognized her son in this young Siberian. Now if this son had first renounced his mother, and if his mother renounced him in her turn, it could occur only from the most weighty motive. Ogareff had therefore no doubt that the pretended Nicholas Korpanoff was Michael Strogoff, courier of the Czar, seeking concealment under a false name, and charged with some mission which it would have been important for him to know. He therefore at once gave orders for his pursuit. Then "Let this woman be conducted to Tomsk," he said.

While the soldiers brutally dragged her off, he added between his teeth, "When the moment arrives I shall know how to make her speak, this old sorceress!"

CHAPTER XV

THE MARSHES OF THE BARABA

IT was fortunate that Michael Strogoff had left the posting-house so promptly. The orders of Ivan Ogareff had been immediately transmitted to all the approaches of the city, and a full description of Michael sent to all the various commandants, in order to prevent his departure from Omsk. But he had already passed through one of the breaches in the wall; his horse was galloping over the steppe, and the chances of escape were in his favor.

It was on the 29th of July, at eight o'clock in the evening, that Michael Strogoff had left Omsk. This town is situated about halfway between Moscow and Irkutsk, where it was necessary that he should arrive within ten days if he wished to get ahead of the Tartar columns. It was evident that the unlucky chance which had brought him into the presence of his mother had betrayed his incognito. Ivan Ogareff was no longer ignorant of the fact that a courier of the Czar had just passed Omsk, taking the direction of Irkutsk. The dispatches which this courier bore must have been of immense importance. Michael Strogoff knew, therefore, that every effort would be made to capture him.

But what he did not know, and could not know, was that Marfa Strogoff was in the hands of Ivan Ogareff, and that she was about to atone, perhaps with her life, for that natural exhibition of her feelings which she had been unable to restrain when she suddenly found herself in the presence of her son. And it was fortunate that he was ignorant of it. Could he have withstood this fresh trial?

Michael Strogoff urged on his horse, imbuing him with all his own feverish impatience, requiring of him one thing only, namely, to bear him rapidly to the next posting-house, where he could be exchanged for a quicker conveyance.

At midnight he had cleared fifty miles, and halted at the station of Koulikovo. But there, as he had feared, he found neither horses nor carriages. Several Tartar detachments had passed along the highway of the steppe. Everything had been stolen or requisitioned both in the villages and in the posting-houses. It was with difficulty that Michael Strogoff was even able to obtain some refreshment for his horse and himself.

It was of great importance, therefore, to spare his horse, for he could not tell when or how he might be able to replace it. Desiring, however, to put the greatest possible distance between himself and the horsemen who had no doubt been dispatched in pursuit, he resolved to push on. After one hour's rest he resumed his course across the steppe.

Hitherto the weather had been propitious for his journey. The temperature was endurable. The nights at this time of the year are very short, and as they are lighted by the moon, the route over the steppe is practicable. Michael Strogoff, moreover, was a man certain of his road and devoid of doubt or hesitation, and in spite of the melancholy thoughts which possessed him he had preserved his clearness of mind, and made for his destined point as though it were visible upon the horizon. When he did halt for a moment at some turn in the road it was to breathe his horse. Now he would dismount to ease his steed for a moment, and again he would place his ear to the ground to listen for the sound of galloping horses upon the steppe. Nothing arousing his suspicions, he resumed his way.

On the 30th of July, at nine o'clock in the morning, Michael Strogoff passed through the station of Touroumoff and entered the swampy district of the Baraba.

There, for a distance of three hundred versts, the natural obstacles would be extremely great. He knew this, but he also knew that he would certainly surmount them.

These vast marshes of the Baraba, form the reservoir to all the rain-water which finds no outlet either towards the Obi or towards the Irtych. The soil of this vast depression is entirely argillaceous, and therefore impermeable, so that the waters remain there and make of it a region very difficult to cross during the hot season. There, however, lies the way to Irkutsk, and it is in the midst of ponds, pools, lakes, and swamps, from which the sun draws poisonous exhalations, that the road winds, and entails upon the traveler the greatest fatigue and danger.

Michael Strogoff spurred his horse into the midst of a grassy prairie, differing greatly from the close-cropped sod of the steppe, where feed the immense Siberian herds. The grass here was five or six feet in height, and had made room for swamp-plants, to which the dampness of the place, assisted by the heat of summer, had given giant proportions. These were principally canes and rushes, which formed a tangled network, an impenetrable undergrowth, sprinkled everywhere with a thousand flowers remarkable for the brightness of their color.

Michael Strogoff, galloping amongst this undergrowth of cane, was no longer visible from the swamps which bordered the road. The tall grass rose above him, and his track was indicated only by the flight of innumerable aquatic birds, which rose from the side of the road and dispersed into the air in screaming flocks.

The way, however, was clearly traceable. Now it would lie straight between the dense thicket of marsh-plants; again it would follow the winding shores of vast pools, some of which, several versts in length and breadth, deserve the name of lakes. In other localities the stagnant waters through which the road lay had been avoided, not by bridges, but by tottering platforms ballasted with thick layers of clay, whose joists shook like a too weak plank thrown across an abyss. Some of these platforms extended over three hundred feet, and travelers by tarantass, when crossing them have experienced a nausea like sea-sickness.

Michael Strogoff, whether the soil beneath his feet was solid or whether it sank under him, galloped on without halt, leaping the space between the rotten joists; but however fast they traveled the horse and the horseman were unable to escape from the sting of the two-winged insects which infest this marshy country.

Travelers who are obliged to cross the Baraba during the summer take care to provide themselves with masks of horse-hair, to which is attached a coat of mail of very fine wire, which covers their shoulders. Notwithstanding these precautions, there are few who come out of these marshes without having their faces, necks, and hands covered with red spots. The atmosphere there seems to bristle with fine needles, and one would almost say that a knight's armor would not protect him against the darts of these dipterals. It is a dreary region, which man dearly disputes with tipulae, gnats, mosquitos, horse-flies, and millions of microscopic insects which are not visible to the naked eye; but, although they are not seen, they make themselves felt by their intolerable stinging, to which the most callous Siberian hunters have never been able to inure themselves.

Michael Strogoff's horse, stung by these venomous insects, sprang forward as if the rowels of a thousand spurs had pierced his flanks. Mad with rage, he tore along over verst after verst with the speed of an express train, lashing his sides with his tail, seeking by the rapidity of his pace an alleviation of his torture.

It required as good a horseman as Michael Strogoff not to be thrown by the plungings of his horse, and the sudden stops and bounds which he made to escape from the stings of his persecutors. Having become insensible, so to speak, to physical suffering, possessed only with the one desire to arrive at his destination at whatever cost, he saw during this mad race only one thing—that the road flew rapidly behind him.

Who would have thought that this district of the Baraba, so unhealthy during the summer, could have afforded an asylum for human beings? Yet it did so. Several Siberian hamlets appeared from time to time among the giant canes. Men, women, children, and old men, clad in the skins of beasts, their faces covered with hardened blisters of skin, pastured their poor herds of sheep. In order to preserve the animals from the attack of the insects, they drove them to the leeward of fires of green wood, which were kept burning night and day, and the pungent smoke of which floated over the vast swamp.

When Michael Strogoff perceived that his horse, tired out, was on the point of succumbing, he halted at one of these wretched hamlets, and there, forgetting his own fatigue, he himself rubbed the wounds of the poor animal with hot grease according to the Siberian custom; then he gave him a good feed; and it was only after he had well groomed and provided for him that he thought of himself, and recruited his strength by a hasty meal of bread and meat and a glass of kwass. One hour afterwards, or at the most two, he resumed with all speed the interminable road to Irkutsk.

On the 30th of July, at four o'clock in the afternoon, Michael Strogoff, insensible of every fatigue, arrived at Elamsk. There it became necessary to give a night's rest to his horse. The brave animal could no longer have continued the journey. At Elamsk, as indeed elsewhere, there existed no means of transport,—for the same reasons as at the previous villages, neither carriages nor horses were to be had.

Michael Strogoff resigned himself therefore to pass the night at Elamsk, to give his horse twelve hours' rest. He recalled the instructions which had been given to him at Moscow—to cross Siberia incognito, to arrive at Irkutsk, but not to sacrifice success to the rapidity of the journey; and consequently it was necessary that he should husband the sole means of transport which remained to him.

On the morrow, Michael Strogoff left Elamsk at the moment when the first Tartar scouts were signaled ten versts behind upon the road to the Baraba, and he plunged again into the swampy region. The road was level, which made it easy, but very tortuous, and therefore long. It was impossible, moreover, to leave it, and to strike a straight line across that impassable network of pools and bogs.

On the next day, the 1st of August, eighty miles farther, Michael Strogoff arrived at midday at the town of Spaskoe, and at two o'clock he halted at Pokrowskoe. His horse, jaded since his departure from Elamsk, could not have taken a single step more.

There Michael Strogoff was again compelled to lose, for necessary rest, the end of that day and the entire night; but starting again on the following morning, and still traversing the semi-inundated soil, on the 2nd of August, at four o'clock in the afternoon, after a stage of fifty miles he reached Kamsk.

The country had changed. This little village of Kamsk lies, like an island, habitable and healthy, in the midst of the uninhabitable district. It is situated in the very center of the Baraba. The emigration caused by the Tartar invasion had not yet depopulated this little town of Kamsk. Its inhabitants probably fancied themselves safe in the center of the Baraba, whence at least they thought they would have time to flee if they were directly menaced.

Michael Strogoff, although exceedingly anxious for news, could ascertain nothing at this place. It would have been rather to him that the Governor would have addressed himself had he known who the pretended merchant of Irkutsk really was. Kamsk, in fact, by its very situation seemed to be outside the Siberian world and the grave events which troubled it.

Besides, Michael Strogoff showed himself little, if at all. To be unperceived was not now enough for him: he would have wished to be invisible. The experience of the past made him more and more circumspect in the present and the future. Therefore he secluded himself, and not caring to traverse the streets of the village, he would not even leave the inn at which he had halted.

As for his horse, he did not even think of exchanging him for another animal. He had become accustomed to this brave creature. He knew to what extent he could rely upon him. In buying him at Omsk he had been lucky, and in taking him to the postmaster the generous mujik had rendered him a great service. Besides, if Michael Strogoff had already become attached to his horse, the horse himself seemed to become inured, by degrees, to the fatigue of such a journey, and provided that he got several hours of repose daily, his rider might hope that he would carry him beyond the invaded provinces.

So, during the evening and night of the 2nd of August, Michael Strogoff remained confined to his inn, at the entrance of the town; which was little frequented and out of the way of the importunate and curious.

Exhausted with fatigue, he went to bed after having seen that his horse lacked nothing; but his sleep was broken. What he had seen since his departure from Moscow showed him the importance of his mission. The rising was an extremely serious one, and the treachery of Ogareff made it still more formidable. And when his eyes fell upon the letter bearing upon it the authority of the imperial seal—the letter which, no doubt, contained the remedy for so many evils, the safety of all this war-ravaged country— Michael Strogoff felt within himself a fierce desire to dash on across the steppe, to accomplish the distance which separated him from Irkutsk as the crow would fly it, to be an eagle that he might overtop all obstacles, to be a hurricane that he might sweep through the air at a hundred versts an hour, and to be at last face to face with the Grand Duke, and to exclaim: "Your highness, from his Majesty the Czar!"

On the next morning at six o'clock, Michael Strogoff started off again. Thanks to his extreme prudence this part of the journey was signalized by no incident whatever. At Oubinsk he gave his horse a whole night's rest, for he wished on the next day to accomplish the hundred versts which lie between Oubinsk and Ikoulskoe without halting. He started therefore at dawn; but unfortunately the Baraba proved more detestable than ever.

In fact, between Oubinsk and Kamakore the very heavy rains of some previous weeks were retained by this shallow depression as in a water-tight bowl. There was, for a long distance, no break in the succession of swamps, pools, and lakes. One of these lakes—large enough to warrant its geographical nomenclature—Tchang, Chinese in name, had to be coasted for more than twenty versts, and this with the greatest difficulty. Hence certain delays occurred, which all the impatience of Michael

Strogoff could not avoid. He had been well advised in not taking a carriage at Kamsk, for his horse passed places which would have been impracticable for a conveyance on wheels.

In the evening, at nine o'clock, Michael Strogoff arrived at Ikoulskoe, and halted there over night. In this remote village of the Baraba news of the war was utterly wanting. From its situation, this part of the province, lying in the fork formed by the two Tartar columns which had bifurcated, one upon Omsk and the other upon Tomsk, had hitherto escaped the horrors of the invasion.

But the natural obstacles were now about to disappear, for, if he experienced no delay, Michael Strogoff should on the morrow be free of the Baraba and arrive at Kolyvan. There he would be within eighty miles of Tomsk. He would then be guided by circumstances, and very probably he would decide to go around Tomsk, which, if the news were true, was occupied by Feofar-Khan.

But if the small towns of Ikoulskoe and Karguinsk, which he passed on the next day, were comparatively quiet, owing to their position in the Baraba, was it not to be dreaded that, upon the right banks of the Obi, Michael Strogoff would have much more to fear from man? It was probable. However, should it become necessary, he would not hesitate to abandon the beaten path to Irkutsk. To journey then across the steppe he would, no doubt, run the risk of finding himself without supplies. There would be, in fact, no longer a well-marked road. Still, there must be no hesitation.

Finally, towards half past three in the afternoon, Michael Strogoff left the last depressions of the Baraba, and the dry and hard soil of Siberia rang out once more beneath his horse's hoofs.

He had left Moscow on the 15th of July. Therefore on this day, the 5th of August, including more than seventy hours lost on the banks of the Irtych, twenty days had gone by since his departure.

One thousand miles still separated him from Irkutsk.

CHAPTER XVI
A FINAL EFFORT

MICHAEL'S fear of meeting the Tartars in the plains beyond the Baraba was by no means ungrounded. The fields, trodden down by horses' hoofs, afforded but too clear evidence that their hordes had passed that way; the same, indeed, might be said of these barbarians as of the Turks: "Where the Turk goes, no grass grows."

Michael saw at once that in traversing this country the greatest caution was necessary. Wreaths of smoke curling upwards on the horizon showed that huts and hamlets were still burning. Had these been fired by the advance guard, or had the Emir's army already advanced beyond the boundaries of the province? Was Feofar-Khan himself in the government of Yeniseisk? Michael could settle on no line of action until these questions were answered. Was the country so deserted that he could not discover a single Siberian to enlighten him?

Michael rode on for two versts without meeting a human being. He looked carefully for some house which had not been deserted. Every one was tenantless.

One hut, however, which he could just see between the trees, was still smoking. As he approached he perceived, at some yards from the ruins of the building, an old man surrounded by weeping children. A woman still young, evidently his daughter and the mother of the poor children, kneeling on the ground, was gazing on the scene of desolation. She had at her breast a baby but a few months old; shortly she would have not even that nourishment to give it. Ruin and desolation were all around!

Michael approached the old man.

"Will you answer me a few questions?" he asked.

"Speak," replied the old man.

"Have the Tartars passed this way?"

"Yes, for my house is in flames."

"Was it an army or a detachment?"

"An army, for, as far as eye can reach, our fields are laid waste."

"Commanded by the Emir?"

"By the Emir; for the Obi's waters are red."

"Has Feofar-Khan entered Tomsk?"

"He has."

"Do you know if his men have entered Kolyvan?"

"No; for Kolyvan does not yet burn."

"Thanks, friend. Can I aid you and yours?"

"No."

"Good-by."

"Farewell."

And Michael, having presented five and twenty roubles to the unfortunate woman, who had not even strength to thank him, put spurs to his horse once more.

One thing he knew; he must not pass through Tomsk. To go to Kolyvan, which the Tartars had not yet reached, was possible. Yes, that is what he must do; there he must prepare himself for another long stage. There was nothing for it but, having crossed the Obi, to take the Irkutsk road and avoid Tomsk.

This new route decided on, Michael must not delay an instant. Nor did he, but, putting his horse into a steady gallop, he took the road towards the left bank of the Obi, which was still forty versts distant. Would there be a ferry boat there, or should he, finding that the Tartars had destroyed all the boats, be obliged to swim across?

As to his horse, it was by this time pretty well worn out, and Michael intended to make it perform this stage only, and then to exchange it for a fresh one at Kolyvan. Kolyvan would be like a fresh starting point, for on leaving that town his journey would take a new form. So long as he traversed a devastated country the difficulties must be very great; but if, having avoided Tomsk, he could resume the road to Irkutsk across the province of Yeniseisk, which was not yet laid waste, he would finish his journey in a few days.

Night came on, bringing with it refreshing coolness after the heat of the day. At midnight the steppe was profoundly dark. The sound of the horses's hoofs alone was heard on the road, except when, every now and then, its master spoke a few encouraging words. In such darkness as this great care was necessary lest he should leave the road, bordered by pools and streams, tributaries of the Obi. Michael therefore advanced as quickly as was consistent with safety. He trusted no less to the excellence of his eyes, which penetrated the gloom, than to the well-proved sagacity of his horse.

Just as Michael dismounted to discover the exact direction of the road, he heard a confused murmuring sound from the west. It was like the noise of horses' hoofs at some distance on the parched ground. Michael listened attentively, putting his ear to the ground.

"It is a detachment of cavalry coming by the road from Omsk," he said to himself. "They are marching very quickly, for the noise is increasing. Are they Russians or Tartars?"

Michael again listened. "Yes," said he, "they are at a sharp trot. My horse cannot outstrip them. If they are Russians I will join them; if Tartars I must avoid them. But how? Where can I hide in this steppe?"

He gave a look around, and, through the darkness, discovered a confused mass at a hundred paces before him on the left of the road. "There is a copse!" he exclaimed. "To take refuge there is to run the risk of being caught, if they are in search of me; but I have no choice."

In a few moments Michael, dragging his horse by the bridle, reached a little larch wood, through which the road lay. Beyond this it was destitute of trees, and wound among bogs and pools, separated by dwarfed bushes, whins, and heather. The ground on either side was quite impracticable, and the detachment must necessarily pass through the wood. They were pursuing the high road to Irkutsk. Plunging in about forty feet, he was stopped by a stream running under the brushwood. But the shadow was so deep that Michael ran no risk of being seen, unless the wood should be carefully searched. He therefore led his horse to the stream and fastened him to a tree, returning to the edge of the road to listen and ascertain with what sort of people he had to do.

Michael had scarcely taken up his position behind a group of larches when a confused light appeared, above which glared brighter lights waving about in the shadow.

"Torches!" said he to himself. And he drew quickly back, gliding like a savage into the thickest underwood.

As they approached the wood the horses' pace was slackened. The horsemen were probably lighting up the road with the intention of examining every turn.

Michael feared this, and instinctively drew near to the bank of the stream, ready to plunge in if necessary.

Arrived at the top of the wood, the detachment halted. The horsemen dismounted. There were about fifty. A dozen of them carried torches, lighting up the road.

By watching their preparations Michael found to his joy that the detachment were not thinking of visiting the copse, but only bivouacking near, to rest their horses and allow the men to take some refreshment. The horses were soon unsaddled, and began to graze on the thick grass which carpeted the ground. The men meantime stretched themselves by the side of the road, and partook of the provisions they produced from their knapsacks.

Michael's self-possession had never deserted him, and creeping amongst the high grass he endeavored not only to examine the new-comers, but to hear what they said. It was a detachment from Omsk, composed of Usbeck horsemen, a race of the Mongolian type. These men, well built, above the medium height, rough, and wild-featured, wore on their heads the "talpak," or black sheep-skin cap, and on their feet yellow high-heeled boots with turned-up toes, like the shoes of the Middle Ages. Their tunics were close-fitting, and confined at the waist by a leathern belt braided with red. They were armed defensively with a shield, and offensively with a curved sword, and a flintlock musket slung at the saddle-bow. From their shoulders hung gay-colored cloaks.

The horses, which were feeding at liberty at the edge of the wood, were, like their masters, of the Usbeck race. These animals are rather smaller than the Turcomanian horses, but are possessed of remarkable strength, and know no other pace than the gallop.

This detachment was commanded by a "pendja-baschi"; that is to say, a commander of fifty men, having under him a "deh-baschi," or simple commander of ten men. These two officers wore helmets and half coats-of-mail; little trumpets fastened to their saddle-bows were the distinctive signs of their rank.

The pendja-baschi had been obliged to let his men rest, fatigued with a long stage. He and the second officer, smoking "beng," the leaf which forms the base of the "has-chisch," strolled up and down the wood, so that Michael Strogoff without being seen, could catch and understand their conversation, which was spoken in the Tartar language.

Michael's attention was singularly excited by their very first words. It was of him they were speaking.

"This courier cannot be much in advance of us," said the pendja-baschi; "and, on the other hand, it is absolutely impossible that he can have followed any other route than that of the Baraba."

"Who knows if he has left Omsk?" replied the deh-baschi. "Perhaps he is still hidden in the town."

"That is to be wished, certainly. Colonel Ogareff would have no fear then that the dispatches he bears should ever reach their destination."

"They say that he is a native, a Siberian," resumed the deh-baschi.

"If so, he must be well acquainted with the country, and it is possible that he has left the Irkutsk road, depending on rejoining it later."

"But then we should be in advance of him," answered the pendja-baschi; "for we left Omsk within an hour after his departure, and have since followed the shortest road with all the speed of our horses. He has either remained in Omsk, or we shall arrive at Tomsk before him, so as to cut him off; in either case he will not reach Irkutsk."

"A rugged woman, that old Siberian, who is evidently his mother," said the deh-baschi.

At this remark Michael's heart beat violently.

"Yes," answered the pendja-baschi. "She stuck to it well that the pretended merchant was not her son, but it was too late. Colonel Ogareff was not to be taken in; and, as he said, he will know how to make the old witch speak when the time comes."

These words were so many dagger-thrusts for Michael. He was known to be a courier of the Czar! A detachment of horsemen on his track could not fail to cut him off. And, worst of all, his mother was in the hands of the Tartars, and the cruel Ogareff had undertaken to make her speak when he wished!

Michael well knew that the brave Siberian would sacrifice her life for him. He had fancied that he could not hate Ivan Ogareff more, yet a fresh tide of hate now rose in his heart. The wretch who had betrayed his country now threatened to torture his mother.

The conversation between the two officers continued, and Michael understood that an engagement was imminent in the neighborhood of Kolyvan, between the Muscovite troops coming from the north and the Tartars. A small Russian force of two thousand men, reported to have reached the lower course of the Obi, were advancing by forced marches towards Tomsk. If such was the case, this force, which would soon find itself engaged with the main body of Feofar-Khan's army, would be inevitably overwhelmed, and the Irkutsk road would be in the entire possession of the invaders.

As to himself, Michael learnt, by some words from the pendja-baschi, that a price was set on his head, and that orders had been given to take him, dead or alive.

It was necessary, therefore, to get the start of the Usbeck horsemen on the Irkutsk road, and put the Obi between himself and them. But to do that, he must escape before the camp was broken up.

His determination taken, Michael prepared to execute it.

Indeed, the halt would not be prolonged, and the pendja-baschi did not intend to give his men more than an hour's rest, although their horses could not have been changed for fresh ones since Omsk, and must be as much fatigued as that of Michael Strogoff.

There was not a moment to lose. It was within an hour of morning. It was needful to profit by the darkness to leave the little wood and dash along the road; but although night favored it the success of such a flight appeared to be almost impossible.

Not wishing to do anything at random, Michael took time for reflection, carefully weighing the chances so as to take the best. From the situation of the place the result was this—that he could not escape through the back of the wood, the stream which bordered it being not only deep, but very wide and muddy. Beneath this thick water was a slimy bog, on which the foot could not rest. There was only one way open, the high-road. To endeavor to reach it by creeping round the edge of the wood, without attracting attention, and then to gallop at headlong speed, required all the remaining strength and energy of his noble steed. Too probably it would fall dead on reaching the banks of the Obi, when, either by boat or by swimming, he must cross this important river. This was what Michael had before him.

His energy and courage increased in sight of danger.

His life, his mission, his country, perhaps the safety of his mother, were at stake. He could not hesitate.

There was not a moment to be lost. Already there was a slight movement among the men of the detachment. A few horsemen were strolling up and down the road in front of the wood. The rest were still lying at the foot of the trees, but their horses were gradually penetrating towards the center of the wood.

Michael had at first thought of seizing one of these horses, but he recollected that, of course, they would be as fatigued as his own. It was better to trust to his own brave steed, which had already rendered him such important service. The good animal, hidden behind a thicket, had escaped the sight of the Usbecks. They, besides, had not penetrated so far into the wood.

Michael crawled up to his horse through the grass, and found him lying down. He patted and spoke gently to him, and managed to raise him without noise. Fortunately, the torches were entirely consumed, and now went out, the darkness being still profound under shelter of the larches. After replacing the bit, Michael looked to his girths and stirrups, and began to lead his horse quietly away. The intelligent animal followed his master without even making the least neigh.

A few Usbeck horses raised their heads, and began to wander towards the edge of the wood. Michael held his revolver in his hand, ready to blow out the brains of the first Tartar who should approach him. But happily the alarm was not given, and he was able to gain the angle made by the wood where it joined the road.

To avoid being seen, Michael's intention was not to mount until after turning a corner some two hundred feet from the wood. Unfortunately, just at the moment that he was issuing from the wood, an Usbeck's horse, scenting him, neighed and began to trot along the road. His master ran to catch him, and seeing a shadowy form moving in the dim light, "Look out!" he shouted.

At the cry, all the men of the bivouac jumped up, and ran to seize their horses. Michael leaped on his steed, and galloped away. The two officers of the detachment urged on their men to follow.

Michael heard a report, and felt a ball pass through his tunic. Without turning his head, without replying, he spurred on, and, clearing the brushwood with a tremendous bound, he galloped at full speed toward the Obi.

The Usbecks' horses being unsaddled gave him a small start, but in less than two minutes he heard the tramp of several horses gradually gaining on him.

Day was now beginning to break, and objects at some distance were becoming visible. Michael turned his head, and perceived a horseman rapidly approaching him. It was the deh-baschi. Being better mounted, this officer had distanced his detachment.

Without drawing rein, Michael extended his revolver, and took a moment's aim. The Usbeck officer, hit in the breast, rolled on the ground.

But the other horsemen followed him closely, and without waiting to assist the deh-baschi, exciting each other by their shouts, digging their spurs into their horses' sides, they gradually diminished the distance between themselves and Michael.

For half an hour only was the latter able to keep out of range of the Tartars, but he well knew that his horse was becoming weaker, and dreaded every instant that he would stumble never to rise again.

It was now light, although the sun had not yet risen above the horizon. Two versts distant could be seen a pale line bordered by a few trees.

This was the Obi, which flows from the southwest to the northeast, the surface almost level with the ground, its bed being but the steppe itself.

Several times shots were fired at Michael, but without hitting him, and several times too he discharged his revolver on those of the soldiers who pressed him too closely. Each time an Usbeck rolled on the ground, midst cries of rage from his companions. But this pursuit could only terminate to Michael's disadvantage. His horse was almost exhausted. He managed to reach the bank of the river. The Usbeck detachment was now not more than fifty paces behind him.

The Obi was deserted—not a boat of any description which could take him over the water!

"Courage, my brave horse!" cried Michael. "Come! A last effort!" And he plunged into the river, which here was half a verst in width.

It would have been difficult to stand against the current—indeed, Michael's horse could get no footing. He must therefore swim across the river, although it was rapid as a torrent. Even to attempt it showed Michael's marvelous courage. The soldiers reached the bank, but hesitated to plunge in.

The pendja-baschi seized his musket and took aim at Michael, whom he could see in the middle of the stream. The shot was fired, and Michael's horse, struck in the side, was borne away by the current.

His master, speedily disentangling himself from his stirrups, struck out boldly for the shore. In the midst of a hailstorm of balls he managed to reach the opposite side, and disappeared in the rushes.

95

CHAPTER XVII
THE RIVALS

MICHAEL was in comparative safety, though his situation was still terrible. Now that the faithful animal who had so bravely borne him had met his death in the waters of the river, how was he to continue his journey?

He was on foot, without provisions, in a country devastated by the invasion, overrun by the Emir's scouts, and still at a considerable distance from the place he was striving to reach. "By Heaven, I will get there!" he exclaimed, in reply to all the reasons for faltering. "God will protect our sacred Russia."

Michael was out of reach of the Usbeck horsemen. They had not dared to pursue him through the river.

Once more on solid ground Michael stopped to consider what he should do next. He wished to avoid Tomsk, now occupied by the Tartar troops. Nevertheless, he must reach some town, or at least a post-house, where he could procure a horse. A horse once found, he would throw himself out of the beaten track, and not again take to the Irkutsk road until in the neighborhood of Krasnoiarsk. From that place, if he were quick, he hoped to find the way still open, and he intended to go through the Lake Baikal provinces in a southeasterly direction.

Michael began by going eastward. By following the course of the Obi two versts further, he reached a picturesque little town lying on a small hill. A few churches, with Byzantine cupolas colored green and gold, stood up against the gray sky. This is Kolyvan, where the officers and people employed at Kamsk and other towns take refuge during the summer from the unhealthy climate of the Baraba. According to the latest news obtained by the Czar's courier, Kolyvan could not be yet in the hands of the invaders. The Tartar troops, divided into two columns, had marched to the left on Omsk, to the right on Tomsk, neglecting the intermediate country.

Michael Strogoff's plan was simply this—to reach Kolyvan before the arrival of the Usbeck horsemen, who would ascend the other bank of the Obi to the ferry. There he would procure clothes and a horse, and resume the road to Irkutsk across the southern steppe.

It was now three o'clock in the morning. The neighborhood of Kolyvan was very still, and appeared to have been totally abandoned. The country population had evidently fled to the northwards, to the province of Yeniseisk, dreading the invasion, which they could not resist.

Michael was walking at a rapid pace towards Kolyvan when distant firing struck his ear. He stopped, and clearly distinguished the dull roar of artillery, and above it a crisp rattle which could not be mistaken.

"It is cannon and musketry!" said he. "The little Russian body is engaged with the Tartar army! Pray Heaven that I may arrive at Kolyvan before them!"

The firing became gradually louder, and soon to the left of Kolyvan a mist collected—not smoke, but those great white clouds produced by discharges of artillery.

The Usbeck horsemen stopped on the left of the Obi, to await the result of the battle. From them Michael had nothing to fear as he hastened towards the town.

In the meanwhile the firing increased, and became sensibly nearer. It was no longer a confused roar, but distinct reports. At the same time the smoke partially cleared, and it became evident that the combatants were rapidly moving southwards. It appeared that Kolyvan was to be attacked on the north side. But were the Russians defending it or the Tartars? It being impossible to decide this, Michael became greatly perplexed.

He was not more than half a verst from Kolyvan when he observed flames shooting up among the houses of the town, and the steeple of a church fell in the midst of clouds of smoke and fire. Was the struggle, then, in Kolyvan? Michael was compelled to think so. It was evident that Russians and Tartars were fighting in the streets of the town. Was this a time to seek refuge there? Would he not run a risk of being taken prisoner? Should he succeed in escaping from Kolyvan, as he had escaped from Omsk? He hesitated and stopped a moment. Would it not be better to try, even on foot, to reach some small town, and there procure a horse at any price? This was the only thing to be done; and Michael, leaving the Obi, went forward to the right of Kolyvan.

The firing had now increased in violence. Flames soon sprang up on the left of the town. Fire was devouring one entire quarter of Kolyvan.

Michael was running across the steppe endeavoring to gain the covert of some trees when a detachment of Tartar cavalry appeared on the right. He dared not continue in that direction. The horsemen advanced rapidly, and it would have been difficult to escape them.

Suddenly, in a thick clump of trees, he saw an isolated house, which it would be possible to reach before he was perceived. Michael had no choice but to run there, hide himself and ask or take something to recruit his strength, for he was exhausted with hunger and fatigue.

He accordingly ran on towards this house, still about half a verst distant. As he approached, he could see that it was a telegraph office. Two wires left it in westerly and easterly directions, and a third went towards Kolyvan.

It was to be supposed that under the circumstances this station was abandoned; but even if it was, Michael could take refuge there, and wait till nightfall, if necessary, to again set out across the steppe covered with Tartar scouts.

He ran up to the door and pushed it open.

A single person was in the room whence the telegraphic messages were dispatched. This was a clerk, calm, phlegmatic, indifferent to all that was passing outside. Faithful to his post, he waited behind his little wicket until the public claimed his services.

Michael ran up to him, and in a voice broken by fatigue, "What do you know?" he asked.

"Nothing," answered the clerk, smiling.

"Are the Russians and Tartars engaged?"

"They say so."

"But who are the victors?"

"I don't know."

Such calmness, such indifference, in the midst of these terrible events, was scarcely credible.

"And is not the wire cut?" said Michael.

"It is cut between Kolyvan and Krasnoiarsk, but it is still working between Kolyvan and the Russian frontier."

"For the government?"

"For the government, when it thinks proper. For the public, when they pay. Ten copecks a word, whenever you like, sir!"

Michael was about to reply to this strange clerk that he had no message to send, that he only implored a little bread and water, when the door of the house was again thrown open.

Thinking that it was invaded by Tartars, Michael made ready to leap out of the window, when two men only entered the room who had nothing of the Tartar soldier about them. One of them held a dispatch, written in pencil, in his hand, and, passing the other, he hurried up to the wicket of the imperturbable clerk.

In these two men Michael recognized with astonishment, which everyone will understand, two personages of whom he was not thinking at all, and whom he had never expected to see again. They were the two reporters, Harry Blount and Alcide Jolivet, no longer traveling companions, but rivals, enemies, now that they were working on the field of battle.

They had left Ichim only a few hours after the departure of Michael Strogoff, and they had arrived at Kolyvan before him, by following the same road, in consequence of his losing three days on the banks of the Irtych. And now, after being both present at the engagement between the Russians and Tartars before the town, they had left just as the struggle broke out in the streets, and ran to the telegraph office, so as to send off their rival dispatches to Europe, and forestall each other in their report of events.

Michael stood aside in the shadow, and without being seen himself he could see and hear all that was going on. He would now hear interesting news, and would find out whether or not he could enter Kolyvan.

Blount, having distanced his companion, took possession of the wicket, whilst Alcide Jolivet, contrary to his usual habit, stamped with impatience.

"Ten copecks a word," said the clerk.

Blount deposited a pile of roubles on the shelf, whilst his rival looked on with a sort of stupefaction.

"Good," said the clerk. And with the greatest coolness in the world he began to telegraph the following dispatch: "Daily Telegraph, London.

"From Kolyvan, Government of Omsk, Siberia, 6th August.

"Engagement between Russian and Tartar troops."

The reading was in a distinct voice, so that Michael heard all that the English correspondent was sending to his paper.

"Russians repulsed with great loss. Tartars entered Kolyvan to-day." These words ended the dispatch.

"My turn now," cried Alcide Jolivet, anxious to send off his dispatch, addressed to his cousin.

But that was not Blount's idea, who did not intend to give up the wicket, but have it in his power to send off the news just as the events occurred. He would therefore not make way for his companion.

"But you have finished!" exclaimed Jolivet.

"I have not finished," returned Harry Blount quietly.

And he proceeded to write some sentences, which he handed in to the clerk, who read out in his calm voice: "John Gilpin was a citizen of credit and renown; a train-band captain eke was he of famous London town."

Harry Blount was telegraphing some verses learned in his childhood, in order to employ the time, and not give up his place to his rival. It would perhaps cost his paper some thousands of roubles, but it would be the first informed. France could wait.

Jolivet's fury may be imagined, though under any other circumstances he would have thought it fair warfare. He even endeavored to force the clerk to take his dispatch in preference to that of his rival.

"It is that gentleman's right," answered the clerk coolly, pointing to Blount, and smiling in the most amiable manner. And he continued faithfully to transmit to the Daily Telegraph the well-known verses of Cowper.

Whilst he was working Blount walked to the window and, his field glass to his eyes, watched all that was going on in the neighborhood of Kolyvan, so as to complete his information. In a few minutes he resumed his place at the wicket, and added to his telegram: "Two churches are in flames. The fire appears to gain on the right. 'John Gilpin's spouse said to her dear, Though wedded we have been these twice ten tedious years, yet we no holiday have seen.'"

Alcide Jolivet would have liked to strangle the honorable correspondent of the Daily Telegraph.

He again interrupted the clerk, who, quite unmoved, merely replied: "It is his right, sir, it is his right—at ten copecks a word."

And he telegraphed the following news, just brought him by Blount: "Russian fugitives are escaping from the town. 'Away went Gilpin—who but he? His fame soon spread around: He carries weight! he rides a race! 'Tis for a thousand pound!'" And Blount turned round with a quizzical look at his rival.

Alcide Jolivet fumed.

In the meanwhile Harry Blount had returned to the window, but this time his attention was diverted by the interest of the scene before him. Therefore, when the clerk had finished telegraphing the last lines dictated by Blount, Alcide Jolivet noiselessly took his place at the wicket, and, just as his rival had done, after quietly depositing a respectable pile of roubles on the shelf, he delivered his dispatch, which the clerk read aloud: "Madeleine Jolivet, 10, Faubourg Montmartre, Paris.

"From Kolyvan, Government of Omsk, Siberia, 6th August.

"Fugitives are escaping from the town. Russians defeated. Fiercely pursued by the Tartar cavalry."

And as Harry Blount returned he heard Jolivet completing his telegram by singing in a mocking tone:

"Il est un petit homme, Tout habille de gris, Dans Paris!"

Imitating his rival, Alcide Jolivet had used a merry refrain of Beranger.

"Hallo!" said Harry Blount.

"Just so," answered Jolivet.

In the meantime the situation at Kolyvan was alarming in the extreme. The battle was raging nearer, and the firing was incessant.

At that moment the telegraph office shook to its foundations. A shell had made a hole in the wall, and a cloud of dust filled the office.

Alcide was just finishing writing his lines; but to stop, dart on the shell, seize it in both hands, throw it out of the window, and return to the wicket, was only the affair of a moment.

Five seconds later the shell burst outside. Continuing with the greatest possible coolness, Alcide wrote: "A six-inch shell has just blown up the wall of the telegraph office. Expecting a few more of the same size."

Michael Strogoff had no doubt that the Russians were driven out of Kolyvan. His last resource was to set out across the southern steppe.

Just then renewed firing broke out close to the telegraph house, and a perfect shower of bullets smashed all the glass in the windows. Harry Blount fell to the ground wounded in the shoulder.

Jolivet even at such a moment, was about to add this postscript to his dispatch: "Harry Blount, correspondent of the Daily Telegraph, has fallen at my side struck by—" when the imperturbable clerk said calmly: "Sir, the wire has broken." And, leaving his wicket, he quietly took his hat, brushed it round with his sleeve, and, still smiling, disappeared through a little door which Michael had not before perceived.

The house was surrounded by Tartar soldiers, and neither Michael nor the reporters could effect their retreat.

Alcide Jolivet, his useless dispatch in his hand, had run to Blount, stretched on the ground, and had bravely lifted him on his shoulders, with the intention of flying with him. He was too late!

Both were prisoners; and, at the same time, Michael, taken unawares as he was about to leap from the window, fell into the hands of the Tartars!

END OF BOOK I

BOOK II

CHAPTER I A TARTAR CAMP

AT a day's march from Kolyvan, several versts beyond the town of Diachinks, stretches a wide plain, planted here and there with great trees, principally pines and cedars. This part of the steppe is usually occupied during the warm season by Siberian shepherds, and their numerous flocks. But now it might have been searched in vain for one of its nomad inhabitants. Not that the plain was deserted. It presented a most animated appearance.

There stood the Tartar tents; there Feofar-Khan, the terrible Emir of Bokhara, was encamped; and there on the following day, the 7th of August, were brought the prisoners taken at Kolyvan after the annihilation of the Russian force, which had vainly attempted to oppose the progress of the invaders. Of the two thousand men who had engaged with the two columns of the enemy, the bases of which rested on Tomsk and Omsk, only a few hundred remained. Thus events were going badly, and the imperial government appeared to have lost its power beyond the frontiers of the Ural—for a time at least, for the Russians could not fail eventually to defeat the savage hordes of the invaders. But in the meantime the invasion had reached the center of Siberia, and it was spreading through the revolted country both to the eastern, and the western provinces. If the troops of the Amoor and the province of Takutsk did not arrive in time to occupy it, Irkutsk, the capital of Asiatic Russia, being insufficiently garrisoned, would fall into the hands of the Tartars, and the Grand Duke, brother of the Emperor, would be sacrificed to the vengeance of Ivan Ogareff.

What had become of Michael Strogoff? Had he broken down under the weight of so many trials? Did he consider himself conquered by the series of disasters which, since the adventure of Ichim, had increased in magnitude? Did he think his cause lost? that his mission had failed? that his orders could no longer be obeyed?

Michael was one of those men who never give in while life exists. He was yet alive; he still had the imperial letter safe; his disguise had been undiscovered. He was included amongst the numerous prisoners whom the Tartars were dragging with them like cattle; but by approaching Tomsk he was at the same time drawing nearer to Irkutsk. Besides, he was still in front of Ivan Ogareff.

"I will get there!" he repeated to himself.

Since the affair of Kolyvan all the powers of his mind were concentrated on one object—to become free! How should he escape from the Emir's soldiers?

Feofar's camp presented a magnificent spectacle.

Numberless tents, of skin, felt, or silk, glistened in the rays of the sun. The lofty plumes which surmounted their conical tops waved amidst banners, flags, and pennons of every color. The richest of these tents belonged to the Seides and Khodjas, who are the principal personages of the khanat. A special pavilion, ornamented with a horse's tail issuing from a sheaf of red and white sticks artistically interlaced, indicated the high rank of these Tartar chiefs. Then in the distance rose several thousand of the Turcoman tents, called "karaoy," which had been carried on the backs of camels.

The camp contained at least a hundred and fifty thousand soldiers, as many foot as horse soldiers, collected under the name of Alamanes. Amongst them, and as the principal types of Turkestan, would have been directly remarked the Tadjiks, from their regular features, white skin, tall forms, and black eyes and hair; they formed the bulk of the Tartar army, and of them the khanats of Khokhand and Koundouge had furnished a contingent nearly equal to that of Bokhara. With the Tadjiks were mingled specimens of different races who either reside in Turkestan or whose native countries border on it. There were Usbecks, red-bearded, small in stature, similar to those who had pursued Michael. Here were Kirghiz, with flat faces like the Kalmucks, dressed in coats of mail: some carried the lance, bows, and arrows of Asiatic manufacture; some the saber, a matchlock gun, and the "tschakane," a little short-handled ax, the wounds from which invariably prove fatal. There were Mongols—of middle height, with black hair plaited into pigtails, which hung down their back; round faces, swarthy complexions, lively deep-set eyes, scanty beards—dressed in blue nankeen trimmed with black plush, sword-belts of leather with silver buckles, coats gayly braided, and silk caps edged with fur and three ribbons fluttering behind. Brown-skinned Afghans, too, might have been seen. Arabs, having the primitive type of the beautiful Semitic races; and Turcomans, with eyes which looked as if they had lost the pupil,—all enrolled under the Emir's flag, the flag of incendiaries and devastators.

Among these free soldiers were a certain number of slave soldiers, principally Persians, commanded by officers of the same nation, and they were certainly not the least esteemed of Feofar-Khan's army.

If to this list are added the Jews, who acted as servants, their robes confined with a cord, and wearing on their heads instead of the turban, which is forbidden them, little caps of dark cloth; if with these groups are mingled some hundreds of "kalenders," a sort of religious mendicants, clothed in rags, covered by a leopard skin, some idea may be formed of the enormous agglomerations of different tribes included under the general denomination of the Tartar army.

Nothing could be more romantic than this picture, in delineating which the most skillful artist would have exhausted all the colors of his palette.

Feofar's tent overlooked the others. Draped in large folds of a brilliant silk looped with golden cords and tassels, surmounted by tall plumes which waved in the wind like fans, it occupied the center of a wide clearing, sheltered by a grove of magnificent birch and pine trees. Before this tent, on a japanned table inlaid with precious stones, was placed the sacred book of the Koran, its pages being of thin gold-leaf delicately engraved. Above floated the Tartar flag, quartered with the Emir's arms.

In a semicircle round the clearing stood the tents of the great functionaries of Bokhara. There resided the chief of the stables, who has the right to follow the Emir on horseback even into the court of his palace; the grand falconer; the "housch-begui," bearer of the royal seal; the "toptschi-baschi," grand master of the artillery; the "khodja," chief of the council, who receives the prince's kiss, and may present himself before him with his girdle untied; the "scheikh-oul-islam," chief of the Ulemas, representing the priests; the "cazi-askev," who, in the Emir's absence settles all disputes raised among the soldiers; and lastly, the chief of the astrologers, whose great business is to consult the stars every time the Khan thinks of changing his quarters.

When the prisoners were brought into the camp, the Emir was in his tent. He did not show himself. This was fortunate, no doubt. A sign, a word from him might have been the signal for some bloody execution. But he intrenched himself in that isolation which constitutes in part the majesty of Eastern kings. He who does not show himself is admired, and, above all, feared.

As to the prisoners, they were to be penned up in some enclosure, where, ill-treated, poorly fed, and exposed to all the inclemencies of the weather, they would await Feofar's pleasure.

The most docile and patient of them all was undoubtedly Michael Strogoff. He allowed himself to be led, for they were leading him where he wished to go, and under conditions of safety which free he could not have found on the road from Kolyvan to Tomsk. To escape before reaching that town was to risk again falling into the hands of the scouts, who were scouring the steppe. The most eastern line occupied by the Tartar columns was not situated beyond the eighty-fifth meridian, which passes through Tomsk. This meridian once passed, Michael considered that he should be beyond the hostile zones, that he could traverse Genisci without danger, and gain Krasnoiarsk before Feofar-Khan had invaded the province.

"Once at Tomsk," he repeated to himself, to repress some feelings of impatience which he could not entirely master, "in a few minutes I should be beyond the outposts; and twelve hours gained on Feofar, twelve hours on Ogareff, that surely would be enough to give me a start of them to Irkutsk."

The thing that Michael dreaded more than everything else was the presence of Ivan Ogareff in the Tartar camp. Besides the danger of being recognized, he felt, by a sort of instinct, that this was the traitor whom it was especially necessary to precede. He understood, too, that the union of Ogareff's troops with those of Feofar would complete the invading army, and that the junction once effected, the army would march en masse on the capital of Eastern Siberia. All his apprehensions came from this quarter,

103

and he dreaded every instant to hear some flourish of trumpets, announcing the arrival of the lieutenant of the Emir.

To this was added the thought of his mother, of Nadia,—the one a prisoner at Omsk; the other dragged on board the Irtych boats, and no doubt a captive, as Marfa Strogoff was. He could do nothing for them. Should he ever see them again? At this question, to which he dared not reply, his heart sank very low.

At the same time with Michael Strogoff and so many other prisoners Harry Blount and Alcide Jolivet had also been taken to the Tartar camp. Their former traveling companion, captured like them at the telegraph office, knew that they were penned up with him in the enclosure, guarded by numerous sentinels, but he did not wish to accost them. It mattered little to him, at this time especially, what they might think of him since the affair at Ichim. Besides, he desired to be alone, that he might act alone, if necessary. He therefore held himself aloof from his former acquaintances.

From the moment that Harry Blount had fallen by his side, Jolivet had not ceased his attentions to him. During the journey from Kolyvan to the camp—that is to say, for several hours—Blount, by leaning on his companion's arm, had been enabled to follow the rest of the prisoners. He tried to make known that he was a British subject; but it had no effect on the barbarians, who only replied by prods with a lance or sword. The correspondent of the Daily Telegraph was, therefore, obliged to submit to the common lot, resolving to protest later, and obtain satisfaction for such treatment. But the journey was not the less disagreeable to him, for his wound caused him much pain, and without Alcide Jolivet's assistance he might never have reached the camp.

Jolivet, whose practical philosophy never abandoned him, had physically and morally strengthened his companion by every means in his power. His first care, when they found themselves definitely established in the enclosure, was to examine Blount's wound. Having managed carefully to draw off his coat, he found that the shoulder had been only grazed by the shot.

"This is nothing," he said. "A mere scratch! After two or three dressings you will be all to rights."

"But these dressings?" asked Blount.

"I will make them for you myself."

"Then you are something of a doctor?"

"All Frenchmen are something of doctors."

And on this affirmation Alcide, tearing his handkerchief, made lint of one piece, bandages of the other, took some water from a well dug in the middle of the enclosure, bathed the wound, and skillfully placed the wet rag on Harry Blount's shoulder.

"I treat you with water," he said. "This liquid is the most efficacious sedative known for the treatment of wounds, and is the most employed now. Doctors have taken six thousand years to discover that! Yes, six thousand years in round numbers!"

"I thank you, M. Jolivet," answered Harry, stretching himself on a bed of dry leaves, which his companion had arranged for him in the shade of a birch tree.

"Bah! it's nothing! You would do as much for me."

"I am not quite so sure," said Blount candidly.

"Nonsense, stupid! All English are generous."

"Doubtless; but the French?"

"Well, the French—they are brutes, if you like! But what redeems them is that they are French. Say nothing more about that, or rather, say nothing more at all. Rest is absolutely necessary for you."

But Harry Blount had no wish to be silent. If the wound, in prudence, required rest, the correspondent of the Daily Telegraph was not a man to indulge himself.

"M. Jolivet," he asked, "do you think that our last dispatches have been able to pass the Russian frontier?"

"Why not?" answered Alcide. "By this time you may be sure that my beloved cousin knows all about the affair at Kolyvan."

"How many copies does your cousin work off of her dispatches?" asked Blount, for the first time putting his question direct to his companion.

"Well," answered Alcide, laughing, "my cousin is a very discreet person, who does not like to be talked about, and who would be in despair if she troubled the sleep of which you are in need."

"I don't wish to sleep," replied the Englishman. "What will your cousin think of the affairs of Russia?"

"That they seem for the time in a bad way. But, bah! the Muscovite government is powerful; it cannot be really uneasy at an invasion of barbarians."

"Too much ambition has lost the greatest empires," answered Blount, who was not exempt from a certain English jealousy with regard to Russian pretensions in Central Asia.

"Oh, do not let us talk politics," cried Jolivet. "It is forbidden by the faculty. Nothing can be worse for wounds in the shoulder—unless it was to put you to sleep."

"Let us, then, talk of what we ought to do," replied Blount. "M. Jolivet, I have no intention at all of remaining a prisoner to these Tartars for an indefinite time."

"Nor I, either, by Jove!"

"We will escape on the first opportunity?"

"Yes, if there is no other way of regaining our liberty."

"Do you know of any other?" asked Blount, looking at his companion.

"Certainly. We are not belligerents; we are neutral, and we will claim our freedom."

"From that brute of a Feofar-Khan?"

"No; he would not understand," answered Jolivet; "but from his lieutenant, Ivan Ogareff."

"He is a villain."

"No doubt; but the villain is a Russian. He knows that it does not do to trifle with the rights of men, and he has no interest to retain us; on the contrary. But to ask a favor of that gentleman does not quite suit my taste."

"But that gentleman is not in the camp, or at least I have not seen him here," observed Blount.

"He will come. He will not fail to do that. He must join the Emir. Siberia is cut in two now, and very certainly Feofar's army is only waiting for him to advance on Irkutsk."

"And once free, what shall we do?"

"Once free, we will continue our campaign, and follow the Tartars, until the time comes when we can make our way into the Russian camp. We must not give up the game. No, indeed; we have only just begun. You, friend, have already had the honor of being wounded in the service of the Daily Telegraph, whilst I—I have as yet suffered nothing in my cousin's service. Well, well! Good," murmured Alcide Jolivet; "there he is asleep. A few hours' sleep and a few cold water compresses are all that are required to set an Englishman on his legs again. These fellows are made of cast iron."

And whilst Harry Blount rested, Alcide watched near him, after having drawn out his note book, which he loaded with notes, determined besides to share them with his companion, for the greater satisfaction of the readers of the Daily Telegraph. Events had united them one with the other. They were no longer jealous of each other. So, then, the thing that Michael Strogoff dreaded above everything was the most lively desire of the two correspondents. Ivan Ogareff's arrival would evidently be of use to them. Blount and Jolivet's interest was, therefore, contrary to that of Michael. The latter well understood the situation, and it was one reason, added to many others, which prevented him from approaching his former traveling companions. He therefore managed so as not to be seen by them.

Four days passed thus without the state of things being in anywise altered. The prisoners heard no talk of the breaking up of the Tartar camp. They were strictly guarded. It would have been impossible for them to pass the cordon of foot and horse soldiers, which watched them night and day. As to the food which was given them it was barely sufficient. Twice in the twenty-four hours they were thrown a piece of the intestines of goats grilled on the coals, or a few bits of that cheese called "kroute," made of sour ewe's milk, and which, soaked in mare's milk, forms the Kirghiz dish, commonly called "koumyss." And this was all. It may be added that the weather had become detestable. There were considerable atmospheric commotions, bringing squalls mingled with rain. The unfortunate prisoners, destitute of shelter, had to bear all the inclemencies of the weather, nor was there the slightest alleviation to their misery. Several wounded women and children died, and the prisoners were themselves compelled to dig graves for the bodies of those whom their jailers would not even take the trouble to bury.

During this trying period Alcide Jolivet and Michael Strogoff worked hard, each in the portions of the enclosure in which they found themselves.

Healthy and vigorous, they suffered less than so many others, and could better endure the hardships to which they were exposed. By their advice, and the assistance they rendered, they were of the greatest possible use to their suffering and despairing fellow-captives.

Was this state of things to last? Would Feofar-Khan, satisfied with his first success, wait some time before marching on Irkutsk? Such, it was to be feared, would be the case. But it was not so. The event so much wished for by Jolivet and Blount, so much dreaded by Michael, occurred on the morning of the 12th of August.

On that day the trumpets sounded, the drums beat, the cannon roared. A huge cloud of dust swept along the road from Kolyvan. Ivan Ogareff, followed by several thousand men, made his entry into the Tartar camp.

CHAPTER II
CORRESPONDENTS IN TROUBLE

IVAN OGAREFF was bringing up the main body of the army of the Emir. The cavalry and infantry now under him had formed part of the column which had taken Omsk. Ogareff, not having been able to reduce the high town, in which, it must be remembered, the governor and garrison had sought refuge, had decided to pass on, not wishing to delay operations which ought to lead to the conquest of Eastern Siberia. He therefore left a garrison in Omsk, and, reinforcing himself en route with the conquerors of Kolyvan, joined Feofar's army.

Ivan Ogareff's soldiers halted at the outposts of the camp. They received no orders to bivouac. Their chief's plan, doubtless, was not to halt there, but to press on and reach Tomsk in the shortest possible time, it being an important town, naturally intended to become the center of future operations.

Besides his soldiers, Ogareff was bringing a convoy of Russian and Siberian prisoners, captured either at Omsk or Kolyvan. These unhappy creatures were not led to the enclosure—already too crowded—but were forced to remain at the outposts without shelter, almost without nourishment. What fate was Feofar-Khan reserving for these unfortunates? Would he imprison them in Tomsk, or would some bloody execution, familiar to the Tartar chiefs, remove them when they were found too inconvenient? This was the secret of the capricious Emir.

This army had not come from Omsk and Kolyvan without bringing in its train the usual crowd of beggars, freebooters, pedlars, and gypsies, which compose the rear-guard of an army on the march.

All these people lived on the country traversed, and left little of anything behind them. There was, therefore, a necessity for pushing forward, if only to secure provisions for the troops. The whole region between Ichim and the Obi, now completely devastated, no longer offered any resources. The Tartars left a desert behind them.

Conspicuous among the gypsies who had hastened from the western provinces was the Tsigane troop, which had accompanied Michael Strogoff as far as Perm. Sangarre was there. This fierce spy, the tool of Ivan Ogareff, had not deserted her master. Ogareff had traveled rapidly to Ichim, whilst Sangarre and her band had proceeded to Omsk by the southern part of the province.

It may be easily understood how useful this woman was to Ogareff. With her gypsy-band she could penetrate anywhere. Ivan Ogareff was kept acquainted with all that was going on in the very heart of the invaded provinces. There were a hundred eyes, a hundred ears, open in his service. Besides, he paid liberally for this espionage, from which he derived so much advantage.

Once Sangarre, being implicated in a very serious affair, had been saved by the Russian officer. She never forgot what she owed him, and had devoted herself to his service body and soul.

When Ivan Ogareff entered on the path of treason, he saw at once how he might turn this woman to account. Whatever order he might give her, Sangarre would execute it. An inexplicable instinct, more powerful still than that of gratitude, had urged her to make herself the slave of the traitor to whom she had been attached since the very beginning of his exile in Siberia.

Confidante and accomplice, Sangarre, without country, without family, had been delighted to put her vagabond life to the service of the invaders thrown by Ogareff on Siberia. To the wonderful cunning natural to her race she added a wild energy, which knew neither forgiveness nor pity. She was a savage worthy to share the wigwam of an Apache or the hut of an Andaman.

Since her arrival at Omsk, where she had rejoined him with her Tsiganes, Sangarre had not again left Ogareff. The circumstance that Michael and Marfa Strogoff had met was known to her. She knew and shared Ogareff's fears concerning the journey of a courier of the Czar. Having Marfa Strogoff in her power, she would have been the woman to torture her with all the refinement of a Redskin in order to wrest her secret from her. But the hour had not yet come in which Ogareff wished the old Siberian to speak. Sangarre had to wait, and she waited, without losing sight of her whom she was watching, observing her slightest gestures, her slightest words, endeavoring to catch the word "son" escaping from her lips, but as yet always baffled by Marfa's taciturnity.

At the first flourish of the trumpets several officers of high rank, followed by a brilliant escort of Usbeck horsemen, moved to the front of the camp to receive Ivan Ogareff. Arrived in his presence, they paid him the greatest respect, and invited him to accompany them to Feofar-Khan's tent.

Imperturbable as usual, Ogareff replied coldly to the deference paid to him. He was plainly dressed; but, from a sort of impudent bravado, he still wore the uniform of a Russian officer.

As he was about to enter the camp, Sangarre, passing among the officers approached and remained motionless before him. "Nothing?" asked Ogareff.

"Nothing."

"Have patience."

"Is the time approaching when you will force the old woman to speak?"

"It is approaching, Sangarre."

"When will the old woman speak?"

"When we reach Tomsk."

"And we shall be there—"

"In three days."

A strange gleam shot from Sangarre's great black eyes, and she retired with a calm step. Ogareff pressed his spurs into his horse's flanks, and, followed by his staff of Tartar officers, rode towards the Emir's tent.

Feofar-Khan was expecting his lieutenant. The council, composed of the bearer of the royal seal, the khodja, and some high officers, had taken their places in the tent. Ivan Ogareff dismounted and entered.

Feofar-Khan was a man of forty, tall, rather pale, of a fierce countenance, and evil eyes. A curly black beard flowed over his chest. With his war costume, coat of mail of gold and silver, cross-belt and scabbard glistening with precious stones, boots with golden spurs, helmet ornamented with an aigrette of brilliant diamonds, Feofar presented an aspect rather strange than imposing for a Tartar Sardana-palus, an undisputed sovereign, who directs at his pleasure the life and fortune of his subjects.

When Ivan Ogareff appeared, the great dignitaries remained seated on their gold-embroidered cushions; but Feofar rose from a rich divan which occupied the back part of the tent, the ground being hidden under the thick velvet-pile of a Bokharian carpet.

The Emir approached Ogareff and gave him a kiss, the meaning of which he could not mistake. This kiss made the lieutenant chief of the council, and placed him temporarily above the khodja.

Then Feofar spoke. "I have no need to question you," said he; "speak, Ivan. You will find here ears very ready to listen to you."

"Takhsir," answered Ogareff, "this is what I have to make known to you." He spoke in the Tartar language, giving to his phrases the emphatic turn which distinguishes the languages of the Orientals. "Takhsir, this is not the time for unnecessary words. What I have done at the head of your troops, you know. The lines of the Ichim and the Irtych are now in our power; and the Turcoman horsemen can bathe their horses in the now Tartar waters. The Kirghiz hordes rose at the voice of Feofar-Khan. You can now push your troops towards the east, and where the sun rises, or towards the west, where he sets."

"And if I march with the sun?" asked the Emir, without his countenance betraying any of his thoughts.

"To march with the sun," answered Ogareff, "is to throw yourself towards Europe; it is to conquer rapidly the Siberian provinces of Tobolsk as far as the Ural Mountains."

"And if I go to meet this luminary of the heavens?"

"It is to subdue to the Tartar dominion, with Irkutsk, the richest countries of Central Asia."

"But the armies of the Sultan of St. Petersburg?" said Feofar-Khan, designating the Emperor of Russia by this strange title.

"You have nothing to fear from them," replied Ivan Ogareff. "The invasion has been sudden; and before the Russian army can succor them, Irkutsk or Tobolsk will have fallen into your power. The Czar's troops have been overwhelmed at Kolyvan, as they will be everywhere where yours meet them."

"And what advice does your devotion to the Tartar cause suggest?" asked the Emir, after a few moments' silence.

"My advice," answered Ivan Ogareff quickly, "is to march to meet the sun. It is to give the grass of the eastern steppes to the Turcoman horses to consume. It is to take Irkutsk, the capital of the eastern provinces, and with it a hostage, the possession of whom is worth a whole country. In the place of the Czar, the Grand Duke his brother must fall into your hands."

This was the great result aimed at by Ivan Ogareff. To listen to him, one would have taken him for one of the cruel descendants of Stephan Razine, the celebrated pirate who ravaged Southern Russia in the eighteenth century. To seize the Grand Duke, murder him pitilessly, would fully satisfy his hatred. Besides, with the capture of Irkutsk, all Eastern Siberia would pass to the Tartars.

"It shall be thus, Ivan," replied Feofar.

"What are your orders, Takhsir?"

"To-day our headquarters shall be removed to Tomsk."

Ogareff bowed, and, followed by the housch-begui, he retired to execute the Emir's orders.

As he was about to mount his horse, to return to the outposts, a tumult broke out at some distance, in the part of the camp reserved for the prisoners. Shouts were heard, and two or three shots fired. Perhaps it was an attempt at revolt or escape, which must be summarily suppressed.

Ivan Ogareff and the housch-begui walked forward and almost immediately two men, whom the soldiers had not been able to keep back appeared before them.

The housch-begui, without more information, made a sign which was an order for death, and the heads of the two prisoners would have rolled on the ground had not Ogareff uttered a few words which arrested the sword already raised aloft. The Russian had perceived that these prisoners were strangers, and he ordered them to be brought to him.

They were Harry Blount and Alcide jolivet.

On Ogareff's arrival in the camp, they had demanded to be conducted to his presence. The soldiers had refused. In consequence, a struggle, an attempt at flight, shots fired which happily missed the two correspondents, but their execution would not have been long delayed, if it had not been for the intervention of the Emir's lieutenant.

The latter observed the prisoners for some moments, they being absolutely unknown to him. They had been present at that scene in the post-house at Ichim, in which Michael Strogoff had been struck by Ogareff; but the brutal traveler had paid no attention to the persons then collected in the common room.

Blount and Jolivet, on the contrary, recognized him at once, and the latter said in a low voice, "Hullo! It seems that Colonel Ogareff and the rude personage of Ichim are one!" Then he added in his companion's ear, "Explain our affair, Blount. You will do me a service. This Russian colonel in the midst of a Tartar camp disgusts me; and although, thanks to him, my head is still on my shoulders, my eyes would exhibit my feelings were I to attempt to look him in the face."

So saying, Alcide Jolivet assumed a look of complete and haughty indifference.

Whether or not Ivan Ogareff perceived that the prisoner's attitude was insulting towards him, he did not let it appear. "Who are you, gentlemen?" he asked in Russian, in a cold tone, but free from its usual rudeness.

"Two correspondents of English and French newspapers," replied Blount laconically.

"You have, doubtless, papers which will establish your identity?"

"Here are letters which accredit us in Russia, from the English and French chancellor's office."

Ivan Ogareff took the letters which Blount held out, and read them attentively. "You ask," said he, "authorization to follow our military operations in Siberia?"

"We ask to be free, that is all," answered the English correspondent dryly.

"You are so, gentlemen," answered Ogareff; "I am curious to read your articles in the Daily Telegraph."

"Sir," replied Blount, with the most imperturbable coolness, "it is sixpence a number, including postage." And thereupon he returned to his companion, who appeared to approve completely of his replies.

Ivan Ogareff, without frowning, mounted his horse, and going to the head of his escort, soon disappeared in a cloud of dust.

"Well, Jolivet, what do you think of Colonel Ivan Ogareff, general-in-chief of the Tartar troops?" asked Blount.

"I think, my dear friend," replied Alcide, smiling, "that the housch-begui made a very graceful gesture when he gave the order for our heads to be cut off."

Whatever was the motive which led Ogareff to act thus in regard to the two correspondents, they were free and could rove at their pleasure

111

over the scene of war. Their intention was not to leave it. The sort of antipathy which formerly they had entertained for each other had given place to a sincere friendship. Circumstances having brought them together, they no longer thought of separating. The petty questions of rivalry were forever extinguished. Harry Blount could never forget what he owed his companion, who, on the other hand, never tried to remind him of it. This friendship too assisted the reporting operations, and was thus to the advantage of their readers.

"And now," asked Blount, "what shall we do with our liberty?"

"Take advantage of it, of course," replied Alcide, "and go quietly to Tomsk to see what is going on there."

"Until the time—very near, I hope—when we may rejoin some Russian regiment?"

"As you say, my dear Blount, it won't do to Tartarise ourselves too much. The best side is that of the most civilized army, and it is evident that the people of Central Asia will have everything to lose and absolutely nothing to gain from this invasion, while the Russians will soon repulse them. It is only a matter of time."

The arrival of Ivan Ogareff, which had given Jolivet and Blount their liberty, was to Michael Strogoff, on the contrary, a serious danger. Should chance bring the Czar's courier into Ogareff's presence, the latter could not fail to recognize in him the traveler whom he had so brutally treated at the Ichim post-house, and although Michael had not replied to the insult as he would have done under any other circumstances, attention would be drawn to him, and at once the accomplishment of his plans would be rendered more difficult.

This was the unpleasant side of the business. A favorable result of his arrival, however, was the order which was given to raise the camp that very day, and remove the headquarters to Tomsk. This was the accomplishment of Michael's most fervent desire. His intention, as has been said, was to reach Tomsk concealed amongst the other prisoners; that is to say, without any risk of falling into the hands of the scouts who swarmed about the approaches to this important town. However, in consequence of the arrival of Ivan Ogareff, he questioned whether it would not be better to give up his first plan and attempt to escape during the journey.

Michael would, no doubt, have kept to the latter plan had he not learnt that Feofar-Khan and Ogareff had already set out for the town with some thousands of horsemen. "I will wait, then," said he to himself; "at least, unless some exceptional opportunity for escape occurs. The adverse chances are numerous on this side of Tomsk, while beyond I shall in a few hours have passed the most advanced Tartar posts to the east. Still three days of patience, and may God aid me!"

It was indeed a journey of three days which the prisoners, under the guard of a numerous detachment of Tartars, were to make across the steppe. A hundred and fifty versts lay between the camp and the town—an easy march for the Emir's soldiers, who wanted for nothing, but a wretched journey for these people, enfeebled by privations. More than one corpse would show the road they had traversed.

It was two o'clock in the afternoon, on the 12th of August, under a hot sun and cloudless sky, that the toptschi-baschi gave the order to start.

Alcide and Blount, having bought horses, had already taken the road to Tomsk, where events were to reunite the principal personages of this story.

Amongst the prisoners brought by Ivan Ogareff to the Tartar camp was an old woman, whose taciturnity seemed to keep her apart from all those who shared her fate. Not a murmur issued from her lips. She was like a statue of grief. This woman was more strictly guarded than anyone else, and, without her appearing to notice, was constantly watched by the Tsigane Sangarre. Notwithstanding her age she was compelled to follow the convoy of prisoners on foot, without any alleviation of her suffering.

However, a kind Providence had placed near her a courageous, kind-hearted being to comfort and assist her. Amongst her companions in misfortune a young girl, remarkable for beauty and taciturnity, seemed to have given herself the task of watching over her. No words had been exchanged between the two captives, but the girl was always at the old woman's side when help was useful. At first the mute assistance of the stranger was accepted with some mistrust. Gradually, however, the young girl's clear glance, her reserve, and the mysterious sympathy which draws together those who are in misfortune, thawed Marfa Strogoff's coldness.

Nadia—for it was she—was thus able, without knowing it, to render to the mother those attentions which she had herself received from the son. Her instinctive kindness had doubly inspired her. In devoting herself to her service, Nadia secured to her youth and beauty the protection afforded by the age of the old prisoner.

On the crowd of unhappy people, embittered by sufferings, this silent pair—one seeming to be the grandmother, the other the grand-daughter—imposed a sort of respect.

After being carried off by the Tartar scouts on the Irtych, Nadia had been taken to Omsk. Kept prisoner in the town, she shared the fate of all those captured by Ivan Ogareff, and consequently that of Marfa Strogoff.

If Nadia had been less energetic, she would have succumbed to this double blow. The interruption to her journey, the death of Michael, made her both desperate and excited. Divided, perhaps forever, from her father, after so many happy efforts had brought her near him, and, to crown her grief, separated from the intrepid companion whom God seemed to have placed in her way to lead her. The image of Michael Strogoff, struck before her eyes with a lance and disappearing beneath the waters of the Irtych, never left her thoughts.

Could such a man have died thus? For whom was God reserving His miracles if this good man, whom a noble object was urging onwards, had been allowed to perish so miserably? Then anger would prevail over grief. The scene of the affront so strangely borne by her companion at the Ichim relay returned to her memory. Her blood boiled at the recollection.

"Who will avenge him who can no longer avenge himself?" she said.

And in her heart, she cried, "May it be I!" If before his death Michael had confided his secret to her, woman, aye girl though she was, she might have been able to carry to a successful conclusion the interrupted task of that brother whom God had so soon taken from her.

Absorbed in these thoughts, it can be understood how Nadia could remain insensible to the miseries even of her captivity. Thus chance had united her to Marfa Strogoff without her having the least suspicion of who she was. How could she imagine that this old woman, a prisoner like herself, was the mother of him, whom she only knew as the merchant Nicholas Korpanoff? And on the other hand, how could Marfa guess that a bond of gratitude connected this young stranger with her son?

The thing that first struck Nadia in Marfa Strogoff was the similarity in the way in which each bore her hard fate. This stoicism of the old woman under the daily hardships, this contempt of bodily suffering, could only be caused by a moral grief equal to her own. So Nadia thought; and she was not mistaken. It was an instinctive sympathy for that part of her misery which Marfa did not show which first drew Nadia towards her. This way of bearing her sorrow went to the proud heart of the young girl. She did not offer her services; she gave them. Marfa had neither to refuse nor accept them. In the difficult parts of the journey, the girl was there to support her. When the provisions were given out, the old woman would not have moved, but Nadia shared her small portion with her; and thus this painful journey was performed. Thanks to her companion, Marfa was able to follow the soldiers who guarded the prisoners without being fastened to a saddle-bow, as were many other unfortunate wretches, and thus dragged along this road of sorrow.

"May God reward you, my daughter, for what you have done for my old age!" said Marfa Strogoff once, and for some time these were the only words exchanged between the two unfortunate beings.

During these few days, which to them appeared like centuries, it would seem that the old woman and the girl would have been led to speak of their situation. But Marfa Strogoff, from a caution which may be easily understood, never spoke about herself except with the greatest brevity. She never made the smallest allusion to her son, nor to the unfortunate meeting.

Nadia also, if not completely silent, spoke little. However, one day her heart overflowed, and she told all the events which had occurred from her departure from Wladimir to the death of Nicholas Korpanoff.

All that her young companion told intensely interested the old Siberian. "Nicholas Korpanoff!" said she. "Tell me again about this Nicholas. I know only one man, one alone, in whom such conduct would not have astonished me. Nicholas Korpanoff! Was that really his name? Are you sure of it, my daughter?"

"Why should he have deceived me in this," replied Nadia, "when he deceived me in no other way?"

Moved, however, by a kind of presentiment, Marfa Strogoff put questions upon questions to Nadia.

"You told me he was fearless, my daughter. You have proved that he has been so?" asked she.

"Yes, fearless indeed!" replied Nadia.

"It was just what my son would have done," said Marfa to herself.

Then she resumed, "Did you not say that nothing stopped him, nor astonished him; that he was so gentle in his strength that you had a sister as well as a brother in him, and he watched over you like a mother?"

"Yes, yes," said Nadia. "Brother, sister, mother—he has been all to me!"

"And defended you like a lion?"

"A lion indeed!" replied Nadia. "A lion, a hero!"

"My son, my son!" thought the old Siberian. "But you said, however, that he bore a terrible insult at that post-house in Ichim?"

"He did bear it," answered Nadia, looking down.

"He bore it!" murmured Marfa, shuddering.

"Mother, mother," cried Nadia, "do not blame him! He had a secret. A secret of which God alone is as yet the judge!"

"And," said Marfa, raising her head and looking at Nadia as though she would read the depths of her heart, "in that hour of humiliation did you not despise this Nicholas Korpanoff?"

"I admired without understanding him," replied the girl. "I never felt him more worthy of respect."

The old woman was silent for a minute.

"Was he tall?" she asked.

"Very tall."

"And very handsome? Come, speak, my daughter."

"He was very handsome," replied Nadia, blushing.

"It was my son! I tell you it was my son!" exclaimed the old woman, embracing Nadia.

"Your son!" said Nadia amazed, "your son!"

"Come," said Marfa; "let us get to the bottom of this, my child. Your companion, your friend, your protector had a mother. Did he never speak to you of his mother?"

"Of his mother?" said Nadia. "He spoke to me of his mother as I spoke to him of my father—often, always. He adored her."

"Nadia, Nadia, you have just told me about my own son," said the old woman.

And she added impetuously, "Was he not going to see this mother, whom you say he loved, in Omsk?"

"No," answered Nadia, "no, he was not."

"Not!" cried Marfa. "You dare to tell me not!"

"I say so: but it remains to me to tell you that from motives which outweighed everything else, motives which I do not know, I understand that Nicholas Korpanoff had to traverse the country completely in secret.

To him it was a question of life and death, and still more, a question of duty and honor."

"Duty, indeed, imperious duty," said the old Siberian, "of those who sacrifice everything, even the joy of giving a kiss, perhaps the last, to his old mother. All that you do not know, Nadia—all that I did not know myself—I now know. You have made me understand everything. But the light which you have thrown on the mysteries of my heart, I cannot return on yours. Since my son has not told you his secret, I must keep it. Forgive me, Nadia; I can never repay what you have done for me."

"Mother, I ask you nothing," replied Nadia.

All was thus explained to the old Siberian, all, even the conduct of her son with regard to herself in the inn at Omsk. There was no doubt that the young girl's companion was Michael Strogoff, and that a secret mission in the invaded country obliged him to conceal his quality of the Czar's courier.

"Ah, my brave boy!" thought Marfa. "No, I will not betray you, and tortures shall not wrest from me the avowal that it was you whom I saw at Omsk."

Marfa could with a word have paid Nadia for all her devotion to her. She could have told her that her companion, Nicholas Korpanoff, or rather Michael Strogoff, had not perished in the waters of the Irtych, since it was some days after that incident that she had met him, that she had spoken to him.

But she restrained herself, she was silent, and contented herself with saying, "Hope, my child! Misfortune will not overwhelm you. You will see your father again; I feel it; and perhaps he who gave you the name of sister is not dead. God cannot have allowed your brave companion to perish. Hope, my child, hope! Do as I do. The mourning which I wear is not yet for my son."

CHAPTER III
BLOW FOR BLOW

SUCH were now the relative situations of Marfa Strogoff and Nadia. All was understood by the old Siberian, and though the young girl was ignorant that her much-regretted companion still lived, she at least knew his relationship to her whom she had made her mother; and she thanked God for having given her the joy of taking the place of the son whom the prisoner had lost.

But what neither of them could know was that Michael, having been captured at Kolyvan, was in the same convoy and was on his way to Tomsk with them.

The prisoners brought by Ivan Ogareff had been added to those already kept by the Emir in the Tartar camp. These unfortunate people, consisting of Russians, Siberians, soldiers and civilians, numbered some thousands, and formed a column which extended over several versts. Some among them being considered dangerous were handcuffed and fastened to a long chain. There were, too, women and children, many of the latter suspended to the pommels of the saddles, while the former were dragged mercilessly along the road on foot, or driven forward as if they were animals. The horsemen compelled them to maintain a certain order, and there were no laggards with the exception of those who fell never to rise again.

In consequence of this arrangement, Michael Strogoff, marching in the first ranks of those who had left the Tartar camp—that is to say, among the Kolyvan prisoners—was unable to mingle with the prisoners who had arrived after him from Omsk. He had therefore no suspicion that his mother and Nadia were present in the convoy, nor did they suppose that he was among those in front. This journey from the camp to Tomsk, performed under the lashes and spear-points of the soldiers, proved fatal to many, and terrible to all. The prisoners traveled across the steppe, over a road made still more dusty by the passage of the Emir and his vanguard. Orders had been given to march rapidly. The short halts were rare. The hundred miles under a burning sky seemed interminable, though they were performed as rapidly as possible.

The country, which extends from the right of the Obi to the base of the spur detached from the Sayanok Mountains, is very sterile. Only a few stunted and burnt-up shrubs here and there break the monotony of the immense plain. There was no cultivation, for there was no water; and it was water that the prisoners, parched by their painful march, most needed. To find a stream they must have diverged fifty versts eastward, to the very foot of the mountains.

There flows the Tom, a little affluent of the Obi, which passes near Tomsk before losing itself in one of the great northern arteries. There water would have been abundant, the steppe less arid, the heat less severe. But the strictest orders had been given to the commanders of the convoy to reach Tomsk by the shortest way, for the Emir was much afraid of being taken in the flank and cut off by some Russian column descending from the northern provinces.

It is useless to dwell upon the sufferings of the unhappy prisoners. Many hundreds fell on the steppe, where their bodies would lie until winter, when the wolves would devour the remnants of their bones.

As Nadia helped the old Siberian, so in the same way did Michael render to his more feeble companions in misfortune such services as his situation allowed. He encouraged some, supported others, going to and fro, until a prick from a soldier's lance obliged him to resume the place which had been assigned him in the ranks.

Why did he not endeavor to escape?

The reason was that he had now quite determined not to venture until the steppe was safe for him. He was resolved in his idea of going as far as Tomsk "at the Emir's expense," and indeed he was right. As he observed the numerous detachments which scoured the plain on the convoy's flanks, now to the south, now to the north, it was evident that before he could have gone two versts he must have been recaptured. The Tartar horsemen swarmed—it actually appeared as if they sprang from the earth—like insects which a thunderstorm brings to the surface of the ground. Flight under these conditions would have been extremely difficult, if not impossible. The soldiers of the escort displayed excessive vigilance, for they would have paid for the slightest carelessness with their heads.

At nightfall of the 15th of August, the convoy reached the little village of Zabediero, thirty versts from Tomsk.

The prisoners' first movement would have been to rush into the river, but they were not allowed to leave the ranks until the halt had been organized. Although the current of the Tom was just now like a torrent, it might have favored the flight of some bold or desperate man, and the strictest measures of vigilance were taken. Boats, requisitioned at Zabediero, were brought up to the Tom and formed a line of obstacles impossible to pass. As to the encampment on the outskirts of the village, it was guarded by a cordon of sentinels.

Michael Strogoff, who now naturally thought of escape, saw, after carefully surveying the situation, that under these conditions it was perfectly impossible; so, not wishing to compromise himself, he waited.

The prisoners were to encamp for the whole night on the banks of the Tom, for the Emir had put off the entrance of his troops into Tomsk. It had been decided that a military fete should mark the inauguration of the Tartar headquarters in this important city. Feofar-Khan already occupied the fortress, but the bulk of his army bivouacked under its walls, waiting until the time came for them to make a solemn entry.

Ivan Ogareff left the Emir at Tomsk, where both had arrived the evening before, and returned to the camp at Zabediero. From here he was to start the next day with the rear-guard of the Tartar army. A house had been arranged for him in which to pass the night. At sunrise horse and foot soldiers were to proceed to Tomsk, where the Emir wished to receive them with the pomp usual to Asiatic sovereigns. As soon as the halt was organized, the prisoners, worn out with their three days' journey, and suffering from burning thirst, could drink and take a little rest. The sun had already set, when Nadia, supporting Marfa Strogoff, reached the banks of the Tom. They had not till then been able to get through those who crowded the banks, but at last they came to drink in their turn.

The old woman bent over the clear stream, and Nadia, plunging in her hand, carried it to Marfa's lips. Then she refreshed herself. They found new life in these welcome waters. Suddenly Nadia started up; an involuntary cry escaped her.

Michael Strogoff was there, a few steps from her. It was he. The dying rays of the sun fell upon him.

At Nadia's cry Michael started. But he had sufficient command over himself not to utter a word by which he might have been compromised. And yet, when he saw Nadia, he also recognized his mother.

Feeling he could not long keep master of himself at this unexpected meeting, he covered his eyes with his hands and walked quickly away.

Nadia's impulse was to run after him, but the old Siberian murmured in her ear, "Stay, my daughter!"

"It is he!" replied Nadia, choking with emotion. "He lives, mother! It is he!"

"It is my son," answered Marfa, "it is Michael Strogoff, and you see that I do not make a step towards him! Imitate me, my daughter."

Michael had just experienced the most violent emotion which a man can feel. His mother and Nadia were there!

The two prisoners who were always together in his heart, God had brought them together in this common misfortune. Did Nadia know who he was? Yes, for he had seen Marfa's gesture, holding her back as she was about to rush towards him. Marfa, then, had understood all, and kept his secret.

During that night, Michael was twenty times on the point of looking for and joining his mother; but he knew that he must resist the longing he felt to take her in his arms, and once more press the hand of his young companion. The least imprudence might be fatal. He had besides sworn not to see his mother. Once at Tomsk, since he could not escape this very night, he would set off without having even embraced the two beings in whom all the happiness of his life was centered, and whom he should leave exposed to so many perils.

Michael hoped that this fresh meeting at the Zabediero camp would have no disastrous consequences either to his mother or to himself. But he did not know that part of this scene, although it passed so rapidly, had been observed by Sangarre, Ogareff's spy.

The Tsigane was there, a few paces off, on the bank, as usual, watching the old Siberian woman. She had not caught sight of Michael, for he disappeared before she had time to look around; but the mother's gesture as she kept back Nadia had not escaped her, and the look in Marfa's eyes told her all.

It was now beyond doubt that Marfa Strogoff's son, the Czar's courier, was at this moment in Zabediero, among Ivan Ogareff's prisoners. Sangarre did not know him, but she knew that he was there. She did not then attempt to discover him, for it would have been impossible in the dark and the immense crowd.

As for again watching Nadia and Marfa Strogoff, that was equally useless. It was evident that the two women would keep on their guard, and it would be impossible to overhear anything of a nature to compromise the courier of the Czar. The Tsigane's first thought was to tell Ivan Ogareff. She therefore immediately left the encampment. A quarter of an hour after, she reached Zabediero, and was shown into the house occupied by the Emir's lieutenant. Ogareff received the Tsigane directly.

"What have you to tell me, Sangarre?" he asked.

"Marfa Strogoff's son is in the encampment."

"A prisoner?"

119

"A prisoner."

"Ah!" exclaimed Ogareff, "I shall know—"

"You will know nothing, Ivan," replied Tsigane; "for you do not even know him by sight."

"But you know him; you have seen him, Sangarre?"

"I have not seen him; but his mother betrayed herself by a gesture, which told me everything."

"Are you not mistaken?"

"I am not mistaken."

"You know the importance which I attach to the apprehension of this courier," said Ivan Ogareff. "If the letter which he has brought from Moscow reaches Irkutsk, if it is given to the Grand Duke, the Grand Duke will be on his guard, and I shall not be able to get at him. I must have that letter at any price. Now you come to tell me that the bearer of this letter is in my power. I repeat, Sangarre, are you not mistaken?"

Ogareff spoke with great animation. His emotion showed the extreme importance he attached to the possession of this letter. Sangarre was not at all put out by the urgency with which Ogareff repeated his question. "I am not mistaken, Ivan," she said.

"But, Sangarre, there are thousands of prisoners; and you say that you do not know Michael Strogoff."

"No," answered the Tsigane, with a look of savage joy, "I do not know him; but his mother knows him. Ivan, we must make his mother speak."

"To-morrow she shall speak!" cried Ogareff. So saying, he extended his hand to the Tsigane, who kissed it; for there is nothing servile in this act of respect, it being usual among the Northern races.

Sangarre returned to the camp. She found out Nadia and Marfa Strogoff, and passed the night in watching them. Although worn out with fatigue, the old woman and the girl did not sleep. Their great anxiety kept them awake. Michael was living, but a prisoner. Did Ogareff know him, or would he not soon find him out? Nadia was occupied by the one thought that he whom she had thought dead still lived. But Marfa saw further into the future: and, although she did not care what became of herself, she had every reason to fear for her son.

Sangarre, under cover of the night, had crept near the two women, and remained there several hours listening. She heard nothing. From an instinctive feeling of prudence not a word was exchanged between Nadia and Marfa Strogoff. The next day, the 16th of August, about ten in the morning, trumpet-calls resounded throughout the encampment. The Tartar soldiers were almost immediately under arms.

Ivan Ogareff arrived, surrounded by a large staff of Tartar officers. His face was more clouded than usual, and his knitted brow gave signs of latent wrath which was waiting for an occasion to break forth.

Michael Strogoff, hidden in a group of prisoners, saw this man pass. He had a presentiment that some catastrophe was imminent: for Ivan Ogareff knew now that Marfa was the mother of Michael Strogoff.

Ogareff dismounted, and his escort cleared a large circle round him. Just then Sangarre approached him, and said, "I have no news."

Ivan Ogareff's only reply was to give an order to one of his officers. Then the ranks of prisoners were brutally hurried up by the soldiers. The unfortunate people, driven on with whips, or pushed on with lances, arranged themselves round the camp. A strong guard of soldiers drawn up behind, rendered escape impossible.

Silence then ensued, and, on a sign from Ivan Ogareff, Sangarre advanced towards the group, in the midst of which stood Marfa.

The old Siberian saw her, and knew what was going to happen. A scornful smile passed over her face. Then leaning towards Nadia, she said in a low tone, "You know me no longer, my daughter. Whatever may happen, and however hard this trial may be, not a word, not a sign. It concerns him, and not me."

At that moment Sangarre, having regarded her for an instant, put her hand on her shoulder.

"What do you want with me?" said Marfa.

"Come!" replied Sangarre, and pushing the old Siberian before her, she took her to Ivan Ogareff, in the middle of the cleared ground. Michael cast down his eyes that their angry flashings might not appear.

Marfa, standing before Ivan Ogareff, drew herself up, crossed her arms on her breast, and waited.

"You are Marfa Strogoff?" asked Ogareff.

"Yes," replied the old Siberian calmly.

"Do you retract what you said to me when, three days ago, I interrogated you at Omsk?"

"No!"

"Then you do not know that your son, Michael Strogoff, courier of the Czar, has passed through Omsk?"

"I do not know it."

"And the man in whom you thought you recognized your son, was not he your son?"

"He was not my son."

"And since then you have not seen him amongst the prisoners?"

"No."

"If he were pointed out, would you recognize him?"

"No."

On this reply, which showed such determined resolution, a murmur was heard amongst the crowd.

Ogareff could not restrain a threatening gesture.

"Listen," said he to Marfa, "your son is here, and you shall immediately point him out to me."

"No."

"All these men, taken at Omsk and Kolyvan, will defile before you; and if you do not show me Michael Strogoff, you shall receive as many blows of the knout as men shall have passed before you."

Ivan Ogareff saw that, whatever might be his threats, whatever

121

might be the tortures to which he submitted her, the indomitable Siberian would not speak. To discover the courier of the Czar, he counted, then, not on her, but on Michael himself. He did not believe it possible that, when mother and son were in each other's presence, some involuntary movement would not betray him. Of course, had he wished to seize the imperial letter, he would simply have given orders to search all the prisoners; but Michael might have destroyed the letter, having learnt its contents; and if he were not recognized, if he were to reach Irkutsk, all Ivan Ogareff's plans would be baffled. It was thus not only the letter which the traitor must have, but the bearer himself.

Nadia had heard all, and she now knew who was Michael Strogoff, and why he had wished to cross, without being recognized, the invaded provinces of Siberia.

On an order from Ivan Ogareff the prisoners defiled, one by one, past Marfa, who remained immovable as a statue, and whose face expressed only perfect indifference.

Her son was among the last. When in his turn he passed before his mother, Nadia shut her eyes that she might not see him. Michael was to all appearance unmoved, but the palm of his hand bled under his nails, which were pressed into them.

Ivan Ogareff was baffled by mother and son.

Sangarre, close to him, said one word, "The knout!"

"Yes," cried Ogareff, who could no longer restrain himself; "the knout for this wretched old woman—the knout to the death!"

A Tartar soldier bearing this terrible instrument of torture approached Marfa. The knout is composed of a certain number of leathern thongs, at the end of which are attached pieces of twisted iron wire. It is reckoned that a sentence to one hundred and twenty blows of this whip is equivalent to a sentence of death.

Marfa knew it, but she knew also that no torture would make her speak. She was sacrificing her life.

Marfa, seized by two soldiers, was forced on her knees on the ground. Her dress torn off left her back bare. A saber was placed before her breast, at a few inches' distance only. Directly she bent beneath her suffering, her breast would be pierced by the sharp steel.

The Tartar drew himself up. He waited. "Begin!" said Ogareff. The whip whistled in the air.

But before it fell a powerful hand stopped the Tartar's arm. Michael was there. He had leapt forward at this horrible scene. If at the relay at Ichim he had restrained himself when Ogareff's whip had struck him, here before his mother, who was about to be struck, he could not do so. Ivan Ogareff had succeeded.

"Michael Strogoff!" cried he. Then advancing, "Ah, the man of Ichim?"

"Himself!" said Michael. And raising the knout he struck Ogareff a sharp blow across the face. "Blow for blow!" said he.

"Well repaid!" cried a voice concealed by the tumult.

Twenty soldiers threw themselves on Michael, and in another instant he would have been slain.

But Ogareff, who on being struck had uttered a cry of rage and pain, stopped them. "This man is reserved for the Emir's judgment," said he. "Search him!"

The letter with the imperial arms was found in Michael's bosom; he had not had time to destroy it; it was handed to Ogareff.

The voice which had pronounced the words, "Well repaid!" was that of no other than Alcide Jolivet. "Par-dieu!" said he to Blount, "they are rough, these people. Acknowledge that we owe our traveling companion a good turn. Korpanoff or Strogoff is worthy of it. Oh, that was fine retaliation for the little affair at Ichim."

"Yes, retaliation truly," replied Blount; "but Strogoff is a dead man. I suspect that, for his own interest at all events, it would have been better had he not possessed quite so lively a recollection of the event."

"And let his mother perish under the knout?"

"Do you think that either she or his sister will be a bit better off from this outbreak of his?"

"I do not know or think anything except that I should have done much the same in his position," replied Alcide. "What a scar the Colonel has received! Bah! one must boil over sometimes. We should have had water in our veins instead of blood had it been incumbent on us to be always and everywhere unmoved to wrath."

"A neat little incident for our journals," observed Blount, "if only Ivan Ogareff would let us know the contents of that letter."

Ivan Ogareff, when he had stanched the blood which was trickling down his face, had broken the seal. He read and re-read the letter deliberately, as if he was determined to discover everything it contained.

Then having ordered that Michael, carefully bound and guarded, should be carried on to Tomsk with the other prisoners, he took command of the troops at Zabediero, and, amid the deafening noise of drums and trumpets, he marched towards the town where the Emir awaited him.

CHAPTER IV
THE TRIUMPHAL ENTRY

TOMSK, founded in 1604, nearly in the heart of the Siberian provinces, is one of the most important towns in Asiatic Russia. Tobolsk, situated above the sixtieth parallel; Irkutsk, built beyond the hundredth meridian—have seen Tomsk increase at their expense.

And yet Tomsk, as has been said, is not the capital of this important province. It is at Omsk that the Governor-General of the province and the official world reside. But Tomsk is the most considerable town of that territory. The country being rich, the town is so likewise, for it is in the

123

center of fruitful mines. In the luxury of its houses, its arrangements, and its equipages, it might rival the greatest European capitals. It is a city of millionaires, enriched by the spade and pickax, and though it has not the honor of being the residence of the Czar's representative, it can boast of including in the first rank of its notables the chief of the merchants of the town, the principal grantees of the imperial government's mines.

But the millionaires were fled now, and except for the crouching poor, the town stood empty to the hordes of Feofar-Khan. At four o'clock the Emir made his entry into the square, greeted by a flourish of trumpets, the rolling sound of the big drums, salvoes of artillery and musketry.

Feofar mounted his favorite horse, which carried on its head an aigrette of diamonds. The Emir still wore his uniform. He was accompanied by a numerous staff, and beside him walked the Khans of Khokhand and Koundouge and the grand dignitaries of the Khanats.

At the same moment appeared on the terrace the chief of Feofar's wives, the queen, if this title may be given to the sultana of the states of Bokhara. But, queen or slave, this woman of Persian origin was wonderfully beautiful. Contrary to the Mahometan custom, and no doubt by some caprice of the Emir, she had her face uncovered. Her hair, divided into four plaits, fell over her dazzling white shoulders, scarcely concealed by a veil of silk worked in gold, which fell from the back of a cap studded with gems of the highest value. Under her blue-silk petticoat, fell the "zirdjameh" of silken gauze, and above the sash lay the "pirahn." But from the head to the little feet, such was the profusion of jewels—gold beads strung on silver threads, chaplets of turquoises, "firouzehs" from the celebrated mines of Elbourz, necklaces of cornelians, agates, emeralds, opals, and sapphires—that her dress seemed to be literally made of precious stones. The thousands of diamonds which sparkled on her neck, arms, hands, at her waist, and at her feet might have been valued at almost countless millions of roubles.

The Emir and the Khans dismounted, as did the dignitaries who escorted them. All entered a magnificent tent erected on the center of the first terrace. Before the tent, as usual, the Koran was laid.

Feofar's lieutenant did not make them wait, and before five o'clock the trumpets announced his arrival. Ivan Ogareff—the Scarred Cheek, as he was already nick-named—wearing the uniform of a Tartar officer, dismounted before the Emir's tent. He was accompanied by a party of soldiers from the camp at Zabediero, who ranged up at the sides of the square, in the middle of which a place for the sports was reserved. A large scar could be distinctly seen cut obliquely across the traitor's face.

Ogareff presented his principal officers to the Emir, who, without departing from the coldness which composed the main part of his dignity, received them in a way which satisfied them that they stood well in the good graces of their chief.

At least so thought Harry Blount and Alcide Jolivet, the two inseparables, now associated together in the chase after news. After leaving Zabediero, they had proceeded rapidly to Tomsk. The plan they had agreed upon was to leave the Tartars as soon as possible, and to join a Russian regiment, and, if they could, to go with them to Irkutsk. All that they had seen of the invasion, its burnings, its pillages, its murders, had perfectly sickened them, and they longed to be among the ranks of the Siberian army. Jolivet had told his companion that he could not leave Tomsk without making a sketch of the triumphal entry of the Tartar troops, if it was only to satisfy his cousin's curiosity; but the same evening they both intended to take the road to Irkutsk, and being well mounted hoped to distance the Emir's scouts.

Alcide and Blount mingled therefore in the crowd, so as to lose no detail of a festival which ought to supply them with a hundred good lines for an article. They admired the magnificence of Feofar-Khan, his wives, his officers, his guards, and all the Eastern pomp, of which the ceremonies of Europe can give not the least idea. But they turned away with disgust when Ivan Ogareff presented himself before the Emir, and waited with some impatience for the amusements to begin.

"You see, my dear Blount," said Alcide, "we have come too soon, like honest citizens who like to get their money's worth. All this is before the curtain rises, it would have been better to arrive only for the ballet."

"What ballet?" asked Blount.

"The compulsory ballet, to be sure. But see, the curtain is going to rise." Alcide Jolivet spoke as if he had been at the Opera, and taking his glass from its case, he prepared, with the air of a connoisseur, "to examine the first act of Feofar's company."

A painful ceremony was to precede the sports. In fact, the triumph of the vanquisher could not be complete without the public humiliation of the vanquished. This was why several hundreds of prisoners were brought under the soldiers' whips. They were destined to march past Feofar-Khan and his allies before being crammed with their companions into the prisons in the town.

In the first ranks of these prisoners figured Michael Strogoff. As Ogareff had ordered, he was specially guarded by a file of soldiers. His mother and Nadia were there also.

The old Siberian, although energetic enough when her own safety was in question, was frightfully pale. She expected some terrible scene. It was not without reason that her son had been brought before the Emir. She therefore trembled for him. Ivan Ogareff was not a man to forgive having been struck in public by the knout, and his vengeance would be merciless. Some frightful punishment familiar to the barbarians of Central Asia would, no doubt, be inflicted on Michael Ogareff had protected him against the soldiers because he well knew what would happen by reserving him for the justice of the Emir.

The mother and son had not been able to speak together since the terrible scene in the camp at Zabediero. They had been pitilessly kept apart—a bitter aggravation of their misery, for it would have been some consolation to have been together during these days of captivity. Marfa longed to ask her son's pardon for the harm she had unintentionally done him, for she reproached herself with not having commanded her maternal feelings. If she had restrained herself in that post-house at Omsk, when she found herself face to face with him, Michael would have passed unrecognized, and all these misfortunes would have been avoided.

Michael, on his side, thought that if his mother was there, if Ogareff had brought her with him, it was to make her suffer with the sight of his own punishment, or perhaps some frightful death was reserved for her also.

As to Nadia, she only asked herself how she could save them both, how come to the aid of son and mother. As yet she could only wonder, but she felt instinctively that she must above everything avoid drawing attention upon herself, that she must conceal herself, make herself insignificant. Perhaps she might at least gnaw through the meshes which imprisoned the lion. At any rate if any opportunity was given her she would seize upon it, and sacrifice herself, if need be, for the son of Marfa Strogoff.

In the meantime the greater part of the prisoners were passing before the Emir, and as they passed each was obliged to prostrate himself, with his forehead in the dust, in token of servitude. Slavery begins by humiliation. When the unfortunate people were too slow in bending, the rough guards threw them violently to the ground.

Alcide Jolivet and his companion could not witness such a sight without feeling indignant.

"It is cowardly—let us go," said Alcide.

"No," answered Blount; "we must see it all."

"See it all!—ah!" cried Alcide, suddenly, grasping his companion's arm.

"What is the matter with you?" asked the latter.

"Look, Blount; it is she!"

"What she?"

"The sister of our traveling companion—alone, and a prisoner! We must save her."

"Calm yourself," replied Blount coolly. "Any interference on our part in behalf of the young girl would be worse than useless."

Alcide Jolivet, who had been about to rush forward, stopped, and Nadia—who had not perceived them, her features being half hidden by her hair—passed in her turn before the Emir without attracting his attention.

However, after Nadia came Marfa Strogoff; and as she did not throw herself quickly in the dust, the guards brutally pushed her. She fell.

Her son struggled so violently that the soldiers who were guarding him could scarcely hold him back. But the old woman rose, and they were about to drag her on, when Ogareff interposed, saying, "Let that woman stay!"

As to Nadia, she happily regained the crowd of prisoners. Ivan Ogareff had taken no notice of her.

Michael was then led before the Emir, and there he remained standing, without casting down his eyes.

"Your forehead to the ground!" cried Ogareff.

"No!" answered Michael.

Two soldiers endeavored to make him bend, but they were themselves laid on the ground by a buffet from the young man's fist.

Ogareff approached Michael. "You shall die!" he said.

"I can die," answered Michael fiercely; "but your traitor's face, Ivan, will not the less carry forever the infamous brand of the knout."

At this reply Ivan Ogareff became perfectly livid.

"Who is this prisoner?" asked the Emir, in a tone of voice terrible from its very calmness.

"A Russian spy," answered Ogareff. In asserting that Michael was a spy he knew that the sentence pronounced against him would be terrible.

The Emir made a sign at which all the crowd bent low their heads. Then he pointed with his hand to the Koran, which was brought him. He opened the sacred book and placed his finger on one of its pages.

It was chance, or rather, according to the ideas of these Orientals, God Himself who was about to decide the fate of Michael Strogoff. The people of Central Asia give the name of "fal" to this practice. After having interpreted the sense of the verse touched by the judge's finger, they apply the sentence whatever it may be.

The Emir had let his finger rest on the page of the Koran. The chief of the Ulemas then approached, and read in a loud voice a verse which ended with these words, "And he will no more see the things of this earth."

"Russian spy!" exclaimed Feofar-Kahn in a voice trembling with fury, "you have come to see what is going on in the Tartar camp. Then look while you may."

CHAPTER V
"LOOK WHILE YOU MAY!"

MICHAEL was held before the Emir's throne, at the foot of the terrace, his hands bound behind his back. His mother overcome at last by mental and physical torture, had sunk to the ground, daring neither to look nor listen.

"Look while you may," exclaimed Feofar-Kahn, stretching his arm towards Michael in a threatening manner. Doubtless Ivan Ogareff, being well acquainted with Tartar customs, had taken in the full meaning of these words, for his lips curled for an instant in a cruel smile; he then took his place by Feofar-Khan.

A trumpet call was heard. This was the signal for the amusements to begin. "Here comes the ballet," said Alcide to Blount; "but, contrary to our customs, these barbarians give it before the drama."

Michael had been commanded to look at everything. He looked. A troop of dancers poured into the open space before the Emir's tent.

Different Tartar instruments, the "doutare," a long-handled guitar, the "kobize," a kind of violoncello, the "tschibyzga," a long reed flute; wind instruments, tom-toms, tambourines, united with the deep voices of the singers, formed a strange harmony. Added to this were the strains of an aerial orchestra, composed of a dozen kites, which, fastened by strings to their centers, resounded in the breeze like AEolian harps.

Then the dancers began. The performers were all of Persian origin; they were no longer slaves, but exercised their profession at liberty. Formerly they figured officially in the ceremonies at the court of Teheran, but since the accession of the reigning family, banished or treated with contempt, they had been compelled to seek their fortune elsewhere. They wore the national costume, and were adorned with a profusion of jewels. Little triangles of gold, studded with jewels, glittered in their ears. Circles of silver, marked with black, surrounded their necks and legs.

These performers gracefully executed various dances, sometimes alone, sometimes in groups. Their faces were uncovered, but from time to time they threw a light veil over their heads, and a gauze cloud passed over their bright eyes as smoke over a starry sky. Some of these Persians wore leathern belts embroidered with pearls, from which hung little triangular bags. From these bags, embroidered with golden filigree, they drew long narrow bands of scarlet silk, on which were braided verses of the Koran. These bands, which they held between them, formed a belt under which the other dancers darted; and, as they passed each verse, following the precept it contained, they either prostrated themselves on the earth or lightly bounded upwards, as though to take a place among the houris of Mohammed's heaven.

But what was remarkable, and what struck Alcide, was that the Persians appeared rather indolent than fiery. Their passion had deserted them, and, by the kind of dances as well as by their execution, they recalled rather the calm and self-possessed nauch girls of India than the impassioned dancers of Egypt.

When this was over, a stern voice was heard saying:

"Look while you may!"

The man who repeated the Emir's words—a tall spare Tartar—was he who carried out the sentences of Feofar-Khan against offenders. He had taken his place behind Michael, holding in his hand a broad curved saber, one of those Damascene blades which are forged by the celebrated armorers of Karschi or Hissar.

Behind him guards were carrying a tripod supporting a chafing-dish filled with live coals. No smoke arose from this, but a light vapor surrounded it, due to the incineration of a certain aromatic and resinous substance which he had thrown on the surface.

The Persians were succeeded by another party of dancers, whom Michael recognized. The journalists also appeared to recognize them, for Blount said to his companion, "These are the Tsiganes of Nijni-Novgorod."

"No doubt of it," cried Alcide. "Their eyes, I imagine, bring more money to these spies than their legs."

128

In putting them down as agents in the Emir's service, Alcide Jolivet was, by all accounts, not mistaken.

In the first rank of the Tsiganes, Sangarre appeared, superb in her strange and picturesque costume, which set off still further her remarkable beauty.

Sangarre did not dance, but she stood as a statue in the midst of the performers, whose style of dancing was a combination of that of all those countries through which their race had passed—Turkey, Bohemia, Egypt, Italy, and Spain. They were enlivened by the sound of cymbals, which clashed on their arms, and by the hollow sounds of the "daires"—a sort of tambourine played with the fingers.

Sangarre, holding one of those daires, which she played between her hands, encouraged this troupe of veritable corybantes. A young Tsigane, of about fifteen years of age, then advanced. He held in his hand a "doutare," strings of which he made to vibrate by a simple movement of the nails. He sung. During the singing of each couplet, of very peculiar rhythm, a dancer took her position by him and remained there immovable, listening to him, but each time that the burden came from the lips of the young singer, she resumed her dance, dinning in his ears with her daire, and deafening him with the clashing of her cymbals. Then, after the last chorus, the remainder surrounded the Tsigane in the windings of their dance.

At that moment a shower of gold fell from the hands of the Emir and his train, and from the hands of his officers of all ranks; to the noise which the pieces made as they struck the cymbals of the dancers, being added the last murmurs of the doutares and tambourines.

"Lavish as robbers," said Alcide in the ear of his companion. And in fact it was the result of plunder which was falling; for, with the Tartar tomans and sequins, rained also Russian ducats and roubles.

Then silence followed for an instant, and the voice of the executioner, who laid his hand on Michael's shoulder, once more pronounced the words, which this repetition rendered more and more sinister:

"Look while you may"

But this time Alcide observed that the executioner no longer held the saber bare in his hand.

Meanwhile the sun had sunk behind the horizon. A semi-obscurity began to envelop the plain. The mass of cedars and pines became blacker and blacker, and the waters of the Tom, totally obscured in the distance, mingled with the approaching shadows.

But at that instant several hundreds of slaves, bearing lighted torches, entered the square. Led by Sangarre, Tsiganes and Persians reappeared before the Emir's throne, and showed off, by the contrast, their dances of styles so different. The instruments of the Tartar orchestra sounded forth in harmony still more savage, accompanied by the guttural cries of the singers. The kites, which had fallen to the ground, once more winged their way into the sky, each bearing a parti-colored lantern, and under a fresher breeze their harps vibrated with intenser sound in the midst of the aerial illumination.

Then a squadron of Tartars, in their brilliant uniforms, mingled in the dances, whose wild fury was increasing rapidly, and then began a performance which produced a very strange effect. Soldiers came on the ground, armed with bare sabers and long pistols, and, as they executed dances, they made the air re-echo with the sudden detonations of their firearms, which immediately set going the rumbling of the tambourines, and grumblings of the daires, and the gnashing of doutares.

Their arms, covered with a colored powder of some metallic ingredient, after the Chinese fashion, threw long jets—red, green, and blue—so that the groups of dancers seemed to be in the midst of fireworks. In some respects, this performance recalled the military dance of the ancients, in the midst of naked swords; but this Tartar dance was rendered yet more fantastic by the colored fire, which wound, serpent-like, above the dancers, whose dresses seemed to be embroidered with fiery hems. It was like a kaleidoscope of sparks, whose infinite combinations varied at each movement of the dancers.

Though it may be thought that a Parisian reporter would be perfectly hardened to any scenic effect, which our modern ideas have carried so far, yet Alcide Jolivet could not restrain a slight movement of the head, which at home, between the Boulevard Montmartre and La Madeleine would have said—"Very fair, very fair."

Then, suddenly, at a signal, all the lights of the fantasia were extinguished, the dances ceased, and the performers disappeared. The ceremony was over, and the torches alone lighted up the plateau, which a few instants before had been so brilliantly illuminated.

On a sign from the Emir, Michael was led into the middle of the square.

"Blount," said Alcide to his companion, "are you going to see the end of all this?"

"No, that I am not," replied Blount.

"The readers of the Daily Telegraph are, I hope, not very eager for the details of an execution a la mode Tartare?"

"No more than your cousin!"

"Poor fellow!" added Alcide, as he watched Michael. "That valiant soldier should have fallen on the field of battle!"

"Can we do nothing to save him?" said Blount.

"Nothing!"

The reporters recalled Michael's generous conduct towards them; they knew now through what trials he must have passed, ever obedient to his duty; and in the midst of these Tartars, to whom pity is unknown, they could do nothing for him. Having little desire to be present at the torture reserved for the unfortunate man, they returned to the town. An hour later, they were on the road to Irkutsk, for it was among the Russians that they intended to follow what Alcide called, by anticipation, "the campaign of revenge."

Meantime, Michael was standing ready, his eyes returning the Emir's haughty glance, while his countenance assumed an expression of intense scorn whenever he cast his looks on Ivan Ogareff. He was prepared to die, yet not a single sign of weakness escaped him.

The spectators, waiting around the square, as well as Feofar-Khan's body-guard, to whom this execution was only one of the attractions, were eagerly expecting it. Then, their curiosity satisfied, they would rush off to enjoy the pleasures of intoxication.

The Emir made a sign. Michael was thrust forward by his guards to the foot of the terrace, and Feofar said to him, "You came to see our goings out and comings in, Russian spy. You have seen for the last time. In an instant your eyes will be forever shut to the day."

Michael's fate was to be not death, but blindness; loss of sight, more terrible perhaps than loss of life. The unhappy man was condemned to be blinded.

However, on hearing the Emir's sentence Michael's heart did not grow faint. He remained unmoved, his eyes wide open, as though he wished to concentrate his whole life into one last look. To entreat pity from these savage men would be useless, besides, it would be unworthy of him. He did not even think of it. His thoughts were condensed on his mission, which had apparently so completely failed; on his mother, on Nadia, whom he should never more see! But he let no sign appear of the emotion he felt. Then, a feeling of vengeance to be accomplished came over him. "Ivan," said he, in a stern voice, "Ivan the Traitor, the last menace of my eyes shall be for you!"

Ivan Ogareff shrugged his shoulders.

But Michael was not to be looking at Ivan when his eyes were put out. Marfa Strogoff stood before him.

"My mother!" cried he. "Yes! yes! my last glance shall be for you, and not for this wretch! Stay there, before me! Now I see once more your well-beloved face! Now shall my eyes close as they rest upon it...!"

The old woman, without uttering a word, advanced.

"Take that woman away!" said Ivan.

Two soldiers were about to seize her, but she stepped back and remained standing a few paces from Michael.

The executioner appeared. This time, he held his saber bare in his hand, and this saber he had just drawn from the chafing-dish, where he had brought it to a white heat. Michael was going to be blinded in the Tartar fashion, with a hot blade passed before his eyes!

Michael did not attempt to resist. Nothing existed before his eyes but his mother, whom his eyes seemed to devour. All his life was in that last look.

Marfa Strogoff, her eyes open wide, her arms extended towards where he stood, was gazing at him. The incandescent blade passed before Michael's eyes.

A despairing cry was heard. His aged mother fell senseless to the ground. Michael Strogoff was blind.

His orders executed, the Emir retired with his train. There remained in the square only Ivan Ogareff and the torch bearers. Did the wretch intend to insult his victim yet further, and yet to give him a parting blow?

Ivan Ogareff slowly approached Michael, who, feeling him coming, drew himself up. Ivan drew from his pocket the Imperial letter, he opened it, and with supreme irony he held it up before the sightless eyes of the Czar's courier, saying, "Read, now, Michael Strogoff, read, and go and repeat at Irkutsk what you have read. The true Courier of the Czar is Ivan Ogareff."

This said, the traitor thrust the letter into his breast. Then, without looking round he left the square, followed by the torch-bearers.

Michael was left alone, at a few paces from his mother, lying lifeless, perhaps dead. He heard in the distance cries and songs, the varied noises of a wild debauch. Tomsk, illuminated, glittered and gleamed.

Michael listened. The square was silent and deserted. He went, groping his way, towards the place where his mother had fallen. He found her with his hand, he bent over her, he put his face close to hers, he listened for the beating of her heart. Then he murmured a few words.

Did Marfa still live, and did she hear her son's words? Whether she did so or not, she made not the slightest movement. Michael kissed her forehead and her white locks. He then raised himself, and, groping with his foot, trying to stretch out his hand to guide himself, he walked by degrees to the edge of the square.

Suddenly Nadia appeared. She walked straight to her companion. A knife in her hand cut the cords which bound Michael's arms. The blind man knew not who had freed him, for Nadia had not spoken a word.

But this done: "Brother!" said she.

"Nadia!" murmured Michael, "Nadia!"

"Come, brother," replied Nadia, "use my eyes whilst yours sleep. I will lead you to Irkutsk."

CHAPTER VI
A FRIEND ON THE HIGHWAY

HALF an hour afterwards, Michael and Nadia
had left Tomsk

Many others of the prisoners were that night able to escape from the Tartars, for officers and soldiers, all more or less intoxicated, had unconsciously relaxed the vigilant guard which they had hitherto maintained. Nadia, after having been carried off with the other prisoners, had been able to escape and return to the square, at the moment when Michael was led before the Emir. There, mingling with the crowd, she had witnessed the terrible scene. Not a cry escaped her when the scorching blade passed before her companion's eyes. She kept, by her strength of will, mute and motionless. A providential inspiration bade her restrain herself and retain her liberty that she might lead Marfa's son to that goal which he had sworn to reach. Her heart for an instant ceased to beat when the aged Siberian woman fell senseless to the ground, but one thought restored her to her former energy. "I will be the blind man's dog," said she.

On Ogareff's departure, Nadia had concealed herself in the shade. She had waited till the crowd left the square. Michael, abandoned as a wretched being from whom nothing was to be feared, was alone. She saw him draw himself towards his mother, bend over her, kiss her forehead, then rise and grope his way in flight.

A few instants later, she and he, hand in hand, had descended the steep slope, when, after having followed the high banks of the Tom to the furthest extremity of the town, they happily found a breach in the inclosure.

The road to Irkutsk was the only one which penetrated towards the east. It could not be mistaken. It was possible that on the morrow, after some hours of carousal, the scouts of the Emir, once more scattering over the steppes, might cut off all communication. It was of the greatest importance therefore to get in advance of them. How could Nadia bear the fatigues of that night, from the 16th to the 17th of August? How could she have found strength for so long a stage? How could her feet, bleeding under that forced march, have carried her thither? It is almost incomprehensible. But it is none the less true that on the next morning, twelve hours after their departure from Tomsk, Michael and she reached the town of Semilowskoe, after a journey of thirty-five miles.

Michael had not uttered a single word. It was not Nadia who held his hand, it was he who held that of his companion during the whole of that night; but, thanks to that trembling little hand which guided him, he had walked at his ordinary pace.

Semilowskoe was almost entirely abandoned. The inhabitants had fled. Not more than two or three houses were still occupied. All that the town contained, useful or precious, had been carried off in wagons. However, Nadia was obliged to make a halt of a few hours. They both required food and rest.

The young girl led her companion to the extremity of the town. There they found an empty house, the door wide open. An old rickety wooden bench stood in the middle of the room, near the high stove which is to be found in all Siberian houses. They silently seated themselves.

Nadia gazed in her companion's face as she had never before gazed. There was more than gratitude, more than pity, in that look. Could Michael have seen her, he would have read in that sweet desolate gaze a world of devotion and tenderness.

The eyelids of the blind man, made red by the heated blade, fell half over his eyes. The pupils seemed to be singularly enlarged. The rich blue of the iris was darker than formerly. The eyelashes and eyebrows were partly burnt, but in appearance, at least, the old penetrating look appeared to have undergone no change. If he could no longer see, if his blindness was complete, it was because the sensibility of the retina and optic nerve was radically destroyed by the fierce heat of the steel.

Then Michael stretched out his hands.

"Are you there, Nadia?" he asked.

"Yes," replied the young girl; "I am close to you, and I will not go away from you, Michael."

At his name, pronounced by Nadia for the first time, a thrill passed through Michael's frame. He perceived that his companion knew all, who he was.

"Nadia," replied he, "we must separate!"

"We separate? How so, Michael?"

"I must not be an obstacle to your journey! Your father is waiting for you at Irkutsk! You must rejoin your father!"

"My father would curse me, Michael, were I to abandon you now, after all you have done for me!"

"Nadia, Nadia," replied Michael, "you should think only of your father!"

"Michael," replied Nadia, "you have more need of me than my father. Do you mean to give up going to Irkutsk?"

"Never!" cried Michael, in a tone which plainly showed that none of his energy was gone.

"But you have not the letter!"

"That letter of which Ivan Ogareff robbed me! Well! I shall manage without it, Nadia! They have treated me as a spy! I will act as a spy! I will go and repeat at Irkutsk all I have seen, all I have heard; I swear it by Heaven above! The traitor shall meet me one day face to face! But I must arrive at Irkutsk before him."

"And yet you speak of our separating, Michael?"

"Nadia, they have taken everything from me!"

"I have some roubles still, and my eyes! I can see for you, Michael; and I will lead you thither, where you could not go alone!"

"And how shall we go?"

"On foot."

"And how shall we live?"

"By begging."

"Let us start, Nadia."

"Come, Michael."

The two young people no longer kept the names "brother" and "sister." In their common misfortune, they felt still closer united. They left the house after an hour's repose. Nadia had procured in the town some morsels of "tchornekhleb," a sort of barley bread, and a little mead, called "meod" in Russia. This had cost her nothing, for she had already begun her plan of begging. The bread and mead had in some degree appeased Michael's hunger and thirst. Nadia gave him the lion's share of this scanty meal. He ate the pieces of bread his companion gave him, drank from the gourd she held to his lips.

134

"Are you eating, Nadia?" he asked several times.

"Yes, Michael," invariably replied the young girl, who contented herself with what her companion left.

Michael and Nadia quitted Semilowskoe, and once more set out on the laborious road to Irkutsk. The girl bore up in a marvelous way against fatigue. Had Michael seen her, perhaps he would not have had the courage to go on. But Nadia never complained, and Michael, hearing no sigh, walked at a speed he was unable to repress. And why? Did he still expect to keep before the Tartars? He was on foot, without money; he was blind, and if Nadia, his only guide, were to be separated from him, he could only lie down by the side of the road and there perish miserably. But if, on the other hand, by energetic perseverance he could reach Krasnoiarsk, all was perhaps not lost, since the governor, to whom he would make himself known, would not hesitate to give him the means of reaching Irkutsk.

Michael walked on, speaking little, absorbed in his own thoughts. He held Nadia's hand. The two were in incessant communication. It seemed to them that they had no need of words to exchange their thoughts. From time to time Michael said, "Speak to me, Nadia."

"Why should I, Michael? We are thinking together!" the young girl would reply, and contrived that her voice should not betray her extreme fatigue.

But sometimes, as if her heart had ceased to beat for an instant, her limbs tottered, her steps flagged, her arms fell to her sides, she dropped behind. Michael then stopped, he fixed his eyes on the poor girl, as though he would try to pierce the gloom which surrounded him; his breast heaved; then, supporting his companion more than before, he started on afresh.

However, amidst these continual miseries, a fortunate circumstance on that day occurred which it appeared likely would considerably ease their fatigue. They had been walking from Semilowskoe for two hours when Michael stopped.

"Is there no one on the road?"

"Not a single soul," replied Nadia.

"Do you not hear some noise behind us? If they are Tartars we must hide. Keep a good look-out!"

"Wait, Michael!" replied Nadia, going back a few steps to where the road turned to the right.

Michael Strogoff waited alone for a minute, listening attentively.

Nadia returned almost immediately and said, "It is a cart. A young man is leading it."

"Is he alone?"

"Alone."

Michael hesitated an instant. Should he hide? or should he, on the contrary, try to find a place in the vehicle, if not for himself, at least for her? For himself, he would be quite content to lay one hand on the cart, to push it if necessary, for his legs showed no sign of failing him; but he felt sure that Nadia, compelled to walk ever since they crossed the Obi, that is, for eight days, must be almost exhausted. He waited.

The cart was soon at the corner of the road. It was a very dilapidated vehicle, known in the country as a kibitka, just capable of holding three persons. Usually the kibitka is drawn by three horses, but this had but one, a beast with long hair and a very long tail. It was of the Mongol breed, known for strength and courage.

A young man was leading it, with a dog beside him. Nadia saw at once that the young man was Russian; his face was phlegmatic, but pleasant, and at once inspired confidence. He did not appear to be in the slightest hurry; he was not walking fast that he might spare his horse, and, to look at him, it would not have been believed that he was following a road which might at any instant be swarming with Tartars.

Nadia, holding Michael by the hand, made way for the vehicle. The kibitka stopped, and the driver smilingly looked at the young girl.

"And where are you going to in this fashion?" he asked, opening wide his great honest eyes.

At the sound of his voice, Michael said to himself that he had heard it before. And it was satisfactory to him to recognize the man for his brow at once cleared.

"Well, where are you going?" repeated the young man, addressing himself more directly to Michael.

"We are going to Irkutsk," he replied.

"Oh! little father, you do not know that there are still versts and versts between you and Irkutsk?"

"I know it."

"And you are going on foot?"

"On foot."

"You, well! but the young lady?"

"She is my sister," said Michael, who judged it prudent to give again this name to Nadia.

"Yes, your sister, little father! But, believe me, she will never be able to get to Irkutsk!"

"Friend," returned Michael, approaching him, "the Tartars have robbed us of everything, and I have not a copeck to offer you; but if you will take my sister with you, I will follow your cart on foot; I will run when necessary, I will not delay you an hour!"

"Brother," exclaimed Nadia, "I will not! I will not! Sir, my brother is blind!"

"Blind!" repeated the young man, much moved.

"The Tartars have burnt out his eyes!" replied Nadia, extending her hands, as if imploring pity.

"Burnt out his eyes! Oh! poor little father! I am going to Krasnoiarsk. Well, why should not you and your sister mount in the kibitka? By sitting a little close, it will hold us all three. Besides, my dog will not refuse to go on foot; only I don't go fast, I spare my horse."

"Friend, what is your name?" asked Michael.

"My name is Nicholas Pigassof."

"It is a name that I will never forget," said Michael.

136

"Well, jump up, little blind father. Your sister will be beside you, in the bottom of the cart; I sit in front to drive. There is plenty of good birch bark and straw in the bottom; it's like a nest. Serko, make room!"

The dog jumped down without more telling. He was an animal of the Siberian race, gray hair, of medium size, with an honest big head, just made to pat, and he, moreover, appeared to be much attached to his master.

In a moment more, Michael and Nadia were seated in the kibitka. Michael held out his hands as if to feel for those of Pigassof. "You wish to shake my hands!" said Nicholas. "There they are, little father! shake them as long as it will give you any pleasure."

The kibitka moved on; the horse, which Nicholas never touched with the whip, ambled along. Though Michael did not gain any in speed, at least some fatigue was spared to Nadia.

Such was the exhaustion of the young girl, that, rocked by the monotonous movement of the kibitka, she soon fell into a sleep, its soundness proving her complete prostration. Michael and Nicholas laid her on the straw as comfortably as possible. The compassionate young man was greatly moved, and if a tear did not escape from Michael's eyes, it was because the red-hot iron had dried up the last!

"She is very pretty," said Nicholas.

"Yes," replied Michael.

"They try to be strong, little father, they are brave, but they are weak after all, these dear little things! Have you come from far."

"Very far."

"Poor young people! It must have hurt you very much when they burnt your eyes!"

"Very much," answered Michael, turning towards Nicholas as if he could see him.

"Did you not weep?"

"Yes."

"I should have wept too. To think that one could never again see those one loves. But they can see you, however; that's perhaps some consolation!"

"Yes, perhaps. Tell me, my friend," continued Michael, "have you never seen me anywhere before?"

"You, little father? No, never."

"The sound of your voice is not unknown to me."

"Why!" returned Nicholas, smiling, "he knows the sound of my voice! Perhaps you ask me that to find out where I come from. I come from Kolyvan."

"From Kolyvan?" repeated Michael. "Then it was there I met you; you were in the telegraph office?"

"That may be," replied Nicholas. "I was stationed there. I was the clerk in charge of the messages."

"And you stayed at your post up to the last moment?"

"Why, it's at that moment one ought to be there!"

"It was the day when an Englishman and a Frenchman were disputing, roubles in hand, for the place at your wicket, and the Englishman telegraphed some poetry."

"That is possible, but I do not remember it."

"What! you do not remember it?"

"I never read the dispatches I send. My duty being to forget them, the shortest way is not to know them."

This reply showed Nicholas Pigassof's character. In the meanwhile the kibitka pursued its way, at a pace which Michael longed to render more rapid. But Nicholas and his horse were accustomed to a pace which neither of them would like to alter. The horse went for two hours and rested one— so on, day and night. During the halts the horse grazed, the travelers ate in company with the faithful Serko. The kibitka was provisioned for at least twenty persons, and Nicholas generously placed his supplies at the disposal of his two guests, whom he believed to be brother and sister.

After a day's rest, Nadia recovered some strength. Nicholas took the best possible care of her. The journey was being made under tolerable circumstances, slowly certainly, but surely. It sometimes happened that during the night, Nicholas, although driving, fell asleep, and snored with a clearness which showed the calmness of his conscience. Perhaps then, by looking close, Michael's hand might have been seen feeling for the reins, and giving the horse a more rapid pace, to the great astonishment of Serko, who, however, said nothing. The trot was exchanged for the amble as soon as Nicholas awoke, but the kibitka had not the less gained some versts.

Thus they passed the river Ichirnsk, the villages of Ichisnokoe, Berikylokoe, Kuskoe, the river Marunsk, the village of the same name, Bogostowskoe, and, lastly, the Ichoula, a little stream which divides Western from Eastern Siberia. The road now lay sometimes across wide moors, which extended as far as the eye could reach, sometimes through thick forests of firs, of which they thought they should never get to the end. Everywhere was a desert; the villages were almost entirely abandoned. The peasants had fled beyond the Yenisei, hoping that this wide river would perhaps stop the Tartars.

On the 22d of August, the kibitka entered the town of Atchinsk, two hundred and fifty miles from Tomsk. Eighty miles still lay between them and Krasnoiarsk.

No incident had marked the journey. For the six days during which they had been together, Nicholas, Michael, and Nadia had remained the same, the one in his unchange-able calm, the other two, uneasy, and thinking of the time when their companion would leave them.

Michael saw the country through which they traveled with the eyes of Nicholas and the young girl. In turns, they each described to him the scenes they passed. He knew whether he was in a forest or on a plain, whether a hut was on the steppe, or whether any Siberian was in sight. Nicholas was never silent, he loved to talk, and, from his peculiar way of viewing things, his friends were amused by his conversation. One day, Michael asked him what sort of weather it was.

"Fine enough, little father," he answered, "but soon we shall feel the first winter frosts. Perhaps the Tartars will go into winter quarters during the bad season."

Michael Strogoff shook his head with a doubtful air.

"You do not think so, little father?" resumed Nicholas. "You think that they will march on to Irkutsk?"

"I fear so," replied Michael.

"Yes... you are right; they have with them a bad man, who will not let them loiter on the way. You have heard speak of Ivan Ogareff?"

"Yes."

"You know that it is not right to betray one's country!"

"No... it is not right..." answered Michael, who wished to remain unmoved.

"Little father," continued Nicholas, "it seems to me that you are not half indignant enough when Ivan Ogareff is spoken of. Your Russian heart ought to leap when his name is uttered."

"Believe me, my friend, I hate him more than you can ever hate him," said Michael.

"It is not possible," replied Nicholas; "no, it is not possible! When I think of Ivan Ogareff, of the harm which he is doing to our sacred Russia, I get into such a rage that if I could get hold of him—"

"If you could get hold of him, friend?"

"I think I should kill him."

"And I, I am sure of it," returned Michael quietly.

CHAPTER VII
THE PASSAGE OF THE YENISEI

AT nightfall, on the 25th of August, the kibitka came in sight of Krasnoiarsk. The journey from Tomsk had taken eight days. If it had not been accomplished as rapidly as it might, it was because Nicholas had slept little. Consequently, it was impossible to increase his horse's pace, though in other hands, the journey would not have taken sixty hours.

Happily, there was no longer any fear of Tartars. Not a scout had appeared on the road over which the kibitka had just traveled. This was strange enough, and evidently some serious cause had prevented the Emir's troops from marching without delay upon Irkutsk. Something had occurred. A new Russian corps, hastily raised in the government of Yeniseisk, had marched to Tomsk to endeavor to retake the town. But, being too weak to withstand the Emir's troops, now concentrated there, they had been forced to effect a retreat. Feofar-Khan, including his own soldiers, and those of the Khanats of Khokhand and Koun-douze, had now under his command two hundred and fifty thousand men, to which the Russian government could not as yet oppose a sufficient force. The invasion could not, therefore, be immediately stopped, and the whole Tartar army might at once march upon Irkutsk. The battle of Tomsk was on the 22nd of August, though this Michael did not know, but it explained why the vanguard of the Emir's army had not appeared at Krasnoiarsk by the 25th.

However, though Michael Strogoff could not know the events which had occurred since his departure, he at least knew that he was several days in advance of the Tartars, and that he need not despair of reaching before them the town of Irkutsk, still six hundred miles distant.

Besides, at Krasnoiarsk, of which the population is about twelve thousand souls, he depended upon obtaining some means of transport. Since Nicholas Pigassof was to stop in that town, it would be necessary to replace him by a guide, and to change the kibitka for another more rapid vehicle. Michael, after having addressed himself to the governor of the town, and established his identity and quality as Courier of the Czar—which would be easy—doubted not that he would be enabled to get to Irkutsk in the shortest possible time. He would thank the good Nicholas Pigassof, and set out immediately with Nadia, for he did not wish to leave her until he had placed her in her father's arms. Though Nicholas had resolved to stop at Krasnoiarsk, it was only as he said, "on condition of finding employment there." In fact, this model clerk, after having stayed to the last minute at his post in Kolyvan, was endeavoring to place himself again at the disposal of the government. "Why should I receive a salary which I have not earned?" he would say.

In the event of his services not being required at Krasnoiarsk, which it was expected would be still in telegraphic communication with Irkutsk, he proposed to go to Oudinsk, or even to the capital of Siberia itself. In the latter case, he would continue to travel with the brother and sister; and where would they find a surer guide, or a more devoted friend?

The kibitka was now only half a verst from Krasnoiarsk. The numerous wooden crosses which are erected at the approaches to the town, could be seen to the right and left of the road. It was seven in the evening; the outline of the churches and of the houses built on the high bank of the Yenisei were clearly defined against the evening sky, and the waters of the river reflected them in the twilight.

"Where are we, sister?" asked Michael.

"Half a verst from the first houses," replied Nadia.

"Can the town be asleep?" observed Michael. "Not a sound strikes my ear."

"And I cannot see the slightest light, nor even smoke mounting into the air," added Nadia.

"What a queer town!" said Nicholas. "They make no noise in it, and go to bed uncommonly early!"

A presentiment of impending misfortune passed across Michael's heart. He had not said to Nadia that he had placed all his hopes on Krasnoiarsk, where he expected to find the means of safely finishing his journey. He much feared that his anticipations would again be disappointed.

But Nadia had guessed his thoughts, although she could not understand why her companion should be so anxious to reach Irkutsk, now that the Imperial letter was gone. She one day said something of the sort to him. "I have sworn to go to Irkutsk," he replied.

But to accomplish his mission, it was necessary that at Krasnoiarsk he should find some more rapid mode of locomotion. "Well, friend," said he to Nicholas, "why are we not going on?"

"Because I am afraid of waking up the inhabitants of the town with the noise of my carriage!" And with a light fleck of the whip, Nicholas put his horse in motion.

Ten minutes after they entered the High Street. Krasnoiarsk was deserted; there was no longer an Athenian in this "Northern Athens," as Madame de Bourboulon has called it. Not one of their dashing equipages swept through the wide, clean streets. Not a pedestrian enlivened the footpaths raised at the bases of the magnificent wooden houses, of monumental aspect! Not a Siberian belle, dressed in the last French fashion, promenaded the beautiful park, cleared in a forest of birch trees, which stretches away to the banks of the Yenisei! The great bell of the cathedral was dumb; the chimes of the churches were silent. Here was complete desolation. There was no longer a living being in this town, lately so lively!

The last telegram sent from the Czar's cabinet, before the rupture of the wire, had ordered the governor, the garrison, the inhabitants, whoever they might be, to leave Krasnoiarsk, to carry with them any articles of value, or which might be of use to the Tartars, and to take refuge at Irkutsk. The same injunction was given to all the villages of the province. It was the intention of the Muscovite government to lay the country desert before the invaders. No one thought for an instant of disputing these orders. They were executed, and this was the reason why not a single human being remained in Krasnoiarsk.

Michael Strogoff, Nadia, and Nicholas passed silently through the streets of the town. They felt half-stupefied. They themselves made the only sound to be heard in this dead city. Michael allowed nothing of what he felt to appear, but he inwardly raged against the bad luck which pursued him, his hopes being again disappointed.

"Alack, alack!" cried Nicholas, "I shall never get any employment in this desert!"

"Friend," said Nadia, "you must go on with us."

"I must indeed!" replied Nicholas. "The wire is no doubt still working between Oudinsk and Irkutsk, and there—Shall we start, little father?"

"Let us wait till to-morrow," answered Michael.

"You are right," said Nicholas. "We have the Yenisei to cross, and need light to see our way there!"

"To see!" murmured Nadia, thinking of her blind companion.

Nicholas heard her, and turning to Michael, "Forgive me, little father," said he. "Alas! night and day, it is true, are all the same to you!"

"Do not reproach yourself, friend," replied Michael, pressing his hand over his eyes. "With you for a guide I can still act. Take a few hours' repose. Nadia must rest too. To-morrow we will recommence our journey!"

Michael and his friends had not to search long for a place of rest. The first house, the door of which they pushed open, was empty, as well as all the others. Nothing could be found within but a few heaps of leaves. For want of better fodder the horse had to content himself with this scanty nourishment. The provisions of the kibitka were not yet exhausted, so each had a share. Then, after having knelt before a small picture of the Panaghia, hung on the wall, and still lighted up by a flickering lamp, Nicholas and the young girl slept, whilst Michael, over whom sleep had no influence, watched.

Before daybreak the next morning, the 26th of August, the horse was drawing the kibitka through the forests of birch trees towards the banks of the Yenisei. Michael was in much anxiety. How was he to cross the river, if, as was probable, all boats had been destroyed to retard the Tartars' march? He knew the Yenisei, its width was considerable, its currents strong. Ordinarily by means of boats specially built for the conveyance of travelers, carriages, and horses, the passage of the Yenisei takes about three hours, and then it is with extreme difficulty that the boats reach the opposite bank. Now, in the absence of any ferry, how was the kibitka to get from one bank to the other?

Day was breaking when the kibitka reached the left bank, where one of the wide alleys of the park ended. They were about a hundred feet above the Yenisei, and could therefore survey the whole of its wide course.

"Do you see a boat?" asked Michael, casting his eyes eagerly about from one side to the other, mechanically, no doubt, as if he could really see.

"It is scarcely light yet, brother," replied Nadia. "The fog is still thick, and we cannot see the water."

"But I hear it roaring," said Michael.

Indeed, from the fog issued a dull roaring sound. The waters being high rushed down with tumultuous violence. All three waited until the misty curtain should rise. The sun would not be long in dispersing the vapors.

"Well?" asked Michael.

"The fog is beginning to roll away, brother," replied Nadia, "and it will soon be clear."

"Then you do not see the surface of the water yet?"

"Not yet."

"Have patience, little father," said Nicholas. "All this will soon disappear. Look! here comes the breeze! It is driving away the fog. The trees on the opposite hills are already appearing. It is sweeping, flying away. The kindly rays of the sun have condensed all that mass of mist. Ah! how beautiful it is, my poor fellow, and how unfortunate that you cannot see such a lovely sight!"

"Do you see a boat?" asked Michael.

"I see nothing of the sort," answered Nicholas.

"Look well, friend, on this and the opposite bank, as far as your eye can reach. A raft, even a canoe?"

Nicholas and Nadia, grasping the bushes on the edge of the cliff, bent over the water. The view they thus obtained was extensive. At this place the Yenisei is not less than a mile in width, and forms two arms, of unequal size, through which the waters flow swiftly. Between these arms lie several islands, covered with alders, willows, and poplars, looking like verdant ships, anchored in the river. Beyond rise the high hills of the Eastern shore, crowned with forests, whose tops were then empurpled with light. The Yenisei stretched on either side as far as the eye could reach. The beautiful panorama lay before them for a distance of fifty versts.

But not a boat was to be seen. All had been taken away or destroyed, according to order. Unless the Tartars should bring with them materials for building a bridge of boats, their march towards Irkutsk would certainly be stopped for some time by this barrier, the Yenisei.

"I remember," said Michael, "that higher up, on the outskirts of Krasnoiarsk, there is a little quay. There the boats touch. Friend, let us go up the river, and see if some boat has not been forgotten on the bank."

Nadia seized Michael's hand and started off at a rapid pace in the direction indicated. If only a boat or a barge large enough to hold the kibitka could be found, or even one that would carry just themselves, Michael would not hesitate to attempt the passage! Twenty minutes after, all three had reached the little quay, with houses on each side quite down to the water's edge. It was like a village standing beyond the town of Krasnoiarsk.

But not a boat was on the shore, not a barge at the little wharf, nothing even of which a raft could be made large enough to carry three people. Michael questioned Nicholas, who made the discouraging reply that the crossing appeared to him absolutely impracticable.

"We shall cross!" answered Michael.

The search was continued. They examined the houses on the shore, abandoned like all the rest of Krasnoiarsk. They had merely to push open the doors and enter. The cottages were evidently those of poor people, and quite empty. Nicholas visited one, Nadia entered another, and even Michael went here and there and felt about, hoping to light upon some article that might be useful.

Nicholas and the girl had each fruitlessly rummaged these cottages and were about to give up the search, when they heard themselves called. Both ran to the bank and saw Michael standing on the threshold of a door.

"Come!" he exclaimed. Nicholas and Nadia went towards him and followed him into the cottage.

"What are these?" asked Michael, touching several objects piled up in a corner.

"They are leathern bottles," answered Nicholas.

"Are they full?"

"Yes, full of koumyss. We have found them very opportunely to renew our provisions!"

"Koumyss" is a drink made of mare's or camel's milk, and is very sustaining, and even intoxicating; so that Nicholas and his companions could not but congratulate themselves on the discovery.

"Save one," said Michael, "but empty the others."

"Directly, little father."

"These will help us to cross the Yenisei."

"And the raft?"

"Will be the kibitka itself, which is light enough to float. Besides, we will sustain it, as well as the horse, with these bottles."

"Well thought of, little father," exclaimed Nicholas, "and by God's help we will get safely over... though perhaps not in a straight line, for the current is very rapid!"

"What does that matter?" replied Michael. "Let us get across first, and we shall soon find out the road to Irkutsk on the other side of the river."

"To work, then," said Nicholas, beginning to empty the bottles.

One full of koumyss was reserved, and the rest, with the air carefully fastened in, were used to form a floating apparatus. Two bottles were fastened to the horse's sides to support it in the water. Two others were attached to the shafts to keep them on a level with the body of the machine, thus transformed into a raft. This work was soon finished.

"You will not be afraid, Nadia?" asked Michael.

"No, brother," answered the girl.

"And you, friend?"

"I?" cried Nicholas. "I am now going to have one of my dreams realized—that of sailing in a cart."

At the spot where they were now standing, the bank sloped, and was suitable for the launching of the kibitka. The horse drew it into the water, and they were soon both floating. As to Serko, he was swimming bravely.

The three passengers, seated in the vehicle, had with due precaution taken off their shoes and stockings; but, thanks to the bottles, the water did not even come over their ankles. Michael held the reins, and, according to Nicholas's directions, guided the animal obliquely, but cautiously, so as not to exhaust him by struggling against the current. So long as the kibitka went with the current all was easy, and in a few minutes it had passed the quays of Krasnoiarsk. It drifted northwards, and it was soon evident that it would only reach the opposite bank far below the town. But that mattered little. The crossing would have been made without great difficulty, even on this imperfect apparatus, had the current been regular; but, unfortunately, there were whirlpools in numbers, and soon the kibitka, notwithstanding all Michael's efforts, was irresistibly drawn into one of these.

There the danger was great. The kibitka no longer drifted, but spun rapidly round, inclining towards the center of the eddy, like a rider in a circus. The horse could scarcely keep his head above water, and ran a great risk of being suffocated. Serko had been obliged to take refuge in the carriage.

Michael knew what was happening. He felt himself drawn round in a gradually narrowing line, from which they could not get free. How he longed to see, to be better able to avoid this peril, but that was no longer possible. Nadia was silent, her hands clinging to the sides of the cart, which was inclining more and more towards the center of depression.

And Nicholas, did he not understand the gravity of the situation? Was it with him phlegm or contempt of danger, courage or indifference? Was his life valueless in his eyes, and, according to the Eastern expression, "an hotel for five days," which, whether one is willing or not, must be left the sixth? At any rate, the smile on his rosy face never faded for an instant.

The kibitka was thus in the whirlpool, and the horse was nearly exhausted, when, all at once, Michael, throwing off such of his garments as might impede him, jumped into the water; then, seizing with a strong hand the bridle of the terrified horse, he gave him such an impulse that he managed to struggle out of the circle, and getting again into the current, the kibitka drifted along anew.

"Hurrah!" exclaimed Nicholas.

Two hours after leaving the wharf, the kibitka had crossed the widest arm of the river, and had landed on an island more than six versts below the starting point.

There the horse drew the cart onto the bank, and an hour's rest was given to the courageous animal; then the island having been crossed under the shade of its magnificent birches, the kibitka found itself on the shore of the smaller arm of the Yenisei.

This passage was much easier; no whirlpools broke the course of the river in this second bed; but the current was so rapid that the kibitka only reached the opposite side five versts below. They had drifted eleven versts in all.

These great Siberian rivers across which no bridges have as yet been thrown, are serious obstacles to the facility of communication. All had been more or less unfortunate to Michael Strogoff. On the Irtych, the boat which carried him and Nadia had been attacked by Tartars. On the Obi, after his horse had been struck by a bullet, he had only by a miracle escaped from the horsemen who were pursuing him. In fact, this passage of the Yenisei had been performed the least disastrously.

"That would not have been so amusing," exclaimed Nicholas, rubbing his hands, as they disembarked on the right bank of the river, "if it had not been so difficult."

"That which has only been difficult to us, friend," answered Michael Strogoff, "will, perhaps, be impossible to the Tartars."

CHAPTER VIII

A HARE CROSSES THE ROAD

MICHAEL STROGOFF might at last hope that the road to Irkutsk was clear. He had distanced the Tartars, now detained at Tomsk, and when the Emir's soldiers should arrive at Krasnoiarsk they would find only a deserted town. There being no communication between the two banks of the Yenisei, a delay of some days would be caused until a bridge of boats could be established, and to accomplish this would be a difficult undertaking. For the first time since the encounter with Ivan Ogareff at Omsk, the courier of the Czar felt less uneasy, and began to hope that no fresh obstacle would delay his progress.

The road was good, for that part of it which extends between Krasnoiarsk and Irkutsk is considered the best in the whole journey; fewer jolts for travelers, large trees to shade them from the heat of the sun, sometimes forests of pines or cedars covering an extent of a hundred versts. It was no longer the wide steppe with limitless horizon; but the rich country was empty. Everywhere they came upon deserted villages. The Siberian peasantry had vanished. It was a desert, but a desert by order of the Czar.

The weather was fine, but the air, which cooled during the night, took some time to get warm again. Indeed it was now near September, and in this high region the days were sensibly shortening. Autumn here lasts but a very little while, although this part of Siberian territory is not situated above the fifty-fifth parallel, that of Edinburgh and Copenhagen. However, winter succeeds summer almost unexpectedly. These winters of Asiatic Russia may be said to be precocious, considering that during them the thermometer falls until the mercury is frozen nearly 42 degrees below zero, and that 20 degrees below zero is considered an unsupportable temperature.

The weather favored our travelers. It was neither stormy nor rainy. The health of Nadia and Michael was good, and since leaving Tomsk they had gradually recovered from their past fatigues.

As to Nicholas Pigassof, he had never been better in his life. To him this journey was a trip, an agreeable excursion in which he employed his enforced holiday.

"Decidedly," said he, "this is pleasanter than sitting twelve hours a day, perched on a stool, working the manip-ulator!"

Michael had managed to get Nicholas to make his horse quicken his pace. To obtain this result, he had confided to Nicholas that Nadia and he were on their way to join their father, exiled at Irkutsk, and that they were very anxious to get there. Certainly, it would not do to overwork the horse, for very probably they would not be able to exchange him for another; but by giving him frequent rests—every ten miles, for instance—forty miles in twenty-four hours could easily be accomplished. Besides, the animal was strong, and of a race calculated to endure great fatigue. He was in no want of rich pasturage along the road, the grass being thick and abundant. Therefore, it was possible to demand an increase of work from him.

Nicholas gave in to all these reasons. He was much moved at the situation of these two young people, going to share their father's exile. Nothing had ever appeared so touching to him. With what a smile he said to Nadia: "Divine goodness! what joy will Mr. Korpanoff feel, when his eyes behold you, when his arms open to receive you! If I go to Irkutsk—and that appears very probable now—will you permit me to be present at that interview! You will, will you not?" Then, striking his forehead: "But, I forgot, what grief too when he sees that his poor son is blind! Ah! everything is mingled in this world!"

However, the result of all this was the kibitka went faster, and, according to Michael's calculations, now made almost eight miles an hour.

After crossing the little river Biriousa, the kibitka reached Biriousensk on the morning of the 4th of September. There, very fortunately, for Nicholas saw that his provisions were becoming exhausted, he found in an oven a dozen "pogatchas," a kind of cake prepared with sheep's fat and a large supply of plain boiled rice. This increase was very opportune, for something would soon have been needed to replace the koumyss with which the kibitka had been stored at Krasnoiarsk.

After a halt, the journey was continued in the afternoon. The distance to Irkutsk was not now much over three hundred miles. There was not a sign of the Tartar vanguard. Michael Strogoff had some grounds for hoping that his journey would not be again delayed, and that in eight days, or at most ten, he would be in the presence of the Grand Duke.

On leaving Biriousinsk, a hare ran across the road, in front of the kibitka. "Ah!" exclaimed Nicholas.

"What is the matter, friend?" asked Michael quickly, like a blind man whom the least sound arouses.

"Did you not see?" said Nicholas, whose bright face had become suddenly clouded. Then he added, "Ah! no! you could not see, and it's lucky for you, little father!"

"But I saw nothing," said Nadia.

"So much the better! So much the better! But I—I saw!"

"What was it then?" asked Michael.

"A hare crossing our road!" answered Nicholas.

In Russia, when a hare crosses the path, the popular belief is that it is the sign of approaching evil. Nicholas, superstitious like the greater number of Russians, stopped the kibitka.

Michael understood his companion's hesitation, without sharing his credulity, and endeavored to reassure him, "There is nothing to fear, friend," said he.

"Nothing for you, nor for her, I know, little father," answered Nicholas, "but for me!"

"It is my fate," he continued. And he put his horse in motion again. However, in spite of these forebodings the day passed without any accident.

At twelve o'clock the next day, the 6th of September, the kibitka halted in the village of Alsalevok, which was as deserted as the surrounding country. There, on a doorstep, Nadia found two of those strong-bladed knives used by Siberian hunters. She gave one to Michael, who concealed it among his clothes, and kept the other herself.

Nicholas had not recovered his usual spirits. The ill-omen had affected him more than could have been believed, and he who formerly was never half an hour without speaking, now fell into long reveries from which Nadia found it difficult to arouse him. The kibitka rolled swiftly along the road. Yes, swiftly! Nicholas no longer thought of being so careful of his horse, and was as anxious to arrive at his journey's end as Michael himself. Notwithstanding his fatalism, and though resigned, he would not believe himself in safety until within the walls of Irkutsk. Many Russians would have thought as he did, and more than one would have turned his horse and gone back again, after a hare had crossed his path.

Some observations made by him, the justice of which was proved by Nadia transmitting them to Michael, made them fear that their trials were not yet over. Though the land from Krasnoiarsk had been respected in its natural productions, its forests now bore trace of fire and steel; and it was evident that some large body of men had passed that way.

Twenty miles before Nijni-Oudinsk, the indications of recent devastation could not be mistaken, and it was impossible to attribute them to others than the Tartars. It was not only that the fields were trampled by horse's feet, and that trees were cut down. The few houses scattered along the road were not only empty, some had been partly demolished, others half burnt down. The marks of bullets could be seen on their walls.

Michael's anxiety may be imagined. He could no longer doubt that a party of Tartars had recently passed that way, and yet it was impossible that they could be the Emir's soldiers, for they could not have passed without being seen. But then, who were these new invaders, and by what out-of-the-way path across the steppe had they been able to join the highroad to Irkutsk? With what new enemies was the Czar's courier now to meet?

He did not communicate his apprehensions either to Nicholas or Nadia, not wishing to make them uneasy. Besides, he had resolved to continue his way, as long as no insurmountable obstacle stopped him. Later, he would see what it was best to do. During the ensuing day, the recent passage of a large body of foot and horse became more and more apparent. Smoke was seen above the horizon. The kibitka advanced cautiously. Several houses in deserted villages still burned, and could not have been set on fire more than four and twenty hours before.

At last, during the day, on the 8th of September, the kibitka stopped suddenly. The horse refused to advance. Serko barked furiously.

"What is the matter?" asked Michael.

"A corpse!" replied Nicholas, who had leapt out of the kibitka. The body was that of a moujik, horribly mutilated, and already cold. Nicholas crossed himself. Then, aided by Michael, he carried the body to the side of the road. He would have liked to give it decent burial, that the wild beasts of the steppe might not feast on the miserable remains, but Michael could not allow him the time.

"Come, friend, come!" he exclaimed, "we must not delay, even for an hour!" And the kibitka was driven on.

Besides, if Nicholas had wished to render the last duties to all the dead bodies they were now to meet with on the Siberian highroad, he would have had enough to do! As they approached Nijni-Oudinsk, they were found by twenties, stretched on the ground.

It was, however, necessary to follow this road until it was manifestly impossible to do so longer without falling into the hands of the invaders. The road they were following could not be abandoned, and yet the signs of devastation and ruin increased at every village they passed through. The blood of the victims was not yet dry. As to gaining information about what had occurred, that was impossible. There was not a living being left to tell the tale.

About four o'clock in the afternoon of this day, Nicholas caught sight of the tall steeples of the churches of Nijni-Oudinsk. Thick vapors, which could not have been clouds, were floating around them.

Nicholas and Nadia looked, and communicated the result of their observations to Michael. They must make up their minds what to do. If the town was abandoned, they could pass through without risk, but if, by some inexplicable maneuver, the Tartars occupied it, they must at every cost avoid the place.

"Advance cautiously," said Michael Strogoff, "but advance!"

A verst was soon traversed.

"Those are not clouds, that is smoke!" exclaimed Nadia. "Brother, they are burning the town!"

It was, indeed, only too plain. Flashes of light appeared in the midst of the vapor. It became thicker and thicker as it mounted upwards. But were they Tartars who had done this? They might be Russians, obeying the orders of the Grand Duke. Had the government of the Czar determined that from Krasnoiarsk, from the Yenisei, not a town, not a village should offer a refuge to the Emir's soldiers? What was Michael to do?

He was undecided. However, having weighed the pros and cons, he thought that whatever might be the difficulties of a journey across the steppe without a beaten path, he ought not to risk capture a second time by the Tartars. He was just proposing to Nicholas to leave the road, when a shot was heard on their right. A ball whistled, and the horse of the kibitka fell dead, shot through the head.

A dozen horsemen dashed forward, and the kibitka was surrounded. Before they knew where they were, Michael, Nadia, and Nicholas were prisoners, and were being dragged rapidly towards Nijni-Oudinsk.

Michael, in this second attack, had lost none of his presence of mind. Being unable to see his enemies, he had not thought of defending himself. Even had he possessed the use of his eyes, he would not have attempted it. The consequences would have been his death and that of his

149

companions. But, though he could not see, he could listen and understand what was said.

From their language he found that these soldiers were Tartars, and from their words, that they preceded the invading army.

In short, what Michael learnt from the talk at the present moment, as well as from the scraps of conversation he overheard later, was this. These men were not under the direct orders of the Emir, who was now detained beyond the Yenisei. They made part of a third column chiefly composed of Tartars from the khanats of Khokland and Koondooz, with which Feofar's army was to affect a junction in the neighborhood of Irkutsk.

By Ogareff's advice, in order to assure the success of the invasion in the Eastern provinces, this column had skirted the base of the Altai Mountains. Pillaging and ravaging, it had reached the upper course of the Yenisei. There, guessing what had been done at Krasnoiarsk by order of the Czar, and to facilitate the passage of the river to the Emir's troops, this column had launched a flotilla of boats, which would enable Feofar to cross and resume the road to Irkutsk. Having done this, it had descended the valley of the Yenisei and struck the road on a level with Alsalevsk. From this little town began the frightful course of ruin which forms the chief part of Tartar warfare. Nijni-Oudinsk had shared the common fate, and the Tartars, to the number of fifty thousand, had now quitted it to take up a position before Irkutsk. Before long, they would be reinforced by the Emir's troops.

Such was the state of affairs at this date, most serious for this isolated part of Eastern Siberia, and for the comparatively few defenders of its capital.

It can be imagined with what thoughts Michael's mind was now occupied! Who could have been astonished had he, in his present situation, lost all hope and all courage? Nothing of the sort, however; his lips muttered no other words than these: "I will get there!"

Half an hour after the attack of the Tartar horsemen, Michael Strogoff, Nadia, and Nicholas entered Nijni-Oudinsk. The faithful dog followed them, though at a distance. They could not stay in the town, as it was in flames, and about to be left by the last of the marauders. The prisoners were therefore thrown on horses and hurried away; Nicholas resigned as usual, Nadia, her faith in Michael unshaken, and Michael himself, apparently indifferent, but ready to seize any opportunity of escaping.

The Tartars were not long in perceiving that one of their prisoners was blind, and their natural barbarity led them to make game of their unfortunate victim. They were traveling fast. Michael's horse, having no one to guide him, often started aside, and so made confusion among the ranks. This drew on his rider such abuse and brutality as wrung Nadia's heart, and filled Nicholas with indignation. But what could they do? They could not speak the Tartar language, and their assistance was mercilessly refused. Soon it occurred to these men, in a refinement of cruelty, to

150

exchange the horse Michael was riding for one which was blind. The motive of the change was explained by a remark which Michael overheard, "Perhaps that Russian can see, after all!"

Michael was placed on this horse, and the reins ironically put into his hand. Then, by dint of lashing, throwing stones, and shouting, the animal was urged into a gallop. The horse, not being guided by his rider, blind as himself, sometimes ran into a tree, sometimes went quite off the road—in consequence, collisions and falls, which might have been extremely dangerous.

Michael did not complain. Not a murmur escaped him. When his horse fell, he waited until it got up. It was, indeed, soon assisted up, and the cruel fun continued. At sight of this wicked treatment, Nicholas could not contain himself; he endeavored to go to his friend's aid. He was prevented, and treated brutally.

This game would have been prolonged, to the Tartars' great amusement, had not a serious accident put an end to it. On the 10th of September the blind horse ran away, and made straight for a pit, some thirty or forty feet deep, at the side of the road.

Nicholas tried to go after him. He was held back. The horse, having no guide, fell with his rider to the bottom. Nicholas and Nadia uttered a piercing cry! They believed that their unfortunate companion had been killed.

However, when they went to his assistance, it was found that Michael, having been able to throw himself out of the saddle, was unhurt, but the miserable horse had two legs broken, and was quite useless. He was left there to die without being put out of his suffering, and Michael, fastened to a Tartar's saddle, was obliged to follow the detachment on foot.

Even now, not a protest, not a complaint! He marched with a rapid step, scarcely drawn by the cord which tied him. He was still "the Man of Iron," of whom General Kissoff had spoken to the Czar!

The next day, the 11th of September, the detachment passed through the village of Chibarlinskoe. Here an incident occurred which had serious consequences. It was nightfall. The Tartar horsemen, having halted, were more or less intoxicated. They were about to start. Nadia, who till then, by a miracle, had been respectfully treated by the soldiers, was insulted by one of them.

Michael could not see the insult, nor the insulter, but Nicholas saw for him. Then, quietly, without thinking, without perhaps knowing what he was doing, Nicholas walked straight up to the man, and, before the latter could make the least movement to stop him, had seized a pistol from his holster and discharged it full at his breast.

The officer in command of the detachment hastened up on hearing the report. The soldiers would have cut the unfortunate Nicholas to pieces, but at a sign from their officer, he was bound instead, placed across a horse, and the detachment galloped off.

The rope which fastened Michael, gnawed through by him, broke by the sudden start of the horse, and the half-tipsy rider galloped on without perceiving that his prisoner had escaped.

Michael and Nadia found themselves alone on the road.

CHAPTER IX
IN THE STEPPE

MICHAEL STROGOFF and Nadia were once more as free as they had been in the journey from Perm to the banks of the Irtych. But how the conditions under which they traveled were altered! Then, a comfortable tarantass, fresh horses, well-kept post-horses assured the rapidity of their journey. Now they were on foot; it was utterly impossible to procure any other means of locomotion, they were without resources, not knowing how to obtain even food, and they had still nearly three hundred miles to go! Moreover, Michael could now only see with Nadia's eyes.

As to the friend whom chance had given them, they had just lost him, and fearful might be his fate. Michael had thrown himself down under the brushwood at the side of the road. Nadia stood beside him, waiting for the word from him to continue the march.

It was ten o'clock. The sun had more than three hours before disappeared below the horizon. There was not a house in sight. The last of the Tartars was lost in the distance. Michael and Nadia were quite alone.

"What will they do with our friend?" exclaimed the girl. "Poor Nicholas! Our meeting will have been fatal to him!" Michael made no response.

"Michael," continued Nadia, "do you not know that he defended you when you were the Tartars' sport; that he risked his life for me?"

Michael was still silent. Motionless, his face buried in his hands; of what was he thinking? Perhaps, although he did not answer, he heard Nadia speak.

Yes! he heard her, for when the young girl added, "Where shall I lead you, Michael?"

"To Irkutsk!" he replied.

"By the highroad?"

"Yes, Nadia."

Michael was still the same man who had sworn, whatever happened, to accomplish his object. To follow the highroad, was certainly to go the shortest way. If the vanguard of Feofar-Khan's troops appeared, it would then be time to strike across the country.

Nadia took Michael's hand, and they started.

The next morning, the 13th of September, twenty versts further, they made a short halt in the village of Joulounov-skoe. It was burnt and deserted. All night Nadia had tried to see if the body of Nicholas had not been left on the road, but it was in vain that she looked among the ruins, and searched among the dead. Was he reserved for some cruel torture at Irkutsk?

Nadia, exhausted with hunger, was fortunate enough to find in one of the houses a quantity of dried meat and "soukharis," pieces of bread, which, dried by evaporation, preserve their nutritive qualities for an indefinite time.

Michael and the girl loaded themselves with as much as they could carry. They had thus a supply of food for several days, and as to water, there would be no want of that in a district rendered fertile by the numerous little affluents of the Angara.

They continued their journey. Michael walked with a firm step, and only slackened his pace for his companion's sake. Nadia, not wishing to retard him, obliged herself to walk. Happily, he could not see to what a miserable state fatigue had reduced her.

However, Michael guessed it. "You are quite done up, poor child," he said sometimes.

"No," she would reply.

"When you can no longer walk, I will carry you."

"Yes, Michael."

During this day they came to the little river Oka, but it was fordable, and they had no difficulty in crossing. The sky was cloudy and the temperature moderate. There was some fear that the rain might come on, which would much have increased their misery. A few showers fell, but they did not last.

They went on as before, hand in hand, speaking little, Nadia looking about on every side; twice a day they halted. Six hours of the night were given to sleep. In a few huts Nadia again found a little mutton; but, contrary to Michael's hopes, there was not a single beast of burden in the country; horses, camels—all had been either killed or carried off. They must still continue to plod on across this weary steppe on foot.

The third Tartar column, on its way to Irkutsk, had left plain traces: here a dead horse, there an abandoned cart. The bodies of unfortunate Siberians lay along the road, principally at the entrances to villages. Nadia, overcoming her repugnance, looked at all these corpses!

The chief danger lay, not before, but behind. The advance guard of the Emir's army, commanded by Ivan Ogareff, might at any moment appear. The boats sent down the lower Yenisei must by this time have reached Krasnoiarsk and been made use of. The road was therefore open to the invaders. No Russian force could be opposed to them between Krasnoiarsk and Lake Baikal, Michael therefore expected before long the appearance of the Tartar scouts.

At each halt, Nadia climbed some hill and looked anxiously to the Westward, but as yet no cloud of dust had signaled the approach of a troop of horse.

Then the march was resumed; and when Michael felt that he was dragging poor Nadia forward too rapidly, he went at a slower pace. They spoke little, and only of Nicholas. The young girl recalled all that this companion of a few days had done for them.

In answering, Michael tried to give Nadia some hope of which he did not feel a spark himself, for he well knew that the unfortunate fellow would not escape death.

One day Michael said to the girl, "You never speak to me of my mother, Nadia."

His mother! Nadia had never wished to do so. Why renew his grief? Was not the old Siberian dead? Had not her son given the last kiss to her corpse stretched on the plain of Tomsk?

"Speak to me of her, Nadia," said Michael. "Speak—you will please me."

And then Nadia did what she had not done before. She told all that had passed between Marfa and herself since their meeting at Omsk, where they had seen each other for the first time. She said how an inexplicable instinct had led her towards the old prisoner without knowing who she was, and what encouragement she had received in return. At that time Michael Strogoff had been to her but Nicholas Korpanoff.

"Whom I ought always to have been," replied Michael, his brow darkening.

Then later he added, "I have broken my oath, Nadia. I had sworn not to see my mother!"

"But you did not try to see her, Michael," replied Nadia. "Chance alone brought you into her presence."

"I had sworn, whatever might happen, not to betray myself."

"Michael, Michael! at sight of the lash raised upon Marfa, could you refrain? No! No oath could prevent a son from succoring his mother!"

"I have broken my oath, Nadia," returned Michael. "May God and the Father pardon me!"

"Michael," resumed the girl, "I have a question to ask you. Do not answer it if you think you ought not. Nothing from you would vex me!"

"Speak, Nadia."

"Why, now that the Czar's letter has been taken from you, are you so anxious to reach Irkutsk?"

Michael tightly pressed his companion's hand, but he did not answer.

"Did you know the contents of that letter before you left Moscow?"

"No, I did not know."

"Must I think, Michael, that the wish alone to place me in my father's hands draws you toward Irkutsk?"

"No, Nadia," replied Michael, gravely. "I should deceive you if I allowed you to believe that it was so. I go where duty orders me to go. As to taking you to Irkutsk, is it not you, Nadia, who are now taking me there? Do I not see with your eyes; and is it not your hand that guides me? Have you not repaid a hundred-fold the help which I was able to give you at first? I do not know if fate will cease to go against us; but the day on which

154

you thank me for having placed you in your father's hands, I in my turn will thank you for having led me to Irkutsk."

"Poor Michael!" answered Nadia, with emotion. "Do not speak so. That does not answer me. Michael, why, now, are you in such haste to reach Irkutsk?"

"Because I must be there before Ivan Ogareff," exclaimed Michael.

"Even now?"

"Even now, and I will be there, too!"

In uttering these words, Michael did not speak solely through hatred to the traitor. Nadia understood that her companion had not told, or could not tell, her all.

On the 15th of September, three days later, the two reached the village of Kouitounskoe. The young girl suffered dreadfully. Her aching feet could scarcely support her; but she fought, she struggled, against her weariness, and her only thought was this: "Since he cannot see me, I will go on till I drop."

There were no obstacles on this part of the journey, no danger either since the departure of the Tartars, only much fatigue. For three days it continued thus. It was plain that the third invading column was advancing rapidly in the East; that could be seen by the ruins which they left after them—the cold cinders and the already decomposing corpses.

There was nothing to be seen in the West; the Emir's advance-guard had not yet appeared. Michael began to consider the various reasons which might have caused this delay. Was a sufficient force of Russians directly menacing Tomsk or Krasnoiarsk? Did the third column, isolated from the others, run a risk of being cut off? If this was the case, it would be easy for the Grand Duke to defend Irkutsk, and any time gained against an invasion was a step towards repulsing it. Michael sometimes let his thoughts run on these hopes, but he soon saw their improbability, and felt that the preservation of the Grand Duke depended alone on him.

Nadia dragged herself along. Whatever might be her moral energy, her physical strength would soon fail her. Michael knew it only too well. If he had not been blind, Nadia would have said to him, "Go, Michael, leave me in some hut! Reach Irkutsk! Accomplish your mission! See my father! Tell him where I am! Tell him that I wait for him, and you both will know where to find me! Start! I am not afraid! I will hide myself from the Tartars! I will take care of myself for him, for you! Go, Michael! I can go no farther!"

Many times Nadia was obliged to stop. Michael then took her in his strong arms and, having no longer to think of her fatigue, walked more rapidly and with his indefatigable step.

On the 18th of September, at ten in the evening, Kimilteiskoe was at last entered. From the top of a hill, Nadia saw in the horizon a long light line. It was the Dinka River. A few lightning flashes were reflected in the water; summer lightning, without thunder. Nadia led her companion through the ruined village. The cinders were quite cold. The last of the Tartars had passed through at least five or six days before.

Beyond the village, Nadia sank down on a stone bench. "Shall we make a halt?" asked Michael.

"It is night, Michael," answered Nadia. "Do you not want to rest a few hours?"

"I would rather have crossed the Dinka," replied Michael, "I should like to put that between us and the Emir's advance-guard. But you can scarcely drag yourself along, my poor Nadia!"

"Come, Michael," returned Nadia, seizing her companion's hand and drawing him forward.

Two or three versts further the Dinka flowed across the Irkutsk road. The young girl wished to attempt this last effort asked by her companion. She found her way by the light from the flashes. They were then crossing a boundless desert, in the midst of which was lost the little river. Not a tree nor a hillock broke the flatness. Not a breath disturbed the atmosphere, whose calmness would allow the slightest sound to travel an immense distance.

Suddenly, Michael and Nadia stopped, as if their feet had been fast to the ground. The barking of a dog came across the steppe. "Do you hear?" said Nadia.

Then a mournful cry succeeded it—a despairing cry, like the last appeal of a human being about to die.

"Nicholas! Nicholas!" cried the girl, with a foreboding of evil. Michael, who was listening, shook his head.

"Come, Michael, come," said Nadia. And she who just now was dragging herself with difficulty along, suddenly recovered strength, under violent excitement.

"We have left the road," said Michael, feeling that he was treading no longer on powdery soil but on short grass.

"Yes, we must!" returned Nadia. "It was there, on the right, from which the cry came!"

In a few minutes they were not more than half a verst from the river. A second bark was heard, but, although more feeble, it was certainly nearer. Nadia stopped.

"Yes!" said Michael. "It is Serko barking!... He has followed his master!"

"Nicholas!" called the girl. Her cry was unanswered.

Michael listened. Nadia gazed over the plain illumined now and again with electric light, but she saw nothing. And yet a voice was again raised, this time murmuring in a plaintive tone, "Michael!"

Then a dog, all bloody, bounded up to Nadia.

It was Serko! Nicholas could not be far off! He alone could have murmured the name of Michael! Where was he? Nadia had no strength to call again. Michael, crawling on the ground, felt about with his hands.

Suddenly Serko uttered a fresh bark and darted towards a gigantic bird which had swooped down. It was a vulture. When Serko ran towards it, it rose, but returning struck at the dog. The latter leapt up at it. A blow from the formidable beak alighted on his head, and this time Serko fell back lifeless on the ground.

At the same moment a cry of horror escaped Nadia. "There... there!" she exclaimed.

A head issued from the ground! She had stumbled against it in the darkness.

Nadia fell on her knees beside it. Nicholas buried up to his neck, according to the atrocious Tartar custom, had been left in the steppe to die of thirst, and perhaps by the teeth of wolves or the beaks of birds of prey!

Frightful torture for the victim imprisoned in the ground—the earth pressed down so that he cannot move, his arms bound to his body like those of a corpse in its coffin! The miserable wretch, living in the mold of clay from which he is powerless to break out, can only long for the death which is so slow in coming!

There the Tartars had buried their prisoner three days before! For three days, Nicholas waited for the help which now came too late! The vultures had caught sight of the head on a level with the ground, and for some hours the dog had been defending his master against these ferocious birds!

Michael dug at the ground with his knife to release his friend! The eyes of Nicholas, which till then had been closed, opened.

He recognized Michael and Nadia. "Farewell, my friends!" he murmured. "I am glad to have seen you again! Pray for me!"

Michael continued to dig, though the ground, having been tightly rammed down, was as hard as stone, and he managed at last to get out the body of the unhappy man. He listened if his heart was still beating.... It was still!

He wished to bury him, that he might not be left exposed; and the hole into which Nicholas had been placed when living, was enlarged, so that he might be laid in it—dead! The faithful Serko was laid by his master.

At that moment, a noise was heard on the road, about half a verst distant. Michael Strogoff listened. It was evidently a detachment of horse advancing towards the Dinka. "Nadia, Nadia!" he said in a low voice.

Nadia, who was kneeling in prayer, arose. "Look, look!" said he.

"The Tartars!" she whispered.

It was indeed the Emir's advance-guard, passing rapidly along the road to Irkutsk.

"They shall not prevent me from burying him!" said Michael. And he continued his work.

Soon, the body of Nicholas, the hands crossed on the breast, was laid in the grave. Michael and Nadia, kneeling, prayed a last time for the poor fellow, inoffensive and good, who had paid for his devotion towards them with his life.

"And now," said Michael, as he threw in the earth, "the wolves of the steppe will not devour him."

Then he shook his fist at the troop of horsemen who were passing. "Forward, Nadia!" he said.

Michael could not follow the road, now occupied by the Tartars. He must cross the steppe and turn to Irkutsk. He had not now to trouble himself about crossing the Dinka. Nadia could not move, but she could see for him. He took her in his arms and went on towards the southwest of the province.

A hundred and forty miles still remained to be traversed. How was the distance to be performed? Should they not succumb to such fatigue? On what were they to live on the way? By what superhuman energy were they to pass the slopes of the Sayansk Mountains? Neither he nor Nadia could answer this!

And yet, twelve days after, on the 2d of October, at six o'clock in the evening, a wide sheet of water lay at Michael Strogoff's feet. It was Lake Baikal.

CHAPTER X
BAIKAL AND ANGARA

LAKE BAIKAL is situated seventeen hundred feet above the level of the sea. Its length is about six hundred miles, its breadth seventy. Its depth is not known. Madame de Bourboulon states that, according to the boatmen, it likes to be spoken of as "Madam Sea." If it is called "Sir Lake," it immediately lashes itself into fury. However, it is reported and believed by the Siberians that a Russian is never drowned in it.

This immense basin of fresh water, fed by more than three hundred rivers, is surrounded by magnificent volcanic mountains. It has no other outlet than the Angara, which after passing Irkutsk throws itself into the Yenisei, a little above the town of Yeniseisk. As to the mountains which encase it, they form a branch of the Toungouzes, and are derived from the vast system of the Altai.

In this territory, subject to peculiar climatical conditions, the autumn appears to be absorbed in the precocious winter. It was now the beginning of October. The sun set at five o'clock in the evening, and during the long nights the temperature fell to zero. The first snows, which would last till summer, already whitened the summits of the neighboring hills. During the Siberian winter this inland sea is frozen over to a thickness of several feet, and is crossed by the sleighs of caravans.

Either because there are people who are so wanting in politeness as to call it "Sir Lake," or for some more meteorological reason, Lake Baikal is subject to violent tempests. Its waves, short like those of all inland seas, are much feared by the rafts, prahms, and steamboats, which furrow it during the summer.

It was the southwest point of the lake which Michael had now reached, carrying Nadia, whose whole life, so to speak, was concentrated in her eyes. But what could these two expect, in this wild region, if it was not to die of exhaustion and famine? And yet, what remained of the long journey of four thousand miles for the Czar's courier to reach his end? Nothing but forty miles on the shore of the lake up to the mouth of the Angara, and sixty miles from the mouth of the Angara to Irkutsk; in all, a hundred miles, or three days' journey for a strong man, even on foot.

Could Michael Strogoff still be that man?

Heaven, no doubt, did not wish to put him to this trial. The fatality which had hitherto pursued his steps seemed for a time to spare him. This end of the Baikal, this part of the steppe, which he believed to be a desert, which it usually is, was not so now. About fifty people were collected at the angle formed by the end of the lake.

Nadia immediately caught sight of this group, when Michael, carrying her in his arms, issued from the mountain pass. The girl feared for a moment that it was a Tartar detachment, sent to beat the shores of the Baikal, in which case flight would have been impossible to them both. But Nadia was soon reassured.

"Russians!" she exclaimed. And with this last effort, her eyes closed and her head fell on Michael's breast.

But they had been seen, and some of these Russians, running to them, led the blind man and the girl to a little point at which was moored a raft.

The raft was just going to start. These Russians were fugitives of different conditions, whom the same interest had united at Lake Baikal. Driven back by the Tartar scouts, they hoped to obtain a refuge at Irkutsk, but not being able to get there by land, the invaders having occupied both banks of the Angara, they hoped to reach it by descending the river which flows through the town.

Their plan made Michael's heart leap; a last chance was before him, but he had strength to conceal this, wishing to keep his incognito more strictly than ever.

The fugitives' plan was very simple. A current in the lake runs along by the upper bank to the mouth of the Angara; this current they hoped to utilize, and with its assistance to reach the outlet of Lake Baikal. From this point to Irkutsk, the rapid waters of the river would bear them along at a rate of eight miles an hour. In a day and a half they might hope to be in sight of the town.

No kind of boat was to be found; they had been obliged to make one; a raft, or rather a float of wood, similar to those which usually are drifted down Siberian rivers, was constructed. A forest of firs, growing on the bank, had supplied the necessary materials; the trunks, fastened together with osiers, made a platform on which a hundred people could have easily found room.

On board this raft Michael and Nadia were taken. The girl had returned to herself; some food was given to her as well as to her companion. Then, lying on a bed of leaves, she soon fell into a deep sleep.

To those who questioned him, Michael Strogoff said nothing of what had taken place at Tomsk. He gave himself out as an inhabitant of

Krasnoiarsk, who had not been able to get to Irkutsk before the Emir's troops arrived on the left bank of the Dinka, and he added that, very probably, the bulk of the Tartar forces had taken up a position before the Siberian capital.

There was not a moment to be lost; besides, the cold was becoming more and more severe. During the night the temperature fell below zero; ice was already forming on the surface of the Baikal. Although the raft managed to pass easily over the lake, it might not be so easy between the banks of the Angara, should pieces of ice be found to block up its course.

At eight in the evening the moorings were cast off, and the raft drifted in the current along the shore. It was steered by means of long poles, under the management of several muscular moujiks. An old Baikal boatman took command of the raft. He was a man of sixty-five, browned by the sun, and lake breezes. A thick white beard flowed over his chest; a fur cap covered his head; his aspect was grave and austere. His large great-coat, fastened in at the waist, reached down to his heels. This taciturn old fellow was seated in the stern, and issued his commands by gestures. Besides, the chief work consisted in keeping the raft in the current, which ran along the shore, without drifting out into the open.

It has been already said that Russians of all conditions had found a place on the raft. Indeed, to the poor moujiks, the women, old men, and children, were joined two or three pilgrims, surprised on their journey by the invasion; a few monks, and a priest. The pilgrims carried a staff, a gourd hung at the belt, and they chanted psalms in a plaintive voice: one came from the Ukraine, another from the Yellow sea, and a third from the Finland provinces. This last, who was an aged man, carried at his waist a little padlocked collecting-box, as if it had been hung at a church door. Of all that he collected during his long and fatiguing pilgrimage, nothing was for himself; he did not even possess the key of the box, which would only be opened on his return.

The monks came from the North of the Empire. Three months before they had left the town of Archangel. They had visited the sacred islands near the coast of Carelia, the convent of Solovetsk, the convent of Troitsa, those of Saint Antony and Saint Theodosia, at Kiev, that of Kazan, as well as the church of the Old Believers, and they were now on their way to Irkutsk, wearing the robe, the cowl, and the clothes of serge.

As to the papa, or priest, he was a plain village pastor, one of the six hundred thousand popular pastors which the Russian Empire contains. He was clothed as miserably as the moujiks, not being above them in social position; in fact, laboring like a peasant on his plot of ground; baptis-ing, marrying, burying. He had been able to protect his wife and children from the brutality of the Tartars by sending them away into the Northern provinces. He himself had stayed in his parish up to the last moment; then he was obliged to fly, and, the Irkutsk road being stopped, had come to Lake Baikal.

These priests, grouped in the forward part of the raft, prayed at regular intervals, raising their voices in the silent night, and at the end of each sentence of their prayer, the "Slava Bogu," Glory to God! issued from their lips.

No incident took place during the night. Nadia remained in a sort of stupor, and Michael watched beside her; sleep only overtook him at long intervals, and even then his brain did not rest. At break of day, the raft, delayed by a strong breeze, which counteracted the course of the current, was still forty versts from the mouth of the Angara. It seemed probable that the fugitives could not reach it before three or four o'clock in the evening. This did not trouble them; on the contrary, for they would then descend the river during the night, and the darkness would also favor their entrance into Irkutsk.

The only anxiety exhibited at times by the old boatman was concerning the formation of ice on the surface of the water. The night had been excessively cold; pieces of ice could be seen drifting towards the West. Nothing was to be dreaded from these, since they could not drift into the Angara, having already passed the mouth; but pieces from the Eastern end of the lake might be drawn by the current between the banks of the river; this would cause difficulty, possibly delay, and perhaps even an insurmountable obstacle which would stop the raft.

Michael therefore took immense interest in ascertaining what was the state of the lake, and whether any large number of ice blocks appeared. Nadia being now awake, he questioned her often, and she gave him an account of all that was going on.

Whilst the blocks were thus drifting, curious phenomena were taking place on the surface of the Baikal. Magnificent jets, from springs of boiling water, shot up from some of those artesian wells which Nature has bored in the very bed of the lake. These jets rose to a great height and spread out in vapor, which was illuminated by the solar rays, and almost immediately condensed by the cold. This curious sight would have assuredly amazed a tourist traveling in peaceful times on this Siberian sea.

At four in the evening, the mouth of the Angara was signaled by the old boatman, between the high granite rocks of the shore. On the right bank could be seen the little port of Livenitchnaia, its church, and its few houses built on the bank. But the serious thing was that the ice blocks from the East were already drifting between the banks of the Angara, and consequently were descending towards Irkutsk. However, their number was not yet great enough to obstruct the course of the raft, nor the cold great enough to increase their number.

The raft arrived at the little port and there stopped. The old boatman wished to put into harbor for an hour, in order to make some repairs. The trunks threatened to separate, and it was important to fasten them more securely together to resist the rapid current of the Angara.

The old boatman did not expect to receive any fresh fugitives at Livenitchnaia, and yet, the moment the raft touched, two passengers, issuing from a deserted house, ran as fast as they could towards the beach.

Nadia seated on the raft, was abstractedly gazing at the shore. A cry was about to escape her. She seized Michael's hand, who at that moment raised his head.

"What is the matter, Nadia?" he asked.

"Our two traveling companions, Michael."

"The Frenchman and the Englishman whom we met in the defiles of the Ural?"

"Yes."

Michael started, for the strict incognito which he wished to keep ran a risk of being betrayed. Indeed, it was no longer as Nicholas Korpanoff that Jolivet and Blount would now see him, but as the true Michael Strogoff, Courier of the Czar. The two correspondents had already met him twice since their separation at the Ichim post-house—the first time at the Zabediero camp, when he laid open Ivan Ogareff's face with the knout; the second time at Tomsk, when he was condemned by the Emir. They therefore knew who he was and what depended on him.

Michael Strogoff rapidly made up his mind. "Nadia," said he, "when they step on board, ask them to come to me!"

It was, in fact, Blount and Jolivet, whom the course of events had brought to the port of Livenitchnaia, as it had brought Michael Strogoff. As we know, after having been present at the entry of the Tartars into Tomsk, they had departed before the savage execution which terminated the fete. They had therefore never suspected that their former traveling companion had not been put to death, but blinded by order of the Emir.

Having procured horses they had left Tomsk the same evening, with the fixed determination of henceforward dating their letters from the Russian camp of Eastern Siberia. They proceeded by forced marches towards Irkutsk. They hoped to distance Feofar-Khan, and would certainly have done so, had it not been for the unexpected apparition of the third column, come from the South, up the valley of the Yenisei. They had been cut off, as had been Michael, before being able even to reach the Dinka, and had been obliged to go back to Lake Baikal.

They had been in the place for three days in much perplexity, when the raft arrived. The fugitives' plan was explained to them. There was certainly a chance that they might be able to pass under cover of the night, and penetrate into Irkutsk. They resolved to make the attempt.

Alcide directly communicated with the old boatman, and asked a passage for himself and his companion, offering to pay anything he demanded, whatever it might be.

"No one pays here," replied the old man gravely; "every one risks his life, that is all!"

The two correspondents came on board, and Nadia saw them take their places in the forepart of the raft. Harry Blount was still the reserved Englishman, who had scarcely addressed a word to her during the whole passage over the Ural Mountains. Alcide Jolivet seemed to be rather more grave than usual, and it may be acknowledged that his gravity was justified by the circumstances.

Jolivet had, as has been said, taken his seat on the raft, when he felt a hand laid on his arm. Turning, he recognized Nadia, the sister of the man who was no longer Nicholas Korpanoff, but Michael Strogoff, Courier of the Czar. He was about to make an exclamation of surprise when he saw the young girl lay her finger on her lips.

"Come," said Nadia. And with a careless air, Alcide rose and followed her, making a sign to Blount to accompany him.

But if the surprise of the correspondents had been great at meeting Nadia on the raft it was boundless when they perceived Michael Strogoff, whom they had believed to be no longer living.

Michael had not moved at their approach. Jolivet turned towards the girl. "He does not see you, gentlemen," said Nadia. "The Tartars have burnt out his eyes! My poor brother is blind!"

A feeling of lively compassion exhibited itself on the faces of Blount and his companion. In a moment they were seated beside Michael, pressing his hand and waiting until he spoke to them.

"Gentlemen," said Michael, in a low voice, "you ought not to know who I am, nor what I am come to do in Siberia. I ask you to keep my secret. Will you promise me to do so?"

"On my honor," answered Jolivet.

"On my word as a gentleman," added Blount.

"Good, gentlemen."

"Can we be of any use to you?" asked Harry Blount. "Could we not help you to accomplish your task?"

"I prefer to act alone," replied Michael.

"But those blackguards have destroyed your sight," said Alcide.

"I have Nadia, and her eyes are enough for me!"

In half an hour the raft left the little port of Livenitchnaia, and entered the river. It was five in the evening and getting dusk. The night promised to be dark and very cold also, for the temperature was already below zero.

Alcide and Blount, though they had promised to keep Michael's secret, did not leave him. They talked in a low voice, and the blind man, adding what they told him to what he already knew, was able to form an exact idea of the state of things. It was certain that the Tartars had actually invested Irkutsk, and that the three columns had effected a junction. There was no doubt that the Emir and Ivan Ogareff were before the capital.

But why did the Czar's courier exhibit such haste to get there, now that the Imperial letter could no longer be given by him to the Grand Duke, and when he did not even know the contents of it? Alcide Jolivet and Blount could not understand it any more than Nadia had done.

No one spoke of the past, except when Jolivet thought it his duty to say to Michael, "We owe you some apology for not shaking hands with you when we separated at Ichim."

"No, you had reason to think me a coward!"

"At any rate," added the Frenchman, "you knouted the face of that villain finely, and he will carry the mark of it for a long time!"

"No, not a long time!" replied Michael quietly.

Half an hour after leaving Livenitchnaia, Blount and his companion were acquainted with the cruel trials through which Michael and his companion had successively passed. They could not but heartily admire his energy, which was only equaled by the young girl's devotion. Their opinion of Michael was exactly what the Czar had expressed at Moscow: "Indeed, this is a Man!"

The raft swiftly threaded its way among the blocks of ice which were carried along in the current of the Angara. A moving panorama was displayed on both sides of the river, and, by an optical illusion, it appeared as if it was the raft which was motionless before a succession of picturesque scenes. Here were high granite cliffs, there wild gorges, down which rushed a torrent; sometimes appeared a clearing with a still smoking village, then thick pine forests blazing. But though the Tartars had left their traces on all sides, they themselves were not to be seen as yet, for they were more especially massed at the approaches to Irkutsk.

All this time the pilgrims were repeating their prayers aloud, and the old boatman, shoving away the blocks of ice which pressed too near them, imperturbably steered the raft in the middle of the rapid current of the Angara.

CHAPTER XI
BETWEEN TWO BANKS

BY eight in the evening, the country, as the state of the sky had foretold, was enveloped in complete darkness. The moon being new had not yet risen. From the middle of the river the banks were invisible. The cliffs were confounded with the heavy, low-hanging clouds. At intervals a puff of wind came from the east, but it soon died away in the narrow valley of the Angara.

The darkness could not fail to favor in a considerable degree the plans of the fugitives. Indeed, although the Tartar outposts must have been drawn up on both banks, the raft had a good chance of passing unperceived. It was not likely either that the besiegers would have barred the river above Irkutsk, since they knew that the Russians could not expect any help from the south of the province. Besides this, before long Nature would herself establish a barrier, by cementing with frost the blocks of ice accumulated between the two banks.

Perfect silence now reigned on board the raft. The voices of the pilgrims were no longer heard. They still prayed, but their prayer was but a murmur, which could not reach as far as either bank. The fugitives lay flat on the platform, so that the raft was scarcely above the level of the water. The old boatman crouched down forward among his men, solely occupied in keeping off the ice blocks, a maneuver which was performed without noise.

The drifting of the ice was a favorable circumstance so long as it did not offer an insurmountable obstacle to the passage of the raft. If that object had been alone on the water, it would have run a risk of being seen, even in the darkness, but, as it was, it was confounded with these moving masses, of all shapes and sizes, and the tumult caused by the crashing of the blocks against each other concealed likewise any suspicious noises.

There was a sharp frost. The fugitives suffered cruelly, having no other shelter than a few branches of birch. They cowered down together, endeavoring to keep each other warm, the temperature being now ten degrees below freezing point. The wind, though slight, having passed over the snow-clad mountains of the east, pierced them through and through.

Michael and Nadia, lying in the afterpart of the raft, bore this increase of suffering without complaint. Jolivet and Blount, placed near them, stood these first assaults of the Siberian winter as well as they could. No one now spoke, even in a low voice. Their situation entirely absorbed them. At any moment an incident might occur, which they could not escape unscathed.

For a man who hoped soon to accomplish his mission, Michael was singularly calm. Even in the gravest conjunctures, his energy had never abandoned him. He already saw the moment when he would be at last allowed to think of his mother, of Nadia, of himself! He now only dreaded one final unhappy chance; this was, that the raft might be completely barred by ice before reaching Irkutsk. He thought but of this, determined beforehand, if necessary, to attempt some bold stroke.

Restored by a few hours' rest, Nadia had regained the physical energy which misery had sometimes overcome, although without ever having shaken her moral energy. She thought, too, that if Michael had to make any fresh effort to attain his end, she must be there to guide him. But in proportion as she drew nearer to Irkutsk, the image of her father rose more and more clearly before her mind. She saw him in the invested town, far from those he loved, but, as she never doubted, struggling against the invaders with all the spirit of his patriotism. In a few hours, if Heaven favored them, she would be in his arms, giving him her mother's last words, and nothing should ever separate them again. If the term of Wassili Fedor's exile should never come to an end, his daughter would remain exiled with him. Then, by a natural transition, she came back to him who would have enabled her to see her father once more, to that generous companion, that "brother," who, the Tartars driven back, would retake the road to Moscow, whom she would perhaps never meet again!

As to Alcide Jolivet and Harry Blount, they had one and the same thought, which was, that the situation was extremely dramatic, and that, well worked up, it would furnish a most deeply interesting article. The Englishman thought of the readers of the Daily Telegraph, and the Frenchman of those of his Cousin Madeleine. At heart, both were not without feeling some emotion.

"Well, so much the better!" thought Alcide Jolivet, "to move others, one must be moved one's self! I believe there is some celebrated verse on the subject, but hang me if I can recollect it!" And with his well-practiced eyes he endeavored to pierce the gloom of the river.

Every now and then a burst of light dispelling the darkness for a time, exhibited the banks under some fantastic aspect—either a forest on fire, or a still burning village. The Angara was occasionally illuminated from one bank to the other. The blocks of ice formed so many mirrors, which, reflecting the flames on every point and in every color, were whirled along by the caprice of the current. The raft passed unperceived in the midst of these floating masses.

The danger was not at these points.

But a peril of another nature menaced the fugitives. One that they could not foresee, and, above all, one that they could not avoid. Chance discovered it to Alcide Jolivet in this way:—Lying at the right side of the raft, he let his hand hang over into the water. Suddenly he was surprised by the impression made on it by the current. It seemed to be of a slimy consistency, as if it had been made of mineral oil. Alcide, aiding his touch by his sense of smell, could not be mistaken. It was really a layer of liquid naphtha, floating on the surface of the river!

Was the raft really floating on this substance, which is in the highest degree combustible? Where had this naphtha come from? Was it a natural phenomenon taking place on the surface of the Angara, or was it to serve as an engine of destruction, put in motion by the Tartars? Did they intend to carry conflagration into Irkutsk?

Such were the questions which Alcide asked himself, but he thought it best to make this incident known only to Harry Blount, and they both agreed in not alarming their companions by revealing to them this new danger.

It is known that the soil of Central Asia is like a sponge impregnated with liquid hydrogen. At the port of Bakou, on the Persian frontier, on the Caspian Sea, in Asia Minor, in China, on the Yuen-Kiang, in the Burman Empire, springs of mineral oil rise in thousands to the surface of the ground. It is an "oil country," similar to the one which bears this name in North America.

During certain religious festivals, principally at the port of Bakou, the natives, who are fire-worshipers, throw liquid naphtha on the surface of the sea, which buoys it up, its density being inferior to that of water. Then at nightfall, when a layer of mineral oil is thus spread over the Caspian, they light it, and exhibit the matchless spectacle of an ocean of fire undulating and breaking into waves under the breeze.

But what is only a sign of rejoicing at Bakou, might prove a fearful disaster on the waters of the Angara. Whether it was set on fire by malevolence or imprudence, in the twinkling of an eye a conflagration might spread beyond Irkutsk. On board the raft no imprudence was to be feared; but everything was to be dreaded from the conflagrations on both banks of the Angara, for should a lighted straw or even a spark blow into the water, it would inevitably set the whole current of naphtha in a blaze.

The apprehensions of Jolivet and Blount may be better understood than described. Would it not be prudent, in face of this new danger, to land on one of the banks and wait there? "At any rate," said Alcide, "whatever the danger may be, I know some one who will not land!"

He alluded to Michael Strogoff.

In the meantime, on glided the raft among the masses of ice which were gradually getting closer and closer together. Up till then, no Tartar detachment had been seen, which showed that the raft was not abreast of the outposts. At about ten o'clock, however, Harry Blount caught sight of a number of black objects moving on the ice blocks. Springing from one to the other, they rapidly approached.

"Tartars!" he thought. And creeping up to the old boatman, he pointed out to him the suspicious objects.

The old man looked attentively. "They are only wolves!" said he. "I like them better than Tartars. But we must defend ourselves, and without noise!"

The fugitives would indeed have to defend themselves against these ferocious beasts, whom hunger and cold had sent roaming through the province. They had smelt out the raft, and would soon attack it. The fugitives must struggle without using firearms, for they could not now be far from the Tartar posts. The women and children were collected in the middle of the raft, and the men, some armed with poles, others with their knives, stood prepared to repulse their assailants. They did not make a sound, but the howls of the wolves filled the air.

Michael did not wish to remain inactive. He lay down at the side attacked by the savage pack. He drew his knife, and every time that a wolf passed within his reach, his hand found out the way to plunge his weapon into its throat. Neither were Jolivet and Blount idle, but fought bravely with the brutes. Their companions gallantly seconded them. The battle was carried on in silence, although many of the fugitives received severe bites.

The struggle did not appear as if it would soon terminate. The pack was being continually reinforced from the right bank of the Angara. "This will never be finished!" said Alcide, brandishing his dagger, red with blood.

In fact, half an hour after the commencement of the attack, the wolves were still coming in hundreds across the ice. The exhausted fugitives were getting weaker. The fight was going against them. At that moment, a group of ten huge wolves, raging with hunger, their eyes glowing in the darkness like red coals, sprang onto the raft. Jolivet and his companion threw themselves into the midst of the fierce beasts, and Michael was finding his way towards them, when a sudden change took place.

In a few moments the wolves had deserted not only the raft, but also the ice on the river. All the black bodies dispersed, and it was soon certain that they had in all haste regained the shore. Wolves, like other beasts of prey, require darkness for their proceedings, and at that moment a bright light illuminated the entire river.

It was the blaze of an immense fire. The whole of the small town of Poshkavsk was burning. The Tartars were indeed there, finishing their work. From this point, they occupied both banks beyond Irkutsk. The fugitives had by this time reached the dangerous part of their voyage, and they were still twenty miles from the capital.

It was now half past eleven. The raft continued to glide on amongst the ice, with which it was quite mingled, but gleams of light sometimes fell upon it. The fugitives stretched on the platform did not permit themselves to make a movement by which they might be betrayed.

The conflagration was going on with frightful rapidity. The houses, built of fir-wood, blazed like torches—a hundred and fifty flaming at once. With the crackling of the fire was mingled the yells of the Tartars. The old boatman, getting a foothold on a near piece of ice, managed to shove the raft towards the right bank, by doing which a distance of from three to four hundred feet divided it from the flames of Poshkavsk.

Nevertheless, the fugitives, lighted every now and then by the glare, would have been undoubtedly perceived had not the incendiaries been too much occupied in their work of destruction.

It may be imagined what were the apprehensions of Jolivet and Blount, when they thought of the combustible liquid on which the raft floated. Sparks flew in millions from the houses, which resembled so many glowing furnaces. They rose among the volumes of smoke to a height of five or six hundred feet. On the right bank, the trees and cliffs exposed to the fire looked as if they likewise were burning. A spark falling on the surface of the Angara would be sufficient to spread the flames along the current, and to carry disaster from one bank to the other. The result of this would be in a short time the destruction of the raft and of all those which it carried.

But, happily, the breeze did not blow from that side. It came from the east, and drove the flames towards the left. It was just possible that the fugitives would escape this danger. The blazing town was at last passed. Little by little the glare grew dimmer, the crackling became fainter, and the flames at last disappeared behind the high cliffs which arose at an abrupt turn of the river.

By this time it was nearly midnight. The deep gloom again threw its protecting shadows over the raft. The Tartars were there, going to and fro near the river. They could not be seen, but they could be heard. The fires of the outposts burned brightly.

In the meantime it had become necessary to steer more carefully among the blocks of ice. The old boatman stood up, and the moujiks resumed their poles. They had plenty of work, the management of the raft becoming more and more difficult as the river was further obstructed.

Michael had crept forward; Jolivet followed; both listened to what the old boatman and his men were saying.

"Look out on the right!"

"There are blocks drifting on to us on the left!"

"Fend! fend off with your boat-hook!"

"Before an hour is past we shall be stopped!"

"If it is God's will!" answered the old man. "Against His will there is nothing to be done."

"You hear them," said Alcide.

"Yes," replied Michael, "but God is with us!"

The situation became more and more serious. Should the raft be stopped, not only would the fugitives not reach Irkutsk, but they would be obliged to leave their floating platform, for it would be very soon smashed to pieces in the ice. The osier ropes would break, the fir trunks torn asunder would drift under the hard crust, and the unhappy people would have no refuge but the ice blocks themselves. Then, when day came, they would be seen by the Tartars, and massacred without mercy!

Michael returned to the spot where Nadia was waiting for him. He approached the girl, took her hand, and put to her the invariable question: "Nadia, are you ready?" to which she replied as usual, "I am ready!"

For a few versts more the raft continued to drift amongst the floating ice. Should the river narrow, it would soon form an impassable barrier. Already they seemed to drift slower. Every moment they encountered severe shocks or were compelled to make detours; now, to avoid running foul of a block, there to enter a channel, of which it was necessary to take advantage. At length the stoppages became still more alarming. There were only a few more hours of night. Could the fugitives not reach Irkutsk by five o'clock in the morning, they must lose all hope of ever getting there at all.

At half-past one, notwithstanding all efforts, the raft came up against a thick barrier and stuck fast. The ice, which was drifting down behind it, pressed it still closer, and kept it motionless, as though it had been stranded.

At this spot the Angara narrowed, it being half its usual breadth. This was the cause of the accumulation of ice, which became gradually soldered together, under the double influence of the increased pressure and of the cold. Five hundred feet beyond, the river widened again, and the blocks, gradually detaching themselves from the floe, continued to drift towards Irkutsk. It was probable that had the banks not narrowed, the barrier would not have formed. But the misfortune was irreparable, and the fugitives must give up all hope of attaining their object.

Had they possessed the tools usually employed by whalers to cut channels through the ice-fields—had they been able to get through to where the river widened—they might have been saved. But they had nothing which could make the least incision in the ice, hard as granite in the excessive frost. What were they to do?

At that moment several shots on the right bank startled the unhappy fugitives. A shower of balls fell on the raft. The devoted passengers had been seen. Immediately afterwards shots were heard fired from the left bank. The fugitives, taken between two fires, became the mark of the Tartar sharpshooters. Several were wounded, although in the darkness it was only by chance that they were hit.

"Come, Nadia," whispered Michael in the girl's ear.

169

Without making a single remark, "ready for anything," Nadia took Michael's hand.

"We must cross the barrier," he said in a low tone. "Guide me, but let no one see us leave the raft."

Nadia obeyed. Michael and she glided rapidly over the floe in the obscurity, only broken now and again by the flashes from the muskets. Nadia crept along in front of Michael. The shot fell around them like a tempest of hail, and pattered on the ice. Their hands were soon covered with blood from the sharp and rugged ice over which they clambered, but still on they went.

In ten minutes, the other side of the barrier was reached. There the waters of the Angara again flowed freely. Several pieces of ice, detached gradually from the floe, were swept along in the current down towards the town. Nadia guessed what Michael wished to attempt. One of the blocks was only held on by a narrow strip.

"Come," said Nadia. And the two crouched on the piece of ice, which their weight detached from the floe.

It began to drift. The river widened, the way was open. Michael and Nadia heard the shots, the cries of distress, the yells of the Tartars. Then, little by little, the sounds of agony and of ferocious joy grew faint in the distance.

"Our poor companions!" murmured Nadia.

For half an hour the current hurried along the block of ice which bore Michael and Nadia. They feared every moment that it would give way beneath them. Swept along in the middle of the current, it was unnecessary to give it an oblique direction until they drew near the quays of Irkutsk. Michael, his teeth tight set, his ear on the strain, did not utter a word. Never had he been so near his object. He felt that he was about to attain it!

Towards two in the morning a double row of lights glittered on the dark horizon in which were confounded the two banks of the Angara. On the right hand were the lights of Irkutsk; on the left, the fires of the Tartar camp.

Michael Strogoff was not more than half a verst from the town. "At last!" he murmured.

But suddenly Nadia uttered a cry.

At the cry Michael stood up on the ice, which was wavering. His hand was extended up the Angara. His face, on which a bluish light cast a peculiar hue, became almost fearful to look at, and then, as if his eyes had been opened to the bright blaze spreading across the river, "Ah!" he exclaimed, "then Heaven itself is against us!"

CHAPTER
XII IRKUTSK

IRKUTSK, the capital of Eastern Siberia, is a populous town, containing, in ordinary times, thirty thousand inhabitants. On the right side of the Angara rises a hill, on which are built numerous churches, a lofty cathedral, and dwellings disposed in picturesque disorder.

Seen at a distance, from the top of the mountain which rises at about twenty versts off along the Siberian highroad, this town, with its cupolas, its bell-towers, its steeples slender as minarets, its domes like pot-bellied Chinese jars, presents something of an oriental aspect. But this similarity vanishes as the traveler enters.

The town, half Byzantine, half Chinese, becomes European as soon as he sees its macadamized roads, bordered with pavements, traversed by canals, planted with gigantic birches, its houses of brick and wood, some of which have several stories, the numerous equipages which drive along, not only tarantasses but broughams and coaches; lastly, its numerous inhabitants far advanced in civilization, to whom the latest Paris fashions are not unknown.

Being the refuge for all the Siberians of the province, Irkutsk was at this time very full. Stores of every kind had been collected in abundance. Irkutsk is the emporium of the innumerable kinds of merchandise which are exchanged between China, Central Asia, and Europe. The authorities had therefore no fear with regard to admitting the peasants of the valley of the Angara, and leaving a desert between the invaders and the town.

Irkutsk is the residence of the governor-general of Eastern Siberia. Below him acts a civil governor, in whose hands is the administration of the province; a head of police, who has much to do in a town where exiles abound; and, lastly, a mayor, chief of the merchants, and a person of some importance, from his immense fortune and the influence which he exercises over the people.

The garrison of Irkutsk was at that time composed of an infantry regiment of Cossacks, consisting of two thousand men, and a body of police wearing helmets and blue uniforms laced with silver. Besides, as has been said, in consequence of the events which had occurred, the brother of the Czar had been shut up in the town since the beginning of the invasion.

A journey of political importance had taken the Grand Duke to these distant provinces of Central Asia. After passing through the principal Siberian cities, the Grand Duke, who traveled en militaire rather than en prince, without any parade, accompanied by his officers, and escorted by a regiment of Cossacks, arrived in the Trans-Baikalcine provinces. Nikolaevsk, the last Russian town situated on the shore of the Sea of Okhotsk, had been honored by a visit from him. Arrived on the confines of the immense Muscovite Empire, the Grand Duke was returning towards Irkutsk, from which place he intended to retake the road to Moscow, when, sudden as a thunder clap, came the news of the invasion.

He hastened to the capital, but only reached it just before communication with Russia had been interrupted. There was time to receive only a few telegrams from St. Petersburg and Moscow, and with difficulty to answer them before the wire was cut. Irkutsk was isolated from the rest of the world.

The Grand Duke had now only to prepare for resistance, and this he did with that determination and coolness of which, under other circumstances, he had given incontestable proofs. The news of the taking of Ichim, Omsk, and Tomsk, successively reached Irkutsk. It was necessary at any price to save the capital of Siberia. Reinforcements could not be expected for some time. The few troops scattered about in the provinces of Siberia could not arrive in sufficiently large numbers to arrest the progress of the Tartar columns. Since therefore it was impossible for Irkutsk to escape attack, the most important thing to be done was to put the town in a state to sustain a siege of some duration.

The preparations were begun on the day Tomsk fell into the hands of the Tartars. At the same time with this last news, the Grand Duke heard that the Emir of Bokhara and the allied Khans were directing the invasion in person, but what he did not know was, that the lieutenant of these barbarous chiefs was Ivan Ogareff, a Russian officer whom he had himself reduced to the ranks, but with whose person he was not acquainted.

First of all, as we have seen, the inhabitants of the province of Irkutsk were compelled to abandon the towns and villages. Those who did not take refuge in the capital had to retire beyond Lake Baikal, a district to which the invasion would probably not extend its ravages. The harvests of corn and fodder were collected and stored up in the town, and Irkutsk, the last bulwark of the Muscovite power in the Far East, was put in a condition to resist the enemy for a lengthened period.

Irkutsk, founded in 1611, is situated at the confluence of the Irkut and the Angara, on the right bank of the latter river. Two wooden draw-bridges, built on piles, connected the town with its suburbs on the left bank. On this side, defence was easy. The suburbs were abandoned, the bridges destroyed. The Angara being here very wide, it would not be possible to pass it under the fire of the besieged.

But the river might be crossed both above and below the town, and consequently, Irkutsk ran a risk of being attacked on its east side, on which there was no wall to protect it.

The whole population were immediately set to work on the fortifications. They labored day and night. The Grand Duke observed with satisfaction the zeal exhibited by the people in the work, whom ere long he would find equally courageous in the defense. Soldiers, merchants, exiles, peasants, all devoted themselves to the common safety. A week before the Tartars appeared on the Angara, earth-works had been raised. A fosse, flooded by the waters of the Angara, was dug between the scarp and counterscarp. The town could not now be taken by a coup de main. It must be invested and besieged.

The third Tartar column—the one which came up the valley of the

Yenisei on the 24th of September—appeared in sight of Irkutsk. It immediately occupied the deserted suburbs, every building in which had been destroyed so as not to impede the fire of the Grand Duke's guns, unfortunately but few in number and of small caliber. The Tartar troops as they arrived organized a camp on the bank of the Angara, whilst waiting the arrival of the two other columns, commanded by the Emir and his allies.

The junction of these different bodies was effected on the 25th of September, in the Angara camp, and the whole of the invading army, except the garrisons left in the principal conquered towns, was concentrated under the command of Feofar-Khan.

The passage of the Angara in front of Irkutsk having been regarded by Ogareff as impracticable, a strong body of troops crossed, several versts up the river, by means of bridges formed with boats. The Grand Duke did not attempt to oppose the enemy in their passage. He could only impede, not prevent it, having no field-artillery at his disposal, and he therefore remained in Irkutsk.

The Tartars now occupied the right bank of the river; then, advancing towards the town, they burnt, in passing, the summer-house of the governor-general, and at last having entirely invested Irkutsk, took up their positions for the siege.

Ivan Ogareff, who was a clever engineer, was perfectly competent to direct a regular siege; but he did not possess the materials for operating rapidly. He was disappointed too in the chief object of all his efforts—the surprise of Irkutsk. Things had not turned out as he hoped. First, the march of the Tartar army was delayed by the battle of Tomsk; and secondly, the preparations for the defense were made far more rapidly than he had supposed possible; these two things had balked his plans. He was now under the necessity of instituting a regular siege of the town.

However, by his suggestion, the Emir twice attempted the capture of the place, at the cost of a large sacrifice of men. He threw soldiers on the earth-works which presented any weak point; but these two assaults were repulsed with the greatest courage. The Grand Duke and his officers did not spare themselves on this occasion. They appeared in person; they led the civil population to the ramparts. Citizens and peasants both did their duty.

At the second attack, the Tartars managed to force one of the gates. A fight took place at the head of Bolchaia Street, two versts long, on the banks of the Angara. But the Cossacks, the police, the citizens, united in so fierce a resistance that the Tartars were driven out.

Ivan Ogareff then thought of obtaining by stratagem what he could not gain by force. We have said that his plan was to penetrate into the town, make his way to the Grand Duke, gain his confidence, and, when the time came, give up the gates to the besiegers; and, that done, wreak his vengeance on the brother of the Czar. The Tsigane Sangarre, who had accompanied him to the Angara, urged him to put this plan in execution.

Indeed, it was necessary to act without delay. The Russian troops from the government of Yakutsk were advancing towards Irkutsk. They had concentrated along the upper course of the Lena. In six days they would arrive. Therefore, before six days had passed, Irkutsk must be betrayed. Ogareff hesitated no longer.

One evening, the 2d of October, a council of war was held in the grand saloon of the palace of the governor-general. This palace, standing at the end of Bolchaia Street, overlooked the river. From its windows could be seen the camp of the Tartars, and had the invaders possessed guns of wider range, they would have rendered the palace uninhabitable.

The Grand Duke, General Voranzoff, the governor of the town, and the chief of the merchants, with several officers, had collected to determine upon various proposals.

"Gentlemen," said the Grand Duke, "you know our situation exactly. I have the firm hope that we shall be able to hold out until the arrival of the Yakutsk troops. We shall then be able to drive off these barbarian hordes, and it will not be my fault if they do not pay dearly for this invasion of the Muscovite territory."

"Your Highness knows that all the population of Irkutsk may be relied on," said General Voranzoff.

"Yes, general," replied the Grand Duke, "and I do justice to their patriotism. Thanks to God, they have not yet been subjected to the horrors of epidemic and famine, and I have reason to hope that they will escape them; but I cannot admire their courage on the ramparts enough. You hear my words, Sir Merchant, and I beg you to repeat such to them."

"I thank your Highness in the name of the town," answered the merchant chief. "May I ask you what is the most distant date when we may expect the relieving army?"

"Six days at most, sir," replied the Grand Duke. "A brave and clever messenger managed this morning to get into the town, and he told me that fifty thousand Russians under General Kisselef, are advancing by forced marches. Two days ago, they were on the banks of the Lena, at Kirensk, and now, neither frost nor snow will keep them back. Fifty thousand good men, taking the Tartars on the flank, will soon set us free."

"I will add," said the chief of the merchants, "that we shall be ready to execute your orders, any day that your Highness may command a sortie."

"Good, sir," replied the Grand Duke. "Wait till the heads of the relieving columns appear on the heights, and we will speedily crush these invaders."

Then turning to General Voranzoff, "To-morrow," said he, "we will visit the works on the right bank. Ice is drifting down the Angara, which will not be long in freezing, and in that case the Tartars might perhaps cross."

"Will your Highness allow me to make an observation?" said the chief of the merchants.

"Do so, sir."

"I have more than once seen the temperature fall to thirty and forty degrees below zero, and the Angara has still carried down drifting ice without entirely freezing. This is no doubt owing to the swiftness of its current. If therefore the Tartars have no other means of crossing the river, I can assure your Highness that they will not enter Irkutsk in that way."

The governor-general confirmed this assertion.

"It is a fortunate circumstance," responded the Grand Duke. "Nevertheless, we must hold ourselves ready for any emergency."

He then, turning towards the head of the police, asked, "Have you nothing to say to me, sir?"

"I have your Highness," answered the head of police, "a petition which is addressed to you through me."

"Addressed by whom?"

"By the Siberian exiles, whom, as your Highness knows, are in the town to the number of five hundred."

The political exiles, distributed over the province, had been collected in Irkutsk, from the beginning of the invasion. They had obeyed the order to rally in the town, and leave the villages where they exercised their different professions, some doctors, some professors, either at the Gymnasium, or at the Japanese School, or at the School of Navigation. The Grand Duke, trusting like the Czar in their patriotism, had armed them, and they had thoroughly proved their bravery.

"What do the exiles ask?" said the Grand Duke.

"They ask the consent of your Highness," answered the head of police, "to their forming a special corps and being placed in the front of the first sortie."

"Yes," replied the Grand Duke with an emotion which he did not seek to hide, "these exiles are Russians, and it is their right to fight for their country!"

"I believe I may assure your Highness," said the governor-general, "you will have no better soldiers."

"But they must have a chief," said the Grand Duke, "who will he be?"

"They wish to recommend to your Highness," said the head of police, "one of their number, who has distinguished himself on several occasions."

"Is he a Russian?"

"Yes, a Russian from the Baltic provinces."

"His name?"

"Is Wassili Fedor."

This exile was Nadia's father. Wassili Fedor, as we have already said, followed his profession of a medical man in Irkutsk. He was clever and charitable, and also possessed the greatest courage and most sincere patriotism. All the time which he did not devote to the sick he employed in organizing the defense. It was he who had united his companions in exile in the common cause. The exiles, till then mingled with the population, had behaved in such a way as to draw on themselves the attention of the Grand Duke. In several sorties, they had paid with their blood their debt to holy Russia—holy as they believe, and adored by her children! Wassili

175

Fedor had behaved heroically; his name had been mentioned several times, but he never asked either thanks or favors, and when the exiles of Irkutsk thought of forming themselves into a special corps, he was ignorant of their intention of choosing him for their captain.

When the head of police mentioned this name, the Grand Duke answered that it was not unknown to him.

"Indeed," remarked General Voranzoff, "Wassili Fedor is a man of worth and courage. His influence over his companions has always been very great."

"How long has he been at Irkutsk?" asked the Duke.

"For two years."

"And his conduct?"

"His conduct," answered the head of police, "is that of a man obedient to the special laws which govern him."

"General," said the Grand Duke, "General, be good enough to present him to me immediately."

The orders of the Grand Duke were obeyed, and before half an hour had passed, Fedor was introduced into his presence. He was a man over forty, tall, of a stern and sad countenance. One felt that his whole life was summed up in a single word—strife—he had striven and suffered. His features bore a marked resemblance to those of his daughter, Nadia Fedor.

This Tartar invasion had severely wounded him in his tenderest affections, and ruined the hope of the father, exiled eight thousand versts from his native town. A letter had apprised him of the death of his wife, and at the same time of the departure of his daughter, who had obtained from the government an authorization to join him at Irkutsk. Nadia must have left Riga on the 10th of July. The invasion had begun on the 15th of July; if at that time Nadia had passed the frontier, what could have become of her in the midst of the invaders? The anxiety of the unhappy father may be supposed when, from that time, he had no further news of his daughter.

Wassili Fedor entered the presence of the Grand Duke, bowed, and waited to be questioned.

"Wassili Fedor," said the Grand Duke, "your companions in exile have asked to be allowed to form a select corps. They are not ignorant that in this corps they must make up their minds to be killed to the last man?"

"They are not ignorant of it," replied Fedor.

"They wish to have you for their captain."

"I, your Highness?"

"Do you consent to be placed at their head?"

"Yes, if it is for the good of Russia."

"Captain Fedor," said the Grand Duke, "you are no longer an exile."

"Thanks, your Highness, but can I command those who are so still?"

"They are so no longer!" The brother of the Czar had granted a pardon to all Fedor's companions in exile, now his companions in arms!

Wassili Fedor wrung, with emotion, the hand which the Grand Duke held out to him, and retired.

The latter, turned to his officers, "The Czar will not refuse to ratify that pardon," said he, smiling; "we need heroes to defend the capital of Siberia, and I have just made some."

This pardon, so generously accorded to the exiles of Irkutsk, was indeed an act of real justice and sound policy.

It was now night. Through the windows of the palace burned the fires of the Tartar camp, flickering beyond the Angara. Down the river drifted numerous blocks of ice, some of which stuck on the piles of the old bridges; others were swept along by the current with great rapidity. It was evident, as the merchant had observed, that it would be very difficult for the Angara to freeze all over. The defenders of Irkutsk had not to dread being attacked on that side. Ten o'clock had just struck. The Grand Duke was about to dismiss his officers and retire to his apartments, when a tumult was heard outside the palace.

Almost immediately the door was thrown open, an aide-de-camp appeared, and advanced rapidly towards the Grand Duke.

"Your Highness," said he, "a courier from the Czar!"

CHAPTER XIII
THE CZAR'S COURIER

ALL the members of the council simultaneously started forward. A courier from the Czar arrived in Irkutsk! Had these officers for a moment considered the improbability of this fact, they would certainly not have credited what they heard.

The Grand Duke advanced quickly to his aide-de-camp. "This courier!" he exclaimed.

A man entered. He appeared exhausted with fatigue. He wore the dress of a Siberian peasant, worn into tatters, and exhibiting several shot-holes. A Muscovite cap was on his head. His face was disfigured by a recently-healed scar. The man had evidently had a long and painful journey; his shoes being in a state which showed that he had been obliged to make part of it on foot.

"His Highness the Grand Duke?" he asked.

The Grand Duke went up to him. "You are a courier from the Czar?" he asked.

"Yes, your Highness."

"You come?"

"From Moscow."

"You left Moscow?"

"On the 15th of July."

"Your name?"

"Michael Strogoff."

It was Ivan Ogareff. He had taken the designation of the man whom he believed that he had rendered powerless. Neither the Grand Duke nor anyone knew him in Irkutsk, and he had not even to disguise his features. As he was in a position to prove his pretended identity, no one could have any reason for doubting him. He came, therefore, sustained by his iron will, to hasten by treason and assassination the great object of the invasion.

After Ogareff had replied, the Grand Duke signed to all his officers to withdraw. He and the false Michael Strogoff remained alone in the saloon.

The Grand Duke looked at Ivan Ogareff for some moments with extreme attention. Then he said, "On the 15th of July you were at Moscow?"

"Yes, your Highness; and on the night of the 14th I saw His Majesty the Czar at the New Palace."

"Have you a letter from the Czar?"

"Here it is."

And Ivan Ogareff handed to the Grand Duke the Imperial letter, crumpled to almost microscopic size.

"Was the letter given you in this state?"

"No, your Highness, but I was obliged to tear the envelope, the better to hide it from the Emir's soldiers."

"Were you taken prisoner by the Tartars?"

"Yes, your Highness, I was their prisoner for several days," answered Ogareff. "That is the reason that, having left Moscow on the 15th of July, as the date of that letter shows, I only reached Irkutsk on the 2d of October, after traveling seventy-nine days."

The Grand Duke took the letter. He unfolded it and recognized the Czar's signature, preceded by the decisive formula, written by his brother's hand. There was no possible doubt of the authenticity of this letter, nor of the identity of the courier. Though Ogareff's countenance had at first inspired the Grand Duke with some distrust, he let nothing of it appear, and it soon vanished.

The Grand Duke remained for a few minutes without speaking. He read the letter slowly, so as to take in its meaning fully. "Michael Strogoff, do you know the contents of this letter?" he asked.

"Yes, your Highness. I might have been obliged to destroy it, to prevent its falling into the hands of the Tartars, and should such have been the case, I wished to be able to bring the contents of it to your Highness."

"You know that this letter enjoins us all to die, rather than give up the town?"

"I know it."

"You know also that it informs me of the movements of the troops which have combined to stop the invasion?"

"Yes, your Highness, but the movements have failed."

"What do you mean?"

"I mean that Ichim, Omsk, Tomsk, to speak only of the more important towns of the two Siberias, have been successively occupied by the soldiers of Feofar-Khan."

"But there has been fighting? Have not our Cossacks met the Tartars?"

"Several times, your Highness."

"And they were repulsed?"

"They were not in sufficient force to oppose the enemy."

"Where did the encounters take place?"

"At Kolyvan, at Tomsk." Until now, Ogareff had only spoken the truth, but, in the hope of troubling the defenders of Irkutsk by exaggerating the defeats, he added, "And a third time before Krasnoiarsk."

"And what of this last engagement?" asked the Grand Duke, through whose compressed lips the words could scarcely pass.

"It was more than an engagement, your Highness," answered Ogareff; "it was a battle."

"A battle?"

"Twenty thousand Russians, from the frontier provinces and the government of Tobolsk, engaged with a hundred and fifty thousand Tartars, and, notwithstanding their courage, were overwhelmed."

"You lie!" exclaimed the Grand Duke, endeavoring in vain to curb his passion.

"I speak the truth, your Highness," replied Ivan Ogareff coldly. "I was present at the battle of Krasnoiarsk, and it was there I was made prisoner!"

The Grand Duke grew calmer, and by a significant gesture he gave Ogareff to understand that he did not doubt his veracity. "What day did this battle of Krasnoiarsk take place?" he asked.

"On the 2d of September."

"And now all the Tartar troops are concentrated here?"

"All."

"And you estimate them?"

"At about four hundred thousand men."

Another exaggeration of Ogareff's in the estimate of the Tartar army, with the same object as before.

"And I must not expect any help from the West provinces?" asked the Grand Duke.

"None, your Highness, at any rate before the end of the winter."

"Well, hear this, Michael Strogoff. Though I must expect no help either from the East or from the West, even were these barbarians six hundred thousand strong, I will never give up Irkutsk!"

Ogareff's evil eye slightly contracted. The traitor thought to himself that the brother of the Czar did not reckon the result of treason.

The Grand Duke, who was of a nervous temperament, had great difficulty in keeping calm whilst hearing this disastrous news. He walked to and fro in the room, under the gaze of Ogareff, who eyed him as a victim reserved for vengeance. He stopped at the windows, he looked forth at the fires in the Tartar camp, he listened to the noise of the ice-blocks drifting down the Angara.

A quarter of an hour passed without his putting any more questions.

Then taking up the letter, he re-read a passage and said, "You know that in this letter I am warned of a traitor, of whom I must beware?"

"Yes, your Highness."

"He will try to enter Irkutsk in disguise; gain my confidence, and betray the town to the Tartars."

"I know all that, your Highness, and I know also that Ivan Ogareff has sworn to revenge himself personally on the Czar's brother."

"Why?"

"It is said that the officer in question was condemned by the Grand Duke to a humiliating degradation."

"Yes, I remember. But it is a proof that the villain, who could afterwards serve against his country and head an invasion of barbarians, deserved it."

"His Majesty the Czar," said Ogareff, "was particularly anxious that you should be warned of the criminal projects of Ivan Ogareff against your person."

"Yes; of that the letter informs me."

"And His Majesty himself spoke to me of it, telling me I was above all things to beware of the traitor."

"Did you meet with him?"

"Yes, your Highness, after the battle of Krasnoiarsk. If he had only guessed that I was the bearer of a letter addressed to your Highness, in which his plans were revealed, I should not have got off so easily."

"No; you would have been lost!" replied the Grand Duke. "And how did you manage to escape?"

"By throwing myself into the Irtych."

"And how did you enter Irkutsk?"

"Under cover of a sortie, which was made this evening to repulse a Tartar detachment. I mingled with the defenders of the town, made myself known, and was immediately conducted before your Highness."

"Good, Michael Strogoff," answered the Grand Duke. "You have shown courage and zeal in your difficult mission. I will not forget you. Have you any favor to ask?"

"None; unless it is to be allowed to fight at the side of your Highness," replied Ogareff.

"So be it, Strogoff. I attach you from to-day to my person, and you shall be lodged in the palace."

"And if according to his intention, Ivan Ogareff should present himself to your Highness under a false name?"

"We will unmask him, thanks to you, who know him, and I will make him die under the knout. Go!"

Ogareff gave a military salute, not forgetting that he was a captain of the couriers of the Czar, and retired.

Ogareff had so far played his unworthy part with success. The Grand Duke's entire confidence had been accorded him. He could now betray it whenever it suited him. He would inhabit the very palace. He would be in the secret of all the operations for the defense of the town. He thus held the situation in his hand, as it were. No one in Irkutsk knew him, no one could snatch off his mask. He resolved therefore to set to work without delay.

Indeed, time pressed. The town must be captured before the arrival of the Russians from the North and East, and that was only a question of a few days. The Tartars once masters of Irkutsk, it would not be easy to take it again from them. At any rate, even if they were obliged to abandon it later, they would not do so before they had utterly destroyed it, and before the head of the Grand Duke had rolled at the feet of Feofar-Khan.

Ivan Ogareff, having every facility for seeing, observing, and acting, occupied himself the next day with visiting the ramparts. He was everywhere received with cordial congratulations from officers, soldiers, and citizens. To them this courier from the Czar was a link which connected them with the empire.

Ogareff recounted, with an assurance which never failed, numerous fictitious events of his journey. Then, with the cunning for which he was noted, without dwelling too much on it at first, he spoke of the gravity of the situation, exaggerating the success of the Tartars and the numbers of the barbarian forces, as he had when speaking to the Grand Duke. According to him, the expected succors would be insufficient, if ever they arrived at all, and it was to be feared that a battle fought under the walls of Irkutsk would be as fatal as the battles of Kolyvan, Tomsk, and Krasnoiarsk.

Ogareff was not too free in these insinuations. He wished to allow them to sink gradually into the minds of the defenders of Irkutsk. He pretended only to answer with reluctance when much pressed with questions. He always added that they must fight to the last man, and blow up the town rather than yield!

These false statements would have done more harm had it been possible; but the garrison and the population of Irkutsk were too patriotic to let themselves be moved. Of all the soldiers and citizens shut up in this town, isolated at the extremity of the Asiatic world, not one dreamed of even speaking of a capitulation. The contempt of the Russians for these barbarians was boundless.

No one suspected the odious part played by Ivan Ogareff; no one guessed that the pretended courier of the Czar was a traitor. It occurred very naturally that on his arrival in Irkutsk, a frequent intercourse was established between Ogareff and one of the bravest defenders of the town, Wassili Fedor. We know what anxiety this unhappy father suffered. If his daughter, Nadia Fedor, had left Russia on the date fixed by the last letter he had received from Riga, what had become of her? Was she still trying to cross the invaded provinces, or had she long since been taken prisoner? The only alleviation to Wassili Fedor's anxiety was when he could obtain an opportunity of engaging in battle with the Tartars—opportunities which came too seldom for his taste. The very evening the pretended courier arrived, Wassili Fedor went to the governor-general's palace and, acquainting Ogareff with the circumstances under which his daughter must have left European Russia, told him all his uneasiness about her.

Ogareff did not know Nadia, although he had met her at Ichim on the day she was there with Michael Strogoff; but then, he had not paid more attention to her than to the two reporters, who at the same time were in the post-house; he therefore could give Wassili Fedor no news of his daughter.

"But at what time," asked Ogareff, "must your daughter have left the Russian territory?"

"About the same time that you did," replied Fedor.

"I left Moscow on the 15th of July."

"Nadia must also have quitted Moscow at that time. Her letter told me so expressly."

"She was in Moscow on the 15th of July?".

"Yes, certainly, by that date."

"Then it was impossible for her—But no, I am mistaken—I was confusing dates. Unfortunately, it is too probable that your daughter must have passed the frontier, and you can only have one hope, that she stopped on learning the news of the Tartar invasion!"

The father's head fell! He knew Nadia, and he knew too well that nothing would have prevented her from setting out. Ivan Ogareff had just committed gratuitously an act of real cruelty. With a word he might have reassured Fedor. Although Nadia had passed the frontier under circumstances with which we are acquainted, Fedor, by comparing the date on which his daughter would have been at Nijni-Novgorod, and the date of the proclamation which forbade anyone to leave it, would no doubt have concluded thus: that Nadia had not been exposed to the dangers of the invasion, and that she was still, in spite of herself, in the European territory of the Empire.

Ogareff obedient to his nature, a man who was never touched by the sufferings of others, might have said that word. He did not say it. Fedor retired with his heart broken. In that interview his last hope was crushed.

During the two following days, the 3rd and 4th of October, the Grand Duke often spoke to the pretended Michael Strogoff, and made him repeat all that he had heard in the Imperial Cabinet of the New Palace. Ogareff, prepared for all these questions, replied without the least hesitation. He intentionally did not conceal that the Czar's government had been utterly surprised by the invasion, that the insurrection had been prepared in the greatest possible secrecy, that the Tartars were already masters of the line of the Obi when the news reached Moscow, and lastly, that none of the necessary preparations were completed in the Russian provinces for sending into Siberia the troops requisite for repulsing the invaders.

Ivan Ogareff, being entirely free in his movements, began to study Irkutsk, the state of its fortifications, their weak points, so as to profit subsequently by his observations, in the event of being prevented from consummating his act of treason. He examined particularly the Bolchaia Gate, the one he wished to deliver up.

Twice in the evening he came upon the glacis of this gate. He walked up and down, without fear of being discovered by the besiegers, whose nearest posts were at least a mile from the ramparts. He fancied that he was recognized by no one, till he caught sight of a shadow gliding along outside the earthworks. Sangarre had come at the risk of her life for the purpose of putting herself in communication with Ivan Ogareff.

For two days the besieged had enjoyed a tranquillity to which the Tartars had not accustomed them since the commencement of the investment. This was by Ogareff's orders. Feofar-Khan's lieutenant wished that all attempts to take the town by force should be suspended. He hoped the watchfulness of the besieged would relax. At any rate, several thousand Tartars were kept in readiness at the outposts, to attack the gate, deserted, as Ogareff anticipated that it would be, by its defenders, whenever he should summon the besiegers to the assault.

This he could not now delay in doing. All must be over by the time that the Russian troops should come in sight of Irkutsk. Ogareff's arrangements were made, and on this evening a note fell from the top of the earthworks into Sangarre's hands.

On the next day, that is to say during the hours of darkness from the 5th to the 6th of October, at two o'clock in the morning, Ivan Ogareff had resolved to deliver up Irkutsk.

CHAPTER XIV
THE NIGHT OF THE FIFTH OF OCTOBER

IVAN OGAREFF'S plan had been contrived with the greatest care, and except for some unforeseen accident he believed that it must succeed. It was of importance that the Bolchaia Gate should be unguarded or only feebly held when he gave it up. The attention of the besieged was therefore to be drawn to another part of the town. A diversion was agreed upon with the Emir.

This diversion was to be effected both up and down the river, on the Irkutsk bank. The attack on these two points was to be conducted in earnest, and at the same time a feigned attempt at crossing the Angara from the left bank was to be made. The Bolchaia Gate, would be probably deserted, so much the more because on this side the Tartar outposts having drawn back, would appear to have broken up.

It was the 5th of October. In four and twenty hours, the capital of Eastern Siberia would be in the hands of the Emir, and the Grand Duke in the power of Ivan Ogareff.

During the day, an unusual stir was going on in the Angara camp. From the windows of the palace important preparations on the opposite shore could be distinctly seen. Numerous Tartar detachments were converging towards the camp, and from hour to hour reinforced the Emir's troops. These movements, intended to deceive the besieged, were conducted in the most open manner possible before their eyes.

Ogareff had warned the Grand Duke that an attack was to be feared. He knew, he said, that an assault was to be made, both above and below the town, and he counselled the Duke to reinforce the two directly threatened points. Accordingly, after a council of war had been held in the palace, orders were issued to concentrate the defense on the bank of the Angara and at the two ends of the town, where the earthworks protected the river.

This was exactly what Ogareff wished. He did not expect that the Bolchaia Gate would be left entirely without defenders, but that there would only be a small number. Besides, Ogareff meant to give such importance to the diversion, that the Grand Duke would be obliged to oppose it with all his available forces. The traitor planned also to produce so frightful a catastrophe that terror must inevitably overwhelm the hearts of the besieged.

All day the garrison and population of Irkutsk were on the alert. The measures to repel an attack on the points hitherto unassailed had been taken. The Grand Duke and General Voranzoff visited the posts, strengthened by their orders. Wassili Fedor's corps occupied the North of the town, but with orders to throw themselves where the danger was greatest. The right bank of the Angara had been protected with the few guns possessed by the defenders. With these measures, taken in time, thanks to the advice so opportunely given by Ivan Ogareff, there was good reason to hope that the expected attack would be repulsed. In that case the Tartars, momentarily discouraged, would no doubt not make another attempt against the town for several days. Now the troops expected by the Grand Duke might arrive at any hour. The safety or the loss of Irkutsk hung only by a thread.

On this day, the sun which had risen at twenty minutes to six, set at forty minutes past five, having traced its diurnal arc for eleven hours above the horizon. The twilight would struggle with the night for another two hours. Then it would be intensely dark, for the sky was cloudy, and there would be no moon. This gloom would favor the plans of Ivan Ogareff.

For a few days already a sharp frost had given warning of the approaching rigor of the Siberian winter, and this evening it was especially severe. The Russians posted by the bank of the Angara, obliged to conceal their position, lighted no fires. They suffered cruelly from the low temperature. A few feet below them, the ice in large masses drifted down the current. All day these masses had been seen passing rapidly between the two banks.

This had been considered by the Grand Duke and his officers as fortunate. Should the channel of the Angara continue to be thus obstructed, the passage must be impracticable. The Tartars could use neither rafts nor boats. As to their crossing the river on the ice, that was not possible. The newly-frozen plain could not bear the weight of an assaulting column.

This circumstance, as it appeared favorable to the defenders of Irkutsk, Ogareff might have regretted. He did not do so, however. The traitor knew well that the Tartars would not try to pass the Angara, and that, on its side at least, their attempt was only a feint.

About ten in the evening, the state of the river sensibly improved, to the great surprise of the besieged and still more to their disadvantage. The passage till then impracticable, became all at once possible. The bed of the Angara was clear. The blocks of ice, which had for some days drifted past in large numbers, disappeared down the current, and five or six only now occupied the space between the banks. The Russian officers reported this change in the river to the Grand Duke. They suggested that it was probably caused by the circumstance that in some narrower part of the Angara, the blocks had accumulated so as to form a barrier.

We know this was the case. The passage of the Angara was thus open to the besiegers. There was great reason for the Russians to be on their guard.

Up to midnight nothing had occurred. On the Eastern side, beyond the Bolchaia Gate, all was quiet. Not a glimmer was seen in the dense forest, which appeared confounded on the horizon with the masses of clouds hanging low down in the sky. Lights flitting to and fro in the Angara camp, showed that a considerable movement was taking place. From a verst above and below the point where the scarp met the river's bank, came a dull murmur, proving that the Tartars were on foot, expecting some signal. An hour passed. Nothing new.

The bell of the Irkutsk cathedral was about to strike two o'clock in the morning, and not a movement amongst the besiegers had yet shown that they were about to commence the assault. The Grand Duke and his officers began to suspect that they had been mistaken. Had it really been the Tartars' plan to surprise the town? The preceding nights had not been nearly so quiet—musketry rattling from the outposts, shells whistling through the air; and this time, nothing. The officers waited, ready to give their orders, according to circumstances.

We have said that Ogareff occupied a room in the palace. It was a large chamber on the ground floor, its windows opening on a side terrace. By taking a few steps along this terrace, a view of the river could be obtained.

Profound darkness reigned in the room. Ogareff stood by a window, awaiting the hour to act. The signal, of course, could come from him, alone. This signal once given, when the greater part of the defenders of Irkutsk would be summoned to the points openly attacked, his plan was to leave the palace and hurry to the Bolchaia Gate. If it was unguarded, he would open it; or at least he would direct the overwhelming mass of its assailants against the few defenders.

He now crouched in the shadow, like a wild beast ready to spring on its prey. A few minutes before two o'clock, the Grand Duke desired that Michael Strogoff—which was the only name they could give to Ivan

Ogareff—should be brought to him. An aide-de-camp came to the room, the door of which was closed. He called.

Ogareff, motionless near the window, and invisible in the shade did not answer. The Grand Duke was therefore informed that the Czar's courier was not at that moment in the palace.

Two o'clock struck. Now was the time to cause the diversion agreed upon with the Tartars, waiting for the assault. Ivan Ogareff opened the window and stationed himself at the North angle of the side terrace.

Below him flowed the roaring waters of the Angara. Ogareff took a match from his pocket, struck it and lighted a small bunch of tow, impregnated with priming powder, which he threw into the river.

It was by the orders of Ivan Ogareff that the torrents of mineral oil had been thrown on the surface of the Angara! There are numerous naphtha springs above Irkutsk, on the right bank, between the suburb of Poshkavsk and the town. Ogareff had resolved to employ this terrible means to carry fire into Irkutsk. He therefore took possession of the immense reservoirs which contained the combustible liquid. It was only necessary to demolish a piece of wall in order to allow it to flow out in a vast stream.

This had been done that night, a few hours previously, and this was the reason that the raft which carried the true Courier of the Czar, Nadia, and the fugitives, floated on a current of mineral oil. Through the breaches in these reservoirs of enormous dimensions rushed the naphtha in torrents, and, following the inclination of the ground, it spread over the surface of the river, where its density allowed it to float. This was the way Ivan Ogareff carried on warfare! Allied with Tartars, he acted like a Tartar, and against his own countrymen!

The tow had been thrown on the waters of the Angara. In an instant, with electrical rapidity, as if the current had been of alcohol, the whole river was in a blaze above and below the town. Columns of blue flames ran between the two banks. Volumes of vapor curled up above. The few pieces of ice which still drifted were seized by the burning liquid, and melted like wax on the top of a furnace, the evaporated water escaping in shrill hisses.

At the same moment, firing broke out on the North and South of the town. The enemy's batteries discharged their guns at random. Several thousand Tartars rushed to the assault of the earth-works. The houses on the bank, built of wood, took fire in every direction. A bright light dissipated the darkness of the night.

"At last!" said Ivan Ogareff.

He had good reason for congratulating himself. The diversion which he had planned was terrible. The defenders of Irkutsk found themselves between the attack of the Tartars and the fearful effects of fire. The bells rang, and all the able-bodied of the population ran, some towards the points attacked, and others towards the houses in the grasp of the flames, which it seemed too probable would ere long envelop the whole town.

The Gate of Bolchaia was nearly free. Only a very small guard had been left there. And by the traitor's suggestion, and in order that the event

186

might be explained apart from him, as if by political hate, this small guard had been chosen from the little band of exiles.

Ogareff re-entered his room, now brilliantly lighted by the flames from the Angara; then he made ready to go out. But scarcely had he opened the door, when a woman rushed into the room, her clothes drenched, her hair in disorder.

"Sangarre!" exclaimed Ogareff, in the first moment of surprise, and not supposing that it could be any other woman than the gypsy.

It was not Sangarre; it was Nadia!

At the moment when, floating on the ice, the girl had uttered a cry on seeing the fire spreading along the current, Michael had seized her in his arms, and plunged with her into the river itself to seek a refuge in its depths from the flames. The block which bore them was not thirty fathoms from the first quay of Irkutsk.

Swimming beneath the water, Michael managed to get a footing with Nadia on the quay. Michael Strogoff had reached his journey's end! He was in Irkutsk!

"To the governor's palace!" said he to Nadia.

In less than ten minutes, they arrived at the entrance to the palace. Long tongues of flame from the Angara licked its walls, but were powerless to set it on fire. Beyond the houses on the bank were in a blaze.

The palace being open to all, Michael and Nadia entered without difficulty. In the confusion, no one remarked them, although their garments were dripping. A crowd of officers coming for orders, and of soldiers running to execute them, filled the great hall on the ground floor. There, in a sudden eddy of the confused multitude, Michael and the young girl were separated from each other.

Nadia ran distracted through the passages, calling her companion, and asking to be taken to the Grand Duke. A door into a room flooded with light opened before her. She entered, and found herself suddenly face to face with the man whom she had met at Ichim, whom she had seen at Tomsk; face to face with the one whose villainous hand would an instant later betray the town!

"Ivan Ogareff!" she cried.

On hearing his name pronounced, the wretch started. His real name known, all his plans would be balked. There was but one thing to be done: to kill the person who had just uttered it. Ogareff darted at Nadia; but the girl, a knife in her hand, retreated against the wall, determined to defend herself.

"Ivan Ogareff!" again cried Nadia, knowing well that so detested a name would soon bring her help.

"Ah! Be silent!" hissed out the traitor between his clenched teeth.

"Ivan Ogareff!" exclaimed a third time the brave young girl, in a voice to which hate had added ten-fold strength.

Mad with fury, Ogareff, drawing a dagger from his belt, again rushed at Nadia and compelled her to retreat into a corner of the room. Her last hope appeared gone, when the villain, suddenly lifted by an irresistible force, was dashed to the ground.

"Michael!" cried Nadia.

It was Michael Strogoff. Michael had heard Nadia's call. Guided by her voice, he had just in time reached Ivan Ogareff's room, and entered by the open door.

"Fear nothing, Nadia," said he, placing himself between her and Ogareff.

"Ah!" cried the girl, "take care, brother! The traitor is armed! He can see!"

Ogareff rose, and, thinking he had an immeasurable advantage over the blind man leaped upon him. But with one hand, the blind man grasped the arm of his enemy, seized his weapon, and hurled him again to the ground.

Pale with rage and shame, Ogareff remembered that he wore a sword. He drew it and returned a second time to the charge. A blind man! Ogareff had only to deal with a blind man! He was more than a match for him!

Nadia, terrified at the danger which threatened her companion ran to the door calling for help!

"Close the door, Nadia!" said Michael. "Call no one, and leave me alone! The Czar's courier has nothing to fear to-day from this villain! Let him come on, if he dares! I am ready for him."

In the mean time, Ogareff, gathering himself together like a tiger about to spring, uttered not a word. The noise of his footsteps, his very breathing, he endeavored to conceal from the ear of the blind man. His object was to strike before his opponent was aware of his approach, to strike him with a deadly blow.

Nadia, terrified and at the same time confident, watched this terrible scene with involuntary admiration. Michael's calm bearing seemed to have inspired her. Michael's sole weapon was his Siberian knife. He did not see his adversary armed with a sword, it is true; but Heaven's support seemed to be afforded him. How, almost without stirring, did he always face the point of the sword?

Ivan Ogareff watched his strange adversary with visible anxiety. His superhuman calm had an effect upon him. In vain, appealing to his reason, did he tell himself that in so unequal a combat all the advantages were on his side. The immobility of the blind man froze him. He had settled on the place where he would strike his victim. He had fixed upon it! What, then, hindered him from putting an end to his blind antagonist?

At last, with a spring he drove his sword full at Michael's breast. An imperceptible movement of the blind man's knife turned aside the blow. Michael had not been touched, and coolly he awaited a second attack.

Cold drops stood on Ogareff's brow. He drew back a step, then again leaped forward. But as had the first, this second attempt failed. The knife had simply parried the blow from the traitor's useless sword.

Mad with rage and terror before this living statue, he gazed into the wide-open eyes of the blind man. Those eyes which seemed to pierce to the bottom of his soul, and yet which did not, could not, see—exercised a sort of dreadful fascination over him.

All at once, Ogareff uttered a cry. A sudden light flashed across his brain. "He sees!" he exclaimed, "he sees!" And like a wild beast trying to retreat into its den, step by step, terrified, he drew back to the end of the room.

Then the statue became animated, the blind man walked straight up to Ivan Ogareff, and placing himself right before him, "Yes, I see!" said he. "I see the mark of the knout which I gave you, traitor and coward! I see the place where I am about to strike you! Defend your life! It is a duel I deign to offer you! My knife against your sword!"

"He sees!" said Nadia. "Gracious Heaven, is it possible!"

Ogareff felt that he was lost. But mustering all his courage, he sprang forward on his impassible adversary. The two blades crossed, but at a touch from Michael's knife, wielded in the hand of the Siberian hunter, the sword flew in splinters, and the wretch, stabbed to the heart, fell lifeless on the ground.

At the same moment, the door was thrown open. The Grand Duke, accompanied by some of his officers, appeared on the threshold. The Grand Duke advanced. In the body lying on the ground, he recognized the man whom he believed to be the Czar's courier.

Then, in a threatening voice, "Who killed that man?" he asked.

"I," replied Michael.

One of the officers put a pistol to his temple, ready to fire.

"Your name?" asked the Grand Duke, before giving the order for his brains to be blown out.

"Your Highness," answered Michael, "ask me rather the name of the man who lies at your feet!"

"That man, I know him! He is a servant of my brother! He is the Czar's courier!"

"That man, your Highness, is not a courier of the Czar! He is Ivan Ogareff!"

"Ivan Ogareff!" exclaimed the Grand Duke.

"Yes, Ivan the Traitor!"

"But who are you, then?"

"Michael Strogoff!"

CHAPTER XV
CONCLUSION

MICHAEL STROGOFF was not, had never been, blind. A purely human phenomenon, at the same time moral and physical, had neutralized the action of the incandescent blade which Feofar's executioner had passed before his eyes.

It may be remembered, that at the moment of the execution, Marfa Strogoff was present, stretching out her hands towards her son. Michael gazed at her as a son would gaze at his mother, when it is for the last time. The tears, which his pride in vain endeavored to subdue, welling up from his heart, gathered under his eyelids, and volatiliz-ing on the cornea, had saved his sight. The vapor formed by his tears interposing between the glowing saber and his eyeballs, had been sufficient to annihilate the action of the heat. A similar effect is produced, when a workman smelter, after dipping his hand in vapor, can with impunity hold it over a stream of melted iron.

Michael had immediately understood the danger in which he would be placed should he make known his secret to anyone. He at once saw, on the other hand, that he might make use of his supposed blindness for the accomplishment of his designs. Because it was believed that he was blind, he would be allowed to go free. He must therefore be blind, blind to all, even to Nadia, blind everywhere, and not a gesture at any moment must let the truth be suspected. His resolution was taken. He must risk his life even to afford to all he might meet the proof of his want of sight. We know how perfectly he acted the part he had determined on.

His mother alone knew the truth, and he had whispered it to her in Tomsk itself, when bending over her in the dark he covered her with kisses.

When Ogareff had in his cruel irony held the Imperial letter before the eyes which he believed were destroyed, Michael had been able to read, and had read the letter which disclosed the odious plans of the traitor. This was the reason of the wonderful resolution he exhibited during the second part of his journey. This was the reason of his unalterable longing to reach Irkutsk, so as to perform his mission by word of mouth. He knew that the town would be betrayed! He knew that the life of the Grand Duke was threatened! The safety of the Czar's brother and of Siberia was in his hands.

This story was told in a few words to the Grand Duke, and Michael repeated also—and with what emotion!—the part Nadia had taken in these events.

"Who is this girl?" asked the Grand Duke.

"The daughter of the exile, Wassili Fedor," replied Michael.

"The daughter of Captain Fedor," said the Grand Duke, "has ceased to be the daughter of an exile. There are no longer exiles in Irkutsk."

Nadia, less strong in joy than she had been in grief, fell on her knees before the Grand Duke, who raised her with one hand, while he extended the other to Michael.

An hour after, Nadia was in her father's arms. Michael Strogoff, Nadia, and Wassili Fedor were united. This was the height of happiness to them all.

The Tartars had been repulsed in their double attack on the town. Wassili Fedor, with his little band, had driven back the first assailants who presented themselves at the Bolchaia Gate, expecting to find it open and which, by an instinctive feeling, often arising from sound judgment, he had determined to remain at and defend.

At the same time as the Tartars were driven back the besieged had mastered the fire. The liquid naphtha having rapidly burnt to the surface of the water, the flames did not go beyond the houses on the shore, and left the other quarters of the town uninjured. Before daybreak the troops of Feofar-Khan had retreated into their camp, leaving a large number of dead on and below the ramparts.

Among the dead was the gypsy Sangarre, who had vainly endeavored to join Ivan Ogareff.

For two days the besiegers attempted no fresh assault. They were discouraged by the death of Ogareff. This man was the mainspring of the invasion, and he alone, by his plots long since contrived, had had sufficient influence over the khans and their hordes to bring them to the conquest of Asiatic Russia.

However, the defenders of Irkutsk kept on their guard, and the investment still continued; but on the 7th of October, at daybreak, cannon boomed out from the heights around Irkutsk. It was the succoring army under the command of General Kisselef, and it was thus that he made known his welcome arrival to the Grand Duke.

The Tartars did not wait to be attacked. Not daring to run the risk of a battle under the walls of Irkutsk, they immediately broke up the Angara camp. Irkutsk was at last relieved.

With the first Russian soldiers, two of Michael's friends entered the city. They were the inseparable Blount and Jolivet. On gaining the right bank of the Angara by means of the icy barrier, they had escaped, as had the other fugitives, before the flames had reached their raft. This had been noted by Alcide Jolivet in his book in this way: "Ran a narrow chance of being finished up like a lemon in a bowl of punch!"

Their joy was great on finding Nadia and Michael safe and sound; above all, when they learnt that their brave companion was not blind. Harry Blount inscribed this observation: "Red-hot iron is insufficient in some cases to destroy the sensibility of the optic nerve."

Then the two correspondents, settled for a time in Irkutsk, busied themselves in putting the notes and impressions of their journey in order. Thence were sent to London and Paris two interesting articles relative to the Tartar invasion, and which—a rare thing—did not contradict each other even on the least important points.

The remainder of the campaign was unfortunate to the Emir and his allies. This invasion, futile as all which attack the Russian Colossus must be, was very fatal to them. They soon found themselves cut off by the Czar's troops, who retook in succession all the conquered towns. Besides this, the winter was terrible, and, decimated by the cold, only a small part of these hordes returned to the steppes of Tartary.

The Irkutsk road, by way of the Ural Mountains, was now open. The Grand Duke was anxious to return to Moscow, but he delayed his journey to be present at a touching ceremony, which took place a few days after the entry of the Russian troops.

Michael Strogoff sought Nadia, and in her father's presence said to her, "Nadia, my sister still, when you left Riga to come to Irkutsk, did you leave it with any other regret than that for your mother?"

"No," replied Nadia, "none of any sort whatever."

"Then, nothing of your heart remains there?"

"Nothing, brother."

"Then, Nadia," said Michael, "I think that God, in allowing us to meet, and to go through so many severe trials together, must have meant us to be united forever."

"Ah!" said Nadia, falling into Michael's arms. Then turning towards Wassili Fedor, "My father," said she, blushing.

"Nadia," said Captain Fedor, "it will be my joy to call you both my children!"

The marriage ceremony took place in Irkutsk cathedral.

Jolivet and Blount very naturally assisted at this marriage, of which they wished to give an account to their readers.

"And doesn't it make you wish to imitate them?" asked Alcide of his friend.

"Pooh!" said Blount. "Now if I had a cousin like you—"

"My cousin isn't to be married!" answered Alcide, laughing.

"So much the better," returned Blount, "for they speak of difficulties arising between London and Pekin. Have you no wish to go and see what is going on there?"

"By Jove, my dear Blount!" exclaimed Alcide Jolivet, "I was just going to make the same proposal to you."

And that was how the two inseparables set off for China.

A few days after the ceremony, Michael and Nadia Strogoff, accompanied by Wassili Fedor, took the route to Europe. The road so full of suffering when going, was a road of joy in returning. They traveled swiftly, in one of those sleighs which glide like an express train across the frozen steppes of Siberia.

However, when they reached the banks of the Dinka, just before Birskoe, they stopped for a while. Michael found the place where he had buried poor Nicholas. A cross was erected there, and Nadia prayed a last time on the grave of the humble and heroic friend, whom neither of them would ever forget.

At Omsk, old Marfa awaited them in the little house of the Strogoffs. She clasped passionately in her arms the girl whom in her heart she had already a hundred times called "daughter." The brave old Siberian, on that day, had the right to recognize her son and say she was proud of him.

After a few days passed at Omsk, Michael and Nadia entered Europe, and, Wassili Fedor settling down in St. Petersburg, neither his son nor his daughter had any occasion to leave him, except to go and see their old mother.

The young courier was received by the Czar, who attached him specially to his own person, and gave him the Cross of St. George. In the course of time, Michael Strogoff reached a high station in the Empire. But it is not the history of his success, but the history of his trials, which deserves to be related.